SPAWN OF NIGHTMARE

Flesh and blood could take no more. The mounted troops broke, riding wildly in all directions. With his flank cover ruined, Marcus drew his line back and to the left, anchoring the end to a small stand of fig trees.

Battlefield din shrieked in his ears. When a great roar swallowed it, Marcus thought for a terrible second that he had been struck a mortal blow and was hearing the sound of death. But the noise was real; troopers on both sides clapped hands to heads and spun about, seeking its source. Then shadow touched the tribune, and terror with it.

The dragon soared over the battle on batwings vast enough to shade a village. It roared again, and flame licked from the fanged cavern of its mouth. The troops scattered before it, clawing at one another in their efforts to escape.

But there *are* no dragons, Marcus' mind yammered.

By Harry Turtledove
Published by Ballantine Books:

The Videssos Cycle:

THE MISPLACED LEGION

AN EMPEROR FOR THE LEGION

THE LEGION OF VIDESSOS

Book Three of *The Videssos Cycle*

The Legion of Videssos

Harry Turtledove

A Del Rey Book

BALLANTINE BOOKS • NEW YORK

A Del Rey Book
Published by Ballantine Books

Library of Congress Catalog Card Number: 87-91144

ISBN 0-345-33069-2

Manufactured in the United States of America

First Edition: August 1987

Cover Art by Romas

Map by Shelly Shapiro

For Kevin, Marcella, Tom, and Kathy.

SHAUMKHIIL
SHAUM RIVER
PARDRAYA
DEGIRD RIVER
THE GODS' DUNG HEAP
KOUPHIS R.
MYLASA
SEA
YEZD
DILBAT MTS.
MASHIZ
GUNIB
ERZERUM MTS.
MOUSH R.
VASPURAKAN MTS.
KHLIAT
MARAGHA
PITYOS
NAKOLEIA
TAVAS
SOLI
APTOS
AMORION
EMPIRE
KYBISTRA
DOXON
SEA OF SALT

HALOGA
BAY OF HALOGA
AGDER
KINGDOM OF AGDER
NORTHERN SEA
THATAGUSH
ASTRIS RIVER
KHATRISH
DUCHY OF NAMDALEN
NUSTAD
SOTEVAG
METEPONT
IMBROS
IDESSOS
OPSIKION
THE KEY
VIDESSOS
SEA

WHAT HAS GONE BEFORE:

Three cohorts of a Roman legion, led by military tribune Marcus Aemilius Scaurus and senior centurion Gaius Philippus, were trying to rejoin Caesar's main army when they were ambushed by Gauls. The Gallic leader Viridovix challenged Marcus to single combat. Both bore druids' swords as battle spoil. When the blades crossed, a dome of light surrounded Viridovix and the Romans. Suddenly they were in the world of the Empire of Videssos, a land where priests of the god Phos could work real magic. There they were hired as mercenaries by the Empire.

In Videssos the city, capital of the Empire, Marcus met the soldier-Emperor Mavrikios Gavras and the prime minister, Vardanes Sphrantzes, a bureaucrat whose enmity Marcus incurred. At a banquet for the Romans, he met Alypia, Mavrikios' daughter, and the sorcerer Avshar. Avshar forced a duel on him; but when the druid's sword neutralized Avshar's spells, Marcus won. Avshar sought revenge by magic. It failed, and Avshar fled to Yezd, western enemy of Videssos. Videssos declared formal war on Yezd.

As native and mercenary troops flooded into the capital, tension broke out between Videssians and the troops from the island kingdom of Namdalen over a small religious difference, with each declaring the other to be heretics. The Videssian patriarch Balsamon preached tolerance, but fanatic monks stirred the trouble into rioting. Marcus led the Romans to control the riots. As those were ending, Marcus saved the Namdalener woman Helvis. They made love, and she and her young son soon joined him in the Roman barracks.

Finally the unwieldy army marched west against Yezd, accompanied by women and dependents. Marcus was pleased to learn Helvis was pregnant, but shocked to discover the left wing was commanded by Sphrantzes' young and wholly inexperienced nephew, Ortaias.

Two Vaspurakaners, Senpat Sviodo and his wife Nevrat, acted as guides to the Romans. Gagik Bagratouni, a Vaspurakaner noble, joined the army. When a fanatic priest, Zemarkhos, cursed him, Bagratouni threw the priest in a sack with his dog and beat the sack. But Marcus, fearing a pogrom, interceded for the priest.

At last the two armies met, with Avshar commanding the Yezda. Battle seemed a draw, until a spell from Avshar panicked Ortaias, who fled. Mavrikios Gavras was killed as the left wing collapsed, and the army of Videssos was routed.

The Romans retreated in order, collecting their womenfolk. They rescued Nepos, a priest and teacher of sorcery, and were joined by Laon Pakhymer and a band of mounted Khatrishers, giving them cavalry support. They marched eastward, harried by the Yezda.

They wintered in the friendly town of Aptos. Marcus learned that Ortaias, calling himself Emperor, had married Alypia. But Mavrikios Gavras' brother Thorisin had retreated with twenty-five hundred troops to a nearby city. In the spring, Marcus joined him to march toward Videssos the city. Cloaked under a spell by Nepos, they crossed the narrow strip of water to the city, but found the gates slammed in their faces. No army had ever penetrated the city's walls.

Days passed futilely, until a desperate band inside the city managed to throw open the gates. Then they drove the city forces under Ortaias' commander Rhavas back to the palace. There Rhavas—Avshar in disguise—resorted to foul magic. But the swords of Marcus and Viridovix overcame the spell. Avshar retreated to where Vardanes and Ortaias Sphrantzes held Alypia hostage. But under pressure, Vardanes attacked Avshar, who killed him and then fled to a small chamber—and suddenly vanished.

Crowned as Emperor, Thorisin annulled Alypia's marriage and banished Ortaias to serve as a humble monk.

But there were still troubles. Tax receipts were far too low, and ships from the island called the Key prevented supplies from reaching the city. Thorisin appointed Marcus to supervise the tax collectors. Marcus soon discovered that rich landowners never paid properly; the worst offender was general Baanes Onomagoulos, an old friend of Mavrikios Gavras. Learning this, Thorisin sent a force of Namdaleners under count Drax to deal with Onomagoulos. Marcus persuaded the Emperor to free a prisoner, Taron Leimmokheir, and give him command of the puny naval forces. By trickery, Leimmokheir managed to defeat the ships of the Key.

Meanwhile, Thorisin was sending a party to far north Arshaum for help. Gorgidas, Greek physician of the legion and close friend of Marcus, decided to go along. And at the last minute, Viridovix, escaping the wrath of Thorisin's mistress, joined Gorgidas.

In a temple ceremony, Thorisin announced that count Drax had won a battle against Onomagoulos, who was now dead. Next—Yezd!

I

"Too hot and sticky," Marcus Aemilius Scaurus complained, wiping his sweaty forehead with the heel of his hand. In late afternoon Videssos' towering walls shaded the practice field just outside them, but it was morning now, and their gray stone reflected heat in waves. The military tribune sheathed his sword. "I've had enough."

"You northerners don't know good weather," Gaius Philippus said. The senior centurion was sweating as hard as his superior, but he reveled in it. Like most Romans, he enjoyed the Empire's climate.

But Marcus sprang from Mediolanum, a north Italian town founded by the Celts, and it was plain some of their blood ran in his veins. "Aye, I'm blond. I can't help it, you know," he said wearily; Gaius Philippus had teased him for his un-Roman looks as long as they had known each other.

The centurion could have been the portrait on a denarius himself, with his wide, squarish face, strong nose and chin, and short cap of graying hair. And like nearly all his countrymen, Scaurus included, he kept on shaving even after two and a half years in Videssos, a bearded land. The Romans were stubborn folk.

"Look at the sun," Marcus suggested.

Gaius Philippus gauged it with a quick, experienced glance. He whistled in surprise. "Have we been at it that long? I was enjoying myself." He turned to the exercising legionaries, shouting, "All right, knock off! Form up for parade to barracks!"

The soldiers, original Romans and the Videssians, Vaspurakaners, and others who had joined their ranks since they came to the Empire, laid down their double-weight wicker swords and heavy practice shields with groans of relief. Gaius Philippus, who was past fifty, had more stamina than most men twenty and thirty years his junior; Scaurus had envied it many times.

"They're looking quite good," he said.

"It could be worse," Gaius Philippus allowed. Coming from the veteran, it was highest praise. A thoroughgoing professional, he would never be truly satisfied by anything short of perfection—or, at least, would never admit it if he was.

He grumbled as he rammed his sword into its bronze scabbard. "I don't like this polluted blade. It's not a proper *gladius*; it's too long, Videssian iron is too springy, and the grip feels wrong in my hand. I should have given it to Gorgidas and kept my good one; the fool Greek wouldn't have known the difference."

"Plenty of legionaries would be happy to trade with you," Marcus said. As he'd known it would, that made the veteran clap a protective hand to the hilt of the sword, which was in fact a fine sample of the swordsmith's art. "As for Gorgidas, you miss him as much as I do, I'd say—and Viridovix, too."

"Nonsense to the one and double nonsense to the other. A sly little Greekling and a wild Gaul? The sun must have addled your wits."

The tribune knew insincerity when he heard it. "You're not happy without something to grouse over."

"Nor are you, unless you're picking at my brains."

Marcus smiled wryly; there was some truth in the charge. Gaius Philippus was a more typical Roman than he in more ways than looks, being practical, straightforward, and inclined to distrust anything that smacked of theory.

They made a formidable pair, with the veteran as shrewd tactician and Scaurus, whose Stoic training and political background gave him a breadth of view Gaius Philippus could never match, as strategist devising the legionaries' best course. Before the tribune's druid-enchanted sword met Viridovix' and propelled the Romans to Videssos, he had not planned on a military career, but any rising young man needed to be able to point to some army time. Now, as mercenary captain in the faction-filled Empire, he needed all his political skill merely to survive among soldiers and courtiers who had been double-dealing, he sometimes thought, since before they left their mothers' breasts.

"You there, Flaccus! Straighten it up!" Gaius Philippus shouted. The Roman shifted his feet an inch or two, then looked back inquiringly. Gaius Philippus glared at him, more from habit than anger. His gaze raked the rest of the soldiers. "All right, move out!" he said grudgingly. The buccinators' cornets and trumpets echoed his command, a metallic blare.

The Videssian guardsmen at the Silver Gate saluted Marcus as they would one of their own officers, with bowed heads and right fists clenched over their hearts. He nodded back, but eyed the great iron-faced gates and spiked portcullis with scant liking; too many irreplaceable Romans had fallen trying unsuccessfully to force them the previous summer. Only rebellion inside the city had let Thorisin Gavras make good his claim to the Empire against Ortaias Sphrantzes, though Ortaias was no leader. With works like the capital's, a defense did not need much leadership.

The legionaries tramped though the gloom of the walled passageway between the city's outer and inner walls, and suddenly Videssos brawled around them. Entering the city was always like taking a big swig of strong wine. The newcomer breathed deeply, opened his eyes a little wider, and braced himself for the next pull.

Middle Street, Videssos' chief thoroughfare, was one Marcus knew well. The Romans had paraded down it the day they first entered the capital, made a desperate dash to the palace complex when Ortaias was toppled from the throne, and marched along it countless times on their way back and forth between barracks and practice field.

It was a slow march today; as usual, Middle Street was packed tight with people. The tribune wished for a herald like that one he'd had the first day in Videssos, to clear the traffic ahead of him, but that was a luxury he no longer enjoyed. The legionaries were just behind a pair of huge, creaking wagons, both full of sand-yellow limestone for some building project or other. A dozen horses hauled each one, but at a snail's pace.

Vendors swarmed like flies round the dawdling soldiers, shouting out the virtues of their wares: sausages and fried fish, which had flies of their own; wine; flavored ices—a favorite winter treat, but brought in by runner in warm weather, and so too expensive for most troopers' wallets—goods of leather, or wicker, or bronze; and aphrodisiacs. "Make you good for seven rounds a night!" the peddler announced dramatically. "Here, you, sir, care to try it?"

He thrust a vial toward Sextus Minucius, newly promoted underofficer. Minucius was tall, handsome, and young, with a perpetual blue-black stubble on his cheeks and chin. In crested helmet and highly polished mail shirt, he cut an impressively masculine figure.

He took the little jar from the Videssian's skinny hand, tossed it up and down as if considering, and gave it back. "No, you keep it," he said. "What do I want with a potion to slow me down?" The legionaries bayed laughter, not least at the sight of one of Videssos' glib hucksters at a loss for words.

Every block or two, it seemed, they passed one of Phos' temples; there were hundreds of them in the city. Blue-robed priests and monks, their shaved heads gleaming almost as brightly as the golden globes atop the temples' spires, were no small part of the street traffic. They drew the circular sun-sign of their faith as they passed Marcus' troopers. Enough men, Videssians and Romans who had come to follow the Empire's god, returned it to hold their ever-ready suspicions of heresay at bay.

The legionaries marched through the plaza of Stavrakios with its gilded statue of that great, conquering Emperor; through the din of the coppersmiths' district, where Middle Street bent to run straight west to the Imperial Palaces; through the plaza called, for no reason Marcus had even been able to learn, the forum of the Ox; past the sprawling red-granite edifice that held Videssos' archives—and its felons as well—and into the plaza of Palamas, the greatest of the imperial capital's fora.

If Videssos the city was a microcosm of Videssos the empire, the plaza of Palamas was Videssos the city in small. Nobles wearing their traditional brocaded robes rubbed shoulders with street toughs in puffed-sleeve tunics and garish hose. Here a drunken whore lolled against a wall, her legs splayed open; there a Namdalener mercenary, the back of his head shaved so it would fit his helmet better, haggled with a fat Videssian jeweler over the price of a ring for his lady; there a monk and a prosperous-looking baker passed the time of day arguing some theological point, both smiling at their sport.

Seeing the mercenary made Scaurus glance at the Milestone, an obelisk of the same ruddy granite as the archives building, from which all distances in the Empire were reckoned. A huge placard at its base lauded the great count Drax, whose regiment of Namdaleni had crushed the revolt Baanes Onomagoulos had raised in the westlands. Onomagoulos' head, just fetched to the city, was displayed above the placard. The late rebel was nearly bald, so instead of being hung by the hair, the head was suspended from a cord tied round its ears. Only a few Videssians paid any attention; in the past couple of generations, unsuccessful rebels had become too common to attract much notice.

Gaius Philippus followed Marcus' eye. "Whoreson had it coming," he said.

The tribune nodded. "After Mavrikios Gavras was killed, he thought the Empire should be his by right. He never could think of Thorisin as anything but Mavrikios' worthless little brother, and if there's any worse mistake to make, I can't think of it offhand."

"Nor I." Gaius Philippus had a soldier's respect for the Avtokrator of the Videssians, one which Thorisin Gavras returned.

The palace compound's calm, uncrowded beauty always came as something of a shock after the ferment of the plaza of Palamas. Marcus was never sure how he would react to the transition; sometimes it soothed him, but about as often he felt he was withdrawing from life itself. Today, he decided, the plaza had been a little too strident for his taste. A quiet afternoon at the barracks doing nothing would suit him down to the ground.

"Sir?" the sentry said hesitantly.

"Eh? What is it, Fostulus?" Marcus looked up from the troops' paysheet listings, looked down again so he would remember where he was, then looked up once more.

"There's a baldy outside, sir, says he needs to talk with you."

"A baldy?" The tribune blinked. "You mean, a priest?"

"What else?" Fostulus said, grinning; he was not one of the Romans who followed Phos. "Big fat fellow, must be rising fifty from the gray in his beard. He's got a mean mouth," the sentry added.

Marcus scratched his head. He knew several priests, but the description did not sound like any of them. Still, it would not do to offend Videssos' religious hierarchy; in some ways it was more powerful than the Emperor himself. He sighed and rolled up the account parchment, tying it shut with a ribbon. "Bring him in, I suppose."

"Yes, sir." Fostulus saluted—Roman-style, with outthrust arm—then spun smartly on his heel and hurried back to the doorway. The hobnails in the soles of his *caligae* clicked on the slate floor.

"Took you long enough," Scaurus heard the man grumbling as Fostulus led him back to the little table in the rear corner of the barracks hall that the tribune used as a makeshift office. Marcus rose to greet him as he approached.

Fostulus had been right; the priest was nearly of a height with Scaurus, whose northern blood gave him more inches than most Romans or Videssians enjoyed. And when they clasped hands, the fellow's firm, dry grip showed considerable strength. "You can go now, Fostulus," the tribune said. With another salute, the sentry returned to his station.

The priest flung himself into a chair, which creaked under his weight. Sweat darkened the armpits of his blue robe and sprayed from his shaved pate; Marcus was glad he had closed the account roll. "Phos' light, standing there in the sun is hot work," the Videssian said accusingly, his voice a rumbling bass. "D'you have any wine for a thirsty man?"

"Well, yes," the tribune said, disconcerted by such

brusqueness; most Videssians were smoother spoken. He found a jug and a couple of earthenware cups, poured, handed one cup to the priest, and raised the other in salute. "Your health, ah—" he paused, not knowing the man's name.

"Styppes," the priest said curtly; like all Videssian clerics, he had abandoned his surname, a symbol of his dedication to Phos alone.

Before he tasted the wine, he raised both hands to the sky, murmuring his faith's basic creed: "We bless thee, Phos, Lord with the great and good mind, by thy grace our protector, watchful beforehand that the great test of life may be decided in our favor." Then he spat on the floor in rejection of Skotos, Phos' evil opponent in the Empire's dualistic religion.

He waited for a moment for the Roman to join him in the ritual, but Scaurus, although he respected Videssos' customs, did not ape the ones he failed to share. Styppes gave him a disdainful glance. "Heathen," he muttered. Marcus saw what Fostulus had meant about his mouth; its narrow, bloodless lips barely covered strong yellow teeth.

Then Styppes drank, and the tribune had to fight to keep contempt from his face in turn. The Videssian drained his cup at a draught, filled it without asking Scaurus' leave, emptied it once more, refilled, and swallowed a third while Marcus' lips were hardly wet. Styppes started to pour again, but the jug gave out with his cup half-empty. He snorted in annoyance and tossed it off.

"Will the wine do you, or was there something else you wanted?" Scaurus asked sharply. He was immediately ashamed of himself; had Stoicism not taught him to accept each man as he was, good and bad together? If this Styppes loved the grape too well, despising him for it would hardly change him.

Marcus tried again, this time without sarcasm. "How can I, or perhaps my men, help you?"

"I doubt it would be possible," Styppes answered, raising the tribune's hackles afresh. "But I have been told to help you." His sour expression did not speak well for his pleasure at the undertaking.

The priest was a veteran drinker. His speech did not slur, and he moved with perfect assurance. Only a slight flush to what had been a rather pallid complexion betrayed the wine he had on board.

Sipping from his own cup, Scaurus took hold of his temper with both hands. "Ah? Told by whom?" he asked, making a game stab at sounding interested. The sooner this sponge in a blue robe left, the better. He wondered whether his priestly friend Nepos or Balsamon the patriarch had sent him and, if so, what they had against the Romans.

But Styppes surprised him, saying, "Mertikes Zigabenos informs me you have lost your healer."

"That's so," Scaurus admitted; he wondered how Gorgidas was faring on the Pardrayan steppe. Zigabenos was commander of the imperial bodyguard, and a very competent young man indeed. If this priest had his favor, perhaps there was something to him after all. "What of it?"

"He suggested I offer you my services. I have been trained in Phos' healing arts, and it is not right for any unit of his Majesty's army to be without such aid—even one full of pagans, as is yours," Styppes ended disparagingly.

Marcus ignored that. "You're a healer-priest? And assigned to us?" It was all he could do to keep from shouting with glee. Using themselves as channels of Phos' energies, some priests could work cures on men Gorgidas had given up for dead; as much as anything, his failure to learn their methods had driven him to the plains. Nepos had healed his share, even though he was no specialist in the art. To have a man who was could prove more precious than rubies, Scaurus thought. "Assigned to us?" he repeated, wanting to hear Styppes say it again.

"Aye." The priest still seemed far from overjoyed; as he was familiar with it, his talent was much less wonderful to him than to the Roman. He looked at the bedrolls neatly checkering the barracks floor. "You'll have quarters for me here, then?"

"Certainly; whatever you like."

"What I'd like is more wine."

Not wanting to antagonize him or seem mean, Marcus struck the seal from another jug and handed it to him. "Care for any?" Styppes asked. When the tribune shook his head, the priest, disdaining his cup, drank the jar dry. Scaurus' worries returned.

"Ahhh," Styppes said when he was done, a long exhalation

of pleasure. He rose—and lurched somewhat; so much neat wine downed so fast would have sozzled a demigod. "Be back," he said, and now the drink was in his speech, too. "Got to get m'gear from the mon'stery, fetch it here." Moving with the carefully steady strides of a man used to walking wine-soaked, he started toward the doorway.

He had only taken a couple of steps when he turned back to Marcus. He studied him with owlish intensity for nearly a minute, then left just as Scaurus was about to ask him what was on his mind. Frustrated, the Roman went back to his paysheets.

That evening, Helvis asked him, "So, how do you like this Styppes?"

"Like him? That has nothing to do with anything—what choice have I? Any healer is better than none." Wondering how frank he should be with her, Marcus leaned back against a thin wood partition; two of the four barracks halls the legionaries used were divided up to give partnered soldiers and their women and children some privacy.

She frowned, sensing his hesitation, but before she could frame her question, her five-year-old son Malric threw aside the wooden cart he had been playing with and started to sing a bawdy Videssian marching song at the top of his lungs: "Little bird with a yellow bill—"

She rolled her eyes, blue like those of many Namdaleni. "Enough of that, young man. Time for bed." He ignored her, singing on until she grabbed his ankles and lifted him. He hung upside down, shrieking laughter. His tunic fell down over his head; he thrashed his way out of it. Helvis caught Marcus' eye. "There's half the battle won."

The tribune smiled, watching as she peeled his stepson's trousers off. Even in such inelegant activity, she was a pleasure to look at. Her skin was fairer and her features less aquiline than the Videssian norm, but strong cheekbones and a generous mouth gave her face a beauty of its own. And her figure was opulent, its rich curves filling her long skirt and lace-bodiced blouse of maroon linen in a way that caught any man's eye. As yet her early pregnancy had not begun to swell her belly.

She swatted Malric lightly on his bare bottom. "Go on,

kiss Marcus goodnight, use the pot, and go to sleep." Her voice was a smooth contralto.

Malric complained and fussed to see if she was serious; the next swat had more authority behind it. "All right, Mama, I'm going," he said, and trotted over to Scaurus. "Goodnight, Papa." He had spoken Namdalener patois with Helvis, but used Latin with the tribune; he had picked up the Roman tongue with a child's ease in the nearly two years Marcus and Helvis had been together.

"Good night, son. Sleep well." Scaurus ruffled the boy's shock of blond hair, so like that of his dead father Hemond. Malric piddled, then slid under the blanket and closed his eyes. Marcus' own son Dosti, not quite a year old, was asleep in a crib close by the sleeping mats. He whimpered, but quieted as soon as Helvis pulled the coverlet up over him. Some nights now, the tribune thought hopefully, he slept all the way through.

When Helvis was sure Malric was asleep, too, she turned back to Scaurus. "What's wrong with the healer-priest?"

At the blunt question, Marcus' hesitation disappeared. "Not much," he said, but before she could do more than begin to raise her eyebrows, he went on, "except that he's an arrogant, greedy, ill-tempered sot—at the moment he's passed out on the floor in one of the bachelor halls, snoring like a sawmill. I doubt he could fix a fleabite, let alone really heal."

Helvis laughed nervously, half amused at Styppes' shortcomings, half scandalized by Scaurus' open contempt for him. She was a zealous follower of Phos, and hearing a priest of any sect maligned made her ill at ease; still, as a Namdalener she reckoned the Videssians heretics and so, in a way, fair game. The ambiguity confused her.

A splinter gouged Marcus' shoulder through his shirt. As he dug it out with a thumbnail, he thought that ambiguity was something he, too, had come to know with Helvis. They were too different to be wholly comfortable with one another, each of them too strong-willed to yield easily. Religion, policy, love-making . . . sometimes it seemed there were few things over which they did not quarrel.

But when things went well, he said to himself with an inward smile, they went very well indeed. Still rubbing his shoulder, he stood and kissed her. She looked at him quizzically. "What was that for?"

"No real reason."

Her face lit. "That's the best reason of all." She pressed herself against him. Her chin fit nicely on his shoulder; she was tall for a woman, as tall, in fact, as many Videssian men. He kissed her again, this time thoroughly. Afterward, he never was sure which one of them blew out the lamp.

Scaurus was spooning up his breakfast porridge—barley flavored with bits of beef and onion—when Junius Blaesus came up to him. The junior centurion looked unhappy. "Mglmpf?" the tribune said, and then, after he had swallowed, "What's the matter?" From Blaesus' hangdog air, he had a fair idea.

The Roman's long face grew glummer yet. A veteran *optio*, or underofficer, he was newly promoted to centurion's rank and did not like to admit there were problems in his maniple that he had trouble handling. Marcus cocked an eyebrow at him and waited; pushing would only make him more sensitive than he was.

At last Blaesus blurted out, "It's Pullo and Vorenus, sir."

The tribune nodded, unsurprised. "Again?" he said. He took a deliberate swig of wine; like almost all Videssian vintages, it was too sweet for his taste. He went on, "Glabrio had nothing but trouble with them. What are they squabbling about now?"

"Which of them threw the *pilum* better at practice yesterday. Pullo swung at Vorenus last night, but they got pulled apart before they could mix it." Relief was flowering on the junior centurion; Quintus Glabrio, whose unit he now led, had been a truly outstanding officer. If, before his death, he had not been able to control the two fractious legionaries, then Blaesus could hardly be blamed for having problems with them.

"Swung on him, you say? We can't have that." Scaurus finished his porridge, wiped off the bone spoon, and put it back in his belt-pouch. He rose. "I'll have a word or two with them. Set your mind at ease, Junius; it won't be the first time."

"Yes, sir." Blaesus saluted and hurried off on other business, relieved to have survived the interview. Marcus watched him go, not quite satisfied. Quintus Glabrio, he thought, would have come with him, instead of being content to have passed the problem on. It seemed an evasion of responsibility, a grave flaw by Scaurus' Stoic-tinged standards. Well, he thought, that must be why Blaesus stayed an *optio* so long.

Titus Pullo sprang to attention when he saw the tribune walking toward him, a fair sign of a guilty conscience. So, interestingly, did Lucius Vorenus. Except for their feud with each other, they were excellent soldiers, probably the two finest in the maniple. Both were in their late twenties, Pullo a bit stockier, Vorenus perhaps a trifle quicker.

Scaurus glared at them, doing his best to project an image of stern reproach. "We've been through all this before," he said. "Docking your pay doesn't do much good, does it?"

"Sir—" Pullo said, and Vorenus said, "Sir, he—"

"Shut up," the tribune snapped. "Both of you are confined to barracks for the next two weeks—and that includes staying here when your mates go out to exercise. Since you're so fond of arguing over your practices, maybe you'll learn to keep your tempers if you have nothing to argue about."

"But, sir," Vorenus protested, "without practice we'll lose our edge." Pullo nodded vigorously; here, at least, was something upon which the two Romans could agree. Both were filled with the pride that marked the best fighting men.

"You should have thought of that before you wrangled," Marcus pointed out. "You won't go soft, not in two weeks' time—cleaning details will see to that. Dismissed!" he said sharply. But as they turned, shamefaced, to go, he had an afterthought. "One thing more: don't make the mistake of keeping this foolish quarrel alive. If there is a next time, I'll make whichever one of you is guilty the other's servant. Think on that before you squabble."

To judge from their faces, neither found the prospect appetizing. Pleased at his ingenuity, the tribune started off to get ready for practice. He wished he could order himself to take a couple of weeks off. The day gave every promise of being another scorcher.

"And how did you handle your battling troopers?" Senpat Sviodo asked him; as usual, the Vaspurankaner's resonant tenor voice held an amused edge.

"You must have heard me," Marcus answered, but then realized that while Senpat might have heard him, he had not understood. Among themselves the Romans clung to their Latin, one of the few reminders they had of their lost homeland. Their comrades understood the strange speech but haltingly, lacking Malric's childish facility for learning new tongues. The tribune explained.

The smile that was never far from the young Vaspurakaner noble's handsome features came into the open. He had a good smile, white teeth flashing against his olive skin, framed by the beard he wore close-trimmed in the Videssian style. "You Romans are a strange folk," he said, only a trace of his throaty native tongue coloring his Videssian. "Who else would punish someone by taking work away from him?"

Marcus snorted. Senpat had enjoyed twitting the legionaries since the day he met them almost two years before, but if there was a better mounted scout than he, it had to be his wife. "Your lady Nevrat would understand," the tribune said.

"So she might," Senpat admitted, chuckling. "But then she enjoys such things, where I merely endure them." He gave a theatrical grimace to indicate his disgust at any and all types of work. "Now I suppose you expect me to bake myself in the broiling sun for the sake of hitting the target a hairsbreadth closer to the center."

"What better way to chastise you for your endless heckling?"

"Oh, what we Firstborn suffer in the cause of truth." The Vaspurakaners traced their ancestry back to an eponymous hero, Vaspur—in their theology, the first man created by Phos. Not surprisingly, the Videssians did not share this view.

Senpat pulled his Vaspurakaner cap rakishly over one eye. On most of his countrymen the three-peaked headgear looked strange and lumpy, but he wore it with such a jaunty air that he carried it off quite well. He tossed his head. The brightly dyed ribbons that hung down from the back of the cap's floppy brim flew round his head.

"Since there's no help for it," he sighed, "I suppose I'll fetch my bow." He started to leave.

"If you carped any more, you'd grow scales," Marcus said. Senpat looked briefly blank; the wordplay did not work in Vaspurakaner. Then he winced, looking back suspiciously in case the tribune had more puns lying in wait for him. Scaurus did not, but he was grinning at managing one in a language not his own . . . and a bad one at that.

"Hold it up a little higher, would you, Gongyles?" Thorisin Gavras said.

Gongyles was a very junior lieutenant, his beard fuzzy; his sudden flush was visible through the straggly growth on his cheeks. "I'm sorry, your Imperial Majesty," he stammered, awed that the Avtokrator of the Videssians would speak to him for any reason. He raised the map of the Empire's westlands so all the officers gathered in the Hall of the Nineteen Couches could see it.

The hall held no couches, nor had it for centuries, but tradition died hard in Videssos. Scaurus, sitting on a plain wooden chair in front of a table that wobbled because one leg was too short, smiled at the homage on the callow soldier's face. He whispered to Gaius Philippus, "Remember when Mavrikios kept Ortaias Sphrantzes standing there for hours holding that damned map? His arms must have been ready to fall off."

The senior centurion laughed softly. "It would've served him right if they had," he said; his scorn for Ortaias was boundless. His face hardened. "Then he wouldn't have come along with us to Maragha, and Mavrikios might be alive. Bloody turntail coward; we had a draw till he ran."

In his contempt, he did not bother to lower his voice much. Thorisin, who stood by the map, looked a question at him, not understanding the veteran's Latin. It was Gaius Philippus' turn to go red, though the color hardly showed under his deep tan. "Nothing, sir," he muttered.

"All right, then." The Emperor shrugged. Mavrikios Gavras had used a wooden pointer to guide his officers' eyes across the map of the westlands in that council a couple of years before. His younger brother was a less patient man. He drew his saber from its well-scuffed leather sheath and pointed his way with that.

For all his impatience, his term as Emperor was beginning to leave its mark on him. The lines on either side of his mouth and proud nose were carved deep into his cheeks, though he was but a few years older than Scaurus. There were lines round his eyes, lines that had not been there before he came to the throne. His hair was thinning, too; what had once been a widow's peak was becoming a forelock.

But he had the active stride of a younger man, and it took but a single glance at his strong mouth and determined eyes to see that he was yet a man of great vigor and bearing up well under the heavy hands of duty and time. "This is what we'll have to do," he said, and his marshals leaned forward as one to listen.

He tapped at the parchment with his sword before he began to speak, mustering his thoughts. As always, the wide peninsula that held the Empire's western provinces reminded Marcus of a knobby thumb. From marching and countermarching through a good part of the westlands, he knew the map was more accurate than anything Rome could have produced. Discouragingly, it also accurately showed the land the Yezda had taken since Maragha. Most of the high central plateau was lost; the nomads were beginning to settle there and pushing eastward toward the fertile plains that ran to the Sailors' Sea.

The Emperor ran his blade west along the Arandos River, which flowed down from the highlands through the broad coastal plain. "The whoresons are using the Arandos valley to come right down our throats. It runs both ways, though. Drax' Namdaleni will plug the gap at Garsavra until we reinforce them. After that, it's our turn to push west again and reclaim what's ours. . . . Yes, this time you have something to say to me, Roman?"

"Aye, or ask you, rather." Gaius Philippus pointed toward the red-filled circle that marked Garsavra. "Your great count Drax may be a canny enough soldier, but how does he propose to hold a town with no putrid wall?"

Hardly any cities in the westlands were walled. Until the Yezda came, the westerners had lived for hundreds of years without fear of invasion. Such fortifications as had once existed were centuries gone, torn down for the building stone they yielded. To Marcus' way of thinking, a land free of walls was Videssos' finest achievement. It told of a security far greater than any his Rome could give its subjects. Even in Italy, an unwalled town would have been as unnatural as a white crow. It had only been fifty years since the Cimbri and

Teutones swarmed over the Alps, asking Marius' legionaries if they had any messages for the barbarians to take to their wives.

"Never fear, outlander, t'ey'll hold it," Utprand son of Dagober said from down the table, his Namdalener accent thick enough to slice. "Drax is a poor excuse for a Namdalener, but his men, t'ey'll hold." The great count had taken on too many Videssian ways for his countryman's liking. They had some old rivalry between them as well; Scaurus was hazy on the details.

"You Romans are good at overnight fieldworks, but we know a few tricks, too," Soteric Dosti's son said, supporting his captain. Helvis' brother had served in the Empire longer than Utprand and lost most of his island accent. He went on, "Give a regiment of ours ten days in one place, and they have a motte-and-bailey up that'll hold 'em all. Garsavra may not have walls, but it won't lack for a strongpoint."

My brother-in-law, Marcus thought—not for the first time—talks too much. Mertikes Zigabenos scowled at Soteric, as did several other Videssian officers. Nor, plainly, was Thorisin overjoyed at the prospect of Namdalener-held castles going up in his land, however necessary they might be for the moment.

The Videssians hired Namdalener mercenaries, but they did not trust them. Namdalen had been a province of the Empire before it fell to Haloga corsairs a couple of centuries ago. The mixed folk that sprang from the conquest combined Videssos' imperial traditions with the ambition and barbaric love of battle the northerners brought. The Dukes of Namdalen dreamed one day of ruling from the imperial capital, a dream that was nightmare to the Videssians.

Zigabenos said to Utprand, "With your heavy cavalry, you islanders shouldn't be reduced to garrison duty. When our main force reaches Garsavra, we'll surely put less valuable troops in whatever fortresses Drax may have built."

"Isn't he slick, now?" Gaius Philippus whispered admiringly. Marcus nodded; what better way to ease the islanders out of positions that could be dangerous to the Empire than to make that easing appear a compliment to their fighting skills? Zigabenos had to an unusual degree the Videssian talent for mixing politics and war; he was the man who had set off the riots in the city that overthrew Ortaias Sphrantzes and won Thorisin Gavras the Empire.

But Utprand had not risen to lead his regiment solely by the strength of his right arm. He was impatient with any sort of subtlety, but there was a considerable wit behind his cold blue eyes. With a shrug he said, "Time will show w'at it shows," a thought that could have come from his pagan Haloga ancestors.

The talk shifted to lines of march, supply centers, and all the other minutiae that went into a major campaign. Despite his travels in the westlands, Marcus listened carefully. Attention to detail was never wasted.

On the other hand, a couple of the Khamorth chieftains looked actively bored. The nomads made fine scouts and raiders, being as mobile as their distant cousins from Yezd. But they were not interested in anything but the fight itself: preparing for it seemed to them a waste of time. One plainsman snored until his seatmate, a Videssian, kicked him in the ankle under the table. He woke with a start, sputtering guttural curses.

However rude they were in manner, the nomads had a firm grip on the realities of the mercenary's trade. One of them caught Thorisin Gavras' eye during a lull in the planning. Thinking he had some point to make, the Emperor asked, "What is it, Sarbaraz?"

"You not run out of money halfway through fight?" Sarbaraz asked anxiously. "We fight for your Ort'iash, he give us more promises than gold, and his gold not much good either." That was true enough; Ortaias Sphrantzes had debased Videssos' coinage until what was styled a goldpiece was less than one-third gold.

"You'll be paid, never fear," Gavras said. His eyes narrowed in annoyance. "And you know I don't coin trash, either."

"True, true—in city. We get away from city, from—how you say?—treasury, then what? Then maybe you run out of money, like I say. My boys not happy if that happen—maybe make up missing pay off countryside." Sarbaraz grinned insolently, exposing crooked teeth. The Khamorth had no use for farmers, except as prey.

"By Phos, I said you'd be paid!" Thorisin shouted, really

angry now. "And if your bandits start plundering, we'll set the rest of the army on you and see how you like that!"

He took a deep breath and then another, trying to calm himself; before he became Emperor, Marcus thought approvingly, he would have let his temper run away with him. When he spoke again, it was with studied reason: "There will be plenty of coin along for the army's needs. And even if the campaign should run longer than we expect, we won't have to send back to the city for more goldpieces, just to the local mint at, at—" He snapped his fingers in irritation, unable to remember the town's name. By inclination he was a soldier, not a financier; he found taxes and revenues as dull as the Khamorth did grain supply and encampment sites.

"Kyzikos," Alypia Gavra supplied. As was her way, the Emperor's niece had sat quietly through most of the council, occasionally scribbling a note for the history she was composing. Most of the officers took no notice of her; they were used to her silent presence.

For his part, Marcus felt the same mixture of longing, guilt, and a touch of fear Alypia always raised in him. He was more than fond of her, which did nothing to help his sometimes-stormy life with Helvis. Moreover, he knew his feelings were returned, at least in part. The fear came there. If a mercenary could not hope to hold a castle in Videssos, what would befall one who held a princess?

"The mint at Kyzikos is not far southeast of Garsavra," she was explaining to Sarbaraz. "In fact, it was first established as a paycenter for our troops in a war against Makuran . . . let me see." Her green eyes grew thoughtful. ". . . Not quite six hundred years ago."

The nomad had not been happy at having to listen to any woman, even one of the imperial family. At her last words he stared, frankly unbelieving. "All right, you have mint, we get money. No need to mock me—who could remember six five-twenties of years?"

He translated his own people's number-system into Videssian. Scaurus wondered what Gorgidas would make of that; he'd probably say it harked back to a time when the Khamorth could not count past their fingers and toes. But then, Gorgidas was seeing Khamorth aplenty himself.

"Skotos take the rude barbarian," the tribune heard one

Videssian officer whisper to another. "Does he doubt the princess' words?"

But Alypia told Sarbaraz, "I did not mean to mock you," as courteously as if apologizing to a great noble. She was without the hot Gavras temper that plagued Thorisin and had sometimes flared in her father Mavrikios as well. Nor were her features as sharply sculptured as those of the male Gavrai, though she shared their rather narrow oval face.

Marcus wondered what her mother had looked like; Mavrikios' wife had died years before he became Avtokrator. Very few Videssians had green eyes, which must have come from that side of the family.

"When do you plan to start the season's fighting?" someone asked Thorisin.

"Weeks ago," the Emperor snapped. "May Onomagoulos rot in Skotos' hell for robbing me of them—aye, and of all the good men his rebellion killed. Civil war costs a country twice, for winners and losers both are its own."

"Too true," Gaius Philippus muttered, remembering his own young manhood and the fight between Sulla and the backers of Marius—to say nothing of the Social War that had matched Rome against its Italian allies. He raised his voice to speak to Gavras. "We can't get ready for weeks ago, you know."

"Not even you Romans?" the Emperor said with a smile. There was honest respect in his voice; the legionaries had taught Videssos more than it ever knew of instant readiness. Thorisin rubbed his chin as he considered. "Eight days' time," he said at last.

Groans came from several officers; one of the Namdaleni, Clozart Leatherbreeches, growled, "Ask for the moon while you're about it!" But Utprand silenced him with a glare. When the Emperor looked a question at the dour mercenary chief, he got a nod back. He returned it, satisfied; Utprand's word on such things was good.

Gavras did not bother checking with the Romans. Scaurus and Gaius Philippus exchanged smug grins. They could have been ready in half Thorisin's eight days and knew it. It was gratifying to see the Emperor did, too.

As the meeting broke up, Marcus hoped for a few words with Alypia Gavra; in ceremony-ridden Videssos such chances came too seldom. But Mertikes Zigabenos buttonholed him as they walked out through the brightly polished bronze doors of the Hall of the Nineteen Couches. The Videssian officer said, "I hope you're pleased with the healer-priest I got for you."

Under most circumstances Scaurus would have passed it off with a polite compliment. After all, Zigabenos had been trying to do him and his men a favor. The sight of Alypia heading off with her uncle toward the imperial family's private chambers, though, left him irritated enough for candor. "Couldn't you have found one who doesn't drink so much?" he asked.

Zigabenos' handsome face froze. "Your pardon, I am sure," he said. "Now if you will excuse me—" With a bow calculated to the fraction of an inch, he stalked off.

Gaius Philippus came up. "How did you step on *his* corns?" he asked, watching the stiff-backed departure. "Don't tell me you gave him a straight answer?"

"I'm afraid so," the tribune admitted. There were times, he thought, when you could make no worse mistake with the Videssians.

The bustle of preparing to move out did not keep the legionaries from their mornings at the practice field. As they were returning one day, Marcus found the barracks halls a good deal grimier and more untidy than even moving's dislocation could have let him put up with. Annoyed, he went looking for Pullo and Vorenus. It was not like them to let down on any job, even one as menial as a housekeeping detail.

He found them standing side by side in the sun behind one of the bachelor halls. They came out of their rather stiff stance as soon as he came round the corner. He filled his lungs for an angry shout.

But Styppes, who was comfortable under the shadow of one of the citrus trees that surrounded the Romans' quarters, anticipated him. "What are you doing breaking your poses, miserable barbarians? Come back this instant—my sketches are hardly begun!"

Scaurus had not noticed the priest in the shade. He rounded on Styppes, ignoring the two legionaries. "Who, sirrah, gave you the authority to take my men away from the duties I assigned them?"

Styppes squinted as he stepped into the sunshine, several sheets of parchment and a charcoal stick in his hand. "Which has the greater weight," he demanded, "the trivial concerns of this existence or Phos' undying glory, which endures forever?"

"This existence is the only one I know," the tribune retorted. Styppes gave back a place in horror, as if confronted by a wild beast. He made the sun-sign of his god on his breast, gabbling out a quick prayer against Marcus' blasphemy. Scaurus realized he had gone too far; in theology-crazed Videssos, an answer like his could launch a riot. He backtracked. "Neither of these soldiers follows Phos, to my knowledge." He glanced at Vorenus and Pullo, who nodded nervously, caught between Styppes and their commander. Marcus turned back to the priest. "What is your concern with them, then?"

"A proper question," Styppes said grudgingly, though he eyed the tribune with scant liking. "While Skotos will doubtless drag their heathen souls down to the eternal ice below, still in body they are images worth commemorating. I sought their likenesses for icons of Phos' holy men Akakios and Gourias, both of whom are to be depicted as young beardless men."

"You paint icons?" Marcus said, hoping he was keeping the skepticism out of his voice. Next, he thought, the fat tosspot would claim he could lay eggs.

Styppes, though, seemed to be taking him seriously. "Aye," he said, offering his parchment scraps to the Roman. "You will understand these are but rough sketches, and poor ones at that. The charcoal is wrong, too; the fools at the monastery use hazelwood, but myrtle gives a finer line and smudges less."

The tribune hardly heard the priest's complaints. He shuffled rapidly through the pieces of parchment, his eyes growing larger at every one. Styppes was an artist, whatever else he was. In a few deft strokes his charcoal picked out the two Romans' salient features: Pullo's strong nose and angular cheekbones, Vorenus' thoughtful mouth beneath heavy eyebrows, the scar that creased his chin.

Pullo was scarred, too, but Styppes' drawing did not show his battle marks. Used to Roman portraiture, which could be brutally realistic, Marcus asked, "Why have you shown one man's wounds, but not the other's?"

"The holy Gourias was a soldier who suffered martyrdom defending an altar of Phos against the Khamorth pagans, and is to be portrayed with a warrior's tokens. Akakios Klimakos, though, gained fame for his charity and had no experience of war."

"But Pullo here is scarred," the tribune protested.

"What of it? I care nothing for your barbarians for their own sakes; why should I? But as representatives of those who were found worthy of Phos, they gain some small importance. Where their features fail to conform to the ideal, am I to betray the ideal for them? My interest is in the holy Klimakos and Gourias, not your Pullus and Voreno, or whatever their names may be." Styppes laughed at the idea.

His theory of art was opposed to everything Scaurus took for granted, but the tribune was too nettled by his scorn to care about that. "You will, in that case, do me the favor of not distracting my men from the tasks assigned them. *My* interest is in seeing those carried out."

Styppes' nostrils flared. "Impudent pagan!"

"Not at all," the tribune said, wary of making him an open enemy. "But just as you have your concerns, I have mine. Your Gourias would understand the duty a soldier owes his commander—and the harm that can come from weakening it."

The healer-priest looked startled. "That is not an argument I would have looked for from an unbeliever." His eyes were red-veined, but also shrewd.

Marcus spread his hands. Anything that works, he said, but only to himself.

"All right, then," the priest finally said. "Perhaps I was hasty."

"What the men do in their free time is their own affair. If they care to pose for you then, I certainly would not mind," the tribune said, relieved he had smoothed things over.

Calculation grew on Styppes' fat face. "And what of you?" he asked.

"Me?"

"Indeed. When I first set eyes on you, I knew you would make a fine model for portraying the holy Kveldulf the Haloga."

"The holy who?" Marcus said in surprise. The Halogai lived in the cold lands far to the north of Videssos. Some served the Empire as mercenaries, but more often they were raiders and pirates. As far as Scaurus knew, they followed their own grim gods, not Phos. "How did a Haloga become a Videssian holy man?"

"Kveldulf exalted the true faith in the reign of Stavrakios of revered memory." Styppes made the sign of the sun over his heart. "He preached it to his kinsmen in their icebound fjords, but they would not hear him. They would have bound him to a tree to spear him to death, but he stood still for their weapons, choosing to die in a way that served Phos' glory."

No wonder the Halogai had not accepted Kveldulf, the tribune thought. Stavrakios had conquered their province of Agder from them, and they must have seen Kveldulf as a stalking-horse for greater encroachment; Videssos often used religion to further political goals. Scaurus did not share that line of reasoning with Styppes. Instead he said, "Why me? I don't really look like a Haloga."

"True; feature for feature you might almost be a Videssian. All the better. You are blond like the northern savages, and through you I can depict the holy Kveldulf so as to make his origin clear even to unlettered worshipers, but symbolically represent his acceptance of the Empire's true faith."

"Oh." Marcus started to scratch his head, then stopped in mid-gesture, unwilling to show his confusion to the healer-priest. He wished Gorgidas was at his side to make sense of Styppes' prototypes and symbols; if anyone could, it would be a Greek. To the hardheaded Romans, a portrait was a portrait, to be judged by how closely it resembled its original.

Still bemused, he nodded vaguely when Styppes again pressed him to pose, and gave Vorenus and Pullo only a quarter of the blistering they deserved. Hardly believing their luck, they saluted and disappeared before he stopped wool-gathering.

If Kveldulf preached like Styppes, he thought, his fellow barbarians had another good reason for martyring him.

* * *

Despite Styppes' interference, the legionaries' preparations went forward smoothly enough. The surviving Romans were old hands at breaking winter quarters and, under their watchful eyes, the recruits who had joined them since they came to Videssos performed well. The spirit that ran through Scaurus' men was powerful; the newcomers wanted to meet the standards the Romans set.

Their performance satisfied even Gaius Philippus, who chivvied them no worse than he did men who sprang from Latium or Apulia. The senior centurion had a different problem to drive him to distraction, one not so easily dealt with as an unruly trooper.

Three days before the Videssian army was due to leave the capital, the veteran came up to Marcus and brought himself to rigid attention. That was a danger sign in itself; he did not bother with such formality unless he was going to say something he did not think Scaurus would want to hear. When the tribune saw the bruise he carried under one eye, his apprehension doubled—had some soldier been stupid enough to swing at Gaius Philippus? If so, the centurion might be about to report a dead legionary.

"Well?" Scaurus said when Gaius Philippus stayed mute.

"Sir," Gaius Philippus acknowledged, and paused so long again Marcus feared his first hasty guess was right. Then, as if some dam inside the senior centurion went down, he burst out, "Sir, is there any way we can leave the damned tarts behind? The men'll be better soldiers for it, really they will, not thinking about the futtering they'll get tonight or whether their brats spit up dinner."

"I'm sorry, but no," Scaurus answered immediately. He knew Gaius Philippus had never truly accepted the Romans taking partners. It went against every tradition of the legions, and also against the veteran's nature. His only use for women was quick pleasure; anything beyond that seemed beyond his comprehension as well.

But Videssos' customs differed from Rome's. Mercenary companies that served the Avtokrators routinely brought their wives and lemans with them on campaign; Marcus had felt unable to deny his men a privilege the rest of the army enjoyed.

"What went wrong?" the tribune asked.

"Wrong?" Gaius Philippus cried, fairly howling the word in his frustration. "Not a bloody fornicating thing goes right with those idiot women; and when it does, they botch it again just for the fun of it. Scaurus, you should have seen what the slut who gave me this—" He gingerly touched his cheek. "—was up to."

"Tell me." Marcus knew the senior centurion had to work the anger out of his system somehow and was willing to be a handy ear.

"By one of Jove's special miracles, this bitch named Myrrha—she's Publius Flaccus' woman, if you don't know—managed—in five days, mind you—to pack up her gear in three sacks, each of 'em big enough to rupture any donkey ever born. But that's as may be; at least she was packed.

"And then her little darling started whining for a sweet, and may the gods shrivel my balls if she didn't dump every bit of her trash on the floor till she found a honeydrop. I was watching all this, you know. It must have taken a good quarter of an hour—and I let her have it. That's when I picked up my shiner here."

Gaius Philippus' parade-ground bellow could peel whitewash off walls; Myrrha, Scaurus decided, had to be a strong-spirited girl to stand up under it. Used to the harsh discipline of the legions, the senior centurion had long forgotten softer ways. Worse, he was furious at being defied without a chance for revenge.

"Come on, enough of this," Marcus said. He put his arm round the older man's shoulder. "You were doing your duty, which was right. Is it worth letting someone who is misled and ignorant of what is proper distract you?"

"Bet your arse it is," Gaius Philippus growled. Scaurus winced; so much for the soothing power of Stoicism.

Despite the veteran's fit of temper—and largely because of his hard work—the legionaries were ready well before Thorisin's deadline. It came and went, though, without the army sailing. Not only were some detachments—mostly Khamorth mercenaries, but a few Videssian units as well—unprepared, but shipping was still inadequate to transport them, despite the best efforts of the drungarios of the fleet, Taron Leimmokheir.

Onomagoulos' revolt had split the Videssian fleet down the middle; here, too, its aftereffects were still being felt.

"Leimmokheir's trying for jail again." Senpat Sviodo laughed, but there was truth behind the joke. The drungarios had spent months in prison when Thorisin Gavras wrongly thought him involved in an assassination plot. If he truly failed the irascible Emperor, he might well return.

Ships of all sizes and descriptions, from great, beamy transports that normally shipped grain to little lateen-rigged fishing smacks, gathered in Videssos' harbors. It seemed the capital held as many sailors as soldiers. The seamen, Videssians all, swarmed into the city's taverns and eateries. They brawled with the mercenaries, sometimes in sport, sometimes for blood.

Marcus thought of Viridovix and wondered how he'd fared sailing to Prista. If the gusty Celt knew what he was missing, he'd likely head back if he had to swim; he had never been known to back away from a tavern row.

With Videssos' docks jammed with ships berthed gunwale to gunwale, the arrival of one more merchantman out of Kypas in the westlands should have made no difference. But it carried more in its hold than a cargo of wine; the news it bore raced through the capital with the speed of fire. In Videssos, what two men knew, everyone knew.

Phostis Apokavkos brought the word to the legionaries' barracks. He was well connected, having scratched out a living in the thieves' quarter of the city before Scaurus adopted him as a Roman. Now he came rushing in, his long face working with anger. "Curse the filthy foreigners!" he shouted.

Heads jerked up and hands reached instinctively for swords. Videssos was cosmopolitan and xenophobic at the same time; a cry like that too often was the rallying call for a mob. The troopers relaxed when they saw it was only Apokavkos and swore at him for startling them.

"Are you including us, Phostis?" Scaurus asked mildly.

"What? Oh, no, sir!" Apokavkos said, shocked. His hand came up in a smart legionary-style salute. There were times, the tribune thought, when he was more Roman than the Romans. They had given him the chance he'd never had on his farm in the far west or in the capital, and won his total allegiance in return. These days he shaved his face like a

Roman, cursed in accented Latin, and, alone among all the recruits who had joined Marcus' men in Videssos, had his hand branded with the legionary mark.

"It's the Phos-detested Namdalener heretics, sir," he started to explain. In some ways he was a Videssian still.

"Utprand's men?" Scaurus' alertness returned, as did his troopers'. The Romans had done riot duty before, holding the city rabble and the men of the Duchy apart. It was soldiering of a kind to turn any man's stomach.

But Apokavkos shook his head. "No, not them buggers—there's enough honest men about to keep 'em in line." He spat on the floor in disgust. "I'm talkin' 'bout Drax' crew."

"What do you mean?" "Let it out, man!" legionaries called to Apokavkos, but Marcus felt his heart sink. He had a horrid feeling he knew what was coming.

"The whoreson pirate," Apokavkos was saying. "Send him over the Cattle-Crossing to put down a rebel, and he thinks he's a king. The dung-chewing Skotos' spawn's stolen the westlands from us!"

II

"LAND!" THE LOOKOUT CALLED FROM HIS PERCH HIGH ON the *Conqueror*'s mast.

"Och, the gods be praised!" Viridovix croaked. "I thought them after forgetting the word." The Gaul's normally ruddy face was sallow and drawn; cold sweat slicked his red hair and long, sweeping mustaches. He clutched the *Conqueror*'s starboard rail, waiting for the next spasm of seasickness to rack him.

He did not wait long. A puff of breeze brought the stink of hot oil and frying fish from the ship's galley astern. It set him retching again. Tears ran down his cheeks. "Three days now! A dead corp I'd be if it was a week."

In his anguish he spoke Celtic, which no one on board—no one in this entire world—understood. That, though, was not why the crew and the diplomats he accompanied eyed him with curiosity and pity. The waters of the Videssian Sea were almost glassy calm; it was a wonder anyone could be taken sick in such fine weather. Viridovix cursed his feeble stomach, then broke off when it took its revenge.

Gorgidas emerged from the galley with a steaming bowl of beef broth. The Greek might claim to renounce medicine for history, but he was still a physician at heart. Viridovix' misery alarmed him, the more so since he did not share and could not understand the strapping Gaul's frailty.

"Here, soak this up," he said.

"Take it away!" Viridovix said. "I dinna want it."

Gorgidas glared at him. If anything could be counted on to kindle his wrath, it was a deliberately foolish patient. "Would you sooner have the dry heaves instead? You'll keep spewing till we reach port—give yourself something to spew."

"Sure and the sea is a hateful place," the Gaul said, but under Gorgidas' implacable stare he slurped the broth down. A few minutes later he gave most of it back. "A pox! Bad cess to the evil kern who thought of boats. The shame of it, me being on one on account of a woman."

"What do you expect, when you fall foul of the Emperor's mistress?" Gorgidas asked rhetorically—Viridovix' foolishness annoyed him. Komitta Rhangavve had a temper fit to roast meat, and when Viridovix refused to abandon his other women for her, she threatened to go to Thorisin Gavras with a tale of rape; thus the Celt's sudden departure from Videssos.

"Aye, belike you're right, teacher; you've no need to lecture me on it." Viridovix' green eyes measured Gorgidas. "At least it's not myself I'm running from."

The doctor grunted. Viridovix' remark had too much truth in it for comfort—he was a barbarian, but far from stupid. After Quintus Glabrio died under Gorgidas' hands, his lifelong art came to look futile and empty. What good was it, he thought bitterly, if it could not save a lover? History gave some hope for usefulness without involvement.

He doubted he could explain that to the Gaul and did not much want to. In any case, Viridovix' one sentence summed up his rationalizations too well.

Arigh Arghun's son strolled across the deck to them and saved him from his dilemma. Even the nomad from the far steppe beyond the River Shaum had no trouble with his sea legs. "How is he?" he asked Gorgidas, his Videssian sharp and clipped with the accent of his people.

"Not very well," the Greek answered candidly, "but if land's in sight we'll make Prista this afternoon. That should cure him."

Arigh's flat, swarthy face was impassive as usual, but mischief danced in his slanted eyes. He said, "A horse goes up and down, too, you know, V'rid'rix. Do you get horsesick? There's lots of riding ahead of us."

"Nay, I willna be horsesick, snake of an Arshaum," Viridovix said. He swore at his friend with all the vigor in his weakened frame. "Now begone with you, before I puke on your fancy sheepskin boots." Chuckling, Arigh departed.

"Horsesick," Viridovix muttered. "There's a notion to send shudders into the marrow of a man. Epona and her mare'd not allow it."

"That's your Celtic horse-goddess?" Gorgidas asked, always interested in such tidbits of lore.

"The same. I've sacrificed to her often enough, though not since I came to the Empire." The Gaul looked guilty. "Sure and it might be wise to make amends for that at Prista, an I live to reach it."

Prista was a town of contrasts, an outpost of empire at the edge of an endless sea of grass. It held fewer than ten thousand souls, yet boasted fortification stouter than any in Videssos save the capital's. For the Empire it was a watchpost on the steppe from which the wandering Khamorth tribes could be played off against each other or cajoled into imperial service. The plainsmen needed it to trade their tallow, their honey, their wax, their furs and slaves for wheat, salt, wine, silk, and incense from Videssos, but many a nomad khagan had coveted it for his own—and so the stonework. Walls were not always enough to hold them at bay; Prista's past was stormy.

Every sort of building could be found inside those walls. Stately homes of the local gray-brown shale in classical Videssian courtyard style stood next to rough-timbered shacks and houses built of slabs of sod from the plain. On unused ground, nomads' tents of hides or brightly dyed felt sprang up like toadstools.

Though Prista held a Videssian governor and garrison, much of its population was of plains blood. The loungers on the dock were squat, heavy-set men with unkempt beards. Most of them wore linen tunics and trousers instead of the steppe's furs and leathers, but almost all affected the low-crowned fur caps the Khamorth wore in cold weather and hot.

And when Pikridios Goudeles asked one of them to help carry his gear to an inn, the fellow sat unmoving.

Goudeles raised an eyebrow in annoyance. "My luck to pick a deaf-mute," he said and turned to another idler, this one baring his broad hairy chest to the sun. The man ignored him. "Dear me, is this the country of the deaf?" the bureaucrat asked, beginning to sound angry; in Videssos he was used to being heeded.

"I'll make them listen, the spirits fry me if I don't," Arigh said, stepping toward the knot of men. They glowered at him; there was no love lost between Arshaum and Khamorth.

Lankinos Skylitzes touched Arigh's arm. The officer was a man of few words and had no liking for Goudeles. He was quite willing to watch the pen-pusher make an ass of himself. But Arigh could cause riot, not embarrassment, and that Skylitzes would not brook.

"Let me," he said, striding forward in Arigh's place. The dock-rats watched him, not much impressed. He was a large man with a soldier's solid frame, but there were enough of them to deal with him and his comrades, too . . . and he kept company with an Arshaum. But their scowls turned to startled grins when he addressed them in their own speech. After a few seconds of chaffering, four of them jumped up to shoulder the envoys' kits. Only Arigh carried his own—and seemed content to do so.

"What a rare useful thing it must be, to be able to bespeak the people wherever you go," Viridovix said admiringly to Skylitzes. The Gaul was already becoming his usual exuberant self once more. Like the giant Antaios in the myth, Gorgidas thought, he drew strength from contact with the earth.

Economical even in gestures, Skylitzes gave a single nod.

That seemed to frustrate Viridovix, who turned to the Greek. "With your history and all, Gorgidas dear, would you no like to have these folk talk your own tongue so you could be asking them all the questions lurking in your head?"

Gorgidas ignored the sarcasm; Viridovix' question touched a deep hurt in him. "By the gods, Gaul, it would give me pleasure if anyone in this abandoned world spoke my tongue, even you. Here the two of us are as closest kin, but I can no more use Hellenic speech with you than you your Celtic with me. Does it not grate you, too, ever speaking Latin and Videssian?"

"It does that," Viridovix said at once. "Even the Romans are better off than we, for they have themselves to jabber with and keep their speech alive. I tried teaching my lassies the Celtic, but they had no thought for sic things. I fear I chose 'em only for their liveliness under a blanket."

And so were you sated but alone, Gorgidas thought. As if to confirm his guess, the Gaul suddenly burst into a torrent of verse in his native tongue. Arigh and the Videssians gaped at him. The local bearers had been stealing glances at him all along, curious at his fair, freckled skin and fiery hair. Now they shrank back, perhaps afraid he was reciting some spell.

Viridovix rolled on for what might have been five or six stanzas. Then he stumbled to a halt, cursing in Celtic, Videssian, and Latin all mixed together.

"Beshrew me, I've forgotten the rest," he mourned and hung his head in shame.

After the imperial capital's broad straight streets paved with cobblestones or flags and its efficient underground drainage system, Prista came as something of a shock. The main thoroughfare was hard-packed dirt. It zigzagged like an alley and was hardly wider than one. Sewage flowed in a channel down the center. Gorgidas saw a nomad undo his trousers and urinate in the channel; no one paid him any mind.

The Greek shook his head. In Elis, where he had grown up, such things were commonplace. The cry of "*Exito!* Here it comes!" warned pedestrians that a fresh load of slops was about to be thrown out. But the Romans had better notions of sanitation, and in their greater cities the Videssians did, too. Here on the frontier they did not bother—and surely paid the price in disease.

Well, what of it? Gorgidas thought; they have healer-priests to set things right. Then he wondered even about that. By the look of things, many of the Pristans kept their plains customs and probably did not follow Phos. He glanced toward the Videssian god's temple. Its discolored stones and weather-softened lines proclaimed it one of the oldest buildings in the town, but streaks of tarnish ran down the gilded dome atop it. Skylitzes saw that, too, and frowned.

If Pikridios Goudeles felt any dismay at the temple's

shabby condition, he hid it well. But he grew voluble when he saw the inside of the inn the natives, through Skylitzes, had assured him was the best Prista offered. "What a bloody hole! I've seen stockyards with better-run pens."

Two of the Pristans scowled; Gorgidas had thought they understood Videssian. In truth, the Greek was with Goudeles. The taproom was small, poorly furnished, and decades overdue for cleaning. Caked-on soot blackened the wall above each torch bracket. The place smelled of smoke, stale liquor, and staler sweat.

Nor was the clientele more prepossessing. Two or three tables were filled by loafers who might have been blood-brothers to the idlers on the docks. Half a dozen Videssians drank at another. Though most of them were in their middle years, they wore gaudy, baggy-sleeved tunics like so many young street ruffians; each looked to have a fortune in gold on his fingers and round his neck. Their voices were loud and sharp, their speech filled with the capital's slang.

In Latin, Viridovix murmured, "Dinna be gambling with these outen your own dice."

"I know thieves when I see them," Gorgidas answered in the same language, "even rich thieves."

If the taverner was one such, he spent his money elsewhere. A short, fat man, his sullen mouth and suspicious eyes belied all the old saws about jolly plump folk. The upstairs room he grudgingly yielded to the embassy was hardly big enough to hold the five straw-stuffed mattresses a servant fetched in.

Goudeles tipped the men with the party's equipment. Once they had gone, he fell down onto a mattress—the thickest one, Gorgidas noted—and burst out laughing. At his companions' curious stares, he said, "I was just thinking: if this is the best Prista has to offer, Phos preserve me from the worst."

"Enjoy it while you may," Skylitzes advised.

"No, the pudgy one is right," Arigh said. Goudeles, unpacking a fresh robe, did not seem overjoyed at his support, if that was what it was. The Arshaum went on, "Even the finest of towns is a prison; only on the plains can a man breathe free."

Someone rapped politely on the door—a soldier. He had the half-Khamorth look of most folk here, being wide-shouldered, dark, and bushy-bearded. But he wore chain mail, instead of the boiled leather of the plains, and spoke good Videssian. "You are the gentlemen from the *Conqueror*, the envoys to the Arshaum?"

He bowed when they admitted it. "His excellency the *hypepoptes* Methodios Sivas greets you, then, and bids you join him at sunset tonight. I will come back then to guide you to his residence." He dipped his head again, sketched a salute, and left as abruptly as he had come. His boots thumped on the narrow stone stairway.

"Is the *hyp*—whatever—a wizard, to be after knowing we're here almost before we are?" Viridovix exclaimed. He had seen enough sorcery in the Empire to mean the question seriously.

"Not a bit of it," Goudeles replied, chuckling at his naïveté. "Surely as Phos' sun rises in the east, one of the leisured gentlemen of the harbor is in his pay."

More sophisticated than the Gaul at governors' wiles, Gorgidas had reasoned that out for himself, but he was not displeased to have it confirmed. This Sivas' main function was to watch the plains for the Empire. If he kept them as closely surveyed as he did his own city, Videssos was well served.

Methodios Sivas was a surprisingly young man, not far past thirty. His outsized nose gave him an air of engaging homeliness, and he was boisterous enough to fit his frontier surroundings. He pounded Arigh on the back, shouting, "Arghun's son, is it? Will you make me put sentries at the wells again?"

Arigh giggled, a startling sound from him. "No need. I'll be good."

"You'd better." Making sure each of his guests had a full wine cup, Sivas explained, "When this demon's sprig came through here on his way to the city, he threw a handful of frogs into every well in town."

Lankinos Skylitzes looked shocked and then guffawed; Goudeles, Viridovix, and Gorgidas were mystified. "Don't you see?" Sivas said, and then answered himself, "No, of course you don't. Why should you? You don't deal with the barbarians every day—sometimes I forget it's me on the edge of nowhere, not the rest of the Empire. Here's the long and short of it, then: all Khamorth are deathly afraid of frogs. They wouldn't drink our water for three days!"

"Hee, hee!" Arigh said, laughing afresh at the memory of his practical joke. "That's not all, and you know it. They had to pay a Videssian to hunt down all the little beasts, and then sacrifice a black lamb over each well to drive away the pollution. And your priest of Phos tried to stop *that*, quacking about heathen rites. It was glorious."

"It was ghastly," Sivas retorted. "One clan packed up an easy five thousand goldpieces' worth of skins and went back to the steppe with 'em. The merchants howled for months."

"Frogs, is it?" Gorgidas said, scribbling a note on a scrap of parchment. The *hypepoptes* noticed and asked him why. Rather hesitantly, he explained about his history. Sivas surprised him with a thoughtful nod and several intelligent questions; sharp wits hid beneath his rough exterior.

The governor had other interests hardly to be expected from a frontiersman. Though his residence, with its thick walls, slit windows, and iron-banded oak doors, could double as a fortress, the garden that bloomed in the courtyard was a riot of colors. Mallows and roses bloomed in neat rows. So did yellow and lavender adder's-tongues, which told Gorgidas of Sivas' skill. The low plants, their leaves mottled green and brown, belonged in moist forests or on the mountainside, not here at the edge of the steppe.

As was only natural, Sivas, isolated from events in the capital, was eager to hear the news the embassy brought with it. He exclaimed in satisfaction when he learned how Thorisin Gavras had regained control of the sea from the rebel forces led by Baanes Onomagoulos and Elissaios Bouraphos. "Damn the traitors anyway," he said. "I've been sending messages with every ship that sailed for the capital for the last two months; they must have sunk them all. That's too long, with Avshar running loose."

"Are you sure it's himself?" Viridovix asked. The name of the wizard-prince was enough to distract him from his flirtation with one of the *hypepotes*' serving girls. A bachelor, Sivas had several comely women in his employ, even if their mixed blood made them too stocky to conform to the Videssian ideal of beauty.

He did not seem put out by the Celt's trifling. Viridovix

had obviously intrigued him from the moment he set eyes on him; men of the Gaul's stature and coloring were rare among the peoples the Videssians knew, and his musical accent was altogether strange.

Now Sivas answered, "Who but shrouds himself in robes so his very eyes are unseen? Who but stirs discord in his wake as the wind stirs waves on the sea? And who but rides a great black charger in a land of ponies? On the plains, that were enough to name him without the other two."

"Sure and it's the spalpeen, all right," Viridovix agreed. "Still and all, my good Celtic blade should do to let the mischief out of him." Methodios Sivas raised a politely skeptical eyebrow, but Gorgidas knew Viridovix was not idly boasting. His sword was twin to the one Scaurus bore, both of them forged and spell-wrapped by Gallic druids and both uncannily mighty in this land where magic flourished.

"Yet another matter has reached me since my last dispatches to Videssos," Sivas said. By his voice, it was one he would rather not have heard. He paused for a moment before going on: "You will understand this is rumor alone, and unsupported, but it's said Varatesh has thrown in his lot with your cursed wizard."

Again Gorgidas was conscious of something important slipping past him; again Viridovix and Goudeles were as mystified. Even Arigh seemed unsure of the name. But Lankinos Skylitzes knew it. "The outlaw," he said, and it was not a question.

"It's but a voice on the breeze, you understand," Sivas repeated.

"Phos grant it stay such," Skylitzes answered, and drew the sun-sign on his breast. Seeing his comrades' incomprehension, he said, "The man is dangerous and wily, and his riders are no bargain. A great clan against us would be worse, but not much."

His obvious concern reached Gorgidas, who did not think Skylitzes one to alarm himself over trifles. Arigh was less impressed. "A Khamorth," he said contemptuously. "Next you'll have me hiding from baby partridges in the grass."

"He's one to be reckoned with, and growing stronger," Sivas said. "You may not know it, but this winter when the rivers froze he raided west over the Shaum."

Arigh gaped, then hissed a curse in his own language. The Arshaum were convinced of their superiority to the Khamorth, and with justice; had they not driven the bushy-beards east over the river? It had been decades since Khamorth, even outlaws, dared strike back.

Sivas shrugged. "He's a ready-for-aught, you see." Arigh was still stormy, so the *hypepoptes* called to his serving maid, "Filennar, why don't you detach yourself from your brick-whiskered friend and fetch us a full skin?"

She swayed away, Viridovix following her hungrily with his eyes.

"A skin?" Arigh said eagerly. He forgot his anger. "Kavass? By the three wolf tails of my clan, it's five years since I set tongue to it. You benighted farmer-folk make do with wine and ale."

"A new tipple?" That was Pikridios Goudeles, sounding intrigued. Gorgidas remembered the Arshaum boasting of the plains drink before, but had forgotten what the nomads brewed it from. Viridovix, a toper born, no longer seemed so dismayed over Filennar's disappearance.

She soon returned, carrying a bulging horsehide with the hair still on the outside. At Sivas' gesture, she handed it to Arigh, who took it as tenderly as he might an infant. He undid the rawhide lace that held the drinking-mouth, raised the skin to his face. He drank noisily; it was good manners on the plains to advertise one's enjoyment.

"Ahhh!" he said at last, pinching the mouth closed after a draught so long his face had begun to darken.

"There's dying scarlet!" Viridovix exclaimed—city slang for drinking deep. He raised the skin for a swig of his own, but at the first taste his anticipation was replaced by a surprised grimace. He spat a large mouthful out on the floor. "Fauggh! What a foul brew! What goes into the making of it, now?"

"Fermented mares' milk," Arigh answered.

Viridovix made a face. "Sure and it tastes like the inside of a dead snail." The Arshaum glowered at him, irritated at hearing his beloved drink maligned.

Lankinos Skylitzes and Methodios Sivas, both long familiar with the steppe brew, showed no qualms at drinking and smacked their lips in best nomad style. When the skin came to

Goudeles he swallowed enough for politeness' sake, but did not seem sorry to pass it on to Gorgidas.

"Get used to it, Pikridios," Skylitzes said, amusement just below the surface of his voice.

"That is a phrase with which I could easily grow bored," the bureaucrat said tartly. More than a little warmed by all he'd drunk, Skylitzes chuckled.

Gorgidas gave a suspicious sniff as he hefted the horsehide, now half empty. He expected a sour, cheesy odor, but the kavass smelled much more like a light, clear ale. He drank. Actually, he thought, it had surprisingly little flavor of any kind, but it put a quick warm glow in his belly. For potency it matched any wine he knew.

"It's not bad, Viridovix. Try it again," he urged. "If you were looking for something as sweet as wine it's no wonder you were startled, but surely you've had worse."

"Aye, and better, too," the Gaul retorted. He reached for a flagon of wine. "On the steppe I'll have no choice, but the now I do and I'm for the grape, begging your pardon, Arigh. Pass him his snail-squeezings, Greek, sith he's so fond of 'em and all." Viridovix' larynx bobbed as he swallowed.

Sivas gave the embassy a token guard of ten men. "Enough to show you're under the Empire's protection," he explained. "Prista's whole garrison wouldn't be enough to save you from real trouble, and if I did send them out, every clan on the plains would unite to burn the town round my ears. They find us useful, but only so long as we don't seem dangerous to them."

The *hypepoptes* did let the envoys choose horses and remounts from the garrison's stables. His generosity saved them from the mercies of their fellow guests at the inn, who had proved to be horse traders. True to Viridovix' prediction, they were also gamblers. Gorgidas sensibly declined to game with them; Arigh and Pikiridios Goudeles were less cautious. The Arshaum lost heavily, but Goudeles held his own.

When Skylitzes heard that he smiled a rare smile, observing, "Seal-stampers are bigger bandits than mere horse copers dream of being."

"To the ice with you, my friend," Goudeles said. Gold clinked in his belt-pouch.

In another area the bureaucrat was wise enough to take expert advice. Like Gorgidas and Viridovix, he asked Arigh to choose a string of horses for him. Only Skylitzes trusted his own judgment enough to pick his beasts, and did so well that the plainsman looked at him with new respect. "There's a couple there I wouldn't mind having for myself," he said.

"Och, how can he bc telling that?" Viridovix complained. "I know summat o' horseflesh, at least as we Celts and the Videssians reckon it, and such a grand lot of garrons I've never seen before, like as so many beans in the pod."

With its Gallic flavor, the word was an apt one to describe the rough-coated steppe ponies. They were small, sturdy beasts, unlovely and not very tame—nothing like the highbred steeds the Videssians prized. But Arigh said, "Who needs a big horse? The plains beasts'll run twice as long and find forage where one of those oat-burners would starve. Isn't that right, my lovely?" He stroked one of his horses on the muzzle, then jerked his hand away as the beast snapped at him.

Gorgidas laughed with the rest, but nervously. He was at best an indifferent horseman, having practiced the art only rarely. Well, then, you can't help getting better, he told himself; but Arigh's promise of months in the saddle made his legs twinge in anticipation.

A week after the *Conqueror* put into Prista, the embassy and its accompanying guards rode out the town's north gate. Though the party numbered only fifteen, from any distance it looked far larger. In steppe fashion, each man rode at the head of five to seven horses, some carrying gear and iron rations, the rest unloaded. The nomad custom was to ride a different animal each day so as not to wear down any of them.

The morning sun shone silver off the Maiotic Bay. The pinched-off arm of the Videssian Sea was several miles to the east, but there were no hills to screen it from view. Beyond the bay a darkness marked another promontory of land jutting south into the ocean. That horizon line, too, was low, flat, and smooth, another portion of the steppe that rolled west—how far? No man knew.

Gorgidas gave such things irregular thought. Most of his attention rested on staying aboard his horse; as beasts will, the cursed animal sensed his inexperience and seemed to take a perverse pleasure in missteps that almost threw him from the saddle. That, luckily, was of the style both Videssians and plainsfolk favored: high-cantled, with pommels before and behind, and with that marvelous invention, stirrups. Without such aids the Greek would have been tossed more than once.

All the improvements, though, did nothing to dull the growing ache in his thighs. He was in good hard shape, able to keep up with the Roman legionaries on march, but riding plainly made different demands. His discomfort was only made worse by the short stirrup leathers the nomads used, which made him draw his knees up and cramped his legs the more.

"Why keep them so short?" he asked the squad leader heading the embassy's guardsmen.

The underofficer shrugged. "Most things in Prista we do Khamorth-style," he said. "They like to stand tall in the saddle for archery." He was a Videssian himself, a lean dark man with heavily muscled forearms. His name was Agathias Psoes. Three or four of his men also looked to have come from across the sea. The rest, like the soldier who had greeted the ambassadors, were obviously locals. Among themselves all the troopers spoke a strange jargon, so thickly laced with Khamorth phrases and turns of syntax that Gorgidas could hardly follow it.

"I have some longer strips," Arigh said. "We Arshaum don't need to get up to know what we're shooting at." He won scowls from his escorts, but ignored them. So did Gorgidas. He took the leathers gratefully. They helped—somewhat.

The Greek's distress was nothing compared to that of Pikridios Goudeles. The seal-stamper was an influential man, but not one who had ever been required to push his body much. When the day's ride ended and he awkwardly scrambled down from his horse, he tottered about like a man of ninety. His hands were soft, too, and chafed from holding the reins. Collapsing to the ground with a groan, he said, "Now I understand Gavras' ploy in making me a legate; he expects my exhausted corpse to be buried on these plains, and may well get his wish."

"He might have wanted you to see the price the Empire pays for your comforts in the city," Lankinos Skylitzes said.

"Hrmmp. Without comforts, what's the point of civilization? When you're in Videssos, my sober friend, you sleep in a bed, too, not rolled in your blanket on the street." Goudeles' bones might ache, but his tongue was still sharp. Skylitzes grunted and went off to help the cavalrymen gather brush for the night's watchfire.

It blazed hot and bright, the only light as far as the eye could reach. Gorgidas felt naked and alone on the vast empty plain. He missed the comforting earthworks and ditches the Romans threw up wherever they went; a whole army could be skulking in the darkness just beyond the sentries' vigilance. He jumped as a nightjar flashed briefly into sight, drawn by the insects the fire lured.

Breakfast the next morning was smoked mutton, hard cheese, and thin, flat wheatcakes one of the troopers cooked on a portable griddle. The nomads seldom ate bread. Ovens were too bulky for a people ever on the move. The cakes were chewy and all but flavorless; Gorgidas was sure he would grow mightily tired of them in short order. Well, he thought, with such fare you need hardly fear a flux of the bowels—more likely the opposite. The climate spoke for that, too—folk in lands with harsh winters and a prevailing north wind tended to constipation, or so Hippokrates taught.

His medical musings annoyed him—that should be over and done. To set his conscience at ease, he jotted a note on the soldier's cooking methods.

Viridovix had been unusually quiet on the first day's journey out of Prista. He was again as the embassy left camp behind. He rode near the rear of the company and kept looking about in all directions, now left, now right, now back over his shoulder. "There's nothing there," Gorgidas said, thinking he was worried they were being followed.

"How right you are, and what a great whacking lot of nothing it is, too!" the Celt exclaimed. "I'm feeling like a wee bug on a plate, the which is no pleasure at all. In the forests of Gaul it was easy to see where the world stopped, if you take my meaning. But here there's no end to it; on and on it goes forever."

The Greek dipped his head, feeling some of the same unhappiness; he, too, had come to manhood in a narrow land. The plains showed a man his insignificance in the world.

Arigh thought them both daft. "I only feel alive on the

steppe," he said, repeating his words back in Prista. "When I first came to Videssos I hardly dared walk down the street for fear the buildings would fall on me. How folk cramp themselves in cities all their lives is past me."

"As Pindar says, convention rules all," Gorgidas said. "Give us time, Arigh, and we'll grow used to your endless spaces."

"Aye, I suppose we will," Viridovix said, "but I'm hanged if I'll like 'em." The Arshaum's shrug showed his indifference.

In one way the broad horizon worked to the traveler's advantage: game was visible at an extraordinary distance. Frightened by the horses, a flock of gray partridges leaped into the air. They flew fast and low, coasting, flapping frantically, coasting again. Several troopers nocked arrows and spurred their mounts after the fleeing birds. Their double-curved bows, strengthened with horn, sent arrows darting faster than any hawk.

"We should have nets," Skylitzes said as he watched three shafts in quick succession miss one dodging bird, but the horsemen were archers trained from childhood, and not every shot went wide. They bagged eight partridges; Gorgidas' mouth watered at the thought of the dark, tender meat.

"Good shooting," Viridovix said to one of Agathias Psoes' men. The soldier, from his looks almost pure Khamorth, held two birds by the feet. He grinned at the Celt. Viridovix went on, "It's a fine flat path your shafts have, too. What's the pull on your bow?"

The trooper passed it to him. Next to the long yew bows the Celts favored, it was small and light, but Viridovix grunted in surprise as he tugged on the sinew bowstring. His arm muscles bunched before the bow began to bend. "Not a bit of a toy, is it?" he said, handing it back.

Pleased at his reaction, the soldier smiled slyly. "Your shield, give him here," he said, his Videssian as accented as the Celt's. Viridovix, who wore it slung over his back when combat was not near, undid its strap and gave it to the horseman. It was a typical Gallic noble's shield: oblong, bronze-faced, with raised spirals of metal emphasized by enameling in bright red and green. Viridovix kept it in good repair; he was fastidious about his arms and armor.

"Pretty," the trooper remarked, propping it upright against a bush. He walked his horse back until he was perhaps a hundred yards from it. With a savage yell he spurred the animal forward, let fly at point-blank range. The shield went spinning, but when Viridovix recovered it there was no shaft stuck in it.

"Sure and the beast kicked it ov—" the Celt began. He stopped in amazement. High in the upper right-hand corner of the shield, a neat hole punched through bronze and wood alike. "By my enemies' heads," he said softly, shaking his own.

The guardsman picked up his arrow, which had flown another ten or twelve feet after piercing the shield. He put it back in his quiver, saying, "A good buckler you have. Through mine it would farther have gone." His own shield was a small round target of wood and leather, good for knocking a sword aside, but not much more.

Viridovix said, "And I was after thinking the plainsmen were light-armored on account of the scrawny little cobs they rode, the which couldna carry the weight o' metal."

"Why else?" Gorgidas said.

"Use your eyes, clodpoll of a Greek," the Celt replied, waving his shield in Gorgidas' face. "Wi' sic bows you're a pincushion with or without ironmongery, so where's the good in muffling up?"

To Viridovix' irritated surprise, Gorgidas burst out laughing. "Where's the jape?"

"Your pardon," the Greek said, jotting a note. "The idea of a weapon so strong as to make defense unprofitable never occurred to me. This steppe bow isn't one, you know; in their mail and plate the Namdaleni stood up to it quite well. But the abstract concept is fascinating."

Trying to poke his little finger through the arrowhole, Viridovix muttered, "The pox take your abstract concepts."

The moving brown smudge in the distance slowly resolved itself into a herd of cattle, their horns pricking up like bare branches from a winter forest. With them were their herders, perhaps a score of Khamorth. Most of them abandoned the herd and came riding up when they spied the approaching envoys.

Their leader shouted several phrases in his own tongue, then, seeing imperials among the newcomers, added in horrible Videssian, "Who you? What here you do?"

He did not wait for an answer. His swarthy face darkened with anger when he noticed Arigh. "Arshaum!" he cried, and his men snarled and grabbed for swords and bows. "What you do with Arshaum?" he asked Goudeles, choosing the bureaucrat perhaps because he was most splendidly dressed. "Arshaum make all Khamorth clans—how you say?—suffer. Your Emperor eat pig guts to deal with them. I, Olbiop son of Vorishtan, say this and I true speak."

"We kill!" one of Olbiop's men cried. The guardsmen were reaching for their weapons, too, and Arigh had an arrow ready to nock. Viridovix and Lankinos Skylitzes both sat warily, each with hand on sword hilt. Gorgidas' Roman blade was still buried in his gear; he waited for whatever fortune might bring.

It was then that Pikridios Goudeles showed his worth. "Stop, O noble Olbiop Vorishtan's son, lest you fall unwittingly into error!" he said dramatically, his voice booming forth with a rhetor's well-trained intonations. Gorgidas doubted if the nomad caught more than his own name, but that was enough to make his head swivel to Goudeles.

"Translate for me, old man, that's a good fellow," the bureaucrat whispered to Skylitzes beside him.

At the soldier's nod he struck a pose and launched into florid Videssian oratory: "O leader of the Khamorth, our being slain by you would be a matter more difficult, grievous, and deadly than death itself. Its—"

"I couldn't repeat that, let alone translate it," Skylitzes said, eyes widening.

"Shut up," Goudeles hissed, and then resumed with a gesture no less graceful for being made atop a scruffy horse rather than in a chamber of the imperial palace. Skylitzes followed gamely as the rhetoric poured out.

"Its defamation would live on to remain among all men; this thing has never been done, but will have been invented by you. There will be clear testimony to your deed, that you killed men on an embassy; and the report's fearfulness will be shown still more fearful by the deed."

The translation was plainly a poor copy of the original,

without its sudden reversals, its alliteration, its twisting tenses. It did not matter; Goudeles had the nomads under his spell whether or not they understood him. Like most unlettered folk, they set great stock in oratory, and the seal-stamper was a master in an older school than theirs.

He went on, "I pray I might know my end by your swords today, now that I have heard my Avtokrator greeted with false words. Let me persist, though, in entreating you, first, to look upon us more gently and to slacken your anger and soften your quick choler with charity; and, second, to be persuaded by the common custom of ambassadors. For we are the shapers of peace and have been established as the dispensers of its holy calm.

"Therefore remember that until the present our relations have been incorruptibly tranquil—surely we shall continue to enjoy the same kindness. I know well that your affairs would not otherwise be secure. For understanding most properly offered to those who are near—understanding, of course, which does not turn aside from that which is suitable—will not be evilly influenced by the yet-unrevealed exchange of fortune."

He bowed to the Khamorth. They nodded back, dazed by his eloquence. "What was all o' that meaning?" Viridovix asked Gorgidas.

"Don't kill us."

"Ah," the Celt said, satisfied. "I thought that's what the omadhaun said, but I wasna sure."

"Don't trouble yourself. Neither were the nomads." The turgid Videssian oratory, awash in rhetorical tricks, never failed to oppress Gorgidas. He was used to a cleaner, sparer style. The height of Videssian eloquence was to say nothing and take hours doing it. Still, Goudeles' harangue had served its purpose; the Khamorth lapped up every gaudy phrase.

"Ha, Silvertongue!" Olbiop was saying to Goudeles. "You come to village with us, eat, spend night, be happy." He leaned forward and planted a kiss on the Videssian's cheek. Goudeles accepted it without change of expression, but, when Olbiop turned to bawl orders to his followers, the pen-pusher gave his comrades a stricken look.

"There are exigencies in the diplomat's art I never anticipated," he murmured plaintively. "Do they never bathe on the plains?" He surreptitiously rubbed at the spot, then wiped his hand on his robe over and over again.

Most of the Khamorth rode back to their herd. A handful stayed with Olbiop to escort the embassy. "Come with me you," the leader said. Agathias Psoes looked a question at Skylitzes, who nodded.

"How do the barbarians come by villages?" Gorgidas asked, Olbiop being safely out of earshot. "I thought they were all nomads, forever following their flocks."

Skylitzes shrugged. "Once Videssos held more of the steppe than Prista alone, and planted colonies of farmers on it. Some linger, as serfs to the plainsmen. In time, I suppose, they will die out or become wanderers themselves. Already most of them have forgotten Phos."

They reached the farming village not long before sunset. Olbiop led them straight through its unkempt fields, trampling the green young wheatstalks with lordly indifference. Gorgidas saw other similar swathes and wondered how the villagers raised enough of their crop to live.

Yapping dogs met the incomers at the edge of the village. Already they had passed crumbling buildings which said it had once been larger. One of the Khamorth shot an arrow at a particularly noisy hound. He grazed it in the leg. It fled, yelping shrilly, while the plainsman's comrades shouted at him. "They mock him for nearly missing," Skylitzes explained, anticipating Gorgidas' question.

"Headman!" Olbiop bellowed in Videssian as he rode down the grass-filled central street. He followed it with a stream of abuse in his own language.

An elderly man in rough, colorless homespun emerged from one of the delapidated houses. The rest of the villagers stayed out of sight, from long experience with their overlords. The headman went down to his belly on the ground before Olbiop, as a citizen of the Empire might to Thorisin Gavras. Skylitzes' mouth tightened at such homage rendered a barbarian of no high rank, but he said nothing.

"We need food, sleep-place, how you say—comfort against cold," Olbiop ordered, ticking off the points on his fingers. A colloquy in the nomads' tongue followed. At length the Khamorth asked a question of Psoes, who nodded easily.

Gorgidas resolved to learn the plains speech; he missed too much by depending on his companions to interpret.

Psoes was still chuckling. "As if the boys'd rust, spending another night in the open. You toffs enjoy yourselves, now." The underofficer spoke briefly to his men, who began to make camp in the village square. At their leader's word, Olbiop's followers joined them. The chieftain stayed with the legates.

The headman bowed to the Videssian party. "An it please you, this way," he said. His accent was plains-roughened, his phrasing archaic; the village was long sundered from living currents of speech in the Empire.

The building he led them to had been a temple once. A wooden spire still topped its roof, though Phos' golden globe had fallen from it. The roof itself was patched with thatch; hunks of sod chinked the walls, which were of rudely cut local stone. There was no door—a leather curtain hung in the entranceway.

"Well, 'tis the guesting house. Climb you down and go in," the village headman said, not understanding the hesitation of some of his visitors. "Your beasts will be seen to. Make free with the fire—there's plenty to burn. I go to ready your victuals and other, ah, comforts. How many be ye?" He counted them twice. "Six, is it? Aye, well," he sighed.

"For your hospitality you have our heartfelt gratitude," Goudeles said courteously, dismounting with obvious relief. "Should we need some trifling assistance, how may we address you?"

The headman gave him a wary glance. Bluster and threats he was used to; what danger lurked behind these honeyed words? Finding none, he grudgingly answered, "I'm called Plinthas."

"Splendid, good Plinthas. Again, we thank you." More suspicious than ever, the villager led their horses away. "Phos, what an ugly name," Goudeles exclaimed as soon as he was gone. The seal-stamper went on, "Let's see what we have here." He sounded as if he expected the worst.

The one-time temple had a musty smell; guests seemed few and far between. The benches that had once surrounded the central worship area were long gone—on the plains, wood was too precious to sit idle in an unused building. Nor had it known an altar for many years; in place of that centerpiece was a fire pit. Skylitzes was right, Gorgidas thought. Not even a memory of Phos remained here.

The Videssian officer drew flint and steel from his pouch and deftly lit the central fire. The envoys stretched out at full length on the hard-packed dirt floor. Goudeles sighed with bliss. As the party's poorest horseman, he was the most saddlesore. His soft hands were no longer merely chafed, but blistered. "Have you a salve for these?" he asked Gorgidas, displaying them.

"I fear I packed few medicines," the Greek replied, not caring to explain to Goudeles his reasons for abandoning the physician's art. Seeing the Videssian's pain though, he added, "A salve of grease and honey would soothe you, I think—you could ask this Plinthas for them."

"Thanks; I'll do that when he comes back."

The fire suddenly flared as a fresh bundle of tight-packed straw caught. Gorgidas glimpsed a hand-sized splotch of blue paint high up on one wall. He walked over for a closer look. It was the last remnant of a religious fresco that probably once covered all the walls of the temple. Neglect, mold, soot, and time had allied to efface the rest—like the nameless village itself, the shabby ruin of a brighter dream.

The leather curtain twitched aside; Goudeles opened his mouth to make his request of Plinthas. But it was not the headman who entered the shrine-turned-serai. Half a dozen young women came in, some carrying food, others cooking tools and soft sleeping mats, the last almost staggering under the weight of several skins of what Gorgidas was sure would be either kavass or beer.

Olbiop gave a roar of approval. He leaped to his feet and grabbed at one of the women, kissing her noisily and folding her into a bear hug. She barely had time to pass the skillet and saucepan she bore to a companion before his hands were greedy on her, squeezing her rump and reaching inside her loose tunic.

"The Khamorth is a pig, aye, but no need for such horror on your face," Skylitzes said softly to Gorgidas. "Giving guests women is a plains courtesy; the unforgivable rudeness is to decline."

The Greek was still dismayed, but for a reason different from the one Skylitzes might have guessed. He could not remember how many years it had been since he last coupled with a woman—fifteen at least, and that final time had been anything but a success. Now it seemed he had no choice—refusal, the Videssian had made clear, was impossible. He tried not to think about the price failure would cost him in the eyes of his fellows.

Viridovix, on the other hand, shouted gleefully when he overheard Skylitzes. He swung one of the girls into his arms; choosier than Olbiop, he picked the prettiest of the six. She was short and slim, with wavy brown hair and large eyes. Unlike the rest, she wore a brooch of polished jet near the neck of her blouse. "And what might your name be now, my fine colleen?" the Celt asked, smiling down at her; he was almost a foot taller than she.

"Evanthia, Plinthas' daughter," she answered shyly.

"You mean himself outside? The headman?" At her nod Viridovix chuckled. "Then it must be your mother you look like, for he's no beauty."

She bobbed in a curtsey, smiling back at him now. Gorgidas had seen him weave that spell before; few were immune to it. Evanthia said, "I never knew there were men with hair the color of rust. Your speech rings strangely, too; what far land are you from?"

With that invitation Viridovix was off, launching into his tale like a man diving into the sea. He paused a few seconds later to take a mat from Evanthia and spread it on the ground. "Here, sit by me, my darling, the which'll make it more comfortable for you to listen." He winked at Gorgidas over her shoulder.

The other partnerings were quickly made. The girls from the village did not seem upset at the arrangement—save perhaps Olbiop's chosen, for he pawed her unceasingly. On reflection, Gorgidas found no reason why they should be. They were but following their people's longtime custom, a practice he had extolled not long before.

His own companion was named Spasia. She was not as well-favored as Viridovix' lady; she was plump and had a faint fuzz above her upper lip. But her voice was pleasant, and Gorgidas soon saw she was not stupid, though she had no more idea of the world around her than any villager would. Her eyes kept flicking to the Greek's face. "Is something wrong?" he asked her, wondering if she could sense she did not rouse him.

But her reply was altogether artless: "Are you what they call a eunuch? Your cheeks are so smooth."

"No," he said, trying not to laugh. "My folk have the custom of shaving their faces, and I follow it even here." He reached into his pack to show her the leaf-shaped razor he used.

She felt the edge. "Why keep such a painful custom?" she asked. He did laugh then, for he had no ready answer.

The women readied the food they had brought: chickens, ducks, rabbits, fresh-baked loaves of bread—real bread, for, being settled, they could have a permanent oven—several kinds of berry tarts, and various herbs and leafy vegetables mixed together into a salad. Roasting meat's welcome smell filled the former temple.

Pleasantly full from a good dinner, his head buzzing a little after several draughts of potent kavass, Gorgidas leaned back on his mat and scratched his belly. With the Videssians and Viridovix, he had laughed at Olbiop and Arigh for refusing the salad; to the nomads, greens were cattle fodder, not food fit for men. "Don't be egging 'em on, now," Viridovix had said. "All the more for the rest of us." The Greek had gone along; some of the vegetables, including a white radish strong enough to bring tears to his eyes, were new to him, while a tasty dressing of spiced vinegar and oil added savor to the serving.

If the plainsmen had no yen for lettuces and cucumbers, they made up for it with their drinking, downing the fermented mare's milk in great gulps. They smacked their lips and belched enormously with the good manners of the steppe. Olbiop's companion kept a kavass skin in his hand as often as she could; Gorgidas wondered if she hoped he would swill himself into insensibility.

If so, she was disappointed. The Khamorth was no inexperienced stripling, to pass out when there were other pleasures yet to enjoy. He pulled the girl to him, worked his hands under her tunic once more, and pulled it off inside out over her head. She yielded with no great enthusiasm; her air was that of someone who had tried a ploy, seen it fail, and now was left with the consequences.

Gorgidas had thought the Khamorth would take the woman out into the night, but he pulled down her skirt, stripped off his own fur jacket, trousers, and boots, and fell to with a will, as if the two of them were alone. The Greek looked away; Pikridios Goudeles pretended not to see, never missing a syllable in the story he was telling his companion; Arigh and Skylitzes, used to steppe ways, were themselves not far behind the Khamorth. Viridovix gaped a moment or two, surprise and rut both on his face, before he grinned and gathered Evanthia in. Her arms tightened around him.

Goudeles caught Gorgidas' eye above the recumbent couples. "When you come to Videssos, you eat fish," he said, and sank down on his sleeping-mat with his partner.

"Push more than your pen, there!" Skylitzes called; the bureaucrat gave back an obscene gesture.

Gorgidas still did not lay a hand on Spasia. The orgy all around raised no lust in him, nor mirth either. With the physician's detachment he could not seem to lose, he watching bodies move, joining and separating, listened to sighs and hard breathing and now and again a gasp of pleasure or a wild fragment of laughter.

He felt Spasia's gaze on him. "I do not please you," she said. It did not sound like a question.

"It's only that I—" he began, but Olbiop's hoarse yell interrupted him.

The Khamorth was leaning on an elbow, waiting for his tool to regain its proper temper. "No stones, woman-face?" he called tauntingly. "Why I get you woman? No good she do you."

Even with the fire playing on them, Gorgidas felt his cheeks grow hot. The thing would have to be essayed, he realized. Spasia's eyes held quiet pity as he slid his arm around her and brought her face toward his. She was kind; maybe that would help.

The very feel of her mouth, soft and small, was strange to him, and the firm pressure of her breasts between them seemed a distraction. He was used to a different kind of embrace, a shared hardness. Awkwardly, still conscious of watching eyes, he helped her out of blouse and skirt. His own clothing slid off easily. His body was slim, stringily muscled, and stronger than it looked. He was one-and-forty; it had looked much the same at twenty-one and would yet if he reached sixty-one. Kissing Spasia again, he pushed her gently down to the soft felt. Her lips were pleasant, her warmth against him comforting, but he remained unstirred.

Viridovix hooted and pointed and shouted to Olbiop: "Will you look at that, Khamorth dear? Silvertongue you were after calling himself this afternoon past; sure and he's earning the name the now!" Plainsman and Gaul cheered Goudeles on.

For a moment Gorgidas hoped it had been the watchers that balked him, but he had no success even after their stares traveled elsewhere. "Your pardon, I beg," he said softly to Spasia. "It's not yourself—"

"May I help you, then? You are gracious to a stranger you will never see again; that deserves some reward."

Startled, the Greek began to toss his head in his nation's no, but stopped. "Maybe you can," he said, and touched the nape of her neck.

Perhaps it was the familiarity of the caress; whatever the reason, he almost shouted when he felt himself respond to it. He lifted her face away from him. Smiling, she rolled invitingly onto her back. "There," she whispered, a half sigh.

Soon her breath came short and fast, her mouth now seeking his, her arms round his back trying to pull him ever closer. He laughed quietly to himself as she quivered in release beneath him; he had come to the steppe to break with his past, but hardly like this.

Even though he had accomplished it, however, it still seemed strange and not a little perverse, nothing he really cared to make a habit of. And, ironically, because he was not truly kindled he was able to go on long after his companions flagged. Spasia's mouth was half-open, her eyes glazed with pleasure; now Olbiop, Viridovix, and Arigh were applauding the Greek's stamina. When he was done at last, the Khamorth came over and slapped his sweaty back. "I wrong," he said, no small admission from one of the overweening plainsmen.

The debauch went on far into the night, with partners shifting kaleidoscopically. Having established his credit—even if in counterfeit coin, he thought—Gorgidas felt free to abstain, and Spasia wanted no other. Lying side by side, they talked quietly of his wanderings and her life in the village until sleep overtook them.

The last thing she said was, "I hope you gave me a son." That brought the Greek back to wakefulness, but the only answer she gave his low-voiced question was a snore. He moved closer to her and drifted off himself.

The next morning Olbiop woke them all with a loud groan. Holding his head in both hands as if afraid it might fall off, the Khamorth shoved the leather curtain aside and, still naked, staggered to the village well. Gorgidas heard him curse the creaking windlass as he drew a bucket of water. He poured it over his pounding head, the other Khamorth laughing at his sorry state.

The nomad returned, his greasy hair dripping. The drenching was his first bath in a very long time; despite it he smelled powerfully of horses and endless years of sweat. He shuddered at the thought of breakfast, but swigged kavass.

"The scales of the snake that stung him," Spasia said, reheating a rabbit leg for Gorgidas. Clothed again, she seemed once more a stranger. The Greek fumbled in his kit, wishing his packing had been less functional. He finally came across a small silver box of powdered ink, an image of Phos on its lid. Spasia tried to refuse it, saying, "You gave of yourself last night. That was enough."

"That was fair exchange," he replied. "Take it, for broadening my horizons if nothing else." She looked at him, uncomprehending, but he did not explain. At last she accepted it with a murmured word of thanks.

Other farewells were going on around them. "Nay, lass, you canna be coming with us. 'Twas but the meeting of a night," Viridovix said patiently, over and over, until Evanthia understood. The Gaul had said many goodbyes in his time, and did not hurry them. For all his ferociousness in battle, for all his delight in strife of any kind, he was not a cruel man.

Along with the rest of the travelers, Gorgidas slung his kit on a packhorse's back, checking to make sure the leather lashings were secure. When he was satisfied, he swung himself up into the saddle of the pony he would ride that day. Skylitzes gestured. Flanked by the squad from Prista and Olbiop's nomads, the embassy rode out of the village. A scrawny yellow dog followed until one of the Khamorth made as if to ride it down. It fled, peering fearfully back over its shoulder. Distance swallowed people, buildings, streets, the hamlet itself.

The plainsmen did not stay with the imperial party long; the herds awaited their return. Olbiop traded gibes with Agathias Psoes and his troopers, boasting of his own prowess. "And then are this one," he said, jabbing a thumb toward Gorgidas. "He futter good, for no-balls man."

"And to the crows with you," the Greek muttered, but in his own language.

Olbiop took no notice in any case. "You careful now, Psoes. We catch you no guard—how you say?—embassies, we kill you."

"Pick your place," the underofficer replied in the same bantering tone, but he and the nomad both knew a day might come when they were not joking. With a last wave, Olbiop and his men turned back toward the south.

"Let's travel," Skylitzes said.

"A moment, please." Gorgidas dismounted and unstrapped his kit from the packhorse, which had begun to graze during the halt. The others watched curiously as he rummaged. When he came upon his razor, he threw it far out onto the steppe. He remounted, dipped his head to Skylitzes. "Very good. Let's travel."

III

A RIPE STRAWBERRY WHIZZED PAST MARCUS' HEAD AND squashed against the barracks wall behind him. "For heaven's sake, Pakhymer," he said wearily, "put your damned toy catapult away and pay attention, will you?"

"I was just checking it," Laon Pakhymer replied innocently. For all his pockmarks and thick beard, he wore a small-boy grin. He led a mercenary regiment of light cavalry from Khatrish, the small Khaganate on Videssos' eastern border. Like all the Khatrishers Scaurus knew, he had trouble taking anything seriously. No *gravitas*, the tribune thought.

Even so, he was glad Pakhymer had chosen to come to the legionary officers' meeting. Though not properly part of Scaurus' command, his horsemen worked well with the Roman infantry.

As if the flying berry had been some strange signal, the tribune's lieutenants left off chattering among themselves and looked toward him to hear what he had to tell them. He rose from his seat at the head of the table and took a couple of paces back and forth to put his thoughts in order. The splash of juice on the clean white plaster behind him was distracting.

"All bets are off—again," he said at last. "Sometimes I

think we'll never fight the Yezda. First the civil war with Ortaias Sphrantzes, then Onomagoulos, and now the great—" He loaded the word with irony, "—count Drax."

"What's the latest?" Sextus Minucius asked hesitantly. He was attending his first council as underofficer and seemed sure everyone else was better informed than he.

Scaurus wished it were so. "You know as much as the rest of us, I fear. It's like Apokavkos said when he brought us the news yesterday. When Drax beat Onomagoulos in the westlands, he found himself left with the only real army there. Appears he's decided to set up on his own."

"But the westlands—Garsavra, Kypas, Kyzikos—they've been ours forever," Zeprin the Red protested, his florid face angry. He was no Videssian, despite that "ours," but a Haloga mercenary who had served the Empire so long he had made it his own, as Phostis Apokavkos had the Romans. Before Maragha, he had held high rank in the Imperial Guards. A lot of things had been different before Maragha.

"Namdalen used to be Videssian, too," the tribune said. Zeprin grunted, nodded ruefully. Marcus went on, "And speaking of that, Drax is making the islanders' old dream of a new Namdalen on the Empire's soil come true. When news of it gets back to the Duchy, we'll see land-hungry barons sailing west to carve out their own little domains while the carving's good. The only way I can see to keep that from happening is to break Drax fast."

Gagik Bagratouni, the *nakharar* who headed the Vaspurakaners in Scaurus' force, raised a hand. "There are—how you say?—more Namdaleni closer to Drax than in the Duchy." His broad, hook-nosed face showed concentration as he spoke; Videssian did not come easily to him. "Utprand plenty of them has, and here. What does—*is*—Thorisin about them going to do?"

"Get that one right and you win the goldpiece," Gaius Philippus muttered. Bagratouni lifted his thick eyebrows, not quite understanding.

"I see three choices, all risky," Marcus said. He ticked them off on his fingers: "He can separate them from the rest of his army and send them, say, toward the Khatrish border. They'd be out of the way there, but who would hold them in check if they decided to imitate Drax?

"Or he can leave them behind, here in the capital, with the same danger. And if they seize Videssos the city, Videssos the Empire is dead." The tribune remembered Soteric talking lovingly of the prospect.

Bagratouni gave a running, low-voiced translation of Scaurus' words to his lieutenant Mesrop Anhoghin. Where his Videssian stumbled, his aide had next to none. The lanky Anhoghin was even more heavily bearded than the *nakharar*.

Marcus finished, "Or he can keep them with the rest of us and hope they don't go over to Drax the first chance they get. I hope so, too," he added, and got a laugh.

"Aye, wouldn't that be just what we needed?" Gaius Philippus said. "Facing the damned Namdalener heavy horse is bad enough head-on. My blood runs cold to think of being taken in flank by treachery."

"I've heard Drax and Utprand are rivals," Minucius said. "Is it so?"

"It's true, I think, though I don't know the why of it," Marcus answered. He looked up and down the table. "Does anyone?"

"I do," Laon Pakhymer said promptly. Somehow Scaurus was unsurprised. Khatrishers, inquisitive as sparrows, were made for gossip. Pakhymer explained, "They were friends and allies once, and joined up to besiege some noble's keep. The place was on a lake; Utprand took the landward side while Drax covered the water. They sat there and sat there, starving this fellow out. He kept fighting, even though it was hopeless —didn't want to surrender to Utprand, I think."

Remembering the Namdalener captain's wintry eyes, Scaurus decided he could not blame the hapless noble.

Pakhymer continued, "So he didn't. He opened the gates on the lakeshore and yielded himself and his castle up to Drax —and Drax only. When Utprand asked for his first share of the spoil, the great count—" He was as sarcastic as Marcus had been. "—told him where to head in. Since then, for some reason they haven't gotten on well." Pakhymer had an infectious grin.

"That is a fair reason," Zeprin the Red rumbled. "The gods spit on the oath-breaking man." For all the holy Kveldulf's labors, the Halogai were pagans yet, worshiping their own band of gloomy deities.

Pakhymer's tale somewhat reassured Marcus; there did seem to be a true and lasting enmity between the two Namdalener leaders. That was the sort of thing Videssos' wily politicians could use to good effect.

The tribune also wondered briefly how loyal Bagratouni and his Vaspurakaners would prove. True, the Yezda had driven them from their homeland into Videssos, but they had suffered worse from a pogrom led by a fanatic Videssian priest. Might they not see Drax and his Namdaleni as allies now instead of foes, even band together with them as fellow heretics? One more thing to worry about, he decided, and filed it away.

The meeting ended soon; there was not enough information to plan further. As the officers wandered away, Scaurus called Gaius Philippus to his side. "What would you do, were you Thorisin?" he asked, thinking the veteran's keen sense of the practical might let him guess what the Emperor intended.

"Me?" The senior centurion scratched at his scarred cheek as he thought. At last he gave the ghost of a chuckle. "I think I'd find another line of work."

"Come on, in you go," sailors urged over and over as the legionaries jumped down into the transports that would take them over the narrow strait the Videssians called the Cattle-Crossing and into the westlands. One of the more considerate ones added, "Mind your feet, you lubbers. The gangplank's bloody slippery in this rain."

"Tell me more," Gaius Philippus said, his cloak wrapped tight around him to protect his armor from the wet. Marcus wished they were embarking from the Neorhesian harbor on the city's northern edge rather than the southern harbor of Kontoskalion. The storm was blowing out of the south, and he had no protection against it here.

Every so often he heard a thump and a volley of curses as a soldier missed a step and tumbled into the waist of a ship. Further down the docks, horses whinnied nervously as their Khatrisher or Namdalener masters coaxed them on board.

Senpat Sviodo landed clumsily beside Scaurus. The strings of the pandoura slung across his back jangled as he staggered to keep his balance. "Graceful as a cat," he declared.

"A drunken, three-legged cat, maybe," Gaius Philippus said. Not a bit put out, Senpat made a face at him.

The young noble's wife leaped down a moment later. She did not need the arm he put out to steady her; her landing truly was cat-smooth. Nevrat Sviodo, Marcus thought, was a remarkable woman for many reasons. To begin with, she was beautiful in the swarthy, strong-featured Vaspurakaner way. Now her finest feature, her wavy, luxuriantly black hair, hung limp and sodden under a bright silk kerchief.

But there was more to Nevrat than her beauty. She wore tunic and baggy trousers like her husband; a slim saber hung at her belt and it had seen use. Moreover, she was a fine horsewoman, with courage any man might envy. No ordinary spirit would have ridden out after Maragha from the safety of the fortress of Khliat, seeking her husband and the legionaries with no idea whether or not they lived—and finding them.

And as if that was not enough, she and Senpat enjoyed a love that seemed to have no room in it for ill. There were times Scaurus had to fight down jealousy.

More women were coming aboard now, and their children as well. Minucius' companion Erene landed nearly as well as Nevrat had, then caught two of her girls as they jumped into her arms. Helvis handed down Erene's third daughter, who was only a few months older than Dosti.

Malric leaped down on his own, laughing as he tumbled and rolled on the ship's rough planking. Helvis started to follow him; Marcus and Nevrat jumped forward together to break her fall. "That was an idiot thing to do," Nevrat said sharply, her brown eyes snapping with anger.

Helvis stared at her. "Who are you to scold me for such trifles?" she replied, not caring for the rebuke. "You've done more dangerous things than hopping off a gangplank."

Nevrat frowned, sadness touching her. "Ah, but I would not, had Phos granted me a child to carry." Her voice was very low; Helvis, suddenly understanding, hugged her.

"That's my job," Senpat said, and attended to it. Merriment danced in his eyes. "We have to keep practicing, that's all, until we do it right." Nevrat poked him in the ribs. He yelped and poked her back.

Thorisin Gavras, his mistress Komitta Rhangavve at his side, came strolling down the docks to watch his army embark. The Emperor still worried about Utprand's Namdaleni, even after deciding to hazard using them. He studied every boarding mercenary, as if seeking treason in the heft of a duffel or the patches on a surcoat.

He relaxed somewhat when he reached the legionaries, giving Marcus a self-mocking smile. "I should have listened, when you warned me of Drax," he said, shaking his head. "Is all well here?"

"Looks to be," the tribune answered, pleased Gavras had remembered, and without anger. "Things are helter-skelter right now."

"They always are, when you're setting out." The Emperor smacked his fist into the palm of his hand. "Phos' light, I wish *I* were coming with you, instead of Zigabenos! This waiting business is hard on the nerves, but I don't dare leave the city until I'm sure the Duchy won't land on my back. It wouldn't do to get stuck inland and then have to try to scramble back east to face maybe Tomond the Duke on ground of his choosing."

A couple of years ago, Marcus thought, Thorisin would have charged blindly at the first foe to show himself. He was more cautious now. The capital was Videssos' central focus as well as its greatest city. It sat astride travel routes by land and sea, and from it all the Empire's holdings could be quickly reached.

Komitta Rhangavve sniffed at such trifles. "You could have stopped all this before it ever began if you'd heeded me," she said to Thorisin. "If you'd made a proper example of Ortaias Sphrantzes, this cursed Drax would have been too afraid to think of rebelling—and Onomagoulos before him, too, for that matter."

"Be quiet, Komitta," the Emperor growled, not caring to hear his fiery paramour take him to task in public.

Her eyes sparked dangerously; her thin, pale face had the fierce loveliness of a bird of prey. "I will not! You cannot speak to me so; I am an aristocrat, though you grant me no decent marriage—" And so you sleep with a Gallic mercenary, Marcus thought, appalled at the line she was taking. Komitta seemed to realize its danger, too, for she returned to her first complaint. "You should have dragged Sphrantzes to the Forum of the Ox and burned him alive, as usurpers deserve. That—"

But Thorisin had heard enough. He could make himself hold his temper for affairs of state, but not for his own. "I should have taken a paddle to your bloodthirsty aristocratic backside the first time you started your 'I-told-you-so's,'" he roared. "You'd see a happier man here today."

"You vain, hulking pisspot!" Komitta screeched, and they were off, standing there in the rain cursing each other like fishmongers. Seamen and soldiers listened, first in shock and then with growing awe. Marcus saw a grizzled sailor, a man with a lifetime of inventive profanity behind him, frowning and nodding every few seconds as he tried to memorize some of the choicer oaths.

"Whew!" Senpat Sviodo said as Gavras, fists clenched, wheeled and stamped away. "Lucky for that lady that she shares his bed. She'd answer for lèse majesté if she didn't."

"She should anyway," Helvis said. Though a Namdalener, she shared the Videssians' venerant attitude toward the imperial dignity. "I can't imagine why he tolerates her."

But Scaurus had seen Thorisin and his mistress row before and come to his own conclusions. He said, "She's like a sluice gate on a dam: she lets him loose all the spleen inside him."

"Aye, and gives it back in double measure," Gaius Philippus said.

"Maybe so," Marcus said, "but without her, he might fall over from a fit of apoplexy."

Gaius Philippus rolled his eyes. "He might anyway."

"And if he did," Senpat Sviodo said, "she'd say it was to spite her."

He looked up in surprise at the crash of the gangplank being hauled on board. Sailors, nearly naked in the warm rain, stowed it under a deck tarpaulin. "Hello! We're really going to sail in this, are we?" Sviodo said.

"Why not? It's only over the Cattle-Crossing, and the wind doesn't seem too bad," Marcus answered. He was no more nautical than most Romans, but felt like a fount of knowledge next to the Vaspurakaner, whose homeland was landlocked. Showing off, he continued, "They say wetting sails actually helps them, for less air slips through their fabric."

His seeming expertise impressed Senpat, but Helvis, from

a nation of true seafarers, laughed out loud. "If that were so, dear, this would be the fastest ship afloat right now. It's like salt in cooking: a little is fine, but too much is worse than none."

Ropes hissed across the wet deck as the sailors wound them into snaky coils. A donkey brayed a few ships away. Two mates and the captain cursed—not half so spendidly as Thorisin and Komitta had—because the big square sail bore Helvis out by hanging from the yardarm like a limp, clinging sheet on a clothesline.

At last a fresh gust filled it; it came away from the mast with a wet sigh. The captain swore again, this time at the man on the steering oar for being slow—whether with reason, Scaurus could not tell. The ship slid away from the dock.

Soteric Dosti's son rode up alongside the marching column of legionaries. Troopers in the front ranks grumbled at the dust his horse kicked up; those further back were already eating their comrades' dust. The Namdalener reined in beside Marcus and shed his conical helmet with a groan of relief. Sweat ran in little clean rills through the dirt on his face. "Whew!" he said. "Hot work, this."

"No argument there," the tribune answered, doubting that his brother-in-law had ridden over to complain about the weather.

Whatever his point was, he seemed in no hurry to make it. "Fine country we're passing through."

Again Scaurus had to agree. The lowlands of the Empire's western provinces were as fertile as any he had known. The rich black soil bore abundantly; the entire countryside seemed clothed in vibrant shades of green. Farmers went out each morning from their villages to the fields and orchards surrounding them to tend their wheat and barley and beans and peas, their vines, their olives, mulberries, peaches, and figs, their nut-trees, and sweet-smelling citruses. A few of the peasants cheered as the army tramped past them to fight the Namdalener heretics. More did their best to give soldiers on any side a wide berth.

The western plain was the breadbasket for Videssos the city, shipping its produce on the barges that constantly plied the rivers running eastward to the sea. It also fed the army as it marched southwest from the suburbs across the strait from the capital. This close to the Cattle-Crossing, the Empire's governors still held the land; with the bureaucratic efficiency Videssos was capable of at its best, they had markets ready to resupply the imperial forces. Marcus wondered how long it would be before the first of Drax'—what was it Soteric had called them?—motte-and-bailey castles would stand by the roadside to block their way. Not long now, he thought.

"Fine country," Soteric repeated. "Too muggy in summer to be perfect, but the land's fruitful enough to grow feathers on an egg. I can see what was in Drax' mind when he decided to take it for his own." He paused a moment, ran his fingers through his light-brown hair, almost the same color as Helvis'. Unlike many of his countrymen, he had a full head; he did not crop the back of his skull. "By the Wager, I wouldn't mind settling here myself one day."

He looked down at Scaurus from horseback, studying him. His eyes might be the same blue as his sister's, the tribune thought, but they had none of her warmth. His high-arched nose put an imperious cast on all his features.

"No?" the Roman said, watching his brother-in-law as closely as he was being watched. Picking his words with care, he went on, "You don't want to go back to the Duchy? Would you sooner take a farm here when your time with the Empire is done?"

"Aye, when my time is done," Soteric said, chuckling silently. He kept scanning the tribune's face. "That may not be so long now."

Marcus did his best to hold a mask of bland innocence. "Really? I thought you'd taken service for a good many years—as I have." He looked the Namdalener in the eye.

Soteric grimaced; his mouth thinned in irritation. "Well, I may be wrong," he said. He jabbed his spurs into his horse's flank so roughly that it started and tried to rear. He fought it down. Wheeling sharply, he trotted away. The tribune watched him go, full of misgivings. He wondered whether Utprand could hold the younger man in check—or whether he intended to try.

* * *

Sunset painted the western sky with blood. Somewhere in a nearby copse an owl, awake too soon, hooted mournfully. The army came to a halt and made camp. Confident they were still in friendly country, the Videssians and Namdaleni built sketchy palisades and ran up their tents higgledy-piggledy inside them. The Khamorth outriders were even less orderly; they stopped where they chose, to rejoin their comrades in the morning.

The legionaries' camp, by contrast, was the usual Roman field fortification, made as automatically in safe territory as when an enemy was on their heels. Gaius Philippus chose a defensible spot with good water; after that the troopers carried on for themselves. Each man had his assigned duty, which never varied. Some dug out a protective ditch in the shape of a square; others piled the excavated dirt into a rampart; still others planted on the earthwork sharp stakes they carried along for that reason. Inside the campground, the legionaries' eight-man tents went up in neat blocks, maniple by maniple, leaving wide streets between them.

No one grumbled at the work that went into a camp, even though it might only be used once and then abandoned forever. To the Romans, such fieldworks were second nature. The men who filled their ranks, for their part, had seen the legionary encampment's value too many times to care to risk getting by with less.

So, for that matter, had Laon Pakhymer and his Khatrishers. Marcus was glad to invite them to share the campsite; they had done so often enough after Maragha. Moreover, they helped cheerfully with the work of setting up. Although not as practiced as the legionaries, they did not shirk.

"They're a sloppy lot," Gaius Philippus said, watching two Khatrisher privates get into a noisy argument with one of their officers. The shouting match, though, did not keep the three of them from filling a shield with dirt and hauling it to the rampart, then trotting back to do it again. The senior centurion scratched his head. "I don't see how they get the job done, but they do."

Khatrisher sentries kept small boys away from their strings of cantankerous little horses. Scaurus was not overjoyed at the presence of women and children in the camp, nor had he ever been. He was more adaptable than Gaius Philippus, but even to him it seemed almost too un-Roman to endure. Two summers before, he had excluded them as the legionaries marched west against the Yezda. But after Maragha's disaster, safety counted for more than Roman custom. And it was little harder to turn cheese back into milk than to revoke a privilege once granted.

The tribune's tent was on the main camp road, the *via principalis*, halfway between the eastern and western gates. Outside it, as Scaurus got there, Malric was playing with a small striped lizard he had caught. He seemed to be enjoying the sport more than the lizard did. "Hello, Papa," he said, looking up. The lizard scuttled away and was gone before he thought about it again. He promptly began to cry and kept right on even after Marcus picked him up and spun him in the air. "I want my lizard back!"

As if in sympathy, Dosti started crying inside the tent. Helvis emerged, looking vexed. "What are you wail—" she began angrily, then stopped in surprise when she saw the tribune. "Hello, darling; I didn't hear you come up. What's the fuss about?"

Marcus explained the tragedy. "Come here, son," she said, taking Malric from him. "I can't give you your lizard," she said, adding parenthetically, "Phos be praised." Malric did not hear that; he was crying louder than ever. Helvis went on, "Would you rather have a candied plum, or even two?"

Malric thought it over. A year ago, Scaurus knew, he would have screeched "No!" and kept howling. But after a few seconds he said, "All right," punctuating it with a hiccup.

"That's a good boy," Helvis said, drying his face on her skirt. "They're inside; come with me." She sighed. "Then I'll see if I can quiet Dosti down." Cheerful again, Malric darted into the tent. Helvis and Marcus followed.

Though commander, Marcus did not carry luxuries on campaign. Apart from sleeping-mats, the only furniture in the tent was Dosti's crib, a collapsible table, and a folding chair made out of canvas and sticks. Helvis' portable altar to Phos sat on the grass, as did the little pine chest that held her private tidbits. Scaurus', of darker wood, was beside it.

Helvis opened her chest to get Malric his sweets, then rocked Dosti in her arms and sang him to sleep. Her rich voice was smooth and gentle in a lullaby. "That wasn't so bad," she said in relief as she carefully put the baby back in the crib. Scaurus lit a clay olive-oil lamp with flint and steel and marked the day's march on the sketch-map he carried with him.

After Malric had gone to sleep, Helvis said, "My brother told me he talked with you today."

"Did he?" the tribune said without inflection. He wrote a note on the map, first in Latin and then, more slowly, in Videssian. So Soteric had ridden back to the women, had he?

"Aye." Helvis watched him with an odd mixture of excitement, hope, and apprehension. "He said I should remind you of the promise you made me in Videssos last year."

"Did he?" Scaurus said again. He winced; he could not help it. When Gavras' siege of the city looked to be failing, he had been on the point of joining the Namdaleni in abandoning the Emperor and traveling back to the Duchy. Only Zigabenos' coup against Ortaias kept the stroke from coming off. Helvis, he knew, had been more disappointed than not when, after unexpected victory, the Namdaleni and Romans stayed in imperial service.

"Yes, he did." Determination thinned her full lips until her mouth was as hard as her brother's. "I was a soldier's woman before you, too, Marcus; I knew you could not do what you planned—" Scaurus grimaced again; it had not been his plan. "—once Thorisin sat the throne. Too often we do what we must, not what we want. But here is the chance come again, finer than before!"

"What chance is that?"

Her eyes glowed with anger. "You are no witling, dear, and you play one poorly. The chance to be our own again, at the call of no foreign heretic master. And better yet, the chance to take a new realm, like the founding heroes in the minstrels' songs."

She had it, too, the tribune thought, the Namdalener lust for Videssian land. "I don't know why you're so eager to pick the Empire's bones," he said. "It's brought peace and safety to a great stretch of this world for so many years I grow dizzy thinking of them. It's base to leap on its back when it's wounded, like a wildcat onto a deer with a broken leg. Tell me, would you islanders do better?"

"Maybe not," she said, and Scaurus had to admire her honesty. "But by the Wager, we deserve the chance to try! Videssos' blood runs thin and cold; only her skill at trickery has kept us from what's ours by right for so long."

"By what right?"

She stepped forward, her right arm moving. Marcus raised his hands to catch a blow, but she seized his sword hilt instead. "By this one!" she said fiercely.

"The same argument the Yezda use," he said; her fingers came away from the blade as if it had burned her. He hitched it away; he did not want anyone but himself touching this sword. "And how would you deal with *them*, here in your new Namdalen?"

In his mind's eye he saw ceaseless petty wars: islander against Yezda, Videssians against nomads, two against one, alliances, betrayals, ambushes, surprise attacks, and the guiltless, prosperous farmers and townsmen of the westlands ground to powder under the iron horseshoes of endlessly marching armies. The picture revolted him, but Avshar, he knew, would laugh at it in chill delight.

He said that and watched Helvis flinch. "The trouble with your brother, and what makes him deadly dangerous," he went on, "is that he has enough imagination to be ruthless, but not enough to see the ruin his ruthlessness will cause." Seeing her outrage, he went on quickly, "This is all quarreling over the reflection of a bone anyhow. It's not Soteric who heads the Namdaleni, but Utprand."

"Utprand? Talk of cold, will you? Utprand eats ice and breathes fog." Her scorn weakened but could not destroy the aptness of the image. A startled laugh jerked from Scaurus.

Helvis was still watching him, with the air of someone studying a waterclock that had once worked but now refused to run. "Tell me one thing," she said. "How is it, if you love this Empire so much—" The scorn was there in her voice again. "—that you would have gone to Namdalen last year?"

Marcus remembered his Stoic teacher, a consumptive Greek named Timanor, wheezing, "If it's not right, boy, don't do it; if it's not true, don't say it." Timanor or no, he wished he had a lie handy.

Because he did not, he sighed and followed his master's advice. "Because then I thought my staying would make the war between Thorisin and Ortaias longer and worse, and help tear Videssos to pieces."

Even in the lamplight he saw the color fade from her cheeks. "Because it would tear Videssos—?" she whispered, as if the words were in some language she did not understand well. "Videssos?" Her voice rose like the tide. "Videssos? Not a thought for me, not a thought for the children, but this moldy, threadbare Empire?"

She was almost screaming; Dosti and Malric both woke, frightened, and began to cry. "Go away, get out!" she shouted at Scaurus. "I don't want to look at you, you flint hearted, scheming marplot!"

"Out? This is my tent," the tribune said reasonably, but Helvis was furious far past reason.

"Get out!" she screamed again, and this time she did swing at him. He threw up his arms; her nails clawed his wrist. He swore, grabbed her hands, and tried to hold her still, but it was like holding a lioness. He pushed her away and strode into the night.

Few legionaries met his eye as he walked past the row of officers' tents. The same thing had happened to some of them, but they did not have a commander's dignity to protect.

Gaius Philippus was talking with a couple of sentries at the palisade. "Thought you'd turned in," he said when he saw the tribune.

"Argument."

"So I see." The senior centurion whistled softly, spying the deep scratches on Marcus' arm. "You can doss with me tonight, if you care to."

"Thanks. Later, maybe." Marcus was too keyed up from the fight to want to sleep.

"I hope you flattened her?"

The tribune knew his lieutenant was trying to show sympathy, but the rough advice did not help. "No," he answered, "it was my fault at least as much as hers."

Gaius Philippus snorted, unbelieving, but Scaurus tasted his own words' bitter truth. He went off to pace round the perimeter of the camp. He knew his past actions had let Helvis—and Soteric with her—believe he would take the islanders' side against the Empire. Saying otherwise would only have touched off a quarrel, and he had thought the question would never arise.

And now he had question and quarrel both, both of them worse for his tacit untruth. He laughed without mirth. Old Timanor proved no donkey after all.

"You snore," the tribune accused Gaius Philippus the next morning.

"Do I?" The veteran bit into an onion. "Well, who's to care?"

Sandy-eyed, Scaurus watched the legionaries break camp, watched their women, chattering with each other, make their way back to their place in the center of the army's line of march. Helvis was already gone; his tent had seemed strangely deserted when he knocked it down. He wondered if she would be back or choose to stay with Soteric and her own people.

It was good to forget such worries as his soldiers shook themselves out into traveling order. Straightforward questions yielded straightforward answers: Blaesus' maniple should march in front of Bagratouni's Vaspurakaners, not behind them; this road looked better than that one; Quintus Eprius should lose three days' pay for gambling with loaded dice.

A Khamorth scout came trotting back past the legionaries toward Mertikes Zigabenos, whose Videssians brought up the rear of the column. In a few minutes another rode by. Wondering if something was in the wind, Marcus called after him. The nomad ignored his hail. "Bastard," Gaius Philippus said.

"We'll find out soon enough, anyway."

"I know," the senior centurion answered gloomily.

An hour or so later, he squinted down the road and said, "Hello! I don't remember passing *that* the last time we were on our way to Garsavra." The veteran's scowl deepened with every forward step he took. "It's a bloody fornicating fortress, that's what it is."

The castle sat athwart the main road south; if the imperial army was to go any farther, it would have to be dealt with. As the legionaries approached, Scaurus watched Namdalener defenders running about on the palisade, and others atop the tower inside. Thin in the distance, he heard the islanders shouting to each other.

Seen at close range, it was easy to understand how Drax'

men had thrown up their fortification so quickly. A ditch surrounded the work, a great gash in the green-covered land around it. The Namdaleni used some of the dirt to form an earthen rampart enclosing a good-sized court—the bailey. In that, at least, thought the tribune, the keep was made like a Roman camp, although here the trench was far deeper and wider and the protecting wall no mere breastwork, but taller than a man.

Inside the bailey, though, the men of the Duchy had heaped the rest of the dirt from their digging into a high mound. And on that motte stood a wooden tower, built in such haste that most of its logs did not have the bark trimmed off them. Archers shooting from atop that tower could command the field. They were already sniping at the imperials' Khatrisher and Khamorth outriders. The nomads shot back, but even their powerful bows could not reach so high.

Zigabenos called a brief council of war. "Just as they want, we'll have to stop and take them out," he declared. "We can't leave a couple of hundred full-armored horsemen on our flank, and I dare not split up my forces to mask the place. Phos alone knows how many more of these pestholes we'll see."

"But starving it out will take forever, and I'd not care to storm it, by the Wager," Soteric said. He seemed so proud of the fieldwork his fellow Namdaleni under Drax had built that even Utprand looked at him in annoyance.

Zigabenos, however, remained suave. "There are ways."

"So there are." Gaius Philippus laughed, understanding him perfectly. He turned to Soteric. "Your toy yonder—" He jerked his chin at the castle. "—is a wonder against hill-bandits or barbarians like the Yezda. But those lads inside are fools to think to hold it when they're facing professionals."

The young Namdalener flushed. "They're professionals, too."

"Aye, belike," Gaius Philippus nodded, still good-humored. "They'll be warm ones, too, bye and bye."

The army's siege train unlimbered that afternoon, at ranges beyond reply from the tower. Soldiers chopped wood to give frameworks to the engines, whose mechanical parts and cordage had been hauled from the capital. Roman engineers worked side by side with their Videssian counterparts.

They sweated together through the night by torchlight. Common troopers cut brush and tied it into bundles to fling into the trench when the time came to storm the castle. Everywhere men were checking blades and armor, shields and shoes, knowing their lives could ride on their precautions.

Marcus was too busy seeing to the legionaries' needs to worry much about Helvis. He could do nothing tonight in any case. With fighting near, the women's camp was at a safe distance behind the army's lines.

Sometime after midnight the drumming of hooves came loud from the Namdalener castle. The men inside had laid planks over their ditch and sent riders pounding out to warn their comrades of the imperials' coming. Whooping, Khamorth and Khatrishers gave chase. They soon ran down two of the messengers, but a third eluded them in the darkness. "Ordure," Gaius Philippus said when the nomads brought that word back.

"Ah, well," Marcus said, trying to make the best of it, "it's not as if Drax didn't know we were moving on him." The senior centurion merely grunted.

Dawn came too early for the tribune's liking, the sun dyeing the clouds first crimson, then golden as the stars faded. A Videssian herald, carrying a white-painted helmet on a spearshaft as a sign of truce, walked up to the very edge of the castle's ditch and called on the Namdalcni to surrender. The islanders yelled obscenities back in their own dialect. An arrow dug into the turf a few feet from the herald. The shot was deliberately wide, but lent his retreat speed, if not dignity.

Zigabenos barked an order. Dart-throwers bucked and crashed. Javelins whizzed at the palisade, making Drax' men keep their heads down. The Namdaleni would pop up, fire at whatever they thought they could hit, and duck behind their earthwork again.

Stone-flingers went into action a few minutes later, hurling rocks as heavy as a man against the tower. They scarred it, and now and then a timber cracked, but it showed no signs of collapse. The islanders had built well. Engineers winched their weapons' twisted gut cords back over and over; oaths filled the air whenever one snapped.

But the machines that hurled darts and stones were only a side show, as were the arrows the Videssians and Khamorth sent flying into the bailey. The Videssian engineers began loading some of their catapults with thin wooden casks full of an incendiary mixture and lobbing them at the tower on the motte.

In their siege warfare the Romans often flung burning pitch or tallow at wooden works. The Empire's fire-brew was deadlier yet. It was compounded of sulfur, quicklime, and a black, foul-smelling oil that seeped up from the ground here and there in imperial territory. As the casks smashed against the tower, sheets of liquid fire dripped down its sides.

The archers inside screamed in terror as the flames took hold. Namdaleni leaped down from the palisade and dashed across the bailey to fight the fire. Marcus heard their dismayed cries as the first buckets of water splashed onto the blaze. Thanks to the quicklime, it burned as enthusiastically wet as dry.

The catapults kept firing; as their cords stretched, the barrels of incendiary they hurled began falling short. Several burst at the top of the motte, splattering flame over the islanders battling the burning tower. Men ran shrieking, blazing like so many torches. The liquid fire dripped under mail shirts and clung to flesh, to hair, to eyes, burning and burning. A Namdalener plunged his sword into a comrade writhing on the ground beside him, afire from head to knees. Thick, black, greasy smoke rose straight into the sky, as sure a message to Drax as any his riders might bring.

Trumpets blared outside the doomed castle. Covered by archery, the legionaries rushed forward, hurling their bundles of brush into the ditch; whether or not he trusted them, Zigabenos held his own islanders out of this first fight with their countrymen. Though no battle-lover, Marcus was glad to run forward at the head of his men. Standing by while Drax' soldiers burned was harder than fighting.

Almost no one was left on the earthwork to hold the legionaries at bay. A spear hurtled past the tribune, but then his *caligae* were chewing at the soft dirt of the palisade's outer face. Shouting at the top of their lungs, the rest of the storming party were close behind.

The Namdalener who had thrown the spear stood at the top of the rampart to engage Scaurus, a big, beefy man with gray stubble on his face. He swung his heavy sword two-handed.

Marcus took the blow on his shield. He grunted at the impact and almost slid down the slope. The islander easily parried his awkward counterthrust, then raised his blade for another swipe.

A *pilum* bit into his neck. The sword flew from his hands. They clutched for a moment at the Roman spear's long iron shank, then slid limply away as his knees buckled and he began to topple. Scaurus charged over his body; already legionaries were dropping down into the bailey.

Only a handful of islanders fell at the rampart. Once it was lost, they wasted little time in dropping swords and helmets in token of surrender. Longtime mercenaries, they saw no point in fighting to the death in a hopeless cause. "Think the Emperor'll take us on again, maybe on the Astris to watch the plainsmen?" one of their officers asked Marcus seriously, not a bit abashed by his revolt.

The tribune could only spread his hands in front of him. Strapped for men, Thorisin might do just that.

"Look out! Heads up!" Namdaleni and Romans cried together. The tower on the motte came crashing down, scattering charred timbers and red-hot embers in all directions. A legionary gasped and swore as a blazing chunk of wood seared his leg; one islander was crushed beneath a falling log. He had already been hideously burned; perhaps, Marcus thought, it was for the best.

A Namdalener healer-priest did what he could for the victims of the rain of fire. That was not much; no healer-priest could call the dead back to life. The islanders' clerics stood out less than their Videssian counterparts. Unlike the Empire's priests, they wore armor and fought alongside other soldiers, a gross barbarism in the imperials' eyes.

Marcus climbed to the top of the earthwork once more. An arrow whistled over his head; he glared out, trying without success to spot the overeager archer who'd loosed it. "Hold up! The place is ours!" he shouted, and gave the thumbs-up signal of the gladiatorial games. The Videssians did not use it, but they understood. The soldiers cheered. Zigabenos waved to the tribune, who returned the salute.

Inside the fortress, islanders recovered their fallen comrades' swords to pass on to their kin, a melancholy ceremony Scaurus knew only too well: he had brought Hemond's sword to Helvis after Avshar's magic killed the islander. Fourteen Namdaleni had died here, most from burns. To the tribune's relief, no legionaries were lost, and only a couple hurt.

As they led their prisoners out of the castle, troopers on both sides were exchanging names and bits of military lore. The legionaries were becoming as much mercenaries as the men of the Duchy, plying their trade with skill but without animosity. And ever since they came to Videssos, the Romans had gotten on well with the Namdaleni, sometimes to the alarm of the Videssians themselves.

When Drax' men saw the Namdaleni in the imperial army, though, they showered abuse on them: "Turncoats! Cowards! You scum are on the wrong side!" The officer who had talked to Scaurus—his name, the tribune had learned, was Stillion of Sotevag—spied a captain he knew and shouted, "Turgot, you should be ashamed!" Turgot looked sheepish and did not answer.

Then Utprand strode forward; his icy glare froze the ragging to silence. "Turncoats you speak of?" he said, not loud but very clear. "T'ose as follow Drax know the word, yes, very well." He turned his back on them, calm and contemptuous.

Mertikes Zigabenos sent the captured rebels back to the capital with a guard of Videssian horsemen. "Very nicely done," he complimented Marcus. "So much for the vaunted Namdalener fortress; taken without losing a man. Yes, nicely done."

"Aye, so much indeed," Gaius Philippus said when Zigabenos had gone off to get the army moving once more. "It held us up for a day and cost us whatever surprise we had. I'd say Drax made a fair bargain."

Styppes dealt capably with one of the Roman casualties, a trooper with a badly gashed calf. As always, the act of healing awed Scaurus. The priest held the cut closed with his hands. Murmuring prayers to focus his concentration, he brought all his will to bear on the wound. The tribune, watching, felt the air—thicken? congeal? Latin lacked the concept, let alone the word—around it as the healing current passed through the priest. And when Styppes drew away his hands, the gaping cut was no more than a thin white scar on the soldier's leg.

"Much obliged, your honor," the legionary said, getting to his feet. He walked with no trace of a limp.

For the second seriously injured soldier, a Vaspurakaner whose skull had been broken by a falling timber when the tower collapsed, Styppes had less to offer. After examining the man, the priest said only, "He will live or die as Phos wills; he is beyond my power to cure." Though disappointed, Marcus did not think he was slacking. Gorgidas could not have helped the luckless trooper, either.

The tribune came up to Styppes, who was—inevitably, Scaurus thought—refreshing himself from a wineskin. In fairness, his craft was exhausting; Scaurus had seen healer-priests fall asleep on their feet.

Styppes wiped his mouth and then his sweat-beaded forehead on the sleeve of his robe. "You took hurt in the fighting, too?" he asked the tribune. "I see no blood."

"Er, no," Scaurus said hesitantly. He held out his wrist to the healer-priest. Helvis' nails had dug deep; the gouges were red and angry-looking. "Our former physician would have given me some salve or other for these. I was hoping you might—"

"What?" Styppes roared, furious. "You want me to squander the substance of my strength on your doxy's claw marks? Get you gone—Phos' service is not to be demeaned by such fribblings, nor do healers waste their time over trifles."

"The poor Vaspurakaner is too much for you, and I too little, eh?" the tribune snapped back, angry in return. Styppes unfailingly found a way to grate on him. "What good are you, then?"

"Ask your Roman," the healer-priest retorted. "If your cursed scratches mortify, I'll see to them. Otherwise leave me be; it wears me no less to heal small hurts than great."

"Oh," Scaurus said in a small voice. He had not known that. There was, he realized, a lot he did not know about the healer-priests' art. Styppes and his kind could work cures that had left Gorgidas in envious despair, but it seemed the Greek also had skills they lacked.

Thinking back to Gaius Philippus' remark of a little while before, the tribune wondered what sort of bargain Styppes was.

* * *

That evening Helvis did not appear. Marcus waited inside his tent until the legionary camp slept around him, hoping she would come. At last, knowing she would not, he blew out the lamp and tried to sleep himself. It was not easy. When Helvis and he were first partnered, sharing the sleeping-mat with her had made it hard for him to doze off. Now, alone, he missed her warm presence beside him.

All what you're used to, he thought. He tossed irritably. What he was getting used to was not sleeping.

Videssos' coastal plain was as flat a land as any, but to the tribune the next day's march was all uphill. There was a brief flurry of excitement late in the afternoon when a couple of Namdalener scouts emerged from a clump of woods to take a long look at the imperial army, but neither the Khatrishers' yells as they gave chase nor Gaius Philippus' lurid oaths after Drax' men escaped succeeded in rousing Scaurus from his torpor.

Munching absently on a husk-filled chunk of journeybread, he walked down the *via principalis* as dusk fell. As always, his own tent was midway between the two entrances on the camp's main street, with the surveyors' white flag just in front of it. He was about to lift the canvas tent flap when the sound of a familiar voice made him spin on his heel.

Yelling, "Papa! Papa!" Malric swarmed down the *via principalis* toward him. Because the Roman camp was always built to the same simple formula, even a five-year-old could find his way in it with confidence.

"I missed you, Papa," Malric said as Marcus bent to hug his stepson. "Where were you? Mama said you were in the fighting yesterday. Were you very brave?"

"I missed you, too," Marcus said, adding, "and your mother," as Helvis, carrying both Dosti and her traveling chest, came up to him. Seeing the tribune, Dosti wriggled in her arms until she set the toddler down. He staggered over to Scaurus; his legs grew steadier under him every day. The tribune gathered his son in.

"Papa," Dosti announced importantly.

"So I am." Marcus stood up; Dosti started undoing the leather straps of one of his *caligae*, reached up to bat at his scabbarded sword.

"You might say hello to me as well," Helvis said.

"Hello," he said cautiously, but she tilted her face up to be kissed as if nothing was wrong. A knot came undone in his chest; he had not known how tight it was till it loosened. Risking a smile, he raised the tent flap. Malric darted in, shouting, "Come on, slowcoach!" to Dosti, who followed as best he could. Helvis stooped to enter. Marcus went in after her.

The talk was deliberately ordinary for a long time: bits of gossip Helvis had picked up among the women, the tribune's account of the storming of the castle. At last he asked it straight out: "Why did you come back?"

She looked at him sidelong. "It's not enough I did? Must you always dig down under everything?"

"Habit," he said, waving at the camp all around them. "I have to."

"The plague take your habits," Helvis flared, "aye, and your senseless love for creaking Videssos, too." Marcus waited for the fire to grow hotter, but instead she laughed, more at herself than to him. "Why did I come back? If it was once, it was five thousand times from Malric: 'Where's Papa? When is he coming back? Well, why don't you know?' And Dosti fussed and cried and wouldn't stop." Even in the flickering lamplight, she looked worn.

"Is that all?"

"What do you want me to say? That I missed you? That I wanted to come back because I cared about you?"

"If that's so, I want very much for you to say it," he answered quietly.

"What does it matter to you, with your precious Empire to care about?" she said, but her face softened. "It is so. Oh, this is hard. There you were fighting against my people—my kinsmen even, for all I know—and what was I doing? Praying to Phos you'd come through safe. I thought I didn't care—until you went into danger. A heart's easy to harden with nothing at stake, but—damn it anyway!" she finished, caught between conflicting feelings.

"Thank you," he said. He went on, "When I was sixteen I was sure everything was simple. Here I am twenty years later and, by the gods, twenty times more confused." Helvis smiled and frowned at the same time, not quite pleased by his automatic translation of the Latin oath. Even there, he thought, I have to be careful. Still . . . "We stumble on somehow, don't we?"

"So far," she said. "So far."

There were more of Drax' men the next day, not scouts but a good fifty hard-looking horsemen who rode, lances couched, not far out of bowshot on the army's flank. They shouted something at Utprand's Namdaleni, but distance blurred their voices so no words were clear. "Bold-faced sods, aren't they?" Gaius Philippus said.

Zigabenos thought so, too. He sent off the Khatrishers to drive the rebel mercenaries away. Drax' men pulled back to forest cover in good order. Laon Pakhymer did not order his archers into the woods after them, unwilling to sacrifice the mobility that was their chief advantage. After a while his men rode off to catch up to the rest of the imperials. Drax' troopers emerged and took up their dogging post once more.

When evening came the rebels did not camp near Zigabenos' army, but trotted purposefully southwest. Watching them go, Gaius Philippus scratched at the scar on his cheek. "We're for it tomorrow, I expect. That troop's not on their own; they're a detachment off a big bunch and act like it."

He pulled out his sword, tested the edge with his middle finger. "Have to do, I suppose. I don't like fighting these bloody islanders. They're big as Gauls and twice as smart."

After full darkness Marcus saw a faint orange glow on the southwestern horizon. He did not remember any good-sized town just ahead of them, which left only Drax' men. His mouth tightened. If they were so close, it would indeed be battle tomorrow.

A messenger came to the Roman camp with orders from Mertikes Zigabenos: "We'll march in extended line tomorrow, not in column." The Videssian general expected it, too, then. His aide continued: "You foot soldiers will be on the left, with the Khatrishers covering you. My lord will take the center, with Utprand's Namdaleni on the right."

"Thanks, spatharios," the tribune said. "Care for a mug of wine?"

"Kind of you, sir," the Videssian said with a grin, looking years younger as his official duty fell away. He took a pull, screwed up his face in surprise. "Rather dry, isn't it?" His second sip was more cautious.

"As dry as we could find," Marcus answered; almost all Videssian wine was too sugary for the Romans' taste. Making conversation, he asked, "Why are the islanders on the right?" If Zigabenos was wary of them, better to put them in the center, where they could be watched—and checked—from either wing.

But the spatharios had an answer that showed his commander had also been thinking, though not along Scaurus' lines: "The right's their place of honor, sir." The tribune nodded thoughtfully; with proud Utprand, an appeal to honor was never wasted. The Videssian finished his wine and hurried away to pass the word to Laon Pakhymer.

Marcus wished the battle had developed sooner; as it was, Helvis and most of the other legionaries' women were here, instead of in a camp of their own farther from the upcoming fight. When he said as much to Gaius Philippus, the senior centurion answered, "They're likely safer here, sir. The imperials take no pains with their fieldworks."

"That's so," the tribune said, consoled. "Still, we'll leave half a maniple behind when we move out tomorrow. Under Minucius, I think."

"Minucius? He'll feel shamed at being left out of the fighting, sir. He's young." The senior centurion spoke as though the word covered a host of faults.

"It's an important job nonetheless, and he's a sensible lad." Marcus' eyes grew crafty. "When you give him the order, explain to him how he'll be protecting his Erene."

Gaius Philippus whistled in admiration. "The very thing. He dotes on the wench." Was that derision or envy in his voice? Scaurus could not tell.

The morning dawned clear and surprisingly cool, with a brisk sea breeze blowing the humidity away. "A fine day," Marcus heard one of the Romans say as they broke camp.

"A fine day to be hamstrung on, beef-head, if you don't tighten that strap on your greave," Gaius Philippus snarled. The soldier checked it; it was quite tight enough. The senior centurion was already rasping away at someone else.

Khamorth irregulars came galloping, waving their fur caps

over their heads and shouting, "Big horses! Lots of big horses!" A ripple of excitement ran through the imperial army. Soon, now.

They topped a slight rise and came down into the almost flat valley of the Sangarios, one of the Arandos' minor tributaries. A wooden bridge spanned the muddy little stream. The rebels' camp was visible on the far side of the river, but their commander had chosen to draw them up in front of the bridge.

"Drax! Drax! The great count Drax!" the Namdaleni shouted as their foes came into sight. The call was deep and steady as the beat of a drum.

"Utprand!" "Videssos!" "Gavras!" The answering battle cries were various but loud.

"I credited this precious Drax with more sense," Gaius Philippus said. "Aye, the land doesn't slope enough to matter, but if we once push them back they'll go into the river, and that'll be the end of 'em."

Marcus remembered something Nephon Khoumnos used to say: "If ifs and buts were candied nuts, then everyone would be fat." If that was an omen, he misliked it; the dour Videssian general was long dead, slain by Avshar's wizardry.

Zigabenos, who had once been Khoumnos' aide, knew better than to exhaust his troops by charging too soon. He kept them well in hand as they advanced. The Namdaleni moved slowly forward to meet them. Drax' men wore sea-green surcoats and had green streamers fluttering from their lances.

Where was Drax' banner? If the right was the islanders' place of honor, Scaurus had expected to see it bearing down on him. But it was nowhere to be found—until the tribune spied it at the opposite end of the Namdalener line. Suspicion flared in him. What was Drax scheming?

Like an armored thunderbolt, Utprand hurled himself at that taunting banner, breaking the steady line the imperial army had maintained. By squads and platoons his men followed, until half a thousand knights bore down on the rebel count.

"Traitor! Robber!" Their war cries rang over the pounding of their horses' hooves.

"Drax! Drax! The great count Drax!" Shouting, too, Drax' horsemen swung lances down and dug spurs into their mounts to meet them. They had another cry as well, and a premonitory shiver went down Scaurus' spine: "Namdalen! Namdalen! Namdalen!"

"Go on! Go on! Back him, you milk-livered, cheese-faced dogturds!" That was Gaius Philippus shouting, profanely praying for some miracle to take his voice across the field and make Soteric's men, and Clozart's, and Turgot's, join Utprand and his loyal retainers in their charge.

A few did, but a trickle, ones, twos, and fives. Most sat their horses, waiting. If Utprand could cast Drax down, perhaps they would advance . . . but Utprand and his followers were alone on the field, and Drax had more than half a thousand knights to throw against them.

Lances shattered. Horses fell, screaming worse than men. Riders flew from saddles to be trampled under iron-shod hooves. The sun sparkled off steel as swords were bared. Utprand's wedge of men, fighting all the more grimly for knowing themselves betrayed, still surged toward their enemy's standard.

Scaurus cheered them on, but not for long, for Drax' right bore down on him, every lance, it seemed, aimed straight at his chest. The Khatrishers were still skirmishing with the onrushing Namdaleni, peppering them with arrows. A knight here, another there, sagged in their saddles as they were hit. But the light horse in front of them could not really stop their charge. One Khatrisher, bolder than his friends, rode in close to slash at an islander with his saber. The Namdalener swerved his horse so it struck his foe's pony shoulder to shoulder. The smaller mount stumbled and went down. An islander speared its rider as if he were a chunk of meat to be impaled on a belt-knife. The sea-green wave rolled over the corpse.

"Stand firm now, you *hastati*! The horses don't want to spear themselves," Gaius Philippus was shouting.

"*Pila* at the ready . . ." Marcus called. He waited, dry-mouthed, as Drax' men neared with frightening speed. "At the ready . . . loose!" He swung his arm down; the buccinators' horns echoed his command.

Hundreds of javelins darted forth as one, followed by another volley and another. Horses and riders went sprawling, killed or wounded; knights behind lost their footing in turn. Some of the horsemen reacted quickly enough to catch the *pila* on their shields—which were shaped, Scaurus thought in one of those strange, clear moments he knew he would remember forever, like the kites Videssian boys flew. It did them less good than they might have hoped. The long, soft-iron shanks of the *pila* bent on impact, making them doubly useless: not only did they foul the shields, but the Namdaleni could not throw them back.

But Drax' men were already fearfully close when the rain of javelins began. Their charge was blunted, slowed. It could not be stopped. A few of their horses drew up rather than running onto the *hastae*; more, spurred on by their riders, crashed through the line of heavy spears. "Drax! Drax! The great count Drax!" Their shout never faltered.

Had it not been for the flexibility of the Romans' maniples, the system that let them fight in small units and shift eight-man squads to meet trouble wherever it occurred, the Namdalener charge would have smashed them to ruin in minutes. Scaurus, Gaius Philippus, Junius Blaesus, Bagratouni—all of them screamed orders, directing legionaries to where they were needed most.

A lancehead, its steel discolored with rust but still deadly, jabbed past the tribune's shoulder. Behind him a Roman grunted, more in surprise than pain. The lance, now dipped in red, ripped free. The legionary's scream drowned in up-bubbling blood.

A hurled stone smashed off the nasal of the lancer's conical helm. He swore in island patois, shook his head groggily. Marcus sprang forward. Sudden fear on his face, the Namdalener tried to beat his thrust aside with the shaft of his lance. The tool was too clumsy, the man too slow. Scaurus' point punched through his chain gorget and into his neck. The lance slipped from his hand. He would have fallen, but in the press he could not for some minutes.

Another Namdalener, also on horseback, slashed down at the tribune, who caught the blow on his shield. The knight grunted and cut, again and again, his sword striking sparks from the bronze facing of Marcus' *scutum*. He was a clever warrior; each cut came from a different, newly dangerous angle. The Roman's shield arm started to ache.

He pivoted on his left foot, thrusting at the rider's jack-booted leg. With a veteran's instinct, the Namdalener twitched it out of the way, but for a horseman that was not enough. His mount took the stab in the barrel. Its eyes wide with pain it could not understand, it reared and then foundered, pinning the islander beneath it before he could kick free of the stirrups. His cry of pain was cut short as another horse trampled him.

Someone pounded the tribune's shoulder. His head whipped round; it was Senpat Sviodo, who waved a scolding finger under his nose. "That was not sporting," the Vaspurakaner said.

"Too bloody bad," Marcus growled, for all the world like Gaius Philippus.

Senpat's mobile features curdled into a frown. "The Romans are a very *serious* people," he declared, and winked at the tribune.

"To the crows with you," Scaurus said, laughing. And one worry, at least, he thought, had come to nothing at all, for Gagik Bagratouni's band of refugee Vaspurakaners was fighting as fiercely as any of Scaurus' troops. The thick-shouldered *nakharar* himself dragged a Namdalener from the saddle, to be finished by his men. Mesrop Anhoghin outdueled another; the Roman thrusting-stroke he had learned let him use his long arms to best advantage.

"This Drax is no great shakes as a general," Senpat yelled in Marcus' ear. "He should have learned from last year's battle that his knights can't break our line. They pay the price for trying, too." That was so. With their charge stalled, the Namdaleni grew vulnerable not only to the legionaries but also to the Khatrishers, who plied them with arrows and began to stretch wide to turn their flank.

But if Drax' tactical skills left something to be desired, the great count was a clever, insightful strategist. Sudden commotion broke out on the imperials' right wing. Scaurus glanced in that direction, but saw nothing—too many horses and riders in the way. He grimaced in annoyance; in most fights his inches gave him a good view of the field, but not today.

All too soon, he had no need to see; the rising tide of battlecries from the right told him all he had to know: "Namdalen! Namdalen! Namdalen!" The shout swelled and swelled, far beyond the noise Drax' men alone could make. Cries of fury and fear came from the Videssian center; the island mercenaries had turned their coats.

There was a lull in the assault on the legionaries. The commander of Drax' right wing, a snub-nosed Namdalener who had to be older than he looked, held up his shield on his lance. It was not painted white, but Marcus guessed he meant it as a sign of truce. "What do you want?" he called to the officer.

"Join us!" the islander shouted back, his accent nearly as thick as that of Utprand, who was surely dead by now. "Why t'row your lives away for not'ing? Up Namdalen and away wit' old Videssos! The future belongs to us!"

The legionaries answered that for themselves, an overwhelming roar of rejection. "Up Namdalen with a hoe handle!" "It'd be us you turned treacher on next!" That one hit home; if the Romans sometimes got on better with the men of the Duchy than they did with the imperials, it was for the islanders' plain speech and straightforwardness. Utprand, although ruthless as a wolf, had been an utterly honest man, while Drax outdid the Videssians in double-dealing. Gaius Philippus' jeer spoke for many: "Why should we give you what you're not men enough to take?"

A slow flush of anger ran up the Namdalener's face. He lowered the upraised shield, settled his helm's bar nasal more firmly on his short nose. "On your heads be it," he said. The islanders surged forward once more.

Their second charge, though, was not half so fierce as the first had been. That puzzled Scaurus, but after a moment he understood. All Drax' knights needed to do here was to keep the legionaries in play. As long as they could not go to the aid of Zigabenos' Videssians in the center, that was enough.

Laon Pakhymer saw that, too, and with bantam courage flung his Khatrishers at the solid Namdalener ranks. The light horsemen's spirit was equal to anything, but man for man, horse for horse, they were grossly overmatched in close combat. "Gutty little bastards, aren't they?" Gaius Philippus said with nothing but respect in his voice. He watched the doomed attack; there was nothing else he could do.

At last flesh and blood could take no more. The Khatrishers broke, riding wildly in all directions, for the time being wrecked as a fighting force. Pakhymer galloped after them, still shouting and trying to bring them back for one more charge, but they would not heed him.

His flank cover ruined, Marcus drew his line back and to the left, anchoring the end of it to a small stand of fig trees. The Namdaleni did not hinder the maneuver; it drew him further from the center. He knew that and hated it, but he could do Zigabenos no good by being surrounded and destroyed, either.

In any case, the Videssian general was being driven leftward, too, pressed from the front by Drax' men and from the right by the Namdaleni who had been his own. But Zigabenos, as Scaurus knew, was resourceful; though his position could hardly have been worse, he still had a stratagem left to try.

The battlefield din shrieked in Scaurus' ears. When a great roar swallowed it as a whale might gulp a spratling, he thought for a terrible second that he had been struck a mortal blow and was hearing the sound of death. But the noise was real; troopers on both sides clapped hands to their heads and spun about, looking for its source. Then the tip of shadow touched the tribune, and terror with it.

Long as the Amphitheater, thick as the city's Middle Street was wide, the dragon soared over the battle on batwings vast enough to shade a village. It roared again, a sound like the end of the world; red-yellow as molten gold, flame licked from the fanged cavern of its mouth. Its eyes, big as shields, wise as time, black as hell, contemptuously scanned the quarreling worms below.

But there are no dragons, Marcus' mind yammered. In his disbelief he must have spoken aloud, for Gaius Philippus jerked his head upward. "Then what do you call that?"

Men shouted and ducked and tried to hide; horses, plunging and rearing, did their best to bolt. Riders jounced on their bucketing mounts and were thrown by the score. Though the Videssians were no more able to defend than the Namdaleni to attack, the pressure which vised them eased.

The dragon sideslipped in the air, sun glinting on silver scales. The great wings beat, once and then again, like the heavy breathing of a god. The beast stooped on the Namdaleni. Fire shot from its mouth now, making the incendiary the imperials brewed seem no more than embers. The islanders scattered before it, clawing at one another in their effort to escape.

Suddenly, incongruously, Gaius Philippus' sweat-streaked face creased in a grin. "Are you daft, man?" Scaurus yelled, waiting for the beast to turn and burn him, too.

"Not a bit of it," the senior centurion answered. "Where's the wind of its passage?" He was right, the tribune realized; those wings, when they worked, should have stirred a gale, but the air was calm and still, even the early morning breeze gone.

"Illusion!" he cried. "It's magicked up!" Battle magic was a touchy thing; most wizardries melted in the heat of combat. Indeed, because that was so, generals often ignored sorcery in their plans. Zigabenos, holding back until the last moment, made the most of it from sheer surprise.

But what one wizard could accomplish, another could undo. Even as the dragon dove toward the islanders' ranks, it began to fade. Its roar grew distant, its shadow faint, its flame transparent. It would not vanish, but a ghost held no terror for man or beast. Now and again it firmed somewhat as the Videssian magicians tried ever more desperate spells to maintain the seeming, but their Namdalener counterparts vitiated each one in turn.

The men of the Duchy re-formed with a trained speed and discipline Marcus had to admire, though it meant ruin for his side. "Namdalen! Namdalen!" Their shout once more dominated the field. And now they fought with greater ferocity than before, as if to make amends for their momentary panic.

The snub-nosed wing commander bawled an order. His horsemen struck forward—not at the legionaries this time, but at the join between their maniples and the Videssian regiment to the right. The move was full of deadly cunning; coordination between units of the polyglot imperial army was never what it should be. Romans and Videssians each hesitated a few seconds too long, and got no chance to repair their mistake. Voices deep-throated in triumph, the Namdaleni swarmed into the gap they had forced.

"Form square!" Marcus ordered. The buccinators echoed him. He bit his lip in anger and dismay. Too late, too late, the islanders were already round his flank.

The Namdalener officer, though, had a feel for the essential. He swung his knights in against the Videssian center, already hard-pressed from right and front. Surrounded on three sides, the imperials shattered. Zigabenos and a forlorn rear guard fought on, but most of the Videssians had no thought beyond saving themselves. The men of the Duchy pounded after them, cutting them down from behind.

Compared to breaking the Videssians, the legionaries were a secondary objective. They formed their hollow square with only token interference from the islanders. "Blow 'retreat,'" Scaurus ordered the buccinators. The bitter call rang out.

"Back to camp?" Gaius Philippus asked.

"Do you think we can do any good here?"

The senior centurion's eyes measured the battlefield. "No, it's buggered right and proper." As if to underscore his words, a fresh burst of shouting from the right had Zigabenos' name in it. Dead or captured, Marcus thought dully. The Videssian general's standard had fallen some time before, the Empire's sky blue and golden sun trampled in the dust . . . and the Empire with it, all too likely.

IV

VARATESH AND HIS FIVE FOLLOWERS RODE SOUTH LIKE WIND-blown leaves, their gray cloaks swirling around them. Their talk was an endless botheration to him, a string of thieveries, rapes, murders, and tortures, all proudly recounted and embellished. He had done worse than any of them, but he did not brag of it. It made him ashamed. Forfeit the company of good men, he thought for the thousandth time, and what you have left is offal—harden yourself to it. He could not.

He had killed his twin brother at seventeen, in a quarrel over a serving girl. No one ever believed Kodoman drew knife on him first, though it was so. Kinslayer his clan named him and punished him accordingly. They did not kill him, for he was the khagan's son, but cast him out, driving him naked from their tents onto the steppe.

In its way that, too, was a death sentence; the spirit went out of ostracized men, so they perished from aloneness as much as from hunger, cold, or wild beasts. But the injustice of it was a flame burning in young Varatesh's breast, a flame to sustain him where a lesser man would have yielded to malignant fate and died. He came back to steal a horse; he had to, he told himself, to survive. The guard was about his size; a swift blow from behind, and he had clothes as well. Of course he only stunned the man; he was sure of that, though the fellow had not moved by the time he rode away.

Bad luck somehow followed him after that. More than once he was on the point of being adopted into a new clan when word of his past caught him up and he was spurned once more. The insult of it rankled still; who were those arrogant chieftains, to presume to judge him on such rumors? One way or another, the insults were avenged. Before long, no khagan in his right mind would have invited Varatesh to join him and his. As his past grew blacker, so did his future; he could not wade to acceptance through blood.

Banned from the clans by no fault of his own—for so he always saw it—Varatesh, ever bold, formed his own. The plains had always known outlaws—scattered skulkers, often starving, distrusting each other and afraid of their betters. Varatesh gave them a standard to rally to, a blank black banner that openly proclaimed them for what they were. At last he was the chief he should have been, with a growing host behind him—and he hated them, almost to a man. Better, he thought sometimes, if Kodoman's dagger had found his heart.

Such thoughts availed him nothing. He reined in to consult the talisman he carried. As always, the crystal sphere was transparent when he first put it in his hands, but at his touch it began to swirl with orange mist. Soon all its depths were suffused with orange—save for one patch, which remained stubbornly clear. He rotated the sphere; however he turned it, the clear area stayed just east of south, as if drawn by some sorcerous lodestone. And it was larger than it had been yesterday.

"We gain," he told his companions. They nodded, smiling like so many wolves.

In fact, Avshar had explained to him, it was not magic that kept the entire crystal from coloring, but the absence of magic. "There is a traveler on the plains who carries a blade proof against my spells," the wizard-prince had said. "We've met before, he and I. If you would, I'd have you take him for me and fetch him here to your tents, where I can pry his secrets from him at leisure."

A cold, greedy hunger was in the white-robed giant's voice, but Varatesh did not hear it. For Avshar he bore admiration and regard not far from love. The sorcerer was outcast, too, driven, he said, far from Videssos in some political convulsion. That alone would have been enough to make a bond between them. But Avshar also used the renegade chieftain's son with exactly the sort of respectful deference Varatesh felt should have been his by right. He rarely received it from his followers, most of whom were ruffians long before they became outlaws. To have the wizard—a mighty one, as he had proved in many more ways than a bit of crystal—freely grant it eased Varatesh's suspicions as nothing else could have. His quality was recognized at last, and by one himself of high estate, even if an outlander.

That had given Varatesh pause, the first few days after Avshar appeared before his tent. The wizard used the steppe tongue like a true Khamorth, not some lisping imperial . . . and no one saw his face. He always wore either a visored helm or mantling so thick only the faintest hint of eyes could be made out. But he was not blind; far from it.

After a very short while, though, doubts somehow disappeared, and both Avshar's curious arrival—*why* had the sentries not reported a traveler?—and personal habits came to be nothing more than matters for idle speculation.

Perhaps he has hideous scars, Varatesh thought compassionately. One day he will see I esteem him for himself, not the fleshly mask he wears.

With a nomad's patience, the plainsman was willing to wait. For now he would help his friend in the task he had been set; it never occurred to him to wonder how Avshar had come to set him tasks. He booted his horse forward.

"No, damn it, I want nothing to do with that miserable piece of pointed iron in my kit," Gorgidas growled at camping time, as he had every day since they left the village. Every day saw him more irritable, too; his face itched and felt rough as a rasp as his beard started growing in. And, to his mortification, it seemed to be mostly white, though his hair was still dark but for a thin dusting of silver at the temples. He wished he had his razor back.

"Listen to the silly man, now!" Viridovix exclaimed to everyone who would listen—the friendly feud between Celt and Greek entertained the whole party. "When you were with the legion, with its thousands of men and all, the lot of 'em could look after you. The now, though, it's but this wee few of us. We have to watch out for our own selves and maybe canna be sparing the time for one puir doit too proud to learn swordplay."

"Oh, go howl. I've managed to come this far in my life without the knack for killing people, and I don't care to pick it up now. I'm too old to learn such tricks anyway." He looked resentfully at the Gaul, who was his own age, near enough, but whose sweeping mustachios were still bright red.

"Too old, is it? Sure and you're a day younger than you'll be tomorrow." Viridovix waited to see if that shot would hit, but the physician merely set his chin. The Celt switched to Latin so only Gorgidas would understand: "Forbye, if you're not too old to start bedding women, now, sure and the sword shouldna come too hard."

The day was warm, but ice leaped up the Greek's spine. "What mean you?" he said sharply.

"Softly, softly," Viridovix said, seeing his alarm. "Naught with harm in it for you. But sith you've tried the one new thing, why not the other?"

Gorgidas sat unmoving, staring past the Gaul. Viridovix left him to himself for most of a minute, then asked with an impudent grin, "Tell me now, how is it by comparison?"

The Greek snorted. "Find out for yourself, you barbarian ape." He had lived under the shadow of the Roman army's law too long to be easy with others knowing he preferred men to women. In the legions, those who did so faced being beaten to death by their fellow soldiers as punishment on discovery.

Even the thought of a *fustuarium* was enough to freeze the smile on his lips. He sat a while, considering; he did not like the idea of being a burden to his companions. Pikridios Goudeles, with more tact than Gorgidas had thought he had, helped solve the dilemma. "Possibly the brave Viridovix," he said, pronouncing the Celt's name with care, though Videssians tended to stumble over it, "would instruct us both. I have no skill at swordplay, either."

Skylitzes had been tossing a handful of dry sheepdung on the fire. At Goudeles' words he looked up, his usually dour features showing amazed delight. The spectacle of the plump bureaucrat wielding a blade promised amusement beyond his wildest dreams. He kept silent, afraid a taunt might make Goudeles change his mind.

Gorgidas unsheathed the *gladius* Gaius Phillippus had given him, hefted it experimentally. It seemed short and stubby compared to the longsword Viridovix bore; the Romans favored blades no more than two feet long, for they relied on the stab rather than the slashing stroke. The leather-wrapped grip fit Gorgidas' hand seductively well; he held a tool perfectly designed for its intended use.

"Heavier than your pens, eh?" Arigh said, stepping toward the fire with the results of his brief hunt: a rabbit, a striped ground squirrel, and a fair-sized tortoise. The Greek nodded, scratching the side of his face for the dozenth time that day. Already his beard was thicker than Arigh's; the Arshaum, unlike the Khamorth, were not a whiskery folk. As if to compensate, they rarely trimmed the few hairs that did appear, but let them grow in a thin tuft at the point of their chins.

Goudeles, of course, had brought no sword. He borrowed a saber from one of Agathias Psoes' troopers, a curved, single-edged blade with a very short back edge, called a shamshir in the Khamorth tongue, a yataghan by Arigh. The Videssian handled it with even more uncertainty than Gorgidas showed; the Greek, at least, had seen combat at first hand.

But after a flourish that almost took off his own ear, Goudeles said grandly to Viridovix, "Impart to us your martial art."

"That I will." As the soldiers gathered round to watch, the Celt set his pupils in the guard position, making sure they carried their left arms well behind them. "Keeping them out o' harm's way and balancing you both, you see. If you've shields you'll stand more face-to-face to get full advantage from 'em, but no use complicating things the now."

He adjusted them once more and stepped back to survey his handiwork. Then, without warning, he tore his own blade free and leaped at his students with a bloodcurdling shriek. They stumbled away, horrified. The watchers guffawed. "There's you first pair of lessons together," Viridovix said, not unkindly. "The one is, never relax around a man with a sword, and t'other, a good loud yell never did you any harm, nor your foe any good."

Even as teacher, the Gaul made a relentless opponent.

Gorgidas' arm and shoulder ached from parrying his slashes. So did his ribs; Viridovix had thumped them with the flat of his blade more than once. The contemptuous ease with which he got through infuriated the Greek, as Viridovix had known it would. Where Gorgidas had been all but forced to take sword in hand, he soon worked in grim earnest, panting breaths hissing out between clenched teeth. Once Viridovix had to pirouette neatly to keep from being spitted on his point; the Greek lacked the experience to know how dangerous his thrust was.

"That poxy Roman blade," the Gaul said. He was sweating as freely as his pupil. "You kern, you were watching the legionaries and never let on—you almost let the air out of me there."

Gorgidas began an apology, but Viridovix slapped him on the back and cut it short. "Nay, 'twas well done." He whirled on Goudeles. "Now, sirrah, your turn. And at ye!"

"Oof!" the pen-pusher said as the Celt's blade spanked his side. He lacked any feel for aggression; whatever strokes he made were purely to defend himself. Within that limitation, though, he showed some promise. His movements were economical, and he had a gift for guessing the direction the next blow was coming from. Lankinos Skylitzes showed disappointment.

"It's good you're not trying to go beyond yourself," Viridovix said. "If you learn enough to stay alive a while, sooner or later a mate'll rescue you, the which would do a dead corp no good at all, at all."

But after a while he grew bored with an opponent who would not take the fight to him. His own strokes grew quicker and harder, and when Goudeles, retreating desperately now, threw up his saber in a counter, the Gallic longsword met it squarely. The pen-pusher's blade snapped clean across; the greater part flew spinning into the fire. Taken by surprise, Viridovix barely managed to turn his sword in his hand so he did not cut Goudeles in two. As it was, the Videssian fell with a groan, clutching his left side.

Viridovix knelt by him, concerned. "Begging your pardon, indeed and I am. That one was not meant to land."

"Mmph." Goudeles sat up gingerly. He hawked and spat. Gorgidas saw the spittle was white, not pink-tinged—the bureaucrat had no truly dangerous hurt, then. Goudeles looked at the stub of his blade. "I did not realize I was facing you with a weapon as flawed as my own skill."

"Not flawed!" protested the trooper from whom he'd borrowed it. He was still young enough for his beard to be soft and fuzzy; his name was Prevalis, Haravash's son, testifying to his mixed blood. "I paid two goldpieces for that sword; it's fine steel from the capital."

Goudeles shrugged, winced, and tossed him the broken saber. He caught the hilt deftly. "Look!" he insisted, showing everyone that what was left of the blade had the suppleness befitting a costly weapon. Once he had satisfied himself and his comrades of that, his eyes slowly traveled to Viridovix. "Phos, how strong are you?" he whispered, awe in his voice.

"Strong enough to eat the pits with the plums—or you without salt." But despite the gibe, the grin stretched thin across Viridovix' strong-cheekboned face. Gorgidas could guess his thoughts. There were times when his sword and Scaurus', spell-wrapped by the druids of Gaul, were far more than ordinary blades in this world where magic was real as a kick in the belly. Usually it took the presence of sorcery to bring out their power, but not always.

The Celt sat cross-legged by the fire. He drew that strangely potent sword, studied the druids' marks that had been stamped into the metal while it was still hot. They meant nothing to him; the druids guarded their secrets well, even from the Gallic nobles.

For a moment the marks seemed to glow with a golden life of their own, but before Gorgidas was sure he had seen it, Viridovix resheathed his blade. Some chance reflection from the firelight, the Greek thought. He yawned and sighed at the same time, too tired to worry about it long.

He also ached. Swordplay, like horsemanship, called on muscles he rarely used. He knew he would be stiff come morning. *Ten years ago I would have been fine*, he protested to himself. The internal answer came too soon: *ten years ago you weren't forty-one.*

He gnawed at a rabbit leg, washed down some of the tasteless nomad-style wheatcakes with swigs of kavass, and fell asleep the moment his feet reached the end of his bedroll.

* * *

Varatesh tested the night breeze with a spit-moistened finger; out of the south, as he had expected. The wind came off the sea in spring and summer, bringing fair weather with it. In fall it would shift, and not even a man born on the plains relished a steppe winter. Every year the shamans begged the wind spirits not to turn, and every year found themselves ignored. Foolishness to waste good prayers thus, the renegade thought.

He had counted on a south wind when he led his little band across the track of the man he sought and his companions. They had ridden on after dusk to catch up with the larger party, using as their guides the stars and Avshar's talisman; in the darkness its orange smoke glowed with a glowworm's pale cold light. Now their quarry's camp lay straight north, the embers of its campfire a red smudge against the horizon.

Luckily there was no moon, or sentries might have seen Varatesh's men approach. But in the faint starglimmer they were so many shadows sliding up, and they moved as quietly as any shades. Varatesh's feet chafed in his boots. He was not used to walking any distance, but he had left the horses behind with one of his men; even muzzled, they were too likely to give themselves away.

"What now?" a nomad whispered. "From the trail the filthy pimps' sons left, they've got twice as many as we do, and then some."

"Much help they'll get from that," Varatesh replied. He checked the wind; it would not do to have it shift now. It was steady. He grunted in satisfaction, reaching inside his leather tunic for the second of Avshar's gifts. The jar was veined alabaster, eggshell-thin, with a wax-sealed silver stopper. Even unopened, it had the feel of magic to it, a magic like the wizard-prince's crystal, subtler and somehow more dangerous than the familiar charms the shamans used. Varatesh's men backed away from their leader, as if wanting no part in what he was about to do.

He cut the sealing wax with a hard thumbnail, stripped it off, and threw it away. Though the jar was still tightly shut, he smelled the faint, sweet odor of narcissus. That was dangerous; he held his breath as a wave of dizziness washed over him, hoping it would pass. It did. Moving quickly now, he yanked the stopper free and tossed the little jar in the direction of the camp a few hundred yards away. He heard it shatter, though the throw was gentle. He did not think the noise would be noticed in the camp, but no matter if it was; any investigator would only meet Avshar's sorcery the sooner.

Varatesh hurried back to his comrades upwind; together they drew back farther, taking no chances—as they had been warned, this was not a magic that chose between friend and foe. "How long do we wait?" someone asked.

"A twelfth part of the night, the wizard said. By then the essence will have dispersed." Varatesh looked west, studying the sky. "When the star that marks the Sheep's left hock sets, we move. Be watchful till then—if they have a sentry posted far enough off to one side, he may not be taken by the spell."

They waited, watching the star creep down the deep-blue bowl of heaven toward the edge of the earth. No outcry came from the camp ahead. Varatesh's spirits rose; all was just as Avshar had foretold.

The white spark of light winked out. The nomads rose from their haunches and walked toward the camp, sabers ready in their hands. "My legs hurt," grumbled one of them, no more comfortable on foot than his leader.

"Shut up," Varatesh snapped, still wary. The outlaw glared at him. He was sorry for his hard words as soon as they were out of his mouth; it hurt him to have to use men so. Back in his own clan, he thought, a simple headshake would have conveyed his meaning. But he rode with his clan no more, and never would again, unless he came one day as conqueror. These oafs with whom he was forced to share his life paid soft manners no mind. Often even curses would not make them listen, and obedience had to be forced with fists or edged steel.

"Look here!" a nomad said, pointing to one side. The huddled shape was a sentry, now curled on his side in unnatural sleep. Varatesh smiled—it was always good to see a magic perform as promised. Not that he doubted Avshar, but a sensible man ran no risks he did not have to. An outlaw's life, even an outlaw chief's life, was risky enough as it was.

The five plainsmen came into the fire's circle of light. Almost as one, they exclaimed at the strange sight of strings of fallen horses, flanks slowly rising and falling in the grip of

Avshar's spell. Varatesh laughed nervously. It had not occurred to him that the sorcery would fell animals along with men.

A dozen men lay unconscious by the fire. With the caution of a beast of prey, Varatesh examined their horses' trappings. He frowned. From the look of things, fifteen of the beasts were being ridden. Counting the sentry he had already seen, that left two men unaccounted for. He trotted back into the darkness. If the sentries spaced themselves in a triangle round the fire, a good sensible plan, the missing ones would be easy to find—unless Avshar's magic had somehow missed them, in which case, he thought, there would be arrows coming out of the night.

The missing guardsmen were close to where he had expected them to be. A drop of sweat ran down his forehead nonetheless; the sorcery's success had been a very near thing. From the awkward way one of the men had fallen, he had been walking back toward the campsite when sleep overcame him. Perhaps he thought he was taken ill and, like a good soldier, headed in for a replacement—as luck would have it, the worst thing he could have done. He had headed straight into the spell instead of away from it.

When Varatesh returned, he found one of his men bending over a sleeper, a thin chap with the scraggly beginnings of a pepper-and-salt beard. The chieftain's foot lashed out, kicking the outlaw's saber away before it could slice the fellow's exposed throat.

The nomad yelped. He cradled his injured right hand in the other. "You've gone soft in the head," he growled, resenting the spoiled kill. "Why ruin my sport?" The other three outlaws, who had been looking forward to the same amusement, grouped themselves behind him.

"Denizli, you are a cur, and the rest of you, too!" Varatesh did not bother to hide his disgust. "Slaying the helpless is women's work—it suits you. If you take such delight in it, here!" His hands well away from sword and dagger, he turned his back on them.

They might have jumped him, but at that moment one of the supposedly ensorceled men by the campfire sat up not six feet from Varatesh and demanded in sleepy, accented Videssian, "Will you spalpeens give over your yattering and let a tired fellow sleep?" His hand was on his sword hilt, just as it had been when he dozed off; he faced away from the outlaws and must have assumed from their Khamorth speech that they were members of his own squad of horsemen arguing among themselves. He did not seem alarmed, only mildly annoyed.

The would-be mutineers froze in surprise; they had thought the members of the embassy party as insensate as so many logs. But Varatesh was more clever than his followers, and knew more. If Avshar's quarry owned a blade that defeated the wizard's magics, why should it not also defend him against this one? Reasoning thus, Varatesh had equipped himself with a bludgeon. He pulled it out now, took two steps forward, and struck the complainer, who was no more than half-awake, a smart blow behind the right ear. Without so much as a groan, the man fell flat, once more as unconscious as his comrades.

The Khamorth chieftain whirled, ready to face his men's challenge. Their uncertain stances, the confusion on their faces, told him they were again his. As if nothing had happened, he ordered them, "Come turn this chap over so we can see what we have." They obeyed without hesitation.

To this point, things had gone as Avshar had predicted, but when Varatesh got a good look at the man he had stunned, he suddenly felt almost as befuddled as his companions had when the fellow sat up and spoke.

Avshar's description of his enemy had been painted with the clarity of hate: a big man, blond, clean-shaven, but otherwise of a Videssian cast. The man at Varatesh's feet was big enough, but there the resemblance to the sorcerer's picture ended. He had blunt features and high, knobby cheekbones; true, he shaved his chin and cheeks, but a great fluffy mustache reached almost to his collarbones. And while his hair was light, it was more nearly fire-colored than golden.

The outlaw scratched his beard, considering. He still had one test to make. He drew forth Avshar's crystal and held it close to the unconscious man. Though he waited and waited, no color appeared in its depths; it might have been any worthless piece of glass. The absence of magic was absolute. Reassured, he said, "This is the one we seek. Denizli, go out and fetch Kubad and the horses."

"What for? And why me?" the nomad asked, not wanting to walk any further than he had to.

Varatesh swallowed a sigh, sick to death of being cursed to work through men unable to see past the tips of their beards. With such patience as he had left, he explained, "If we bring the horses here, we won't have to carry this great hulk out to them." He let some iron come into his voice, "And you because I say so."

Denizli realized he would get no backing from his companions, who were all relieved Varatesh had not chosen them. He trotted clumsily away, pausing once or twice to rub at his blistering heels.

Donkey, Varatesh thought. But then, it seemed even Avshar's wisdom had its limits. When he had time, he would have to ponder that.

The man he had clubbed moaned and tried to roll over. Varatesh hit him again, a precisely calculated blow delivered without passion. It would not do to strike too hard; he remembered the sentry in his father's clan. No, no, he told himself for the thousandth time, the fellow had only been knocked cold. Still, he was more careful now.

Hoofbeats in the darkness heralded Kubad's approach. Denizli with him looked happier on horseback. At least he had the wit to remount, Varatesh thought. Kubad looked around the campfire with interest. "Worked, did it?" he remarked economically. "Can we plunder them?"

"No."

"Pity." Of the five Varatesh had with him, Kubad was far the best. He slid down from his horse, walked to the side of his chief, who was still standing over the red-haired man. "This the one the wizard wants?"

"Yes. Get one of the remounts over here; we'll tie him aboard." They slung the unconscious man over the horse's back like a hunting trophy, bound his hands and feet beneath the beast's belly. Varatesh took his sword.

"How long is your charm good for?" Kubad asked. "You don't want to butcher these sheep—" Denizli had been talking, then. "—so likely they'll come after us when they wake. And there's more o' them than there is of us."

"We'll have a day's start, from what I was told. That should be plenty. Smell the air—the night's clear, aye, but rain's coming before long. What trail will they follow?"

In the crimson glow of the campfire, Kubad's smile seemed dipped in blood.

Viridovix awoke to nightmare. The driving pain in his head left him queasy and weak, and when his eyes came open he groaned and squinched them shut again. He was facing directly into the rising sun, whose brilliance sent new needles of agony drilling into his brain. Worse even than that was the work of some malevolent sorcerer, who had reversed sky and horizon and set both of them bobbing like a bowl of calf's-foot jelly. His sensitive stomach heaved. Only when he tried to reach up to shield his face from the sun did he discover his hands were tied.

His moan alerted his takers to his returning awareness. Someone said something in the plains speech. The jouncing stopped. Very carefully, Viridovix opened one eye. The world was steady, but still upside down. He let his head hang loosely. Gray-brown dirt swooped toward him; a sharp stem of grass poked up to within a couple of inches from his forehead. There was a brown, shaggy-haired leg on either side of him. *I'm on a horse,* he told himself, pleased he could think at all.

After more talk in the Khamorth tongue, one of the nomads came over to him. In his undignified posture, Viridovix could only see the man from the thighs down. That was enough to send alarm shooting through him, for alongside a saber the plainsman bore the Gaul's sword.

Viridovix had learned only a few words of the plains language, none of them polite. He used one now, his voice a ghastly croak. Almost instantly he realized his rashness; his captor could enjoy revenge at leisure. He tried to gather his wits so he could take a blow manfully, if nothing else.

But the nomad only laughed, and there seemed to be no menace under the mirth. "I will cut you loose, yes?" he said in good Videssian, with only a trace of his people's guttural accent. His voice was a surprisingly light tenor, a young man's voice. He went on, "Please do not plan any folly. There are two men with bows covering you. I ask again, shall I cut you down?"

"Aye, an you will." The Celt saw no point in refusing; trussed as he was, he could do nothing, even without the pounding in his head. The Khamorth bent beneath the horse's barrel. His dagger bit through the rawhide thongs that lashed Viridovix' wrist to his ankles.

The Gaul tumbled to the ground, limp as a sack of meal. His nausea abruptly overwhelmed him. As he spewed, the Khamorth held his head so he would not foul himself, then gave him water to clean his mouth. The kindness was in its way more frightening than brutality would have been. To brutality, at least, he would have known how to respond.

After two or three tries he managed to sit. He studied his captor as best he could, though his vision was still blurred and went double on and off. The Khamorth *was* young, likely less than thirty, though the great bushy beard he wore after his people's custom helped obscure his youth. He was a bit taller than most plainsmen and carried himself like one used to leading. His eyes, though, were strange; even when he looked straight at Viridovix, they seemed far away, peering at something only he could see.

Fighting dizziness, the Gaul turned his head to see what allies the nomad had. As promised, two plainsmen had nocked arrows in their short bows. One drew his shaft back a few inches when Viridovix' eyes met his. He had a most unpleasant smile.

"Hold, Denizli!" the chief said in Videssian for the Gaul's benefit, then repeated the command in his own speech. Denizli scowled, but did as he was told.

There were three more Khamorth simply relaxing on their horses. They watched Viridovix as they might a wildcat they had ridden down, a dangerous beast who should get no chance to use his fangs. The lot of them were typical enough plainsmen, if on the hard-bitten side. It was their leader who put trepidation in the Celt's heart, the more so because he did not seem to belong on the steppe. He had more depth than his followers and, with his beard trimmed, would not have been out of place at the imperial court. Finesse, thought Viridovix, that was the word.

In his pain and confusion the Gaul took a bit of time to notice that none of his comrades had been taken. When he did, he burst out, "What ha' ye done wi' my mates, y'black-hearted omadhaun?"

The nomad chieftain frowned a moment; as was often true, Viridovix' brogue thickened in times of stress. But when he understood, the Khamorth laughed and spread his empty hands. "Nothing at all."

Oddly, Viridovix believed him. He was sure any of the other five would have delighted in the killing, but not this man. "What is it you want o' me, then?" the Celt asked, not reassured.

The answer, though, was mild enough. "For now, let me wash your head, so your cuts do not fester." Varatesh poured some kavass onto a scrap of wool, then knelt by Viridovix. The Celt winced when the stinging stuff touched his cut and swollen scalp, but the nomad daubed away as gently as Gorgidas might have done. "I am called Varatesh, by the way," he remarked.

"I'd be lying if I said I was pleased to make your acquaintance," the Gaul told him. Varatesh smiled and nodded, quite kindly—or so it would have seemed had Viridovix not been his prisoner.

The nomad's body screened him from one of the archers. As if his weight were too much for him, Viridovix slumped against Varatesh's shoulder—and then grappled for the longsword at the plainsman's belt. Only then did he realize how hurt and fuddled he was; Varatesh twisted away and bounced to his feet before the Celt's move was well begun.

The nomad shouted for his bowmen not to fire. He looked down at Viridovix, and there was no kindness on his handsome face now. With chilling deliberation, he kicked the Gaul in the point of the elbow. "Play no games with me," he said, still quiet-voiced.

Viridovix barely heard; sheets of red and black fire were passing in front of his eyes. The pain in his head, anguish a moment before, receded to a dull, all but friendly ache. Varatesh might not slaughter for the sport of it, but that only made his torments worse when they came.

"I doubt whether Avshar cares what shape you are in when he meets you," the Khamorth said. He paused, waiting to see how Viridovix met the name.

"Och, be damned to you and him both," the Gaul said, trying not to show the chill he felt. He blustered, "My comrades'll be catching up with you long before you can bring me to him." He had no idea how true that was; but if Varatesh had let them live, he might as well worry about them.

One of the other nomads laughed. "Hush, Kubad," Varatesh said, then turned back to Viridovix. "They're welcome to try," he went on placidly. "In fact, I wish them luck."

When the Celt could stand, his captors put him on one of their remounts. They took no chances on his escape, tying his feet under the horse and his hands behind him; the plainsman called Kubad guided his mount on a lead. Trying to gain more freedom of any sort, he protested, "At least be letting me have hold of the reins. What if I slip off?" He meant it; he felt anything but well.

Kubad had enough Videssian to answer him. "Then you drag." Viridovix gave up.

As the nomads rode north over the plains, the Gaul began to see that, by comparison, his own party had been lazing along. The steppe ponies trotted on and on, tireless as if driven by some clockwork. Despite the wide detour the plainsmen took round the herds of some clan, they covered nearly as much ground in one day as Viridovix was used to doing in two.

The only stops they made were to answer nature's calls; Viridovix found it hard to relieve himself with an arrow aimed at his midriff. The Khamorth ate in the saddle, gnawing on barklike sun-dried strips of beef and lamb. They did not pause to feed their prisoner, but halfway through the day Varatesh, courteous as if he'd never killed a man, held a flask of kavass to Viridovix' lips. He drank, both from thirst and in an effort to dull the pounding hurt in his head. The fermented milk did not help much.

Dirty-gray clouds like the underbellies of so many sheep came scudding up out of the south as the afternoon wore to a close. Kubad said something in his own language to Varatesh, who bobbed his head as if acknowledging a compliment. The wind grew brisker and began to feel damp.

The Khamorth leader picked a small creek with an overhanging bank as a campsite. "Rain tonight," he told Viridovix, "but we sleep dry here—unless the stream rises. I do not think it will."

"And what if it does?" The Gaul, hurt and also exhausted from staying in the saddle without being able to use his hands, did not really care, but tried to discommode Varatesh in any small way he could.

He failed. "Then we move," the nomad answered, busying himself with the fire. It was tiny and smokeless, not one to advertise their presence. This time the Khamorth shared their travelers' fare with Viridovix, untying him so he could eat, but always watching him so closely he could do nothing more. When he was through Varatesh bound him once more, testing each knot so carefully that the Gaul hated him for his thoroughness.

The plainsmen drew straw for their watches; Viridovix gathered himself to do something—he knew not what—as soon as he saw the chance. But his body betrayed him. Despite the misery in his head, despite the discomfort of having his arms tied behind his back, he yielded to sleep almost at once.

The gentle plashing of rain in the rivulet a few feet away woke him some hours later; Denizli, who had drawn third watch, was on sentry go. Varatesh had chosen his campsite perfectly. The projecting streambank left it snug and dry, just as he had said. Actually, the Celt had not doubted him; even in his cruelty, the outlaw chief was competent.

Viridovix rolled out toward the rain. Denizli growled something threatening in his own tongue and hefted his bow. "Sure and I just want to soak my puir battered noddle," the Celt said, but Denizli only grunted and lifted the bow a couple of inches further.

Swearing at his luck, Viridovix perforce drew back. "Arse-licking eunuch," he said. He knew he was gambling, but beyond grunting again Denizli did not respond. Here, at least, was one nomad who had no Videssian. The Gaul cursed him for several minutes, a profane stew of the imperial tongue, Latin, and Celtic. Feelings slightly eased, he tried to find some tolerable position in which to go back to sleep. The rain, he thought, looked to be lasting a while.

Gorgidas stirred and grumbled as a raindrop splashed against his cheek. Another coldly kissed his ear, a third spattered off his left eyelid. He scrabbled at his bedroll, trying to pull it over his head without really rousing. Before he could, half a dozen more drops landed on his face, leaving him irretrievably awake. "By the dog," he muttered in Greek, an oath of annoyance. The weather had seemed good enough when he fell asleep.

He winced as he sat, for his head gave a savage twinge. He wished for raw cabbage to deal with his hangover, but wondered what he had done to deserve one. Kavass was potent, aye, but the little he'd had at the evening meal should not have left him as crapulent as this.

Others were waking, too, and groaning and cursing in such a way that the Greek guessed they felt no better than he. Only when he began to look around did he notice the campfire had gone out. He frowned. The ground, as yet, was barely damp —why were only ashes left of the good-sized blaze they'd set not long before?

Agathias Psoes had the same thought. "What's wrong with you sheeps' heads?" he shouted to his troopers. "Can't you even keep a bloody fire going?" Their replies were mumbles; the evidence of their failure was only too plain.

"How many Khamorth does it take to start a fire?" Arigh asked rhetorically, and then answered his own question: "Ten —one gathers the brushwood while the other nine try to figure out what to do next."

"Heh, heh." Psoes barked a short fragment of laugh, enough for politeness' sake. Though he was not of Khamorth blood himself, most of his squad was, and he naturally took their part when an outsider taunted them.

Pikridios Goudeles, on the other hand, found the Arshaum's gibe funny, chuckling quietly for nearly a minute. Gorgidas allowed himself a wry smile; Arigh took every chance, it seemed, to twit his people's eastern neighbors on the steppe.

It was then that Gorgidas realized Viridovix' booming laugh had failed to ring out at his friend's joke. Was the accursed Gaul still sleeping? Gorgidas peered through the darkness and the raindrops, which were coming thicker now. He could not see the Celt. "Viridovix?" he called.

There was no answer. He called again, with equal lack of success. "Probably gone off somewhere to drop his trousers," Lankinos Skylitzes guessed.

Gorgidas heard footsteps squelching toward the camp and thought for a moment Skylitzes was right. But it was one of the sentries. "Hallo the camp!" the trooper said. "Are you daft there, to let your fire die? Keep talking, the lot of you, so I can find you."

When the sentry came in, he asked, "Is everything well? I had something odd happen to me." He spoke with elaborate unconcern, trying to mask his worry. "I was out there watching and started to feel faint. I headed in to get a relief, but I reckon I didn't make it—next thing I knew, it was raining on me. Very strange—seems like there's a smith pounding out stirrups in my head, but I drank water because I knew I had to be sober for watch. What hour is it, anyway?"

As it turned out, no one knew. Nor did they argue about it long, for just then one of the horses gave a puzzled-sounding snort and scrambled to its feet, followed within minutes by the rest of the animals. Ignoring their own headaches, Psoes' men and Skylitzes rushed over to them, shouting in mixed Videssian and the Khamorth tongue. For the first time, Gorgidas understood something was truly amiss; horses did not go down of their own accord.

The horsemen clucked and fussed over their beasts, trying to learn why they had fallen. Lankinos Skylitzes walked back toward the dead campfire. "Gorgidas?"

"Here."

"Where? Oh." The soldier almost stumbled over him. "Sorry—bloody dark." Skylitzes' voice softened. "I've heard you are a healer. Would you see to the horses? They seem all right, but—" He spread his hands, a motion the Greek saw only dimly.

Gorgidas understood the request, but it did not please him. "I'm a physician no more," he said shortly. That was too abrupt, he decided, so he went on, "Even if I were, I know nothing of animals. Horseleeching is a different art from doctoring men." And a good deal lower one, he did not add.

Skylitzes caught his annoyance nonetheless. "I meant no offense." Gorgidas dipped his head impatiently, then regretted it as his headache flared. Skylitzes asked, "Has Viridovix turned up?"

"No. Where could he have wandered off to, anyhow? Where did he lay out his sleeping-mat? If he's on it snoring, I'll wring his lazy neck."

"You'd need to wait your turn, I think." Skylitzes squinted

as he peered through the rain. He pointed. "Over there, wasn't it?"

"Was it?" Gorgidas took himself to task for not paying closer heed before he slept; if a historian—or a doctor, for that matter—failed to notice details, what good was he? He was proud of his powers of observation, and here, when he needed them, they let him down.

Skirting the ashes of the campfire—and still wondering why they were so cold—the Greek walked in the direction Skylitzes had indicated. Sure enough, there were blankets and a thin traveling mat spread on the ground; they were beginning to get soaked now. Beside them was a knapsack Gorgidas recognized as Viridovix' and the Celt's helmet with its seven-spoked bronze wheel of a crest. Of Viridovix himself there was no sign.

The commotion in the camp made the two remaining sentries come in to see what was toward; both reluctantly admitted falling asleep at their posts. "Trouble yourselves not," Pikridios Goudeles said pompously, "for no harm resulted."

Agathias Psoes growled, as any good underofficer would at the notion of his men dozing on watch. And Gorgidas shouted, "No harm? Where's Viridovix?"

"To that I must confess my ignorance. The man is your comrade, and of your people. Why should he choose to wander off?"

Gorgidas opened his mouth, shut it again; he had no idea. He did know how useless it was to explain that he and the Celt were no more of the same people than Goudeles and a Khamorth.

The rest of the night was dank and miserable. No one went back to sleep, and not just the pattering rain stopped them. The entire party was much more awake than their midnight rousing called for, but unpleasantly so; a good part of the desultory talk centered on their aching heads.

"Been drunk without a hangover before," Arigh remarked, "but I never had the hangover without the drunk." As if to correct the fault, he swigged from the kavass-skin that was almost always near him.

Toward morning the clouds grew tattered for a while, revealing a thin cheese-paring of a moon low in the east. Too thin, too low—"We've lost a day!" Gorgidas exclaimed.

"Phos, you're right," Skylitzes said, making his god's circular sun-sign over his breast. He raised his hands to the damp heavens and muttered a prayer. Nor was he the only one; Psoes and the Videssians in his squad imitated him, while the troopers who still followed Khamorth ways poured kavass out on the ground to propitiate the less abstract powers they worshiped. Even Goudeles, as worldly a man as Videssos grew, prayed with the soldiers.

"Some spirit has touched us. We should sacrifice a horse," Arigh said, and the Khamorth cried out in agreement.

Gorgidas listened to his companions with growing exasperation. While they babbled of gods and spirits, his logical mind saw the answer only too clearly. "We've been magicked asleep so someone could snatch Viridovix," he said, and, a moment later, carrying his train of thought to its conclusion, added, "Avshar!"

"No," Skylitzes replied at once. "Were it Avshar, we should be waking in the next world. There is no mercy in him."

"His minions, then," the Greek insisted. He remembered the potent blade the Gaul carried, but did not mention it; the fewer who knew of it, the less likely word of it would reach the wizard, should Gorgidas prove wrong by some lucky chance.

He did not think he was. It was growing steadily lighter; he walked over to examine Viridovix' bedroll once more. His breath hissed out as he saw the bloodstains on the Celt's blankets. He held them up, displaying them to the rest of the party. "A kidnapping while we were spelled to sleep!" he said.

"And even so, what of that?" Goudeles said. The seal-stamper sounded petulant; he was used to the comforts of Videssos and did not relish sitting unprotected in the rain and mud of the trackless steppe. He went on, "When weighed against the mission with which we were entrusted, what is the fate of one barbarian mercenary? Once our embassy is successfully completed—which boon Phos grant—then, with the augmentation of manpower the addition of the Arshaum will yield us, we may properly search for him. But until such augmentation should come to pass, he remains a secondary consideration."

Gorgidas gasped, not wanting to believe his ears. "But he

may be hurt, dying—he surely is hurt," the Greek said, touching the brown stains on the cloth. "You would not leave him in the enemy's hands?"

If Goudeles was embarrassed, he did not show it. "I would not cast myself into them, either, and bring to nothing the purpose for which I was dispatched."

"The pen-pusher is right," Skylitzes said, looking as though the admission left a bad taste in his mouth. "The Empire's safety overrides that of any one man. Your countryman is a doughty fighter, but he is only one. We need hundreds."

Neither of the Videssians knew Viridovix, save on the journey. Gorgidas turned to Arigh, who had roistered with the Celt for two years. "He is your friend!"

Arigh tugged at his straggling chin whiskers, plainly uncomfortable with the Greek's bald appeal. Personal ties counted for more with him than with the imperials, but he was a khagan's son and understood reasons of state. "It grieves me, but no. The farmer-folk speak true, I fear. I betray a trust now whatever I do, but I act for my clan before I act for myself. V'ridrish is no easy prey; he may yet win free."

"Curse you all!" Gorgidas said. "If you care nothing for what happens to your comrade, stand aside for one who does. I'll ride after him myself."

"That is well said," Arigh said quietly. Several of the troopers echoed him. Furious, Gorgidas ignored them all, sweeping possessions into his rucksack.

But Skylitzes came over to put a hand on the Greek's shoulder. Gorgidas cursed again and tried to shake free, but the stocky Videssian officer was stronger than he. "Let loose of me, you god-detested oaf! Why should you care if I seek my friend? I cannot matter to you any more than he does."

"Think like a man, not an angry child," Skylitzes said softly. The rebuke was calculated to touch the Greek, who prided himself on his rationality. Skylitzes waved, an all-encompassing gesture that swept round the horizon. "Go after Viridovix—" Like Goudeles, he said the name carefully. "—if you will, but where will you go?"

"Why—" the Greek began, and then stopped in confusion. He rubbed his bristly chin; a beard, he was finding, could be a useful adjunct to thought. "Where do your reports place Avshar?" he asked at last.

"North and west of where we are now, but that news is weeks old and worth nothing now. You've seen how the plainsmen move, and no law makes the damned wizard-prince stay with any one clan."

"Northwest is good enough."

"Is it? I've seen you, outlander; you lack the skill to follow a trail—not that the rain will leave you one." Skylitzes went on remorselessly, "And if you do somehow catch up to your foes, what then? Are you warrior enough to slay them all singlehanded? Are you warrior enough even to protect yourself if a nomad chooses to make sport of you? Will that sword of yours help, should you buckle it on instead of leaving it in your kit?"

Gorgidas started; sure enough, he had not thought of the *gladius* Gaius Philippus had given him, and had left it tucked away with his scrolls of parchment. For the first time in many years, he wished he were skilled with weapons. It was humiliating that he could not stop some chance-met, unwashed, illiterate barbarian who might enjoy killing him simply to watch him die.

He rummaged through his sack for the sword, but threw it angrily back in when he found it. It could not cut Lankinos Skylitzes' logic. "West, then," he said, hating the necessity that impelled his words. *Ananke*, he thought: life's harshest master.

When Skylitzes offered a sympathetic handclasp, the Greek did not take his hand. Instead he said, "Keep drilling me on my swordplay, will you?" The officer nodded.

Gorgidas' thoughts were full of irony as he scrambled onto his horse. He had left Videssos for the plains to change from doctor to historian. Change he was finding aplenty, but hardly what he had wanted. Things long excluded from his life were forcing their way in: women, weapons—but precious little history yet. It might have been funny, had he been without greater concerns.

The rain poured down from an indifferent sky.

V

THE RETREAT FARED BETTER THAN MARCUS HAD DARED hope. With victory in their hands, the Namdaleni were more eager to chase small bands of fugitives than to tackle a good-sized detachment still under arms. A couple of companies of horsemen made tentative runs at the legionaries, but went off in search of easier prey when they failed to dissolve in panic flight.

"Cowards get what they deserve," Nevrat Sviodo remarked as she passed the body of a Videssian speared in the back. Scorn filled her voice. She had fought side by side with her husband. Her quiver was almost empty, her saber had blood on it, and her forehead was cut and bruised from a thrown stone, luckily only a glancing blow.

"Aye, that's the reward for running higgledy-piggledy," Gaius Philippus agreed. The senior centurion was not downcast in defeat; he had seen it before. "There's ways to lose as well as ways to win. By the Sucro, now, my mates did well even though we lost, and at Turia, too. If the old woman hadn't shown up, we'd have given the boy a good drubbing and sent him back to Rome." He smiled at the memory.

"The old woman? The boy?" Nevrat looked at him in confusion.

"Never mind, lass; it was a long time ago, back where the lot of us came from. These Videssians aren't the only ones with civil wars, and I chose the wrong side in one."

"So you were with Sertorius, then?" Marcus said. He knew the senior centurion had been of Marius' party. After Sulla beat the last of the Marians in Italy, Quintus Sertorius refused to yield Spain to the winners. Winning the Spanish natives to his side, he fought on guerilla-style for eight years, until one of his own subordinates murdered him.

"So I was. What of it?" Gaius Philippus challenged. His loyalty, once given, died hard.

"Not a thing," the tribune said. "He must have been a fine soldier, to face up to Pompey the Great."

"'The Great?'" Gaius Philippus spat in the dusty roadway. "Compared to what? As I said, if Metellus hadn't saved his bacon at Turia, he'd be running yet—if he could. We wounded him there, you know."

"I hadn't realized that. I was still in my teens then."

"Yes, I suppose you would have been. I was a little younger than you are now, I think." He wiped his face with the back of his hand. Most of the hair on his scarred forearm was silver. "Time wins the war, no matter what becomes of the battles."

The sun was still high in the west when the legionaries came into sight of their camp again. There were dead horses and riders outside, and a squad of Namdaleni studying the palisade at a respectful distance. They trotted off when they recognized the newcomers.

Minucius met Scaurus at one of the entrances to the *via principalis*. The young underofficer's salute was as much a gesture of relief as of respect. "Good to see you, sir," he managed.

"And you," Marcus said. He raised his voice so everyone could hear: "Half an hour! Knock down the tents, find your women and tots, and then we travel. Anyone slow can make his excuses to the islanders—we won't be here to listen to them."

"I knew it went wrong," Minucius was saying. "First the

plainsmen running, and then the Videssians, with Drax' men on their heels. Did Utprand turn traitor, then?"

"No, but his men did. He's dead."

"So that was the way of it," Minucius growled. His large hands folded into fists. "I thought I knew some of the good-for-naughts who tried coming over the stakes. You saw the welcome we gave 'em—they went off to have a go at something less lively, like the imperials' camp over past the trees." He hesitated; uncertainty seemed out of place on his rugged features. "I hope we did right, sir. There was, ah, some as wanted us to open up and join 'em."

"Some, eh?" the tribune said, seeing through Minucius' clumsy directions. "I'll tend to that; don't you worry about it." He slapped the underofficer on the back. "You did well, Sextus. Go on, get Erene and your children. I want some distance between us and Drax before he decides to make his lads stop plundering and finish us off."

Drax might do that at any time, Marcus thought as Minucius hurried away—perhaps this moment, perhaps not until morning. Had the tribune been leading the Namdaleni, he would have attacked the legionaries at once. But Drax had been a mercenary far longer than Scaurus: with booty in front of his men, he might not dare pull them away. Might, might, might . . . Marcus wished the Namdalener count were less opaque.

The camp bubbled and seethed like limestone splashed with vinegar. Soldiers and their kin shouted each other's names over and over, wandering here and there as they searched for one another. "Lackwits," Gaius Philippus muttered. "If the silly hens'd stay by their men's tents they'd get found easy enough."

"Those whose men are still here to find them," Marcus said, and the senior centurion had to nod. As fights went, this one had not cost the legionaries overmuch; the center of the imperial army had borne the brunt. Still, men were down who would never rise again; too many, too many. How long would it be before there were no Romans left?

In the camp's central forum, Styppes was doing his best to hold off that evil day. Scaurus gave credit where due; the healer-priest's fat face was dead pale from the strain of his labor. He hurried from one moaning, wounded soldier to the next, never pausing long enough to heal a man completely, but giving him a chance at life before going on to another bleeding trooper. He gulped wine in the moments between patients, but, seeing his work, Marcus did not care.

Helvis stood by the tribune's tent. They shared a quick hug, then Scaurus began uprooting tent pegs. Malric gave what he thought was help until Marcus growled at him to get out of the way. His hands automatically went through the motions of folding the tent for travel.

"Even after we've won, you have no use for us?" Helvis asked.

"Look around you," Scaurus suggested. "This is the only 'we' I know; it's far past time you understood that."

Outside the camp a Namdalener yelled something. Marcus could not tell what it was through the din, but the island drawl was unmistakable. "The only 'we'?" Helvis said dangerously. "What would you do if that was Soteric out there?"

Marcus squeezed air from between layers of the collapsed tent, tied the tent cord around it. He thought of his brother-in-law's work of the day. "Right now I believe I'd kill him."

Whatever answer she had started to make froze on her lips. The tribune went on wearily, "There are no chains on you, dear, but if you come with me you'd best see the folk here inside as 'we.' Come or not, as you please. I haven't the time to argue."

He thought for a long moment the brutality of that was more than she would bear. But Dosti squirmed in her arms; she comforted him, at first absently, then with real attention. She looked at him, at Scaurus, while the palm of her left hand lightly touched her belly. "I'll come with you," she said at last.

Marcus only grunted. He was wrestling the folded tent into his pack. As with a snake swallowing a rabbit, the engulfing looked impossible but was accomplished even so. Somehow his little wooden chest fit, too. The chair and table would have to stay behind—no time to load them on a mule. He swung the pack onto his shoulders; Romans were their own best mules.

Helvis wore an odd, wistful look. He impatiently started to turn away, but her words spun him back: "There are times, dear, when you make me think so much of Hemond."

"What? Why?" he asked, startled. She seldom spoke of Malric's father to the tribune, knowing the mention of Hemond made him touchy and remembering how annoyed he grew when she carelessly called him by her dead husband's name.

"By the Wager, it's not for how you act!" Remembering, she smiled, her eyes soft. "When he wanted something of me, he'd laugh and joke and poke me in the ribs, jolly me along." She cocked a rueful eyebrow at him. "Where you set things out like a butcher slapping a hunk of meat on the table, and if I don't like it, to the ice with me."

Marcus felt his ears grow hot. "Where's the likeness, then?"

"You knew Hemond. He'd have his way, come fire or flood—and so will you. And so do you, again." She sighed. "I'm ready."

The legionaries traveled in a hollow square, with their families and the wounded in the center. The Namdaleni dogged their tracks, as Marcus had known they would. Without cavalry of his own, he could do nothing about it. He counted himself lucky only to be watched. From the noise coming out of the captured Videssian camp, Drax was treating most of his men to a good round of plundering.

Videssian stragglers attached themselves to Scaurus' band by ones and twos, some afoot, others on horseback. He let them join; some were still soldiers, and any mounted troops could be useful, as scouts if nothing more.

One of them brought word of Zigabenos' fate: captured by the Namdaleni. One more piece of bad news among the many —Marcus was dismayed but not surprised. It was also something he had expected to hear, whether true or not. He asked the imperial, "How do you know that's so?"

"Well, I ought to. I seen it," the trooper answered; his upcountry accent made Scaurus think of Phostis Apokavkos. He glared at the tribune, as spikily indignant as any Videssian at having his word questioned. "They drug him off his horse; Skotos' hell, if he hadn't been wounded, they never would a-done it. He gave 'em all the fight they wanted and some besides. The plague take all Namdaleni anyways."

"You saw him taken and did nought to stay it?" Zeprin the Red rumbled ominously. The burly Haloga, long an imperial guard, still carried in his heart the shame of not dying with the regiment of his countrymen who vainly defended Mavrikios at Maragha. It was no fault of his own; the Emperor had sent him away to take command of the imperial left wing. He blamed himself regardless. Now, axe in hand, he glowered at the bedraggled Videssian before him. "What sort of soldier do you call yourself?"

The trooper hawked and spat. "A live one," he retorted, "which is a sight better than the other kind." He stared back with deliberate insolence.

Zeprin's always florid complexion darkened to the color of blood. He roared out something in his own tongue that sounded like red-hot iron screaming as it was quenched. Before either Marcus or the Videssian could move, his axe jerked up, then smashed down through the man's helmet, splitting his skull almost to the teeth. He toppled, jerking, dead before the blow was through.

The Haloga tugged his axe free. "Craven carrion," he growled, cleaning the weapon on a clump of purslane. "A man who will not stand by his lord deserves no better."

"We might have learned something more from him," Marcus said, but that was all. If legionaries broke and ran in large numbers, they could be decimated: one in ten chosen at random for execution to requite their cowardice. Before he took service, the tribune had reckoned the punishment hideous in its barbarity; now he thought of it without revulsion. The change shamed him. War fouled everyone it touched.

The Arandos was a fat brown stream, several hundred yards across. Bridges spanned it, but Drax' men held their watchtowers. Perhaps they could be forced, but that would take time, time the legionaries did not have. Had Drax not had so many bands of fugitives to hunt down, he would have overrun them already instead of giving them these three days of grace. The Namdalener was like a dog surrounded by so many bones he did not know which one to take up and gnaw. Scaurus, on the other hand, felt like a hare with the nets closing in.

Hoping against hope, he sent out Videssians to ask the peasants if they knew of a ford, reasoning that they would be more inclined to talk to their countrymen than to aliens like the Romans. He almost shouted when Apokavkos brought back a big-eared codger who came straight to the point: "What's it worth to ye?"

Another twanger, the tribune thought. He answered, "Ten goldpieces—on the other side of the river."

"You on a cross if you're lying," Gaius Philippus added. The local scratched his head at that—the Videssians did not practice crucifixion. But the threat in the senior centurion's voice could not be missed. Still, the farmer nodded agreement.

He led the legionaries east along the Arandos until they were well out of sight of any bridge. Then he slowed, squinting across the river for some landmark he did not name. At last he grunted. "There y'are," he said, pointing.

"Where?" To Scaurus, the stretch of water looked no different from any other part of the Arandos.

"Nail the lying bastard up," Gaius Philippus said, but in Latin. Not understanding him, the farmer pulled the knee-length tunic that was his only garment over his head and, naked, stepped into the river.

He was promptly in up to his outsized ears, and Marcus thought seriously of what to do with him. The peasant, though, seemed unabashed. He turned around, grinning a wet grin. "Spring flood's not as near done as I'd'a liked, but come ahead. It don't get no deeper."

Holding his sword over his head, the tribune followed. His inches were an advantage; the water reached his chin, but no higher. Two and three at a time, the legionaries followed. "No more'n that," their guide warned. "The track ain't what you call wide." He splashed forward, now bearing a few paces left, now a few right, now pausing as if to feel about with his toes.

"The gods help us if the damned islanders come on us," Gaius Philippus said, looking back nervously. He stepped into a deep place and vanished, to emerge a moment later, spluttering and choking. "Ordure," he growled.

Marcus was glad for the Romans' training, which included swimming as an essential part. Even when they stumbled off the narrow ford, they were able to save themselves; luckily the Arandos' current was not strong. Only one man was lost, a Vaspurakaner who sank and drowned before he could be rescued. The mountaineers, alas, were no swimmers; their streams were tiny trickles in summer, torrents spring and fall, and frozen solid when winter came.

When the tribune squelched up onto the south bank of the river, the Videssian peasant greeted him with outstretched palm. Scaurus eyed him meditatively as he fumbled in his wet belt-pouch. "How do I know you'll not sell the secret of the ford to the first Namdaleni who ride by?"

If he expected some guilty start, he was disappointed. With mercenary candor, the fellow answered, "I'd do it, excepting they wouldn't buy. Why would they? They hold the bridges." His regret was perfectly genuine.

"Listen to the man!" Senpat Sviodo exclaimed. He was checking to make sure his pandoura had taken no harm during the crossing. "Is it any wonder these Videssians are ever at strife with themselves?"

"Probably not." Marcus paid his guide, who examined each coin carefully, biting a couple of them to see if they were real soft gold.

"Not bad," the farmer remarked. "I could've broken a tooth on that one of Ortaias' you gave me, but it's only the one." In lieu of anywhere else to carry them, he popped the coins into his mouth; his left cheek sagged under their weight. "Much obliged to you, I'm sure," he said blurrily.

"Likewise," Scaurus answered. Children were squealing and splashing each other as their mothers and the legionaries carried them across the stream. Some of the women got carried, too: the very short ones, and those whom pregnancy had made awkward. Helvis, tall and strong, made the passage on her own. She brought Dosti herself; a trooper carried Malric. Her linen blouse and long, heavy wool skirt clung to her magnificently as she came out of the water.

With regret, the tribune pulled his eyes away and looked down along the riverbank to where several of Gagik Bagratouni's men were sitting glumly, mourning their drowned comrade. The sight made him ask the peasant, "Why not drive a row of stakes into the riverbed so the ford would be safe?"

"And let everyone know where it's at?" The local shook his head in amazement. "Thank ye, nay."

"What do you use it for that's so secret?" Marcus asked,

but when he saw the Videssian's hand come out he said hastily, "Never mind. I don't want to know enough to pay for it."

"Thought not." The farmer waited until the last legionaries were done with the ford, then waded back into the Arandos. When he got to the north bank he discovered someone had made off with his tunic. Peering across the river, Marcus waited for an angry outburst. There was none. Mother-naked, the Videssian disappeared into the brush that crowded close to the stream.

"Why should he care?" Senpat said. He bulged his own cheek out comically. "He's still ahead nine goldpieces and change, even without the old rag."

There were Namdaleni on the far side of the Arandos. The legionaries were two days south of the river when they came headlong onto a pair of the islanders, sitting their mounts with the easy arrogance of men who feel themselves lords of all they survey. That arrogance vanished like smoke in the wind when they came out from behind a stand of scrubby oaks and spied Scaurus' column. He saw them exchange horrified glances. Then they were riding madly across a wheat field, spurring their heavy horses like racing steeds as they dashed toward the river.

For a moment Marcus rocked back on his heels, as startled by the encounter as the men of the Duchy. Then he remembered he, too, had horsemen, a good score of Zigabenos' men. "After them!" he shouted.

The Videssians moved hesitantly at first, as if fighting had not occurred to them. The foot soldiers' cheers, though, put fresh heart in them, as did the sight of the Namdaleni in full flight. The islanders were a bare hundred yards ahead of their pursuers when they disappeared over a low rise.

The imperials soon returned, trotting proudly now. They led one horse and held up a pair of fine mail shirts and two conical helms with bar nasals. "Where's the other beast?" someone called.

"We had to shoot it," one of them said.

"Idiots!" "Bunglers!" "A pack of damned incompetents, the lot of you!" The Videssians accepted the good-natured chaffing for the praise it was.

"That's all to the good," Gaius Philippus said. "They feel like men again; we'll get some use out of them."

"You're right," Marcus said. "But how many men does Drax have, anyway? I'd hoped he was just holding the line of the Arandos against whatever the Videssian grandees south of the river could scrape up to throw at him, but he looks to be coming right at them. Whatever you say about him, he doesn't think small, does he?"

"Hmm." The senior centurion considered that. "If he spreads himself too thin, the Yezda will see to him, whether we do nor not."

"That's so," Marcus admitted, disquieted. He had not even seen one of the invading nomads for almost a year and a half; it was easy to forget them in the tangles of the Empire's civil wars. Yet without them, those wars would not have happened, and they roamed the highlands like distant thunderheads.

"Not distant enough," Gaius Philippus said when Scaurus spoke his conceit aloud.

The stand of oaks was bigger than the tribune had guessed. It went on for miles. Part of some noble's estate? he wondered. Half-ripe acorns, dirty green with tan, ribbed tops, nestled between sharp-lobed leaves. He heard a boar grunting somewhere out of sight among the trees; all pigs loved acorns.

The legionaries scuffed through the gray-brown, tattered remnants of last autumn's fallen leaves. The sound was soothing, like surf on a beach.

Discordant footfalls ahead roused Scaurus to alertness once more. A man burst round a corner of the forest path. His chest heaved with his exertion; blood splashed his tunic and the dust of the road from a great cut across his forehead. The terror on his face turned to disbelieving joy as he recognized the Videssian horsemen with the legionaries.

"Phos be praised!" he gasped. His words stumbled over each other in his urgency: "A rescue! Quick, my lord, the outland devils—murder!"

"Namdaleni?" Marcus demanded—was there no end to them? At the fellow's nod, he snapped, "How many?"

The man spread his hands. "A hundred, at least." He hopped up and down, ignoring his wound. "Phos' mercy, hurry!"

"Two maniples," the tribune decided. Gaius Philippus

nodded in grim agreement; the men of the Duchy were no bargain. In the same breath, Scaurus went on, "Blaesus, your men; aye, and yours, Gagik!" Bagratouni understood the order, though it was in Latin. He shouted in his own throaty tongue; his Vaspurakaners yelled back, clashing their spears on their shields. The *nakharar*'s contingent was oversized for a proper maniple; a hundred Namdaleni would be outnumbered three to one.

Gaius Philippus shook the wounded Videssian, who was wobbling now that he had stopped his dash for life. "Which way, man?" the veteran demanded.

"Left at the first fork, then right at the next," the man said. He daubed at his forehead with his sleeve, staring in disbelief at the bright blood. Then he doubled over and was sick in the road. Gaius Philippus grunted in disgust, but shouted out the directions for all the troopers to hear.

Marcus pulled his sword free. "At a trot!" he said, and added, "The shout is 'Gavras!'" The legionaries pounded after him.

The first fork was only a furlong or so down the forest track, but the second was a long time coming. Feeling the sweat running itchily under his corselet, Scaurus began to wonder if he'd missed it. But the Videssian's gory trail told him he had not. The blood in the roadway was still fresh and unclotted; the man must have run as if the Furies nipped his heels.

The Romans were not as fast, but the pace they set was enough to make their Vaspurakaner comrades, most of them heavy-set, rather short-legged men, struggle to keep up. "There up ahead, past the rotten stump," Gaius Philippus said, pointing; sure enough, the path did split. The senior centurion's voice was easy; he could jog along far longer than this without growing winded.

As the fork neared, Marcus heard shouts and the clash of steel on steel. "Gavras!" he yelled, the legionaries echoing him. There was a startled pause ahead, then the cry came back in Videssian accents, along with roars of anger and dismay from Namdalener throats.

The legionaries charged down the right fork of the path, which opened out into a clearing in the oak woods. A double handful of Videssians, four mounted and the rest on foot, were pushed into a compact, desperate circle by hard-pressing Namdalener horsemen. Men were down on either side; the islanders looked to be gathering themselves for a last charge to sweep their enemies away.

As his maniple deployed into battle line, *pila* ready to cast, even stolid Junius Blaesus burst out laughing. "A hundred?" he said to Scaurus. "Looks to me, sir, like we've brought a mountain to drop on a fly."

If the little clearing held thirty islanders, the tribune would have been surprised. The men of the Duchy gauped as legionaries kept pouring out of the woods. Finally the fellow Marcus took to be their commander because of his fine saddle and horse and the gold inlay on his helm threw back his head and laughed louder than Blaesus had. "Down spears, lads," he called to his knights. "They have us, and no mistake."

The Namdaleni followed his order, warily in the case of those still fronting their intended victims. But the Videssians, as surprised as their foes by their deliverance, were content to lean on their weapons and sob in great breaths of air; they were in no condition to attack.

The mercenary captain rode slowly up to Scaurus. The Romans around the tribune raised javelins threateningly, but the islander paid them no mind. He held his shield out to Scaurus. "Give me a blow for my honor's sake," he said, and Marcus tapped the metal facing with his sword. "Well struck! I yield me!" He took off his helmet to show he had surrendered. His men followed suit.

Under the helm the Namdalener had a smiling, freckled face and a thick head of light brown hair; like most of his countrymen, he shaved the back of his head. As had been true of the islanders in the motte-and-bailey fort north of the Sangarios, he did not seem disturbed at yielding; these things were part of a professional soldier's life.

His squadron was as casual; one of them said, quite without rancor, to the imperials they had just fought, "We'd have had you if these whoreson Romans hadn't come along." Having served side-by-side with them in the capital, the Namdaleni knew more about the legionaries than did the Videssians they had saved.

Scaurus set his troopers to disarming the islanders, then walked over to salute the Videssian leader. The man's highbred horse and the air of authority he wore like a good cloak made him easy to pick out. He must have been nearly sixty, but a vigorous sixty. His hair and close-trimmed beard were iron gray, and, while his middle was thick, his shoulders did not sag under the weight of armor.

His eye held a twinkle of irony as he returned Marcus' salute. "You do me too much honor. The weaker should bow and scrape, not the stronger. Sittas Zonaras, at your service." He bowed in the saddle. "My rank is spatharios, for all that tells you."

Even as the tribune gave his name, he decided he liked this Zonaras. In the cloud-cuckoo-land of Videssian honorifics, spatharios was the vaguest, but few imperials would poke fun at their own pretensions.

"I've heard of you, young fellow," Zonaras remarked, apparently adding the last phrase to see if Scaurus would squirm. When he got no response, he probed harder. "Baanes Onomagoulos had things to say about you, none of which I'd care to repeat to you face-to-face." One of the noble's retainers shot him an alarmed look.

"Did he?" Marcus said, alert beneath his casual mask. It was not surprising Zonaras knew the late rebel; this was the country from which Onomagoulos came. That he would admit knowing him was something else, an extraordinary gesture of trust when offered to a man who served Baanes' foe.

"Onomagoulos rarely said much good about anyone," the tribune said, and Zonaras nodded, his own face impassive now, as if wondering whether he had made a mistake. His eyes cleared as Marcus went on, "I think being lamed embittered him. He wasn't so sour before Maragha."

"That's so," the Videssian said. As if relieved to back away from a dangerous subject, he glanced toward the men of the Duchy. "What will you do with them? They think they own the country for no better reason than their bandit chief's say-so."

After the Sangarios, Marcus thought gloomily, they had better reason than that. He thought for a few seconds. "Perhaps Drax will exchange them for Mertikes Zigabenos."

The legionaries must have outmarched news of the battle, for Zonaras blinked in amazement, and his men exclaimed in alarm. "Drax holds the guards commander?" Zonaras said. "Grave news. Tell it me."

Scaurus set it forth. Zonaras listened impassively until he spoke of the desertion of the Namdaleni who had marched with the Imperial Army, then cursed in black anger. "Skotos freeze all treachers' privates," he growled, and from that moment on the tribune was sure he had taken no part in Onomagoulos' revolt. When Marcus was done, Zonaras sat silent a long while. At last he asked, "What will you do now?"

"What I can," the tribune answered. "How much that may be, I don't know."

He thought Zonaras might snort in contempt, but the Videssian noble gave a sober nod. "You carry an old man's head on your shoulders, to fight shy of promising Phos' sun when you don't carry it on your belt." Zonaras scratched his knee as he watched Scaurus. "You know, outlander, you shame me," he said slowly. "It is not right for hired troops to be more willing to save Videssos than her own men."

Marcus had thought that since his first weeks in the Empire, but few Videssians agreed. Long used to their power, they took it for granted—or had, until Maragha. The Roman, whose homeland had grown mighty only in the century and a half before his birth, was not so complacent.

Zonaras broke into his thoughts, reaching down to take his hand. "What I and mine can do for you, we will," he pledged, and squeezed with a strength that belied his years. Scaurus returned the clasp, but wondered how much help one backwoods noble was likely to give.

The next day's march was a revelation to the tribune, not least because all of it was over Sittas Zonaras' land. Toward evening the legionaries made camp beside his sprawling villa, which nestled in a narrow valley. The setting sun shone purple off the highlands to the south and east. "We've done well," Zonaras said with no little pride.

"Aye, belike, and an elephant's plump," Gaius Philippus said.

Marcus had known intellectually of the broad estates and peasant villages Videssian grandees controlled. Only now did he start to feel what that control meant. Around the capital, brawling city life replaced the nobles' holdings, and in the westlands' central plateau the soil was too poor to allow a concentration of wealth such as Zonaras enjoyed.

His acres included fine vineyards and gardens; a willow plantation by the stream that ran past him home; meadows where horses and donkeys, cattle, sheep, and goats grazed; forests for timber and animal fodder; poor grapevines climbing up hillside trees; and the oak woods where he had met first the Namdaleni and then Scaurus, which yielded acorns not only to be the wild boar he hunted, but also to his own herd of pigs.

On the march the tribune had seen no fewer than five presses for squeezing out olive oil. There were herders in the fields with the flock; the chief herdsman, a solid, middle-aged man without the least touch of servility, had warily come up to greet Zonaras after the noble assured him at some distance that the long column of legionaries behind him was friendly.

"Glad of it, sir," the man had answered, "else I'd have raised the countryside against 'em." He tore up a scrap of parchment with something written on it; probably the numbers and direction of the intruders, Marcus thought. He was not surprised the herder chief knew his letters. In Rome, too, a man with such a responsible job would have to be able to read and write.

And while the legionaries who heard the fellow's promise to his lord snickered at it, Scaurus suspected it should not be taken lightly. Nor was Gaius Philippus laughing. Unlike most of the Romans, he knew the other side of irregular warfare. "All the folk in all these villages we've passed through seem plenty fond of Zonaras here," he said to the tribune. "It'd be no fun having them bushwhack us and then fade off through the woods or into the hills before we could chase 'em." He spoke Latin, so Zonaras caught his name but no more.

Marcus understood the senior centurion's logic and also suddenly understood why the bureaucrats back in Videssos the city so hated and feared the provincial nobles. It would literally take an army to make Zonaras do anything he did not care to do, and there were scores of nobles like him.

Indeed, even an army might not have sufficed to bring Zonaras back to obedience. He could defend with more than an armed peasantry. As the legionaries discovered when they reached his family seat, the noble kept a band of half a hundred armed retainers. They were not quite professional troops, as they made most of their living by farming, but what they lacked in spit and polish they made up for with unmatched knowledge of the area and the same strong devotion to their lord the chief herdsman had shown.

Once, Scaurus knew, the farmer-soldiers' first loyalty had been to the Empire. But years of harsh taxes made them seek protection from the grandees against the central government's greed. The local nobles, ambitious and powerful, were glad to use them to try to throw off the bureaucrats' yoke once for all. To survive, the pen-pushers in the capital hired mercenaries to hold them in line . . . and so, Marcus thought as the legionaries planted stakes on their rampart, these endless civil wars, first an Onomagoulos rebelling, then a Drax. He grunted. Without Videssos' civil strife, the Yezda would be out beyond the borders of Vaspurakan, not looking down like vultures over Garsavra.

"Well, what of it?" Helvis responded when he remarked on that. "If Videssos used no mercenaries, the two of us would not have met. Or would that thought please you these days?" There were challenge and sadness both in her voice; the question was not rhetorical.

"No, love," he said, touching her hand. "The gods know we're not perfect, but then only they are. Or Phos, if you'd rather," he amended quickly, seeing her mouth tighten. He cursed his clumsy tongue; he had no real belief in the Roman gods, but spoke merely from habit.

Gaius Philippus had also heard the tribune's first comment. "Hrmp," he said. "If the Videssians didn't hire mercenaries, they'd have killed the lot of us as soon as we came into this crazy world."

"There is that," Scaurus admitted. Gaius Philippus nodded, then hurried off to swear at a Vaspurakaner who had been foolish enough to start to relieve himself upstream from the camp. The luckless trooper found himself with a week of latrine duty.

Marcus was left thoughtful. Gaius Philippus rarely broke in when he and Helvis were talking. Was the senior centurion trying in his gruff way to keep things smooth between them? Considering his misogynism, the notion was strange, but the tribune was strapped for any other explanation. He murmured a sentence in archaic, rhythmic Greek. Helvis looked at him strangely.

"'Everything you say, my friend, is to the point,'" he translated. Everything was in Homer somewhere.

Zonaras' wife was a competent, gray-haired woman named Thekla. His widowed sister Erythro lived with them. Several years younger than Sittas, she was flighty and talkative, and had a gift for puncturing the calm front he cherished.

Erythro was childless; her brother and Thekla had had a daughter and three sons. The girl, Ypatia, reminded Marcus a little of Alypia Gavra in her quiet intelligence. She was betrothed to one of the nobles in the hills to the south. The man stood to inherit Zonaras' estates, for his only surviving son, Tarasios, was a pale, consumptive youth. He bore his illness with courage and laughed at the coughing fits that wracked his thin frame, but death's mark was on him. Along with many men of lower rank from the holding, his two brothers had fallen at Maragha, fighting under Onomagoulos.

Despite that, Zonaras had not supported his neighbor's rebellion against Thorisin Gavras. "As Kalokyres says, in civil war the prudent man sits tight." Scaurus smothered a smile when he heard that; the last man he had known who was fond of quoting the Videssian military writer was Ortaias Sphrantzes, a miscast soldier if ever there was one.

Framed in black, portraits of the grandee's dead sons hung in his dining hall. "They're crude daubs," Erythro told Marcus in the confidential manner she liked to affect. "I'll have you know my nephews were handsome lads."

"All your taste is in your mouth, darling sister," Sittas Zonaras rumbled. He and Erythro argued constantly, with great enjoyment on both sides. If she spoke well of wine, he would drink ale for the next fortnight to irritate her, while she kept urging him to drown all the cats on the estate—but stroked them when he was not there to see it.

Actually, Scaurus agreed with Erythro here. By the standards of the capital, the paintings were the product of a half-schooled man, no doubt a local. Still, they gave Marcus an idea. A couple of days after the legionaries encamped by Zonaras' villa, he went to Styppes, saying, "I'd ask a favor of you."

"Ask," Styppes grunted, ungracious as usual. At least, thought the tribune, he was sober.

"I'd like you to paint an icon for me."

"For you?" Styppes' eyes narrowed within their folds of flesh. "Why should an unbeliever want a holy image?" he asked suspiciously.

"As a gift for my lady Helvis."

"Who is a heretic." The healer-priest still sounded surly, but Scaurus had his arguments ready; he had played this game with Videssians before. It took some time and some shouting, but after a while Styppes sullenly admitted that right devotion could lead even heretics toward the true faith—his own. "Which holy man would you have me depict, then?"

The tribune remembered the temple in Videssos Helvis had been visiting when rioting broke out against the Namdaleni in the city. "I don't know the name of the saint," he said, as Styppes curled his lip, "but he lived on Namdalen before it was lost to the Empire—Kalavria, it was called, wasn't it? He has a shrine dedicated to him in the capital, not far from the harbor of Kontoskalion."

"Ah!" the healer-priest said, surprised Scaurus had a choice in mind. "I know the man you mean: the holy Nestorios. He is portrayed as an old bald man with his beard in two points. So the heretics of the Duchy revere him yet, do they? Very well, you shall have your icon."

"My thanks." Marcus paused, then felt he had to add, "A favor for a favor. When I find time, I'll pose for your image of the holy—what did you call him?—Kveldulf, that was it."

"Yes, yes, that's good of you, I'm sure," Styppes said, abstracted. The tribune thought he was already starting to plan the icon, but as he turned to go he heard the priest mutter under his breath, "Phos, I'm thirsty." Not for the first time, he wished jolly, capable Nepos preferred life in the field to his chair in theoretical thaumaturgy at the Videssian Academy.

Over the next few days Scaurus was too busy to give Styppes or the icon much thought. Zonaras' villa and his little private army were well enough to face a rival grandee, but the tribune had few illusions about their ability to withstand Drax' veterans. The legionaries dug like badgers, strengthening the place as best they could, but his worries only deepened. The best, he knew, was none too good; he simply did not have enough men.

He used Zonaras' retainers and his other Videssian horsemen to spy out the Namdaleni. Every day they reported more islanders south of the Arandos, but not the great column of knights the tribune feared. The men of the Duchy began building a motte-and-bailey fort a couple of hours' ride north of Zonaras' oak woods. "Drax is busy somewhere and doesn't want us interfering," Gaius Philippus said.

Marcus spread his hands in bewilderment. Not all of what the Namdalener count did made sense. "No, all it does is work," the senior centurion replied. A good Roman, he valued results more than methods.

The tribune released one of his Namdalener prisoners at the edge of the woods, using him as a messenger to offer Drax the exchange of his fellows for Mertikes Zigabenos. Their freckled captain, who called himself Persic Fishhook from a curved scar on his arm, said confidently, "No problem. We'll be free in a week, is my guess. Thirty of us are worth a Videssian general any day, and then some." While they waited to be swapped, the islanders cheerfully fetched and carried for the legionaries; even as captives, they and the Romans got on well.

When he got back to Zonaras' holding, Marcus was intrigued to find Styppes on his hands and knees in the garden by the villa, turning up lettuce leaves. "What are you after?" he called to the healer-priest, wondering what sort of medicinal herbs grew along with the salad greens.

He blinked when Styppes answered, "I need a good fat snail or two. Ah, here!" The priest put his catch in a small burlap bag.

"Now I understand," the tribune laughed. "Snails and lettuce make a good supper. Will you boil some eggs with them?"

Styppes grunted in exasperation as he got to his feet. He brushed once at the mud on the knees of his blue robe, then let it go. "No, lackwit. I want them to let me finish the image of the holy Nestorios." He made Phos' sun-sign over his heart.

"Snails?" Marcus heard his voice rise in disbelief.

"Come see then, scoffer." Wondering whether Styppes was playing a prank on him, the Roman followed him to his tent.

They squatted together on the dirt floor. Styppes lit a tallow candle that filled the tight space with the smell of burning fat. The priest rummaged in his kit, finding at last a large oyster shell. "Good, good," he said to himself. He took one of the snails from his bag, held it over the candle flame. The unfortunate mollusc bubbled and emitted a thick, clear slime. As it dripped, Styppes caught it in the oyster shell. The other snail suffered the same fate. "You see?" the healer-priest said, holding the shell under Scaurus' nose.

"Well, no," the tribune said, more distressed at the snails' torment than he had been in several fights.

"Bah. You will." Styppes poured the slime onto a hand-sized marble slab and added powdered gold. "You will pay me back, and not in new coin," he warned Scaurus. Next came a little whitish powder—"Alum"—and some sticky gum, then he stirred the mix with a brass pestle. "Now we are ready—you will admire it," he said. He took out a pair of badger-fur brushes, one so fine the hairs were fitted into a goosequill, the other larger, with a wooden handle.

Marcus drew in a breath of wonder when he saw the icon for the first time. Styppes' sketches had shown him the priest had a gift, but they were only sketches. The delicate colors and fine line, the holy Nestorios' ascetic yet kindly face, the subtled shadings of his blue robe, his long, thin hands upraised in a gesture of blessing that reminded the tribune of the awesome mosaic image of Phos in the High Temple in the capital . . . "Almost I believe in your god now," he said, and knew no higher praise.

"That is what an image is for, to instruct the ignorant and guide them toward its prototype's virtues," the healer-priest replied. His plump hand deft as a jeweler's, he dipped his tiny feather-brush in the gold pigment on his piece of marble. Though he held the icon close to his face as he worked, his calligraphy was elegant; the gilding, even wet, shone and sparkled in the dim candlelight. "Nestorios the holy," Marcus read. Styppes used the larger brush to surround the saint's head with a gleaming circle of gold. "Thus we portray Phos' sun-disk, to show the holy man's closeness to the good god," he explained, but the tribune had already grasped the halo's meaning.

"May I?" he said, and when Styppes nodded, he took the

wooden panel into his own hands. "How soon will it be ready for giving?" he asked eagerly.

Styppes' smile, for once, was not sour. "A day for the gilding to dry, then two coats of varnish to protect the colors underneath." He scratched his shaved head. "Say, four days' time."

"I wish it were sooner," Marcus said. He was still not won over to this Videssian art of symbol and allegory, but there was no denying that in Styppes' talented hands its results were powerfully moving.

The priest reclaimed the icon and set it to one side to dry undisturbed. "Now," he said with an abrupt change of manner, "where did I toss those snails? Your supper idea wasn't half bad, outlander; have you any garlic to go with them?"

Laon Pakhymer appeared at the legionaries' camp like the god from a machine in a Roman play: no one set eyes on him until suddenly he was there. He flipped Scaurus the wave that passed for a salute among his easygoing folk; when the tribune asked how he had managed to ride through not only Zonaras' picket posts but also the Namdaleni, he answered airily, "There's ways," and put a finger by the side of his nose.

Sextus Minucius exclaimed, "I'll bet you used that old geezer's ford."

"Aren't you the clever young fellow?" Pakhymer said with mild irony. "And what if I did?"

"What did he gouge you for?" Gaius Philippus asked.

The Khatrisher gave a resigned shrug. "A dozen goldpieces."

The senior centurion choked on his wine. "Jove's hairy arse! You ought to go back and kill the bugger—he only got ten for the lot of us."

"Maybe so," Pakhymer answered, "but then, you hadn't just come from Kyzikos." He looked uncommonly smug, like a cat that knew where cream came from.

"What difference does it make where you—" Marcus began, and then stopped, awe on his face. Kyzikos housed an imperial mint. No one in this world had ever heard of Midas, but in Kyzikos the Khatrishers could come close to making his dream real. The tribune did not even think of pointing out that they were stealing the Empire's gold; he had learned mercenaries served themselves first. What he did say was, "Drax won't love you for emptying the till."

"Too bad for Drax. You're right, though; he's thrown a good deal at us, trying to drive us out. And so he has, but our pockets are full. I never did see such a payday." His pockmarked face was dirty, his beard wind-matted and snarled, his clothes ragged, but he was blissful nonetheless. Gaius Philippus stared at him with honest envy.

"No wonder the Namdaleni have been so easy on us, with Kyzikos to go after," Minucius said.

"It's like I guessed, sir," Gaius Philippus said to Scaurus. "But Drax is making a mistake, grabbing at the treasure first. Once his enemies are gone, it falls into his lap, but if he takes the gold and leaves us around, we may find some way to get it back."

"He doesn't have it," Pakhymer pointed out. "Still, I take your meaning even so. I have something planned to make old Drax jump and shout."

"What will you do?" Marcus asked with interest. For all his slapdash ways, that Khatrisher was a clever, imaginative soldier.

"Oh, it's done already." Pakhymer seemed pleased at his own shrewdness. "I spread some of Kyzikos' gold around where it would do the most good—it's on its way up to the central plateau. If the damned islanders are busy fighting Yezda, they can't very well fight us."

The tribune gaped. "You bribed the nomads to attack Drax?"

"So we fought them a couple of years ago. What of it?" Pakhymer was defiant and defensive at the same time. "We fought the islanders last year when they served Ortaias, and now again. One war at a time, I say."

"There's a difference," Marcus insisted. "Drax is an enemy, aye, but not wicked, only power-hungry. But the nomads kill for the joy of killing. Think on what we saw on the road to Maragha—and after." He remembered Avshar's gift, hurled into the legionaries' camp after the fight—Mavrikios Gavras' head.

Pakhymer flushed, perhaps recalling that, too, but he answered, "Any man who tries to kill me is wicked in my eyes, and my foe's foe my friend. And have a care the way you say 'nomad,' Scaurus; my people came off the same steppe the Yezda did."

"Your pardon," the tribune said at once, yielding the small point so he could have another go at the large one. "Bear this in mind, then—once you invite the, ah, Yezda down into the lowlands, even if they do hurt Drax, still you set the scene for endless fighting to push them back again."

"Is that bad? Why would the Videssians hire mercenaries, if they had no one to fight?" Pakhymer was looking at him strangely, the same look, he realized, he had seen several times on Helvis.

He sighed. Without meaning to, the Khatrisher had fingered the essential difference between himself and Scaurus. To Laon Pakhymer, the Empire was a paymaster and nothing more; its fate meant nothing to him, save as it affected his own interests. But Marcus found Videssos, despite its flaws, worth preserving for its own sake. It was doing—had done for centuries—what Rome aspired to: letting the folk within its borders build their lives free from fear. The chaos and destruction that would follow a collapse filled him with dread.

How to explain that to Pakhymer, who, for the sake of a temporary triumph, would have two packs of wolves fight over the body of the state he thought he was serving? Marcus sighed again; he saw no way. Here was his quarrel with Helvis, come to frightening life. The Khatrisher would make a desert and call it peace.

His gloom lifted somewhat as the council shifted focus. Pakhymer intended bringing all his countrymen south of the Arandos; that would give the Romans the scouts and raiders they badly needed. If Thorisin could piece together some kind of force to keep Drax at play in the north, perhaps the legionaries would not be outnumbered to the point of uselessness. And if Gaius Philippus could do with these half-trained Videssians what Sertorius had with the Spaniards, they might yet make nuisances of themselves. If, if, if . . .

He was so caught up in his worries that, when the officers' meeting broke up, he walked past Styppes as if the healer was not there. "I like that," the fat priest said. "Do a favor and see the thanks you get for it."

"Huh?" Scaurus brightened. "It's done, then?" he asked,

glad to have something to think about beside Namdaleni on the march.

"Aye, so it is. Now you notice me, eh?" Marcus held his peace under the reproach; whatever he said to the healer-priest was generally wrong. Styppes grumbled something into his beard, then said, "Well, come along, come along."

When the tribune had the icon in his hands, his praise was as unstinting as it was sincere. Styppes was ill-tempered and overfond of wine, but his hands held more gifts than healing alone. Unmoved by Scaurus' compliments, he began, "Why I waste my talent for a heathen's heretic tart—" but Scaurus retreated before he was at full spate.

He found Helvis sitting under a peach tree outside the camp, mending a tunic. She looked up as he came toward her. When she saw he was going to sit by her, she jabbed her needle into the shirt, one of Malric's—and put it aside. "Hello," she said coolly; she did not try to hide her anger over the tribune's refusal to take her countrymen's side against Videssos. He was tired of the way policy kept getting between the two of them.

"Hello. I have something for you." The words seemed flat and awkward as soon as they were out of his mouth. With a sudden stab of shame, he realized he had too little practice saying such things, had been taking Helvis too much for granted except when they fought.

"What is it?" Her tone was still neutral; probably, Marcus guessed unhappily, she thinks I have underwear for her to darn.

"Here, see for yourself," he said, embarrassment making his voice gruff as he handed her the icon.

The way her eyes grew wide made him sure his guess had been all too close to the mark. "Is it for me? Truly? Where did you get it?" She did not really want an answer; her surprise was speaking. "Thank you so much!" She hugged him one-armed, not wanting to lay the image down, then made Phos' sun-sign at her breast.

Her joy made Scaurus glad and contrite at the same time. While happy to have pleased her, he knew in his heart he should have thought to do so long ago. He had ill repaid her love and loyalty—for why else would she stay with him despite their many differences? Nor did he think of her as only a bed warmer, a pleasure for his nights; love, he thought with profound unoriginality, is very strange.

"Who is it?" Helvis demanded, breaking his reverie. Then in the same breath she went on, "No, you don't tell me, let me work it out for myself." Her lips moved as she sounded out Styppes' golden letters one by one; in less than three years Marcus, already literate in two other tongues, had gained a grasp of written Videssian far better than hers. "Nes-to-ri-os," she read, and, putting the pieces together, "Nestorios! The island saint! However did you remember him?"

The tribune shrugged, not wanting to admit Styppes had provided the name. He felt no guilt over that; in a faith he did not share, it was enough he had recalled the holy man's existence. "Because I knew you cared for him," he said, and from the touch of her hand he knew he had the answer right.

Sentries escorted a pair of Namdaleni into Scaurus' presence. "They've come under truce-sign, sir," a Roman explained. "Gave themselves up to our pickets at the oak woods, they did." The men of the Duchy favored the tribune with crisp salutes, although one looked distinctly unhappy. And no wonder, Marcus thought; it was the islander he had sent to Drax with his exchange offer.

"Hello, Dardel," he said. "I didn't expect to see you again."

"Nor I you," Dardel answered mournfully.

The other Namdalener saluted again. Scaurus had seen that handsome, snub-nosed face before, too, on the right wing of Drax' army at the Sangarios. Now the officer looked elegant in silk surcoat and gold-inlaid ceremonial helm. "Bailli of Ecrisi, at your service," he said smoothly, his Videssian almost without trace of island accent. "Allow me to explain. As my suzerain the great count and protector Drax must decline your gracious proposal, he deemed it only just to return to you the person of your prisoner."

So Drax had a new title, did he? Well, no matter, thought Marcus; he could call himself whatever he chose. "That is most honorable of him," the tribune said. He bowed to Bailli. Not to be outdone in generosity by Drax, he added, "Of course Dardel will be free to return with you when you leave here."

Bailli and Dardel both bowed, the latter in delight. Scaurus said, "Why does the great count reject my offer? We are not rich here, but if he wants ransom for Zigabenos as well as his men free, we will do what we can."

"You misunderstand the great count and protector's reasons, sir," Bailli said. Marcus suddenly distrusted his smile; it said too plainly he knew something the tribune did not. The Namdalener went on, still smiling, "Chief among them is the fact that, being a loyal lieutenant to my lord Zigabenos, he cannot compel him to accept an exchange he does not wish."

"What?" Marcus blurted, astonished out of suaveness. "What farce is this?"

Bailli reached under his surcoat. His guards growled in warning, but all he produced was a sealed roll of parchment. "This will explain matters better than I could," he said, handing it to Scaurus. The tribune examined the seals. One he knew—the sun in golden wax, the mark of the Empire of Videssos. The other seal was green, its symbol a pair of dice in a wine cup. That would have to be Drax' mark. Scaurus broke the seals and unrolled the parchment.

The great count's man had been eyeing his exotic gear. He said, "I don't know, sir, if you read Videssian. If not, I'd be happy to—"

"I read it," Marcus said curtly, and proceeded to do so. He recognized Drax' style at once; the great count wrote the imperial tongue as ornately as any Videssian official. That was part of what made him such a deadly foe; he aped the Empire's ways too well, including, Scaurus saw as he read on, its gift for underhanded politics.

The document was not long, nor did it need be. In four convoluted sentences it proclaimed Mertikes Zigabenos rightful Avtokrator of the Videssians, named the great count Drax his "respected commander-in-chief and Protector of the Realm," urged all citizens and "soldiery whether Videssian or foreign" to support the newly declared regime, and threatened outlawry and destruction for any who resisted. Drax' signature, in fancy script with a great flourish underneath, completed the proclamation; Zigabenos' was conspicuously absent.

Marcus read it all through again, damning the great count at every word. The man had to be a genius at intrigue, to do so much damage in so little space. By working through a Videssian puppet, he took away the stigma of being an invader and permanently compromised Zigabenos in Thorisin Gavras' eyes. The rightful Emperor could not be sure Zigabenos was not willingly cooperating with Drax. And Zigabenos, no mean machinator himself, would see that for himself—and might really help the great count from fear of what would happen to him if Drax' revolt failed. The tribune's head started to ache. The more he thought, the worse things looked.

He rolled up the parchment to hand it back to Bailli. The two pieces of Drax' seal fit neatly together, edge to edge. In his choice of emblem, at least, Scaurus thought, he was a Namdalener; the men of the Duchy loved to gamble.

Bailli sniggered when he remarked on that. "Look again."

The tribune did, then swore and threw the parchment to the floor, for what were dice in a wine cup but loaded dice?

VI

"TELL ME," VARATESH SAID TO VIRIDOVIX AS HE HELPED HIS prisoner dismount after another long day of travel, "why did you dye your hair and mustache that hideous shade? And why have you grown the mustache but no beard? By the spirits, you stand out more among plainsmen this way than as you were."

"Will you give over havering anent my looks? It's no beauty y'are your own self." He tried to smooth his long mustachioes, sadly draggled by days of steady rain. With a rawhide strap binding his wrists, he made a clumsy job of it.

"Do not toy with me," Varatesh said, mild-voiced as usual. "I will only ask my question once more." The outlaw chief made no threats, as his riders would have. His cruelty was subtler, letting the Gaul find his own terrors to imagine.

"A pox take you, man. My own face this is on the front o' my head, and nought but." Viridovix glared at the Khamorth, afraid and exasperated at the same time. "What is it I'm supposed to look like, anyway?" he demanded.

"As Avshar set you forth," Varatesh said, and Viridovix felt a chill at the wizard-prince's name. Every day the roughgaited steppe pony he unwillingly rode brought him closer to a meeting he did not want.

"Well, how is that, you kern? I'm not likely to be reading the villain's mind, nor wanting to, either."

Kubad snarled at the insults and fingered his knife in its sheath. What Videssian he understood was mostly vile, just as Viridovix could curse in the plains speech. But Varatesh waved his rider to silence. When he was on the trail of something, such trifles were like false scents to a hunting hound, distractions to be screened out. "As you wish," he said to the Celt. "Your height matches Avshar's picture of you, but he makes your hair out to be dark yellow, not this roan of yours, and calls you clean shaven, though that, I know, means not much. Nor do you look like any imperial I've seen, and he said you might be a Videssian but for fair hair and light eyes."

"Sure and I'd never be that, Varatesh dear," Viridovix said, and then laughed in the Khamorth's face.

"What do you find so funny?" The outlaw chief's tone was dangerous; like most men habitually unsure of themselves, he could not stand being mocked.

"Only that your puir soft-noodled wizard sent you off chasing fish, fur, or virgin's milk. I ken the man you mean, and he's no friend of Avshar, Scaurus isn't, nor a bad wight for all he's a Roman." The alien names meant nothing to Varatesh, who waited with angry impatience. Enjoying himself for the first time since he was taken, the Gaul went on, "If it's the Scaurus you're after, lad, you've a farther ride than the one you took to nab me, for he's still back in the Empire, indeed and he is."

"What?" Varatesh barked. He did not doubt his prisoner's word; the relish Viridovix took in making him look a fool was too obvious. His men were shouting questions at him. With poor grace, he translated what the Celt had said. That his own men lost respect for him was worse than Viridovix' glee; who cared what an enemy thought?

"Avshar won't be pleased," Kubad said, a remark that hung in the air like the smell of lightning.

It was Denizli's turn to half draw his dagger. He smiled evilly. "If this son of a spotted mare's no one Avshar wants, we can have our sport with him here and now." He did pull the knife free, held it under Viridovix' eyes.

"Loose my hands and do that, hero," the Celt growled.

"What does he say?" Denizli said. When Varatesh told him, his smile grew wider. "Tell him I will loose his hands for him—one finger at a time." He stepped toward Viridovix again.

Varatesh nearly let him have his way, but a sudden thought made him cry, "No! Wait!" and knock his rider's blade to one side. Twice now in days he had robbed Denizli of the pleasure of the kill. The renegade sprang at him with an oath, dagger slashing out. But it bit only empty air; Varatesh, who seemed impossible to surprise, had already danced aside. His own knife leaped into his hand. The other Khamorth—Kubad and his comrades Khuraz, Akes, and Bikni—made no move to interfere. In their brutal world, strength alone gave the right to lead.

Varatesh took a cut arm, but a moment later Denizli was writhing in the mud, shrieking as he clutched his hands to his gashed belly. Varatesh stooped over him and cut his throat, as a merciful man would.

Viridovix caught his eye. "Well fought," he said. "I wish it had been me to do it." He meant the compliment; he took fighting too seriously for idle flattery. Varatesh was fast and supple as a striking snake.

The Khamorth shrugged. "Bury this garbage," he said to the four remaining riders. Obeying with no back answers, they stripped the corpse and started to dig; the sodden ground made the work easy. Varatesh turned back to the Gaul. "Riddle me this: if you are not the man my comrade Avshar seeks, how did his magic lead me to you? How did his sleeping-charm not fell you? And how is it you bear a sword like the one this—what was his name?—Scaurus carries?" His Khamorth accent made it sound like "Skrush."

"Begging your pardon and all, but if I'm not the man himself is after, how should I know the answers to your fool questions?"

Varatesh smiled, but thinly. "Just what Avshar will ask you, I think. I will leave it to him, then." For the first time Viridovix was glad of the rain. It hid the sweat that sprang out on his forehead. That sword—he wished he knew more about the sorceries the druids had laid in it. But the Celtic priests revealed their secrets to no one outside their caste. Initiates spent up to twenty years memorizing their lore, for they would not commit it to writing . . . and now they were a world away, and a lost world, to boot.

"Your honor!" he called as Varatesh started to leave. When the Khamorth paused, he went on, "Now that that pig's bladder of a Denizli is after having no further use for his cloak, could I sleep under it tonight? A dry snooze'd be a rare pleasure after this cursed soppy weather." The nomads' cloaks, of greasy wool, shed the rain like ducks' feathers, while the Gaul, in his cloth, had been constantly sodden. Luckily it was warm; a chill likely would have put a fever in his lungs.

"Well, why not? You do have the look of a drowned pup." Varatesh gave his men the order. There were a couple of startled looks, and Kubad quickly spoke up in protest, but Varatesh's answer seemed to satisfy the nomad. The outlaw leader said to Viridovix, "You'll take Kubad's instead. It has a hole in it, and he'll keep Denizli's for himself."

"That will do me, and I thank you."

The Khamorth untied his hands so he could eat, but, as always, kept him covered while loose and rebound them with a fresh strip of rawhide as soon as he was done. When he asked to go out to answer a call of nature, they also bound his ankles together so he had to take tiny hobbling steps. Again, an archer accompanied him.

He had not gone far when he slipped and fell with a splash into a man-sized puddle. His guard laughed and made no effort to help him up. Suspecting a trap, he watched from a safe distance, bow drawn, as the Celt floundered. At last Viridovix struggled back onto his feet. If he had been wet before, he was drenched now. "Och, for a copper I'd piss on *you*," he said to the nomad, but in Gaulish. Recognizing the tone if not the words, the Khamorth kept on laughing. Viridovix glowered at him. "Well, you blackguard, you're not so smart as you think y'are," he said, and his guard laughed even more.

Sodden as he was, the sheepskin cloak did nothing to keep him dry. He curled under it nonetheless. Four of the five nomads slept; Varatesh drew first watch. After his stint was done he woke Akes, who sat grumpily in the rain waiting until it was time for him to rouse Kubad. Every so often, as Varatesh had done, he would glance over at Viridovix, but the Celt was no more than an unmoving lump in the darkness.

For all his pretended sleep, Viridovix was frantically if quietly busy under the sheepskin. His thrashings in the puddle had not been accidental; he had thoroughly soaked the rawhide straps that tied him. Wet, the hide had far more stretch in it than it did dry. Ever so slowly and carefully, not daring to risk detection, he moved his wrists back and forth, up and down, until at last—it was halfway through Kubad's watch—he hooked a thumb under the edge of the hide strip and worked it up over his hands. He clenched his fists over and over, trying to get full feeling back.

Kubad had a skin of kavass with him to help while away the time. All the better, Viridovix thought. The top of the cloak hid his smile. He yawned loudly and half sat, making sure he kept his arms behind him. He looked around as if just locating the sentry he had been anxiously watching all the while.

At the motion Kubad eyed him, but the nomad knew his captive was safely tied. He lifted the skin to his mouth. "How about a nip for me, too, Khamorth darling?" Viridovix called. He kept his voice very low; he hardly wanted to wake Kubad's mates—least of all Varatesh. Varatesh smelled trouble as a bear smelled honey.

But Kubad ambled over and squatted by the Gaul. "You wake thirsty, eh?" he said, holding the skin to Viridovix' lips.

As he drank, Viridovix felt a tiny twinge of guilt at betraying the nomad's friendly act. He stifled it—how friendly had Varatesh's bandits been when they kidnapped him?

"Another?" Kubad asked. The Gaul nodded. The nomad bent closer to present the skin again, and Viridovix lunged forward to take him by the throat. The skin of kavass went flying. By good fortune, it landed on the wool cloak so it did not splash and give the Celt away.

Kubad was an experienced fighter, but he was taken by surprise and made a mistake that proved fatal. Instead of reaching for his dagger, his first, instinctive reaction was to try to break Viridovix' grip on his neck. But the Gaul had desperation's strength, his strangling fingers pressing up under the angle of Kubad's jaw. Too late the nomad remembered the knife. It was his last thought, and his hands would not obey him, falling limp at his sides.

Viridovix let the corpse down into the mud. He took the

dagger himself—a curved weapon with a heavy, lozenge-shaped pommel—and cut the strip of hide that bound his ankles. He made himself wait until the aches and tingles of returning circulation were gone before he moved. "You've only the one chance, now, so don't go wasting it from impatience," he muttered.

The rain drumming down masked his noise as he slid toward the nomads; here was revenge for the taking. But he paused as he stooped over the first of them. Kubad had been a fair fight, but he could not bring himself to murder sleeping men. Eighty-nine kinds of a fool Gaius Philippus'd call you, he said to himself as he sheathed the weapon. Reversed, it would do for a club.

Three times he struck—none of them gentle, for he did not intend to have any of the Khamorth wake with a howl. That left Varatesh.

The outlaw chief woke with a blade tickling his throat. Self-possessed as usual, he sent his right hand slithering toward his belt-knife, hoping the motion would be invisible under the thick cloak. "Dinna try it," Viridovix advised. He held a second dagger, sheathed and reversed, in his left hand. "Sure and I'll slit your weasand for you or ever you get it out." Varatesh considered, decided he was right, and seemed to relax. Viridovix was undeceived.

"Not knowing how hard-pated your lads are, I'll make the farewells brief," the Gaul said.

That startled Varatesh as the reversal of fortunes had not. "You're free and did not kill them?"

"Kubad's dead," Viridovix answered matter-of-factly, "but the rest'll have no worse than the fierce sore head you gave me. As will you," he added, and clubbed the outlaw chief. Varatesh slumped.

Thinking the Khamorth might be shamming, Viridovix drew back warily, but his left-handed blow had been strong enough. Working quickly, he tied all four of the unconscious plainsmen. One wasn't, quite, and had to be flattened a second time. He took all their weapons he could find, loaded them onto a packhorse, then buckled on his own sword. It made a pleasant weight at his hip.

Varatesh's eyes opened while the Celt was still tying the horses' lead lines together. He started working at his bonds at once, making no effort to disguise it—had Viridovix intended to kill him, he would have been dead by now. "We'll meet again, outlander," he promised.

"Aye, belike, but not soon, I'm thinking, e'en once you do get loose," Viridovix said, finishing his work with the animals. "You'd look the proper set o' mooncalves, now, chasing after me afoot, and me with your horses and all."

Varatesh paused, looked at him with grudging respect. "I hoped you would not think of that; many southrons would not have." He started to shake his head, then winced and gave it up as a bad job.

"And besides," Viridovix went on, grinning, "you'll have the demons' own time finding a trail in this muck." The Khamorth scowled, remembering how he had said that to Kubad about Viridovix' comrades. Now the shoe was on his foot and it pinched. So would his boots, soon enough, he thought sourly.

The Gaul swung himself into the saddle. "A pox on your skimpy stirrup leathers," he grumbled; with his long legs, his knees were nearly under his chin. He dug a heel into the steppe pony's ribs, cuffed it when it tried to buck. "None o' that, now!" One by one, as their leads went taut, the nomads' three dozen horses followed the beast he rode. The lilting air he was whistling came straight from the Gallic forests. And why not? he thought, there's just myself the now, so I can be me—aye, and like it, too, with none to say they don't understand.

He whistled louder.

Gorgidas muttered an obscenity as a raindrop hit him in the eye, blurring his vision for a few seconds. "I thought we were done with this cursed weather," he complained.

"Why wait till now to carp?" Lankinos Skylitzes asked. "We've been out from under the worst of it almost all day. If you'd ridden north instead of west, you'd still be soaking it up like a sponge."

Arigh nodded. "It'll get drier the further west you go. In Shaumkhiil, my people's land, these week-long summer storms don't happen much. Winter, now, is another tale." He shuddered at the thought of it. "Videssos has spoiled me."

"I wonder why that's so," Gorgidas said, curious in spite of himself. "Perhaps your being further from the sea has something to do with it. But no—how could you have wet, snowy winters if that were so?" He thought briefly, then asked. "Or is there some other sea to the north, from which your winter storms could gather moisture?"

"Never heard of one," Arigh said without much interest. "There's the Mylasa Sea between the plains and Yezd, but that's south of my folk, not north, and hardly more than a big lake anyhow."

Surprisingly, Goudeles said to Gorgidas, "Well reasoned, outlander. The Northern Sea does run some distance west of the Haloga lands, how far no man knows, but cold and drear throughout." He gave an elegant grimace of distaste. "It must be the cause of the harsh weather good Arigh mentions."

"How do you know that, Pikridios?" Skylitzes challenged. "Far as I've heard, you never set foot outside Videssos till now."

"A fragment of poetry I came across in the archives," the bureaucrat replied blandly. "Written by a naval officer—a Mourtzouphlos, I think; they're an old family—not long after Stavrakios' time, when the Halogai still minded their manners. Quite an arresting little thing, really; one is quite taken with the strangeness of it, almost as if the author were portraying another world. Rocks and ice and wind and odd, bright-beaked shore birds with some flatulent name he must have borrowed from the local barbarians: 'auks,' I think it was."

"Well, auks to you, too," Skylitzes said, defeated by the pen-pusher's barrage of detail. Goudeles dipped his head in a smug half-bow. Gorgidas thought he heard Skylitzes grind his teeth.

"Your pardon, gents," Agathias Psoes broke in, practical as a Roman, "but that looks to be a good place to camp, there up ahead by the stream." The underofficer pointed; as if at the motion, a small flock of ducks came quacking down from the gray sky. Psoes smiled like a successful conjurer; his men unshipped their bows. Gorgidas' stomach rumbled at the thought of roast duck.

But the first bird that was shot let out a loud squawk, and its flockmates took wing, evading the fusillade of arrows the troopers aimed at them. "Shut up in there," the Greek said as his belly growled again. "It's cheese and wheatcakes after all."

Sword drill came before supper. To his dismay, Gorgidas was starting to look forward to it. There was an animal pleasure in feeling his body begin to learn the right response to an overhand cut, a thrust at his belly, a slash at his calf. The practice was like the Videssian board game that mimicked war, but played with arm and eye and feet as well as mind.

Feet—at last he was working on ground firm enough to make footwork mean something more than just staying upright. "A man-killer soon," Skylitzes said, dancing back from a stab.

"I don't want to be a man-killer," the Greek insisted. Skylitzes ignored that and came back to show him how he had given the thrust away. The taciturn Videssian officer was a good teacher; better, Gorgidas thought, than Viridovix would have been. He was more patient and more systematic than the mercurial Celt and remembered his pupils were altogether untrained. Where Viridovix would have thrown up his hands in disgust, Skylitzes was willing to repeat a parry, a lunge, a sidestep thirty times if need be, until it was understood.

When Gorgidas was done, he went down to bathe in the stream, leaving Pikridios Goudeles to Skylitzes' tender mercies. Skylitzes worked the seal-stamper harder than Gorgidas; the Greek was not sure how much of that was because he was a better student than Goudeles and how much because Goudeles and the soldier did not get along. He heard Goudeles yelp as Skylitzes spanked his knuckles—getting some of his own back for that arctic epic.

A green and brown frog no bigger than the last joint of Gorgidas' finger sat in a bush near the edge of the stream. If it had not peeped suddenly, he never would have noticed it. He shook his finger at it. "Hush," he said severely, "before you send all our Khamorth running for their lives." His stomach gurgled again. "And you, too."

They came to a good-sized river the next day; Psoes identified it as the Kouphis. "This is as far west on the Pardrayan steppe as I've come," he said.

"We're halfway to the Shaum, near enough," Arigh said, and Skylitzes nodded. He spoke little of his travels, but if he knew the Arshaum speech along with that of the Khamorth, likely he had gone much farther than the Kouphis.

The river ran north and south. They rode upstream, looking for a ford, and came level with what looked like a heap of building-stones on the far bank. They set Gorgidas scratching his head—what were they doing here in the middle of the flat, empty plain? Two of Psoes' troopers had heard of the stone-pile, but they were little help; they called it "the gods' dung heap."

Skylitzes gave a rare laugh. "Or the Khamorth's," he said quietly, so Psoes' men would not hear. "It's what's left of a Videssian fort, after two hundred-odd years of sacks and no upkeep."

"What?" Gorgidas said. "The Empire ruled here once?"

"No, no," Skylitzes explained. "It was a gift from the Avtokrator to a powerful khagan. But when the khagan died, his sons quarreled, and the nomads went back to living clan by clan."

Pikridios Goudeles stared across the Kouphis at the ruin and burst into laughter himself. "That? That pile of rubble is Khoirosphaktes' Folly?"

"You know of it, too?" Gorgidas asked, forestalling Lankinos Skylitzes; the soldier, it seemed, was not willing to believe Goudeles knew anything.

The bureaucrat rolled his eyes, a gesture that somehow brought with it a whiff of the capital despite the shabby traveling clothes that had quickly replaced his fine robes. "Know of it? My inquisitive friend, in Videssos' accounting schools it is the paradigm of failing to measure cost against results. The goldpieces squandered on shipping artisans and stone from the Empire! And for what? You see it for yourself." He shook his head. "And that says nothing of the elephant."

"Elephant?" the Greek and Skylitzes said together. In Videssos as in Rome they were rare breasts, coming from the little-known lands south of the Sailors' Sea.

"Oh, indeed. One of the khagan's envoys had seen one—at a menagerie, I suppose—and told his master about it. So there was nothing for it but that the barbarian had to have a look at it, too. And the Avtokrator Khoirosphaktes, who, I fear, drank too much to know when to leave well enough alone, shipped it to him. Oh, the gold!" Goudeles looked pained to the bottom of his parsimonious soul.

"Well, out with it, man!" Gorgidas exclaimed. "What did the khagan do with his elephant?"

"Took one look and shipped it back, of course. What would *you* do?"

"Och, beshrew me, sure and I've gone and made a hash of it," Viridovix said, cocking hands on hips in irritation. The inky-black night was at last graying toward another cloudy morning, and the Celt, to his disgust, realized he had been riding east ever since he escaped from Varatesh. The corners of his eyes crinkled. "There's a bit o' good in everything," he told himself, "that there is. The omadhaun'd never think to look for me going this way—he must credit me for better sense."

He gnawed at his mustache as he thought, then swung south, planning to ride in a large circle around Varatesh's camp; he had a healthy respect for the outlaw chief. "I should have put paid to the son of a mangy ferret, for all he spared my mates," he said, speaking aloud again to hear the good Celtic words flow off his tongue. "One fine day he'll cause me more grief, sure as sure."

A horse which had started to graze while he paused jerked its head up with a sharp neigh of protest as its lead rope came taut again. "Dinna say me nay," the Gaul told it, still unhappy with himself. "Too late for your regrets, as for mine."

As the day wore on, the sun finally began to burn its way through the storm clouds. The rain grew fitful, then stopped. "Well, the gods be praised," Viridovix said, and looked about for a rainbow. He did not find one. "Likely that knave of a Varatesh stole it," he muttered, only half joking.

In one small way, the rain and clouds and mist had been a comfort to him, for they closed in his circle of vision and did not make him cope with the plains' vast spaces along with his other miseries. But with the clearing weather, the horizon seemed to draw back veil after veil until, as in his first days on the steppe, he felt like a tiny speck moving through infinity. "If there were but one wee star in all the sky, sure and it'd be no lonelier than I," he said, and bellowed out endless songs to hold aloneness at arm's length.

His banshee shout of glee when he spied a herd of cattle moving far to the south sent his horses' ears pricking up in alarm. After a moment's reflection, though, he squelched it, wondering which was worse, no neighbors or bad ones. "For if I can see them, sure as sure they can see me. Och, wouldn't the little Greek be proud now, to hear me play the logician?"

His reasoning was rewarded, if that was the word, within minutes. A handful of Khamorth peeled away from their cattle and came toward him at a trot. "And what will they do when they find a stranger with these horses and all?" he asked himself; he did not care for the answer he reached. Then he recalled the heavy bows the nomads carried and grew unhappier yet.

He wished for his helm and his cape of scarlet skins to let him cut an impressive figure. His traveling clothes were muddy, wet, and drab to begin with; he surveyed himself with distaste. "Sure and it's a proper cowflop I look," he said mournfully. He cursed Varatesh anew. The outlaw, a scrupulous thief, had stolen only the Gaul and his sword.

At that thought he yelled laughter; his lively spirits could not hold gloom for long. He leaped down from his horse, pulled his ragged tunic over his head, and scrambled out of baggy trousers. He threw them on his pony's back. Naked, blade in hand, he waited for the plainsmen.

"Now they'll have somewhat to think on," he said, still grinning widely. The breeze ran light fingers over his skin. He felt no strangeness, readying himself to fight bare. For as long as the bards recalled, there had been Celts who went naked into battle, wanting no more armor than their fighting rage. He roared out a challenge and strode toward the nomads.

The grin turned sour on his face as he saw the arrows nocked in their double-curved bows, but he was not shot out of hand. The Khamorth gaped at him—what sort of crazy man was this pale, copper-haired giant? They talked back and forth in their own language. One pointed at Viridovix' crotch and said something that was probably rude; they all laughed. Curiosity would not keep this pack at bay long; already the arrows were beginning to bear on him.

He took another long step forward; the plainsmen raised their bows menacingly. "Is it that any o' you lumping buggers is after having the Videssian?" he shouted, his whole stance a defial.

As it happened, none of them spoke the imperial tongue. But their colloquy after the question let him pick out their leader, a lean, hard-faced barbarian whose curly beard tumbled halfway down his chest. "You!" the Celt shouted, and pointed at the Khamorth with his sword.

The nomad gave back a stony glare. "Aye, you, you sheep-futtering spalpeen!" Viridovix said, repeating the insult in his vile Khamorth. As the plainsman slowly reddened, the Gaul gestured, daring him to come out face to face in single combat.

He knew the risk he ran. If the Khamorth was secure in his dominance over his comrades, he would just order them to kill the Celt and then ride on, unruffled. But if not . . . The plainsmen were watching their chief very closely. Silence stretched.

The nomad snarled something; he was angry, not afraid. He reminded Viridovix of a stoat as he slipped off his pony—his motions had a fluid, quick purposefulness that warned the Celt at once he would be no easy meat. The nomad's shamshir slid from its leather sheath, down which writhed polychrome beasts of prey in the contorted Khamorth style. He sidled forward, taking the Gaul's measure as he advanced.

Curved sword met straight one, and at the first pass Viridovix gave back a pace. Quick as a ferret indeed, he thought. He parried a cut at his upper thigh, then threw his arm back to avoid another. Smiling now, enjoying the game, the plainsman bored in to finish him, only to be brought up short by the Celt's straight-armed thrust—not for nothing had Viridovix spent years with the Romans. But his sword, unlike Scaurus', had no sharp stabbing point, and the nomad's shirt of thick sueded leather kept it from his vitals. The Khamorth grunted and stepped back himself.

Each having surprised the other, they fenced warily for a time, both looking for some flaw to use to advantage. Viridovix hissed as the very point of his foe's blade drew a thin line across his chest, then growled in disgust at his own clumsiness when he was pinked again, this time on the left arm. His ancestors, he decided, were great fools—fighting naked, there was just too much to guard. The nomad was unmarked.

Viridovix was stronger than the Khamorth and had a longer reach, but in the long run speed would likely count for more.

"Well, then, we maun be keepin' it brief," he said to himself and leaped at the plainsman, raining blows from all directions, trying to overwhelm him by sheer dint of muscle. His opponent danced away, but his boot heel skidded in the trampled mud, and he had to block desperately as Viridovix' blade came slashing down. He turned the stroke, but his own sword went flying, to land point down in the muck.

"Ahh," said the Khamorth from their horses.

With their leader at his mercy, as he thought, Viridovix had no intention of killing him—there was no telling what the plainsmen might do after that. But when he stepped confidently forward to pluck the nomad's knife from his belt in token of victory, the Khamorth chopped at his wrist with the hard edge of his hand, and his own sword dropped from suddenly nerveless fingers.

"No you don't, you blackhearted omadhaun!" the Gaul shouted as his foe grabbed for the dagger. He grappled, wrapping the nomad in a bear hug. The Khamorth butted like a goat, crashing the top of his head up into Viridovix' chin. The Celt saw stars, spat blood from a bitten tongue, but his left hand kept its clamp on his opponent's right wrist. He punched the plainsman in the back of the neck again and again—not sporting, maybe, but effective. At last, with a soft little groan, the Khamorth slumped to the mud.

Sweat glistening all over his body, Viridovix retrieved his sword and faced the mounted nomads. They stared back, as uncertain as he was. "I've not killed him, you know," the Gaul said, gesturing toward their chief, "though he'll wish I had for the next few days." He still got blinding headaches from the clubbing Varatesh had given him.

He squatted beside the plainsman, who was just beginning to revive. The rest of the nomads hefted their bows in warning. "It's no harm I mean him," Viridovix said; they did not understand that any more than they had his previous speech, but relaxed somewhat when they saw him help their comrade sit. The barbarian moaned and held his head in his hands, still half unconscious.

One of the Khamorth tossed his bow to the man beside him, dismounted, and walked up to Viridovix, his empty hands spread in front of him. He pointed to the Celt. "You," he said. Viridovix nodded; that was a word he knew. The nomad pointed to the string of steppe ponies the Gaul was leading. "Where?" he asked. He repeated it several times, with gestures, until Viridovix understood.

"Oh, it's these beauties you'd be knowing about, is it? I stole 'em from Varatesh, indeed and I did," the Celt said, proud of his exploit, not just because it had let him escape, but for its own sake as well. In Gaul as among the nomads, stock raiding was a sport, in fact almost an art.

"Varatesh?" Three of the Khamorth spoke the name at the same time; it was all they had caught of what Viridovix had said. Even their stunned leader jerked his head up, but let it fall with a groan. They hurled excited questions at the Gaul. He waved his hands to show he could not follow.

The dismounted nomad shouted his friends down. "You and Varatesh?" he asked Viridovix with a wide, artificial smile, then repeated the question, this time with a fearsome scowl on his face.

"Aren't you the clever one, now?" the Celt exclaimed. "Me and Varatesh," he said, and screwed up his face into the most terrible grimace he could imagine, slashing the air with his sword for good measure. Only then did he realize the nomads might be friendly to the outlaw. Well, no help for it, and a lie had the same chance of getting him into trouble as the truth.

But he got the answer right. The plainsmen broke into smiles for the first time. The dismounted one offered his hand for Viridovix to clasp. He took it warily, shifting his sword to his own left hand, but the Khamorth's friendliness was genuine. "Yaramna," he said, tapping himself on the chest. He pointed to his companions on their horses: "Nerseh, Zamasp, Valash," then to his chief: "Rambehisht."

"More sneeze-names," Viridovix sighed, and gave his own. Then he had two inspirations, one on the other's heels. He retrieved Rambehisht's saber and gave it back to the plainsman. Rambehisht was hardly up to standing yet, let alone showing thanks, but his comrades murmured appreciatively.

Then the Gaul walked back to his horses, retrieving his trousers and tunic from the back of the one he had been riding.

He used his sword to cut some of the animals' leads, and presented each of the plainsmen with half a dozen beasts. The string he kept for himself had been Varatesh's; in such matters he trusted the outlaw chief's judgment.

He could not have picked a better friendship-offering from all the world's wealth. All the Khamorth but Rambehisht crowded round Viridovix, wringing his hand, pounding his back, and shouting in their own language. Even their leader managed a wan smile, though it looked as if moving his face in any way hurt. Viridovix had tried to give him some of the best animals he had, not wanting to make a permanent enemy if he could help it.

With more gestures and the few words the Celt knew, Yaramna indicated they would soon be riding back to his clanmates' tents. "The very thing I was hoping you'd say," Viridovix replied. Yaramna understood his grin and nod better. The Khamorth made a wry face at his failure to communicate; he finally made Viridovix realize that some men of his clan did speak Videssian. "We do the best we can, is all," the Celt shrugged. He had already made up his mind to learn the plains tongue.

He laughed suddenly. Yaramna and the other Khamorth looked at him, puzzled. "Nay, it's nought to do with you," Viridovix said. He had never thought a day would come when he started to sound like Scaurus.

Varatesh's hands were puffy and swollen still, the marks from the thongs Viridovix had used to bind him carved deep and red and angry on his wrists. If the Gaul had not missed the little knife he always carried in a slit pouch on the side of one boot, he would still be tied. But Khuraz had wriggled over through the mud to get it out and then, working back-to-back with Varatesh, managed to cut his bonds—and his wrists and hands, more than once.

The outlaw clenched painful fists and tried with little success to ignore the hoofbeats of agony in his skull. He did not like to lose at anything, least of all to a man who should have been his helpless prisoner. Nor did he relish the week or more of a hiking he and his comrades had ahead of them unless they could steal horses. And least of all he liked the prospect of explaining to Avshar how the fat partridge had slipped through his nets. Avshar's anger would be bad enough, but to have the wizard-prince think him nothing but a thick-witted barbarian after all . . . he bit his lip in humiliated fury.

When the wave of black anger passed, he found he could think again, despite the pain. He reached inside his tunic for the crystal charm Avshar had given him. Holding it carefully in clumsy fingers, he watched the orange mist suffuse its depths.

"East," he grunted in surprise, peering at the clear patch the orange would not enter. "Why is the worthless dog moving east?" He wondered if the crystal had gone awry, decided it had not. But when captured, the red-haired stranger had been heading west, and in company with an Arshaum. Varatesh tugged at his beard. He distrusted what he did not understand.

"Who gives a sheep turd where he's going?" Bikni asked from the ground. "Good riddance, says I," Akes echoed, also sitting in the wet dirt. Varatesh's three surviving followers were all sick and shaken from Viridovix' bludgeoning. So was their chief, but his will drove him, while they were content to lie like dogs in their own vomit.

"Avshar will care," he answered; battered as they were, his henchmen flinched. "And I care," he added. He had made sure to get the knife back from Khuraz and showed it now.

"It's a long walk back to our mates," Bikni whined. "No horses, no food, no arms—and you know what your bloody toy dagger is worth, Varatesh. Not much."

"So we walk. I will get home if I have to eat all three of you along the way. And," Varatesh said very softly, "I will be even."

When he strode north, the other three Khamorth, moaning and lurching and grumbling, followed, just as a lodestone will draw dead iron in its wake.

Prevalis, Haravash's son, came galloping back toward the embassy party from his station at point. "Something up ahead," the young trooper called.

"'Something,'" Agathias Psoes muttered, rolling his eyes. The underofficer shouted, "Well, what is it?"

At that point they both dropped into the Videssian-Khamorth lingua franca used at Prista, and Gorgidas lost the thread of their conversation. After days with no more than an occasional herd on the horizon, anything would be a relief, simply to break the boredom of travel. Arigh claimed the Shaum river, the great stream that marked the border between the Khamorth and his own Arshaum, was close. The Greek had no idea how he knew. One piece of the endless steppe was identical to the next.

"What are they jabbering about?" Goudeles said impatiently. The bureaucrat from the capital could no more follow the bastard frontier dialect than could Gorgidas.

"Your pardon, sir," Psoes said, returning to the formal imperial speech. "There's a nomad encampment in sight, but it doesn't seem right somehow."

"Where are their flocks?" Skylitzes asked. He turned to Prevalis. "This place of many tents, where is?" He was at home in the jargon Videssians and nomads used together.

"You'll see it as soon as you top the next rise," the trooper answered, smiling as he switched styles so Goudeles, Arigh, and Gorgidas could understand.

Skylitzes' habitual frown deepened. "That close? Then where *are* their bloody flocks?" He looked this way and that, as if expecting them to pop out of thin air.

Just as Haravash's son had said, the encampment was visible when the embassy party rode to the top of the gentle swell of land ahead. Recalling the bright tents of the Yezda he had seen too often in Vaspurakan and western Videssos, Gorgidas was looking for a similar gaudy spectacle. He did not find one. The camp seemed somber and quiet—too quiet, the Greek thought. Even at this distance, he should have been able to see cookfires' smokes against the sky and horsemen riding from one tent to the next, if as no more than fly-sized specks.

"A plague?" he wondered aloud, remembering his Thucydides, and Athens wasted at the start of the Peloponnesian War. His scalp prickled. Plagues were beyond any doctor's power to cure—though who knew what wonders a healer-priest could work?

Goudeles, who should have known, said, "The expedient course, to my mind, would be to take a broad detour and avoid the risk." For some obscure reason, it comforted Gorgidas that the Videssian feared disease as much as he.

"No," Lankinos Skylitzes said. Goudeles started a protest,

but the officer cut through it: "Plague might have killed the plainsmen's herds, or it might have left them untouched. It would not have made them run away."

"You're right, Empire man," Arigh said. "Plagues only make people run." His slanted eyes mocked Goudeles.

"As you wish, then," the bureaucrat answered, doing his best to show unconcern. "If the fever melts the marrow inside my bones, at least I know I shall be dying in brave company." Still an awkward horseman, he urged his mount into a trot and rode past Arigh toward the encampment. Looking less sly and smug than he had a few seconds before, the Arshaum followed, with the rest of the embassy behind them.

Skylitzes' logic only partly reassured Gorgidas; what if a pestilence had struck some time before, and the nomads' animals wandered off in the interim? But when his comrades exclaimed in alarm as three or four ravens and a great black vulture flapped into the sky on spying the oncoming horsemen, the Greek leaned back in his high-cantled saddle in relief. "When did death-birds become a glad sign?" Psoes asked.

"Now," Gorgidas replied, "for they mean there is no plague. Scavengers either shun corpses that die of pestilence or, eating of them, fall victim to the same disease." Unless, of course, the fearful part of his mind whispered, Thucydides had it wrong.

But as the embassy party came closer, it grew clear no pestilence had brought the camp low—or none save the pestilence of war. Wagons were gutted shells, some tilting drunkenly with one wheel burned away. Tent-frames held only charred remnants of the felts and leathers that had stretched across them. The tatters waved in the wind like a skeleton's fleshless fingers; death had ruled long here.

A few more carrion birds rose as the riders entered the murdered encampment—not many, for the best pickings were mostly gone. The stench of death was fading; more bone than rotted flesh leered sightlessly up at the newcomers, as if resenting life's intrusion into their unmoving world.

The bodies of men and women, children and beasts lay strewn about the tents. Here was a plainsman with the stub of his blade in his hand, the rest a few feet away. Broken, it was not worth looting. An axe had cleaved the man's skull. Close by him was what once had been a woman. Her corpse was naked, legs brutally spread wide. Enough flesh clung to her to let Gorgidas see her throat had been slashed.

With the legions and then in Videssos, the Greek had known more violent death than he liked to remember, but here he saw a thoroughness, a wantonness of destruction for its own sake that had made his flesh crawl. He looked from one of his companions to the next. Goudeles, who knew little of war, was pale and sickened, but he was not alone. Psoes' soldiers, Skylitzes, even Arigh, who seemed to pride himself for hardness—what they saw shocked them all.

No one seemed able to speak first, to break the silent spell of horror. At last Gorgidas said, as much to himself as to the rest, "So this is how they wage war, here on the plains."

"No!" That was Skylitzes, Agathias Psoes, and three of his troopers all together. Another raven cawed indignantly at the near-shout and waddled away, too stuffed to fly. Psoes, quicker-tongued than Skylitzes, went on, "This is not war, outlander. This is madness." To that Gorgidas could only dip his head in agreement.

"Even the Yezda are no worse than this," the Greek said, and then, his agile mind leaping: "And they, too, came off the steppe—"

"But it was in Makuran—Yezd, now—they learned to follow Skotos," Psoes said, and all the Videssians spat in rejection of the dark god. "The plainsfolk are heathen, aye, but fairly clean as heathens go." Gorgidas had heard otherwise in Videssos, but then Psoes was closer to the Khamorth than men who lived in the Empire proper. He wondered whether that intimacy made the underofficer more reliable or less. The Greek tossed his head. History was proving as maddeningly indefinite as medicine.

The brief moment of abstraction was shattered when his sharp eyes spied the symbol hacked into the shattered side of a cedar box. He had seen those paired side-by-side three-slash lightning bolts too often in the ruins of Videssian towns and monasteries to fail to recognize Skotos' mark now. He pointed. Psoes followed his finger, jerked as if stung; he, too, knew what the mark meant. He spat again, sketched Phos' sun-circle on his breast. Skylitzes, Goudeles, and the Videssian troopers followed suit.

Arigh and the Khamorth, though, were puzzled, wondering why their companions chose to excite themselves over a rude carving in the midst of far worse destruction.

"I would not have thought it," Skylitzes and Psoes said in the same breath. Skylitzes dismounted, squatted beside the profaned chest. The pious officer spat yet a third time, this time directly on the mark of Skotos. Pulling flint and steel from his belt, he cracked them together over a little pile of dead grass. The fire did not want to catch; the grass was still a bit damp from the recent rain.

"Varatesh's renegades. It must be," Psoes said over and over while Skylitzes fumed and his fire did not. The underofficer sounded badly shaken, as if searching for any explanation he could find for the butchery all around him. "Varatesh's renegades."

"Ah." Skylitzes had coaxed his blaze to life. He put the cedar box at one corner of it. As the flames fed on the tinder, they began licking the wood as well. Skotos' symbol charred, vanished. "Thus in the end light will cast out darkness forevermore," Skylitzes said. He and all the Videssians made the sun-sign again.

As the embassy party left the raped camp behind, Gorgidas wondered aloud, "Where are the nomads learning of Skotos?"

"A wicked god for wicked men," Goudeles replied sententiously. To the Greek, that sort of answer was worse than useless. Until this horror, the plainsmen had struck him as men like any others—barbarous, yes, but their natures a mix of good and bad. Nor was Skotos native to the steppe; neither the troopers of Khamorth blood nor Arigh had recognized his mark.

Yet in Yezd the incoming nomads took to the evil deity with savage enthusiasm—and, on reflection, that was not right either. Before the nomad conquest, Yezd had been Makuran, an imperial rival to Videssos, but a civilized one. And the Makurani had a religion of their own, following their beloved Four Prophets. Whence the cult of Skotos, then, and where the link between distant Yezd and an encampment still all too close?

Lankinos Skylitzes had no trouble making a connection. "Avshar travels with Varatesh," he said, as to a stupid child.

The explanation satisfied him completely, and Gorgidas

flushed, angry he had not seen it himself. But the Yezda, the Greek remembered, were already entering Makuran half a century ago. A chill ran up his spine—what, then, did that make Avshar?

Valash came galloping back toward the horsemen from his station at point. He called something in his own language. The rest of the Khamorth shouted back, glee on their bearded faces. Even dour Rambehisht grudged a smile, though the look he gave Viridovix was unreadable.

"Camp at last, I'll be bound, and about time, too. Now we get down to it," the Gaul said. He had spent four days helping the nomads tend their cattle while Zamasp rode in to fetch herders to replace them. The work was thoroughly dull; cattle were stupid, and the more of them there were together, the stupider the lot of them seemed to get. Even so, he had not been able to enjoy the release mindless tasks sometimes bring, not with his life still held by nomads who were not his friends.

Yaramna rode close to the Celt. The plainsman was on one of the animals Viridovix had given him. "Good horse," he said, slapping its neck affectionately. Viridovix understood the second word from a Khamorth obscenity; the plainsman's action gave him the first.

"Glad you like him, indeed and I am," he answered, and Yaramna was as quick to grasp his meaning, if not the sense of each word.

The Khamorth camp sprawled across the plain, with tents and wagons set down wherever their owners chose. Viridovix guffawed. "Sure and Gaius Philippus'd spit blood, could he see these slovens. Not a proper Roman camp at all, at all. Welladay, free and easy always did suit me better."

And yet, his years with the legionaries made him frown when he saw—and smelled—piles of garbage by each tent, when men pissed wherever they happened to be when they felt the urge, as casually as the grazing horses that wandered through the camp. That was no way to make a proper encampment, either. His own Celts were a cleanly folk, if not so much given to order as the Romans.

The sight of a stranger in the camp, especially one as exotic as the Gaul, made the nomads shout and point. Some shied away, others came crowding in for a closer look. One toddler, bolder than some warriors, ran forward from a cookfire to touch the tip of the stranger's boot as he rode by. Viridovix, who was fond of children, brought his pony to a careful stop. "Boo!" he said. The tot's eyes went very round. He turned and fled. Viridovix laughed again; the child's trousers, otherwise like his elders', had no seat in them. "Foosh! Isn't that a sly way to do things, now!" he exclaimed.

The tot's mother snatched it up and spanked its bare rump, a use for the bottomless pants the Celt had not thought of. "Puir bairn!" he said, listening to its outraged howls.

Valash led his comrades and Viridovix to a round, dome-shaped tent larger and more splendid than any of the rest. A wolfskin on a pole in front of it marked it as the clan-chief's; so did the two sentries eating curded cheese by the entranceway. Beasts and demons in the writhing nomad style were embroidered on the green felt tent; similar scenes were painted on the frame of the wagon that would haul the disassembled tent across the steppe. Rank on rank of baggage carts stood beside it. The chests they carried were shiny with tallow to protect them from the rain.

All that was wealth only a chief enjoyed, the Gaul saw. Most of the tents were smaller and of thinner stuffs, light enough so one man could pitch them and so a horse could bear their fabric and the sticks that made up their framework along with a goodly part of the rest of a nomad family's goods. Where the clan leader had dozens of carts by his tent, most of the tribesmen made do with three or four—or sometimes none. Viridovix revised his estimate; the plains life might be free, but it was far from easy.

One of the sentries licked his horn spoon clean and glanced up at Valash's group. He pointed at Viridovix, asked something in the Khamorth tongue. They went back and forth for a few seconds. The Celt caught the name "Targitaus" repeated several times; he gathered it belonged to the chief. Then the sentry surprised him by saying in accented Videssian, "You wait. Targitaus, I tell him you here."

As the plainsman started to duck inside the tent, Viridovix called after him, "Your honor, is himself after having the Empire's speech?"

"Oh, yes. He go Prista many times—trade. Raid once, but long time gone." The sentry disappeared. Viridovix sighed in relief; at least he would not have explain himself through an interpreter. Trying to use an interpreter for vigorous speech was like trying to yell underwater—noise came through, but not much sense.

The sentry came out. He spoke to the Khamorth, then to Viridovix: "You go in now. You see Targitaus, you bow, yes?"

"I will that," the Celt promised. He dismounted, as did the plainsmen. The second sentry took charge of their horses while the first one held the tent flap open; it faced west, away from the wind. Sensible, Viridovix thought, but the idea of passing a steppe winter in a tent made the red-gold hairs on his arms stand up as if he were a squirrel puffing out its fur against bad weather.

He dipped his head to pass through the entranceway, which was low even for the stocky Khamorth. When he raised his eyes again he whistled in admiration. The Romans, he discovered, were tyros when it came to tents. This one was big as any four legionary tents, a good dozen paces across. White fabric lined the inside, making in seem larger still by reflecting the light of the fire in the very center and butter-burning lamps all around the edge. Leather bags along the northern side held more of Targitaus' goods; the men of his household had hung their bows and swords above them. Cooking utensils, spindles, and other women's tools went along the southern edge of the tent. Between them, opposite the entrance, was a great bed of fleeces and felt-covered cushions. Not an inch of space was wasted, but the tent did not seem cramped.

That was a small miracle, for it was full of people, men on the northern side, women to the south. There was a low couch—the only bit of real furniture in the tent—between the cookfire and piled-up bedding. Remembering what the sentry had told him, Viridovix bowed to the man reclining on it, surely Targitaus himself.

"So. You take long enough to notice me," the nomad chief said to the Gaul; Valash and the rest of the Khamorth had already made their bows. Targitaus' Videssian was much more fluent than his sentry's but not as good as Varatesh's. He did not seem much angered. The Celt studied the man who would decide his fate. Targitaus was middle-aged and far from handsome—paunchy, scarred, with a big, hooked nose that had been well broken a long time ago and now pointed toward the right corner of his mouth. His full gray beard and the uncut hair under his fur cap gave him something of the look of a gone-to-seed dandelion. But in their nest of wrinkles, his brown eyes were disconcertingly keen. A noble himself in Gaul, Viridovix knew a leader when he saw one.

"You look like an 'Alugh," Targitaus remarked; with his guttural accent it took the Gaul a moment to recognize "Haloga." The Khamorth went on, "Come round the fire so I get a better see at you." Accompanied by Rambehisht, Yaramna, and the others, Viridovix picked his way through the men's side of the tent. Nomads sitting on pillows or round cloths leaned aside to let them pass.

"Big man," Targitaus said when the Celt stood before him. "Why you so big? You wear out any horse you ride."

"Aye, well, so long as it's not the lassies complaining," Viridovix murmured. Targitaus blinked, then chuckled. The Gaul smiled to himself; he had gauged his man aright.

The men on the ground to the right of the chief's couch translated his words and the Celt's so the plainsmen could understand. He was the first smooth-faced Khamorth Viridovix had seen; his cheeks were pink and shiny in the firelight. His voice was between tenor and contralto. He wore a robe that his corpulent frame stretched tight.

Seeing the Celt's glance, Targitaus said, "This Lipoxais. He is *enaree* of clan."

"'Shaman,' you would say in Videssian," Lipoxais added, his command of the imperial speech near perfect. The melting look he gave Viridovix made the Gaul wonder whether the *enaree* was a eunuch, as he had first thought, or simply effeminate.

"Shaman, yes," Targitaus nodded impatiently. "Not to talk of words now." He measured Viridovix up and down, his eyes flicking to the longsword at the Celt's hip. "You tell me your story, hey, then we see what words need saying."

"That I will," Viridovix said, and began at the point of his kidnaping.

The chief stopped him. "No, wait. What you doing Pardraya in first place? You no Empire man, no Khamorth, no Arshaum either—that plain enough, by wind spirits!" His laugh had a wheeze in it.

With a sinking feeling, Viridovix told the truth. As Lipoxais translated, an angry muttering rose from the plainsmen round the fire. "You go to lead Arshaum through Pardraya and you want my thanks and help?" Targitaus growled. He touched his saber, as if to remind himself where it was.

"And why not? I deserve the both of 'em." Targitaus stared; Lipoxais raised a plucked eyebrow. Outface the lot of them, Viridovix told himself; if they see you yielding so much as a digit, it's all up. He stood straighter, looking down his long nose at the Khamorth chief. "The more o' the Arshaum are after fighting in Videssos, the fewer to tangle with you. Is it not so?"

Targitaus scratched his chin. Lipoxais' smooth, high voice finished rendering the Gaul's words into the plains tongue. Viridovix did not dare look around to see how the nomads were taking what he said, but the hostile rumbling died away. "All right. You go on," Targitaus said at last.

The hurdle leaped, Viridovix warmed to his tale and won his listeners to him when they understood he and Varatesh were foes. "The brother-slayer, eh?" Targitaus said, and spat in the dirt in front of his couch. "Few years gone by, he try to join clan. His story even worse than yours—he not just leave things out, he tell lies, too." He looked Viridovix full in the face, and the Celt could not help flushing. "Go on," Targitaus said. "What next?"

Viridovix started to warn the nomads of Avshar, but they did not know the wizard-prince's name and so did not fear him. The gods grant they don't find out, the Gaul thought, and went on to tell of his escape from Varatesh. That brought shouts from the plainsmen as it was interpreted, and a "Not bad," from Targitaus. Viridovix grinned; he suspected the Khamorth was short with praise.

"In the dark and all I rode east instead of west and came on your lads here," the Celt finished. "Belike you'd sooner have the tale o' that from them."

Interrupting each other from time to time, the nomads told their side of the meeting with Viridovix. Early on, Targitaus' jaw fell. "Naked?" he said to the Gaul.

"It's a way my people have betimes."

"Could be painful," was all the chief said. His men went on to describe the fight with Rambehisht. Targitaus snapped a question at the stern-featured nomad. "What do you have to say for yourself, losing to a naked man?" Lipoxais translated.

The Gaul tensed. Rambehisht was fairly important in the clan; if he shouted denunciations now, it might not be pleasant. But he answered his chief with a shrug and a short phrase. "He beat me," Lipoxais rendered tersely. Rambehisht added another, slightly longer, sentence: "My head still hurts—what more can I say?"

"So." After that single syllable, Targitaus was quiet for a long time. At last the Khamorth chief turned to Viridovix. "Well, outlander, you are a fighter if nothing else. You have gall, to meet a man like that."

"Have gall? Indeed and I am one."

"So," the plainsman repeated, scratching his head. "What next?"

"If I were after asking you for an escort to the Arshaum country, you'd have my head for fair, I'll wager," Viridovix said. He did not need the nomads' growls as Lipoxais translated; he had put out the idea to let it be knocked down and make his real proposal the more attractive. "How's this, then, your honor? It's a nasty neighbor you have in this kern of a Varatesh, the which ye can hardly say nay to. Now you've a grudge against him, and I've one, too, the gods know—" No Videssians were here to shout "Heresy!" at that. "—and like enough some o' your other clans hereabouts, too. Would it not be a fine thing to put the boot to him once for all, aye, and the mangy curs as run with him?" And Avshar, too, he thought, but did not name him again.

Guttural mumbles round the fire as the listening nomads considered. "Grudge?" Targitaus said softly. "Oh my yes, grudge." He leaped to his feet, shouted something in the plains speech. "Does it please you, brothers?" Lipoxais gave the words to Viridovix. The roar that came back could only be "Aye!" A meat-eater's smile on his face, Valash slapped the Gaul on the back.

But Targitaus, as leader, had learned caution. "*Enaree!*" he said, and Lipoxais stood beside him. "Take your omens, say if this will be good or bad for clan."

Lipoxais bowed his head and put both hands over his face in token of obedience. Then he turned to Viridovix, saying quietly, "Come round here behind me and put your hands on my shoulders." The *enaree*'s flesh was very warm and almost as soft as a feather cushion.

From inside his robe Lipoxais drew a piece of smooth white bark two fingers wide and about as long as his arm. He cut it into three equal lengths, wrapped it loosely round his hands. Viridovix felt him suddenly go rigid; his head snapped back, as a man's will in the throes of lockjaw. The Celt could look down at the *enaree*'s face. His mouth was clenched shut, his eyes open and staring, but they did not see Viridovix. Lipoxais' hands moved as if they had a will of their own, twisting and untwisting the lengths of bark round his fingers.

The mantic fit went on and on. Viridovix had no idea how long it should last, but saw from the worry growing in Targitaus' eyes that this was not normal. He wondered whether he should shake Lipoxais out of his trance, but hesitated, afraid to interfere with a magic he did not understand.

The *enaree* returned to himself about when Viridovix was making up his mind to shake him whether it ruined the charm or not. Sweat dripped from his face; his robe was wet under the Gaul's hands. He staggered, righted himself with the air of someone getting his land legs after a long time at sea. This time no longing was on his face when he looked at Viridovix, only awe and a little fear. "There is strong magic around you," he said, "your own and others." He shook his head, as if to clear it.

Targitaus barked something at Lipoxais, who answered at some length before turning back to Celt. "I could see little," he explained, "through so much sorcery, and that little was blurred: fifty eyes, a doorway in the mountains, and two swords. Whether these are signs of goods or ill I do not know."

Plainly unhappy at not learning more, Targitaus reflected, his chin in his hand. At last he straightened, stepping forward to clasp Viridovix' hand. "As much chance for good as for bad," he said, "and Varatesh's ears need trimming—down to the neck, I think." He sounded jovial, but the Gaul thought he would not be a good enemy to have.

"So," the Khamorth chieftain went on; he seemed to use the word as a pause to gather his thoughts. "You swear oath with us, yes?"

"Whatever pleases your honor," Viridovix said at once.

"Good." Targitaus switched to the plains tongue. A young man who had his eyes and his prominent nose—the later unkinked—brought a large earthenware bowl and a full skin of kavass. No ordinary nomad brew was this, but dark, strong, and heady, with a rich aroma like ale's. "Karakavass—black kavass," Targitaus said, pouring it into the bowl. "The lords' drink."

But he did not drink of it yet; instead, he pulled a couple of arrows from a quiver and put them point-down in the bowl, then followed them with his shamshir. "Your sword, too," he said to Viridovix. The Celt drew it and put as much of the blade as would fit—a bit more than half—into the bowl. Targitaus nodded, then unsheathed his dagger and took Viridovix' hand. "Do not flinch," he warned, and made a small cut on the Celt's forefinger. Viridovix' blood dripped into the bowl. "Now you me," Targitaus said, giving him the knife. He might have been carved from stone as the Gaul cut him. Their bloods mingled now—a strong magic, Viridovix thought approvingly.

Lipoxais began a chanted prayer; the gutturals of the Khamorth language sounded strange in his high voice. From time to time Targitaus spoke in response. As the *enaree* prayed on, Targitaus said to Viridovix, "Swear by your powers to act always as a brother to this clan and never to betray it or any man of it."

The Gaul paused only a moment, to think which of his gods would best hear his oath. "By Epona and Teutates I swear it," he said loudly. Horse-goddess and war-god—what better powers to call on with the nomads? As he spoke their names, the druids' marks on his enchanted blade glowed golden. Lipoxais' eyes were closed, but Targitaus saw.

"Magics of your own, yes," he muttered, staring at his new-sworn ally.

When Lipoxais' chant was done, the Khamorth chief took his weapons from the bowl. Viridovix did the same, drying his sword on his shirttail before putting it back in its sheath. Targitaus stooped, carefully lifted the bowl to his lips. He drank, then handed it to the Celt. "We share blood, we share fate," he said, with the air of one translating a proverb. Viridovix drank, too; the karakavass was mouth-filling, smooth on his tongue as fine wine, warm and comforting in his belly.

Once the Gaul's drinking sealed him to them, Targitaus' lieutenants rose from their sitting-cloths and came up to share the bowl. Servants rolled the cloths into tight cylinders so not a crumb of precious food would be spilled.

"You are one with us now," Targitaus said, punctuating the remark with a belch. "More kavass!" he called, and new skins were broached: not the dark, earthy brew in the ceremonial bowl, but strong enough. Viridovix drank deep, passed the skin to Valash next to him. Another came his way a moment later, then another. His ears began to buzz.

Targitaus' wolfskin cap kept wanting to slide down over the chief's left eye. He pushed it back, looked owlishly at Viridovix. "You one with us," he said again, his accent rougher than it had been a few minutes before. "You should be glad; it is the right of a man. Do you see a wench who pleases you?"

"Well, fry me for a sausage!" the Gaul exclaimed. "I never looked." That he had paid no attention to the women in the tent was a measure of his anxiety.

Now he made amends for the lapse. There were times when loneliness stabbed like a knife, remembering the pale Celtic women with hair sun-colored or red to match his own. But he was not one to live in the past for long and took his chances where he found them. He grinned, thinking of Komitta Rhangavve.

It was not that he expected any such high-strung beauties in Targitaus' tent. Like the Vaspurakaners, the Khamorth were heavier-featured than the Videssians. The faces of their men often held great character, but the women tended to have a stern, forbidding aspect to them. Their clothes did not soften their appearance, either; they wore trousers, tunics, and cloaks identical in cut to those of the plainsmen, and of the same furs and leathers. In place of the men's inevitable fur caps, though, they wore conical headdresses of silk, ornamented with bright stones, and topped by crests of iridescent feathers from ducks and pheasants. That helped, but not enough.

Worse still, Viridovix thought as his eye roved, a good many of the women on the southern side of the tent had to be the wives of Targitaus' officers: chunky, far from young, and some of them looking as used to command as the nomad chief. He had had enough of that last from Komitta. They were surveying him, too, with a disconcerting frankness; he was as glad he could not understand their comments.

Then he paused. Not far from Targitaus' couch was a girl whose strong features, as with Nevrat Sviodo, had their own kind of beauty. It was her eyes, the Celt decided—they seemed to smile even when the rest of her face was still. She met his glance as readily as did the older women by her, but without their coarse near-mockery. "That's a likely-looking lass," he said to Targitaus.

The Khamorth's thick eyebrows went up like signal flags. "Glad you think so," he said dryly, "but pick again, a serving-girl, if you please. That is Seirem, my daughter."

"Och, begging your pardon I am," Viridovix said, reddening. He was very much aware of his fragile place here. "How is it I'm to tell the wenches from some laird's lady?"

"By the bughtaq, of course," Targitaus answered. When he saw the Gaul did not know the word, he gestured to show he meant the Khamorth women's headdress. Viridovix nodded, chiding himself for not noticing that detail. Along with jade and polished opals, Videssian goldpieces ornamented Seirem's bughtaq; she was plainly no slavey.

The Celt's gaze settled on a woman of perhaps twenty-five, without Seirem's lively face, but attractive enough and nicely rounded. Except for a few reddish stones and a very small piece of jade, her headdress was plain. "She'll do me, an it suit you," he said.

"Who?" Targitaus put down the skin of kavass from which he had been slurping. "Oh, Azarmi. Aye, why not? She serves my wife Borane."

Viridovix waved her over to him. One of the richly adorned women, a particularly heavy-set one, said something that set all her companions rolling in helpless mirth. Azarmi shook her head, which only made the old women laugh harder.

The Gaul offered her kavass from the skin Targitaus had laid aside. With no language in common, it was hard to put her at ease. She did not pull away when he touched her, but did not warm to him either.

So it proved later, too, when the bedding was spread round the banked fire. She was compliant and did not seem resentful, but he could not excite her. Piqued and disappointed, he thought hungrily of Seirem asleep a few feet away until he drifted off himself.

"My father has it from his grandfather," Arigh said, "that when the Arshaum first saw the Shaum, they took it for an arm of the sea."

"I believe it," Gorgidas said, looking down at the slate-blue river flowing majestically southwest toward the distant Mylasa Sea. He shaded his eyes; the reflection of the afternoon sun sparkled dazzlingly bright. He tried to guess how wide the river was, and failed—a mile and a half? Two miles? Whatever the answer, the Shaum made the Kouphis, the Arandos, any stream Gorgidas had seen in Gaul or Italy or Greece, into a pygmy by comparison.

He wiped his forehead with the back of his hand, felt grit rasp his skin. Goudeles, still foppish even in plains costume, brushed a bit of dry grass from his sleeve. "As if reaching this stream was not trial enough, however shall we cross it?" he asked no one in particular.

A good question, the Greek thought. The nearest ford would be hundreds of miles north. It would take a demigod to bridge the Shaum, and who on the wood-scarce steppe knew anything of boatbuilding?

Skylitzes bared his teeth in a smile. "How well do you swim, Pikridios?"

"Over that distance? At least as well as you, by Phos."

"The horses are better than either of you," Arigh said. "Come on." He led them down to the bank of the Shaum, dismounted and stripped, then climbed back on his horse. The rest of the embassy party did likewise. Arigh directed, "Ride your lead beast out until he has to swim, then slide off and keep a good grip round his neck. I'll go last; here, Psoes, you lead my string with yours. I'll take just the one animal and make sure nobody else's horses decide to stay on land." He drew his saber, tested the point with his thumb.

Gorgidas hefted the oiled leather sack in which he kept his precious manuscript. Catching the Arshaum's eye, he said, "I'll hold on with one hand—this has to stay dry." The nomad shrugged; if the Greek cared to take chances for the sake of some scratchings, that was his affair.

Surveying Goudeles' pudgy form, Lankinos Skylitzes said,

"You'll float better than I do, anyhow, pen-pusher." Goudeles sniffed.

Gorgidas twitched the reins and urged his mount forward. It tried to swerve when it realized he wanted it to go in the river, but he kicked it in the ribs and kept it on a straight course. It swung its head back resentfully. He booted it again. Like a bather testing the water with one toe, it stepped daintily in, then paused once more. *"Ithi!"* the exasperated Greek shouted in his own tongue. "Go on!" As he swung a foot free of the stirrups for another kick, the horse did.

It gave a frightened snort when its hooves no longer touched ground, but then struck out strongly for the far bank. Seen from only a few inches above the water, that seemed impossibly far away. Back on the eastern bank, a trooper's remount balked at entering the Shaum. Arigh prodded it with his sword. It neighed shrilly and bolted in, dragging the two beasts behind it along willy-nilly.

The Shaum's current was not as strong as Gorgidas had expected. It pulled the swimming horses and their masters south somewhat, making the journey across the river longer than it would have been, but did not really hamper their swim. The water was cool and very clear. The Greek could look down to the rocks and river plants on the bottom. About halfway through the crossing he started in alarm—the dun-colored fish rooting about on the bottom was longer from nose to wickedly forked tail than his horse was. "Shark!" he shouted.

"Nay, no sharks in the Shaum," Skylitzes reassured him. "They call it a mourzoulin hereabouts; the Videssian name is sturgeon."

"I don't care what they call it," the Greek said, frightened out of curiosity. "Does it bite?"

"No, it only has a little toothless sucker-mouth for worms and such."

"Salted, the eggs are very fine," Goudeles said with relish. "A rare delicacy."

"The flesh is good smoked," Prevalis Haravash's son added. "And from the swim bladder we make—what is the word for letting some light through?"

"Translucent," Goudeles supplied.

"Thank you, sir. Yes, we make translucent windows to fit into tent panels."

"And if it had a song, I suppose you'd use that, too," Gorgidas said darkly. The ugly brute still looked dangerous.

Prevalis took the Greek seriously. "On the plains we use everything. There is too little to waste." Gorgidas only grunted, keeping an eye on the sturgeon, or mourzoulin, or whatever it was. It paid him no attention. After a while, he could not see it any more.

By the time the western bank drew near, his arms were exhausted from holding the mouth of his leather bag above water, even though he had taken to switching it from one to the other. That also meant his grip on his horse was not what it should have been. The shore was only about thirty yards away when he and the animal parted company. He thrashed frantically—and felt his feet scrape bottom; the steppe pony was still too short to touch. Now it was his turn to help his horse. Sighing with relief, he did so, and led the beast and his remounts up onto the land of Shaumkhiil. Save that the river was behind him, it seemed no different from Pardraya to the east.

Skylitzes splashed ashore a few feet away from him. He reached into the bag and dug out a stylus. "How do you spell 'mourzoulin'?" he demanded. Looking resigned, Skylitzes told him.

Robes swirling about him, Avshar paced his tent like a caged panther. His great height and long strides made it seem cramped and tiny, built for a race of dwarfs. The sorcerer lashed out with a booted foot. A cushion flew across the tent, rebounded from the tight-stretched felt of the wall, and an image of a black-corseleted warrior hurling a brace of three-spiked thunderbolts thumped to the ground.

The wizard-prince swung round on Varatesh. "Incompetent!" he snarled. "Lackwitted, poxy maggot! You puling, milk-livered pile of festering dung, cutting your filthy heart out would be revenge too small for your botchery!"

They were alone; even in his rage, Avshar knew better than to revile the outlaw chief in front of his men. The wizard's contempt, the lash of his words, burned like fire. Varatesh bowed his head. More than anything else, he wanted the regard of this man, and bore abuse for which he would have killed any other.

But he reckoned himself slave to no one and said, "I was not the only one to make mistakes on this venture. The man you sent me after was not the one I found. He—"

Avshar dealt him a tremendous backhand buffet that stretched him in the dirt of the tent floor. He rose tasting blood, his head ringing. He slid into fighter's crouch. He had loved Kodoman, too, and Kodoman also stuck first . . . "Who are you, to use me so?" he whispered, tears stinging his eyes.

Avshar laughed, a laugh as black as the mail his icon showed. He swept aside the mantlings that always hid his face. "Well, worm," he said, "who am I?"

Varatesh whimpered and fell to his knees.

VII

"HERE," THEKLA ZONARA SAID, HANDING A SERVANT A silver candlestick. "This will fit in the load you're packing." When the man held it in confusion, she took it from him and stowed it away. "And this," she added, edging in beside it a gilded silver plate decorated with a hunting scene in low relief.

"We must save these, too," her sister-in-law Erythro cried, running up with an armload of brightly glazed earthenware cups. "They're too lovely to be left for the Namdaleni."

"Merciful Phos!" Sittas Zonaras said. "Why not pack up the pigs' swill troughs while you're about it? That's worthless junk; the islanders are welcome to it. There's little enough time for this move as is. Don't waste it worrying over excess baggage." He shook his head in mock annoyance.

"And don't you waste it bickering with Erythro," his daughter Ypatia told him.

The nobleman sighed and turned to Scaurus. "Women should never be allowed to be sensible, don't you think, outlander?"

Still holding her cups, Erythro faced up to the Roman like a pugnacious sparrow. "Why ask him? What does he know of sensible? He brought the Namdaleni down on us in the first place. Were it not for him, we'd still be snug here instead of trekking into the hills like so many Khamorth following their herds."

"Enough!" Sittas said; now his irritation was real. "Were it not for him, I'd be dead in the woods or captive with all the estate for ransom. Had you forgotten that?"

"Well, yes, I had," Erythro said, not a bit abashed. "This move has me all in a frenzy, and no wonder, too!" She bent and piled the cups on top of the candlestick and plate. Her brother rolled his eyes and looked pointedly at Ypatia, who pretended not to notice.

Though at first Marcus had thought Erythro's comment monumentally unfair, on reflection he was not so sure. Plenty of nobles in the westlands were coming to terms with the Namdaleni and the "Emperor" Mertikes. "You might have been able to do the same, Sittas, were it not for my men being here," the tribune finished. Erythro smirked.

"Don't encourage her," Zonaras said. He went on, "Me, make common cause with bandits and heretics? I'd sooner see this villa burned over my head than bend the knee to Drax and his straw man. Nay, I'm glad to be with you."

The villa might burn regardless, the tribune thought unhappily. For all their entrenching, for all the manpower Pakhymer and his Khatrishers added, if Drax threw the whole weight of his army against the legionaries, they would be crushed. And that full weight was coming; Pakhymer's scouts said the Namdalener column would cross the Arandos tomorrow. So it was retreat again, this time south into the hills.

Leaving the Zonarai still arguing over what was to go and what had to be left behind, Scaurus went outside. Lowing cattle and milling sheep streamed past; the herdsmen needed no urging to get their flocks out of the oncoming army's way. "Come on, keep them moving!" the chief herder was shouting. "No, Stotzas, don't let them drink now. Time enough for that later, when everyone's passed through."

Gaius Philippus, who already had the Romans ready to travel, watched the herder with respect. "He'd make a good officer," he said to the tribune.

Marcus had an inspiration. "Well, why not make him one, then? Who better to lead your irregulars?"

The senior centurion stared. "By the gods, sir, that's a triple six!" The two Romans smiled at each other briefly. In Videssian dice, sixes were the worst throw, not the best—the sort of little thing that left the legionaries permanently alien here. "You there!" Gaius Philippus called.

"You want me?" the herder chief said without turning his head. "Wait a bit." He deftly disentangled two flocks, sent them up separate passes so they would not compete for fodder. That done, he walked over to the Romans, nodded in the same respectful but unservile way he had to Zonaras. "Do something for you?"

"Yes, ah—" Marcus paused, not knowing his name.

"Tarasikodissa Simokattes," he said. Seeing the Romans flinch, he relented. "They call me Ras."

"And a good thing, too," Gaius Philippus muttered, but in Latin.

Scaurus felt much the same, but went on, "When you first saw us, you spoke of raising the countryside." Ras nodded again. "You know weapons, then?"

"Aye, somewhat. Bow, spear, axe. I'm no great shakes with a sword in my hand—not enough practice."

"Like to fight, do you?" Gaius Philippus asked.

"No." The answer was quick and definite.

The senior centurion beamed, the expression sitting oddly on his usually dour face. "You were right, Scaurus. I can use this one." He turned back to Simokattes. "How would you like to make a lot of Namdaleni wish they'd never been born?"

Ras studied him, his face as elaborately guileless as Gaius Philippus'. The two of them, bearded Videssian herdsman and Roman veteran, had a good deal in common, Marcus thought. But the senior centurion's bait was too tasty not to be nibbled. "Tell me more," Simokattes said.

Gaius Philippus smiled.

The senior centurion was less happy two mornings later, when he looked back on Zonaras' villa as the legionaries tramped up into the hills. "We should have torched the place," he said to Marcus. "It'll make Drax a lovely strong point."

"I know," the tribune said, "but if we did burn it, what would the highland nobles think they had to gain by siding with us? If we don't leave what they have unharmed, they'll see us as just another set of barbarians, bad as the Namdaleni."

"Maybe so," Gaius Philippus said, "but they don't have much use for us if they see us as weak, either." Scaurus grunted; there was too much truth in that for comfort. Would antagonizing Zonaras by destroying the villa do more harm than leaving Drax a base? He wished for a surer sense of when tactics had to override strategy.

"It's something you learn by doing it wrong every so often at first," Gaius Philippus said when he complained about that. The veteran added, "Of course, if your mistake is too big, it kills you, and you don't learn much after that."

"You always relieve my mind," Marcus said dryly. He saw a stir of motion to the north, at the head of the valley that sheltered Zonaras' villa. "We pulled out none too soon—here come the islanders. Think the rear guard will do any good?"

"Under young Tarasios? Not a chance." The senior centurion sounded regretful but certain. He called to a trooper, "You there, Florus—run fetch that herder fellow Ras back here. He ought to see this." The Roman saluted and trotted off.

The hectic flush of fever in his face, Tarasios Zonaras had refused to join the retreat to the hills. "No," he had said in the bubbling whisper that was all he had left of his voice, "here I stand. I have little enough time anyway. Fighting for my land is a faster and better end than I looked for." His kinsfolk had not been able to sway him, and Scaurus had not tried; his Stoic training taught that a man could decide when to let go of life. About a score of his father's troopers had chosen to stand with him.

Ras Simokattes came back with the Roman. "What is it, outlander?"

"Just watch," Gaius Philippus said.

The men of the Duchy, sensible veterans, fanned out into a skirmish line as they entered the valley, taking no chances on an ambush. Their advance quickened as they saw the abandoned legionary camp, and looked up into the hills and spied their opponents' withdrawing column.

They were close to the villa when Tarasios and his followers burst from the cover of a stand of apple trees and charged, sabers gleaming as they spurred their horses forward. In the distance everything was tiny and silent and perfect, a realistic painting that somehow moved. An islander toppled from his saddle, then another. But the Namdaleni, after a panicky moment, fought back. More and more knights rode up, to ring Tarasios' band with steel.

Simokattes' glance flicked to the young Zonaras' kin. His face carved by harsh lines of grief, Sittas watched the unequal fight; now and again his hands twitched on his horse's reins as he pantomimed a blow that should be struck. His wife and daughter wordlessly embraced, while Erythro wept. The herder-chief, his own strong rough hands curling into fists, gave his attention back to the battle below. It was already almost over.

"What do you see?" Gaius Philippus asked him.

"A brave man," Simokattes replied quietly.

"Aye, maybe so, but a stupid one regardless." Simokattes turned in anger, but the senior centurion went on as earnestly as Marcus had ever heard him. "Think on it, Ras, and think well. Soon enough it'll be you leading men against the islanders, and not ones with the skill or arms Tarasios had behind him. What did he do? He broke cover instead of fighting from it, and he attacked a great many men with a few instead of the other way round. Brave? What good was his bravery to him—or to the troopers who followed him?" In the valley, no Videssians were still horsed. "The task is to hurt the enemy, not your own men."

The chief herdsman was silent for some time. At last he said, "You're a hard man, Roman."

"That's as may be, but I've been at this filthy trade thirty-odd years now and I know what's so. This is what you signed on for, you and your talk of raising the countryside. If you haven't the stomach for it, go back to your cows."

Simokattes swung at him, a blow born largely of frustration. With unhurried quickness, Gaius Philippus ducked and stepped forward, at the same time seizing the herder's arm and twisting it behind his back until he gasped with pain. The senior centurion let him go at once, slapped him on the shoulder. "What you think of me is your affair, but listen to me. It'll save your neck one day." Simokattes gave a brusque nod and walked away.

"He'll do," Gaius Philippus said, watching his back.

"Did you have to be so hard on him?" the tribune asked.

"I think so. Amateurs come to this business with all sorts of stupid ideas."

Marcus' own bitter knowledge, gained the past three years, made him add, "Precious little room for gallantry, is there?"

"That for gallantry." The senior centurion spat in the dust. "It wasn't Achilles who took Troy." Scaurus stared; if Gaius Philippus, with hardly a letter to his name, could draw lessons from Homer, he was the prince of poets indeed!

Judging from what Drax had done in the past, the tribune thought he would try to seal off the passes leading south, but not do any serious campaigning in the hills south of the Arandos. But the great count, perhaps seeing final victory just ahead of him, showed more aggressiveness than Scaurus expected of him. Not only did quick motte-and-bailey forts got up in well-placed spots at valley mouths and on hillsides, but Namdalener patrols slashed into the hill country, looting and burning right up to the legionaries' heels.

Marcus did not need Sittas Zonaras' reproachful gaze to tell him he had to stop that quickly, if he could. If the islanders could raid where they chose, what use for the Videssians to back the legionaries against them? He thought for a while, then went to see Laon Pakhymer.

The Khatrisher was firing grapes at a miniature motte-and-bailey made of dirt and sticks. "I wish it were that easy," Scaurus said; Pakhymer's toy catapult was doing a good job of destruction.

"It's simpler when they don't shoot back," Pakhymer agreed, taking careful aim. He touched the trigger; the little catapult bucked. A bit of wood flew from the castle on the bailey. Marcus waited with increasing impatience as the Khatrisher reloaded. At last Pakhymer looked up, a sly smile on his pockmarked face. "Ready to burst yet?"

The tribune had to laugh at his impudence. "Not quite."

"I was afraid you'd say that. You expect my lads to earn what they got at Kyzikos, then? Aye, do you; I can see it in your eyes. What is it this time?"

Marcus told him. He tugged at his unkempt beard as he

considered. "Yes, that could happen, if we have a proper guide riding with us."

"I'll see to it Simokattes gets you one."

"All right, you're on. Three days from now, you said?" At Scaurus' nod, the Khatrisher remarked, "The problem, as I see it, will be not biting off too big a chunk."

"Exactly." As usual, the tribune thought, Pakhymer had a keen sense of what was required—and not much inclination to use it. The Khatrisher examined another grape. He shook his head sadly. "Not round enough," he said, and ate it. "Care for one?" He laughed when Marcus pretended not to hear.

Scaurus thought the fat green bush he was crouching behind was wild parsley. Whatever it was, its little pale yellow flowers were pungent enough to make his eyes water. He bit down hard on his upper lip to keep from sneezing. Nothing was happening yet, but if he started he did not think he could stop, and it would be soon now.

Half a dozen Khatrishers entered the valley, spurring their little ponies for all they were worth. Now and again one would turn to fire at the men of the Duchy close behind.

The Namdalener leader was a stocky youngster named Grus. Though young, he had learned caution; he ordered his double squadron to halt and craned his neck to study the canyon walls. But Ras Simokattes and Gaius Philippus had set their trap well. Though Junius Blaesus' maniple lay in wait for the islanders to advance, no telltale glint of sun off steel, no untoward motion gave them away. Grus whooped and waved his men on.

Hand clutching sword, Marcus waited until all the Namdaleni, even the rear guard, had entered the valley. He nodded to the buccinator beside him. The cornet blared, a single long note. With cries of "Gavras!" legionaries leaped from behind shrubs and tree trunks and stands of brush and dashed down the steep-sloping canyon walls at the islanders.

The two knights of the rear guard brutally jerked their horses round and started up the valley again—not cowardice but sense, to bring help to their mates. A *pilum* thudded into the belly of one beast. It crashed to the ground, screaming, and rolled over its rider. The other horseman was nearly at the mouth of the canyon when three legionaries pulled him out of the saddle.

Grus, cursing, tried to pull his men into a circle. But one Roman came rushing down toward them, far ahead of his comrades. It was Titus Pullo; he bellowed, "Come on, Vorenus! We'll see which of us is the better man!" Another legionary bolted out of the pack; Lucius Vorenus was pounding after his rival and swearing at the top of his lungs.

Pullo cast his *pilum* at very long range, but his throw was true; a Namdalener on the fringe of Grus' milling circle took the javelin in his thigh. He screamed and fell from his horse. Pullo darted forward to finish him off and strip his corpse, but a pair of islanders covered their wounded comrade. One of them rammed his own heavy lance clean through the thick wood and leather of the Roman's *scutum*. The iron point caught the buckle of his sword belt and twisted it to one side; when he reached for the *gladius* he grabbed only air. The Namdaleni rained sword strokes on him. He went over on his back to get the most use from his fouled shield.

Then Lucius Vorenus, in a berserk fury Viridovix might have envied, was on the islanders, screaming, "Get off him, you pimps, you dogs, you bleeding vultures! He's a fig-sucker, but even a fig-sucking Roman's worth the lot of you!" He killed the Namdalener who had thrust his spear at Pullo, beating the man's light kite-shaped shield aside with his own heavier one and then stabbing him in the side at the join in his shirt and mail.

The second islander and one of his countrymen, perhaps thinking Pullo dead and out of the fight, turned all their attention to Vorenus, who was hard-pressed to defend himself. But Pullo was far from dead. Having finally managed to draw his sword, he cast aside his worthless *scutum*, scrambled to his feet, and jabbed the *gladius* into a horse's rump. Blood spurting, the beast bucketed away, its rider clinging to its neck and trying in vain to bring it under control.

"Bastard!" Vorenus panted.

"You're the whore's get, not me!" Pullo retorted. They fought back-to-back, raving at each other all the while. By then the rest of the Romans were reaching the Namdaleni, and the pressure on the two of them eased.

Trapped, outnumbered, pelted by javelins, the islanders

began surrendering one after the other. But Grus, mortified at falling into the ambush, came rushing at Marcus on foot; his horse was down, hamstrung by a *gladius*. "Yield yourself!" the Roman called.

"To the ice with you!" Grus shouted, almost crying with age and chagrin. The tribune raised his shield against a whirlwind attack. Grus must have been drawing on the same furious energy that powered Vorenus and Pullo; he struck and struck and struck, as if driven by clockwork. He paid no thought to defense. More than once he left himself open to a killing blow, but Marcus held back. The little battle was already won, and the Namdalener officer might be worth more as prisoner than corpse.

Gaius Philippus bent, found a stone of good hand-filling size. He let fly at close range; the rock clanked off the side of grus' conical helmet. The Namdalener staggered, dropped his guard. Marcus and the senior centurion wrestled him to the ground and disarmed him. "Nice throw," the tribune said.

"I saw you didn't want to kill him."

Ras Simokattes looked in confusion from the two officers to where Pullo and Vorenus were accepting their comrades' praise. "What are you foreigners, anyway?" he asked Scaurus. "Here you two go out of your way to keep from letting the air out of this one—" He nudged Grus with his foot. "—while that pair yonder's a couple of bloodthirsty madmen."

The tribune glanced over to the two rival legionaries. Junius Blaesus was congratulating them now. Marcus frowned; the junior centurion seemed unable to see past the obvious, something the tribune had noticed before. He turned back to Simokattes. "Bide a moment, Ras. You'll see what we are." Then, to the Romans: "Pullo, Vorenus—over here, if you would."

The troopers exchanged apprehensive looks. They broke away at once from their mates, came to attention before Scaurus. "I hope your rivalry is done," he said mildly. "Now each of you has saved the other; that should be plenty to put you at quits." He spoke Videssian, for the chief herdsman's benefit.

"Yes, sir," they said together, and actually sounded as if they meant it.

"To say it was bravely done would be to waste words. I'm glad the both of you came through alive."

"Thank you, sir," Pullo said, smiling; Vorenus relaxed with him.

"No one said at ease, you!" Gaius Philippus rasped. The legionaries stiffened. The apprehension returned to their faces.

"Both of you are fined a week's pay for breaking ranks in the charge," Scaurus went on, no longer mild. "Not only do you endanger yourselves by bringing your feud along to combat, you also gamble with your comrades' safety. Never again—d'you understand me?"

"Aye, sir," they answered, both very low.

"What were you playing at?" Gaius Philippus demanded. "You might as well have been a couple of Gauls over there." That was his worst condemnation for disorderly soldiers; Vorenus flushed, while Pullo shuffled his feet like a small, naughty boy. Both were a far cry from the ferocious warriors of a few minutes before. When Scaurus dismissed them, they went quietly back to their comrades.

"Well, what are we, Ras?" the tribune asked Simokattes.

"A pack of bastards, if you want to know," Grus said from the ground.

"Quiet, you," Gaius Philippus said.

Simokattes had watched in disbelief as the Romans took their dressing-down; he had never known soldiers trained to such obedience. He scratched his head, rubbed at a leathery cheek. "Damned if I could tell you, but I'm glad you're not against me."

"Bah!" said Grus.

Isolated in the southeastern hills, Marcus longed for news of the wider world, but had all but given up hope of having any when an imperial messenger, a dapper, foxy-faced little man, made his way through the Namdaleni and was scooped up by a Khatrisher patrol. "Karbeas Antakinos, I'm called," he said when they brought him to the tribune. His sharp eyes flicked round the legionary camp, missing nothing.

"Good to see you, good to see you," Marcus said, pumping his hand.

"Very good to be here, let me tell you," the courier said. His speech had the quick, staccato rhythm of the capital. "The ride was hellish—damned Gamblers all over the lot." He used the Videssians' insulting nickname for the men of the Duchy, who returned the favor by calling the imperials Cocksures. The Roman swallowed a sigh; he had no patience for the bickering between Phos' sects.

He also remembered Drax' gift for treachery. "Let me have your bona fides," he said to Antakinos.

"Yes indeed." The Videssian rubbed his hands together briskly. "I was to ask you his Imperial Majesty's opinion of hot-tempered women."

Scaurus relaxed; Thorisin had used that recognition signal before. "That they're great fun, but wearing."

"Has a point, does he?" Antakinos chuckled. He had an easy laugh that went well with his resonant tenor. "I remember a girl named Panthia—but that's another story. To business: how do you stand here?"

"It's stalemate, for now. The islanders don't go poking their noses into these hills any more, not after a couple of little lessons we taught them, but I can't get loose, either. There's too many of them down here. Can Gavras draw them off?"

The messenger grimaced. "Not a prayer. He just led two regiments to Opsikion, opposite the Duchy, to fight off a Namdalener landing there."

"Bloody wonderful," Gaius Philippus said. "I suppose we might have known it was coming."

"Aye," Antakinos said. "Phos be praised it's only freebooters and not the Duke. Speaking of which, pirates from the Duchy have shown up off the westlands, too. Three days before I set out, Leimmokheir came into port after chasing four of them away and sinking a fifth. And you can be sure more than those are lurking about."

"By the gods," Scaurus said, dismayed into Latin. He returned to the imperial tongue. "You're telling me, then, that we are as great a force as the Avtokrator has left."

"In essence, yes," the courier agreed unhappily. "In truth, I'll be glad to tell him how strong you are. After the, ah, misfortune at the Sangarios, he feared all of Zigabenos' army had been destroyed or turned traitor with its general." Damn the great count Drax, Marcus thought, while Antakinos finished, "But you do not have the look of defeated men to you."

"I should hope not," Gaius Philippus snorted.

Laon Pakhymer walked up in time to hear the last exchange. "No indeed," he said, eyes twinkling, "for your men fear you worse than Drax. All he can do is kill them." The senior centurion snorted again, but did not seem displeased.

"You traveled through the lands the islanders hold," Marcus said to Antakinos. "How are the folk there taking to their rule?"

"Interesting question." Antakinos eyed him with respect. "Thinking of stirring them up, maybe? His Majesty said you were a tricksy one. Well, here's how it is: out in the countryside they'd take kindly to roasting Gamblers over a slow fire, the peasants 'cause they steal and the nobles because some of their number have been dispossessed to give their estates to men from the Duchy." The messenger pursed his lips. "The towns, I fear, are the other way round. Drax takes tribute from 'em, aye, but less than they paid Videssos—and the townsfolk count on the Namdaleni to protect them from the Yezda."

Laon Pakhymer shook his head very slightly, but Antakinos noticed and raised a curious eyebrow. To Scaurus' relief, the Khatrisher did not explain himself. That ploy still made the tribune's hackles rise.

"Well, what if there's more of the sods coming by than we thought when we laid the ambush?" The speaker was a tall, lanky farmer in rough homespun and a thick leather jerkin. He clutched his boar spear uncertainly.

Gaius Philippus held onto his patience with both hands. These raw Videssian recruits had neither Roman discipline nor the impetuosity of the Spaniards Sertorius had forged into so dangerous a guerilla army. But all the two hundred or so men hunkered down around him were volunteers, either refugees from the lowlands or hillmen who wanted more of soldiering than squabbling with the noble a couple of valleys over.

The senior centurion said to his listeners, "You don't need me to answer a question like that. Who'll tell him?" A score of hands rose, Ras Simokattes' first. Gaius Philippus pretended not to see Zonaras' chief herdsman. "You, there—yes, you with the gray streak in your hair."

The man stood, clasped his hands behind his back and dipped his head, as if to some half-forgotten childhood teacher. "If there's too many, we stay in hiding," he said diffidently. A light hunting bow was at his feet.

"That's the way of it!" Gaius Philippus approved. "And don't be ashamed to do it, either. Unless the odds are all with you, don't get gay with the islanders. They have better gear than you and they know what to do with it, too. Just like me." He grinned a lazy grin.

Watching the lesson, Marcus saw the veteran's would-be marauders sober as they remembered his demonstration of a couple of days before. In full panoply, he had invited any four of his pupils to come at him with the hand-weapons they had. The fight did not last long. Reversing his *pilum*, he knocked the wind out of one assailant, ducked the scythe-stroke of another and broke the spearshaft over his head. Whirling, he let the third Videssian's club whack into his shield, then hit him under the chin with the *scutum*'s metal-faced edge. Even as the man sank, Gaius Philippus was drawing his sword and sidling toward his last foe, who carried a short pike. The fellow was brave enough, rushing forward to jab at the Roman, but Gaius Philippus, graceful as a dancer, stepped inside the thrust and tapped him on the chest with his sword. Two men unconscious, one helpless on the ground, the fourth white-faced and shaking—not bad, for a minute's work.

A good dozen men slipped out of camp that night.

But for the ones who stayed, the senior centurion was proving a better teacher than Scaurus had expected. In fact, he showed a zest for the assignment he did not always bring to his ordinary duties. Like any job, those had become largely routine as the years went by. The new role seemed to take him back to his youth, and he plunged into it with more enthusiasm than the tribune had seen from him since they knew each other.

The veteran was saying, "Make your strike, do as much mischief as you can, and get away fast. Sometimes it doesn't hurt to ditch your weapons." That would have been blasphemous advice to give to full-time soldiers. But to guerillas, it made sense. "Without 'em, who's to know who you are?"

"And when they chase us?" someone asked.

"Scatter, of course. And if you get out of sight for a minute or two, you can stop running. Just bend down in a field and pull weeds like you belonged there. They'll ride past you every time." Gaius Philippus' smile was altogether without the cynical cast it usually bore. "You can have a lot of fun at this business."

Marcus dug a finger into his ear. The senior centurion, as hardened a professional as ever lived, calling soldiering fun? Reliving one's youth was all very well, but from Gaius Philippus that seemed like second childhood.

Ruelm Ranulf's son was pleased with himself as he and his squad of Namdaleni rode south toward the hills where resistance still simmered against his liege lord Drax. Not for a moment did he think of himself as subject to any Emperor Zigabenos. That piece of play-acting was for the Videssians to chew on.

He paused to light a torch. Twilight was almost gone, but he wanted to keep moving. With luck, he could join Bailli by midnight. That was what pleased him; when he'd set out from Kyzikos, he had expected to be on the road another day, but the ford over the Arandos that gaffer had shown him saved hours skirting the bank looking for a bridge and then doubling back. He touched his wallet. It had been well worth the goldpiece, and the old man looked as though he hadn't seen many lately.

A moth flew in tight circles round his torch. The night was warm and very still; he could hear the faint whirr of its wings. A bat swooped out of the blackness, snatched the bug, and was gone almost before he was sure he'd seen it.

"Damned flittermouse," he said, making the sun-sign on his breast to ward off the evil omen. His men did the same. The Namdaleni called bats "Skotos' chickens," for without the dark god's help, how could they see to fly so unerringly by night?

As the hills came nearer, stands of brush and shadowy clumps of trees grew more common than they had been north of the Arandos. That rich low plain was the most intensively farmed and most productive land Ruelm had ever seen. By the austere standards of the duchy, even this was plenty fine enough.

A lapwing piped in the undergrowth to the side of the roads. "Pee-wit!" it said, following the call with a long whistle. Ruelm was mildly surprised to hear a day bird so long after dusk. Then the first arrow whispered out of the night, and the knight behind him swore in startlement and pain as it stuck in his calf.

For a second Ruelm sat frozen—no enemies were supposed to be here. The Romans and the Videssian and Khatrisher ragtag and bobtail clinging to their skirts had been driven well up into the hills.

Another arrow hissed past his face, so close a rough feather of the fletching tickled his cheek. Suddenly he was soldier again. He threw the torch as far as he could—whoever these night-runners were, no sense lighting a target for them. He was drawing his sword as they broke cover and rushed.

He slashed out blindly, still half dazzled by the torchlight, felt the blade bite. Behind him, the trooper who was first wounded yelled as he was dragged from the saddle; his cry cut off abruptly. Others replaced it—backcountry Videssian voices shouting in mixed triumph and, he would have taken oath, fear.

The darkness gave the savage little fight a nightmare quality. Whirling his horse round to go to the aid of his men, Ruelm saw his foes as shifting black shadows, impossible to count, almost impossible to strike.

"Drax!" he shouted, and tasted sour fear in his mouth when only two men answered.

A hand pulled at his thigh. He kicked at his assailant; though his boot met only air, the man skipped back. He roweled his horse's flank with his spurs. The gelding reared, whinnying. Well-trained as a warhorse, it lashed out with iron-shod hooves. A man's skull shattered like a smashed melon; a bit of brain, warm, wet, and sticky, splashed on Ruelm's forehead, just below his helmet.

Then, with a great scream, the gelding foundered. As he kicked free of the stirrups, Ruelm heard a Videssian cry, "Hamstrung, by Phos!" Boots and bare feet scuffed in the dirt of the roadway as more came running up like so many jackals.

The islander lit rolling and started to scramble to his feet, but a club smashed against the chain-mail neckguard that hung from his helm. Stunned, he fell to his knees and then to his belly. His sword was torn away; greedy hands ripped at the fastenings of his hauberk. He groaned and tried to reach for his dagger. "'Ware!" someone shouted. "He's not done yet!"

A harsh chuckle. "We'll fix that!" Still dazed, he felt rough fingers grope under his chin, jerk his head back. "Jist like a sheep," the Videssian said. The knife stung, but not for long.

Accompanied by Sittas Zonaras and Gaius Philippus, Scaurus walked toward the truce-site Bailli of Ecrisi had suggested. "Here, Minucius," the tribune said, pausing, "this is close enough for you and your squad." The young underofficer saluted; they were a good bowshot away from where Bailli and a pair of his lieutenants were waiting. A double handful of dismounted Namdaleni lounged on the ground a similar distance north of their leaders.

"Hello, islander," Scaurus called as he came up. "What do we need to talk about?"

But Bailli was not the suave, self-assured officer who had delivered Drax' proclamation a few weeks before. "You scum," he snarled, his neck corded with fury. "For two coppers I'd stake you out for the crows. I thought you a man of honor." He spat at the Roman's feet.

"If I'm not, why risk a parley with me? We're enemies, true, but there's no need to hate each other."

"Go howl, you and your pretty talk," Bailli said. "We took you and yours for honest mercenaries, men who'd do their best for him who pays them, aye, but not stoop to such foulness as you're wading in. Murders in the night, tavern stabbings, maimed horses, thefts to drive a man mad—"

"Why blame us?" Marcus asked. "First off, you know we Romans don't war like that—as I say, you must, or you'd not be here talking with me. And second, even if we did, we couldn't, for it's you who pinned us back in these hills."

"Seems someone in the flatlands isn't fond of you," Gaius Philippus said, as casually as if remarking on the weather.

Bailli was near the bursting point. "All right! All right! Loose your stupid peasants, if that's how you care to play this game. We'll root them out if we have to chip down every tree and burn every cottage from here back to the city. And then we'll come back to deal with you, and you'll wish for what we gave your cowardly skulkers."

Gaius Philippus said nothing, but an eyebrow twitched. To Bailli it could have meant anything; to Marcus, it showed he was not worried by the threat.

"Will there be anything more, Bailli?" the tribune asked.

"Just this," the Namdalener officer said heavily. "At the Sangarios you fought your men as well as you could and as cleanly, too. Then afterwards in the talks over your exchange scheme, you were gracious even when they did not turn out as you wanted. So why this?"

The honest perplexity in his voice deserved a straight answer. Marcus thought for a moment, then said, "'Doing me best,' as you call it, is all very well, but it's not my job. My job is to hold things together, and one way or another I intend to do it."

He treasured the look of unreserved approval Gaius Philippus gave him, but knew he had made no sense to Bailli. Roman stubbornness was a trait without counterpart in this world; neither sly Videssians, happy-go-lucky Khatrishers, nor proud upstart Namdaleni fully appreciated it.

Yet Bailli was no fool. Just as Scaurus had quoted him, now he threw the tribune's words back in his face. "'One way or another,' is it? How much thanks do you think you'll win from the Empire's nobles, outlanders, if you teach the assassin's trade to peasants with manure between their toes?" He looked Zonaras in the eye. "And you, sirrah. When you go out to collect your rents, will you feel safe riding past any bush big enough for a man to hide behind?"

"Safer than when your bravoes set on me," the Videssian retorted, but he tugged thoughtfully at his beard all the same.

"You remind me of the man in the story, who threw himself on the fire because he was chilly. On your head be it—and it probably will." Bailli turned back to Scaurus. "We buried that northbound rider of yours—Antakinos, wasn't it?"

If he knew the name, he was not bluffing. Marcus wondered how many couriers had been taken before they ever reached him. "Did you?" he said. "Well, *vale*—farewell!"

Bailli grunted, plainly hoping for some larger reaction. He nodded to his lieutenants, who had been glowering at the tribune and his comrades with even less liking than their leader showed. "Come on; we've given him his warning, and more than he deserves." With almost legionary precision, the Namdaleni turned on their heels and tramped back to their waiting knights.

As Scaurus, Gaius Philippus, and Zonaras moved toward

Minucius' guard squad, the senior centurion had all he could do to keep from smirking. "That one'll be the best recruiter we ever had. There's nothing like seeing your farm torn to bits and your neighbors killed to give you the idea of which side you should be on."

"Aye, likely so," Marcus said, but abstractedly. Bailli's jab over the consequences of encouraging a guerilla among the Videssian peasantry troubled him more than he had shown the islander. When he gave Gaius Philippus a free hand, he had not thought past the immediate goal of making Drax' life miserable. He was doing that, no doubt; Bailli's spleen was a good measure of it. But the Namdalener, blast him, was right—the marauders who took up arms against the men of the Duchy would not magically unlearn their use once the war was done. How long before they realized a disliked landowner or imperial tax-agent bled as red as an islander?

Zonaras might have been reading his thoughts. He clapped the tribune on the back, saying, "I don't expect to be bushwhacked tomorrow, Scaurus, no, nor next year either."

"I'm glad," Marcus answered. He consoled himself by thinking that in Videssos, as in Rome, the great landowners were too powerful. Their grip needed loosening. The Empire had been stronger when it relied on its freeholding peasantry than now, with the provincial nobles at odds with the pen-pushers in the capital, and with the state's defenses in the hands of unreliable mercenaries like the Namdaleni—or the Romans.

But that evening Pakhymer laughed at him when he retorted what Bailli had said. "And you were the one who got huffy at me for doing what needed doing with the Yezda."

"There's a difference," Marcus insisted.

"In a pig's arse," the Khatrisher said cheerfully; the tribune had known he would not see it. "You load your side of the Balance as heavily as you can, then hope for the best." Orthodox Videssian thought held that Phos would one day vanquish his wicked rival Skotos. Pakhymer's folk, whose very nation sprang from the chaos of barbarian invasion, were not so optimistic. In their view the fight between good and evil was evenly matched, thus the metaphor of the balance. To the imperials, even to the Namdaleni, it was foul heresy. Independent as always, the Khatrishers clung to it regardless.

Marcus was glad he was indifferent to theology.

Gaius Philippus had come to respect Pakhymer's opinions; the pockmarked little cavalry commander had a habit of being right. Picking a bit of raisin out from between his teeth, he said to Scaurus, "You're the one who keeps track of these cursed imperial politics, sir. Will they see us as ogres for using their clients to fight the islanders?"

"Only the ones who are ogres themselves, is my guess. They're the ones who have something to fear." Marcus eyed the veteran curiously; such worries were unlike him. "Why should it trouble you?"

"No reason, really," the senior centurion said, but his sheepish smile rang false. Marcus waited. Gaius Philippus stumbled on, "After all, what with the Yezda and Zemarkhos' fanatics between here and Aptos, likely no trouble from this would ever reach there."

"Aptos?" The Romans had wintered there after Maragha, but it was more than a year since they left the small town, and Scaurus had hardly thought of it since.

Gaius Philippus seemed to regret opening his mouth in the first place. The tribune thought he was going to clam up, but he plunged ahead: "The local noble's widow there—what was her name? Nerse Phorkaina, that was it—is a fine lady. What with raising up her son, and the Yezda, and Zemarkhos' holy war against everything, I'd rather she didn't think we'd given her a new headache. That would be a poor return for good guesting."

"So it would," Marcus agreed solemnly. What was her name, indeed, he thought. He was sure Gaius Philippus remembered everything there was to remember about Phorkos' widow, down to what stones she favored in her rings. But the senior centurion was so used to despising women that Scaurus doubted he would ever admit feeling otherwise, even to himself.

The short-hafted axe bit into the black mulberry's trunk again and again. Chips flew. Bryennios the woodcutter grunted in satisfaction as the tree began to totter. Long years of use had polished the axe handle smooth as a maiden's skin beneath his callused palms. He walked round to the other side of the mulberry, deepened his undercut with a few strokes, then went back to the main cut. He grunted again. Sure enough, he'd be able to drop the tree in the space where the old alder had stood until the storm three winters past. That would make chopping it into timber so much easier.

The breeze shifted, bringing with it the sharp odor of wood smoke. Bryennios made another wordless noise, this one anything but pleasant—it was not Tralles the charcoal-burner at work. Houses in his hamlet were going up in flames. He could hear women wailing in the distance, and Namdaleni shouting to each other.

As if thinking of the men of the Duchy had conjured them up, three came riding toward him down the forest track. "You, there!" one shouted; his lazy island accent swallowed the last *r*. Bryennios sneered, but to himself. The Namdaleni were all armored and carried their long lances at the ready. The woodcutter swung his axe again. The mulberry groaned. A few more strokes and it would fall.

"Belay that!" the islander shouted. The seaman's word meant nothing to Bryennios, who had seen no water greater than a pond, but the sense was plain. He lowered the axe.

Pretending not to, he eyed the Namdaleni as they approached. Two might have been Videssians for looks had they not shaved; the third was fair-haired, with eyes of a startling green. All of them were big, strapping men, overtopping him by half a head or more, but his shoulders were wider than theirs, his arms thick with muscle from his trade.

"What do you want of me?" he asked. "I have work to do—more work, thanks to the lot of you." He did not bother hiding his bitterness.

The older of the two dark Namdaleni, their spokesman, wiped at his forehead with the sleeve of his green surcoat. Soot and rusty sweat came away in a short clean streak. The rest of his face was filthy. "You want to be spared such visits, eh?" he said.

Bryennios looked at him as at any idiot. "Who would not?"

"A point." The islander smiled thinly. "Well, we aren't pleased to have a supply wagon torched and two guards knocked over the head. Have any ideas about whose clever scheme that was? We'd pay well to learn his name."

The woodcutter shrugged, spread his hands. The Namdalener snarled in disgust, mockingly imitated his gesture. "You see how it is, then. If we can't find out who these rebels are, we have to teach everyone the price of sheltering them." Bryennios shrugged again.

"You mi' as well talk to the clot's axe," the blond islander said. "It'd tell you more." His emerald stare stabbed at Bryennios; the down-pointing bar nasal on his helmet gave him the aspect of a brooding falcon. At last he jerked hard on his horse's reins, wheeling the beast around. His comrades followed.

Bryennios attacked the mulberry again. After a few savage swings it fell just where he had known it would. He stepped forward to lop off the bigger branches. He muttered a short prayer of thanks that the men of the Duchy had not taken the blond knight's sour advice and examined his axe. The dark red crusted stain at the top of the handle did not come from sap.

"Why are they pulling out? I haven't a clue," the Khatrisher scout said to Scaurus, as cheeky as any of his people. "You want whys, see a magician. Whats I'm pretty good at, and I tell you the Namdaleni are breaking camp."

The tribune fumbled in his pouch, tossed the horseman a goldpiece. "Whatever the reason, good news deserves a reward." The Khatrisher made it disappear before Marcus thumped his forehead at his folly. "After Kyzikos, you should be paying me."

"It won't go to waste, even so." The Khatrisher grinned smugly.

The tribune rode back to his vantage point with him. No great horseman, Scaurus blessed the stirrups that gave him a fighting chance to stay on the large, unreliable beast between his thighs.

A glance from the hilltop crag told him the scout was right. Bailli's Namdaleni had used the legionary camp by Zonaras' villa as their own main base. Now it lay deserted; Marcus reached the observation post in time to see the last of the Namdalener column ride north out of the valley. Even at some distance, he could see how tightly bunched they were—a hostile countryside was the best argument against straggling.

Watching the retreat as he was, he took a while to notice that a garrison still held Zonaras' strong-walled home. So it proved over the next few days all along the line the islanders had set up to contain the legionaries. Their striking force was gone, but they still stood strongly on the defensive.

When the riders who did sneak past the Namdalener forts reported that the main body of islanders was hurrying northwest toward Garsavra, Laon Pakhymer looked so pleased with himself that Marcus wanted to throttle him. "You see, even the Yezda can be useful," the Khatrisher general said. "One man's trouble is the next fellow's chance."

"Hmmp," Scaurus said. He still hoped the men of the Duchy would smash the Yezda, though he had to admit he would not be brokenhearted to see them weakened in the smashing. He did not mean to sit idly by while they battled. If a couple of the islanders' motte-and-baileys fell, the way would open for the legionaries to go down into the coastal plain once more. The hills made a good refuge, but nothing would be decided here—and the lush lowlands were much better able to feed any army. He was sick of barley and lentils, and even those were running low.

Naturally, Zonaras wanted his villa to be the first strong point freed, but the tribune had to tell him no—its approaches were too open, and the building itself too strong. The elderly noble shook his head ruefully. "There's praise I could do without."

Marcus chose several more likely targets to attack. For himself he picked a fort that was new Namdalener construction, a few miles west of Zonaras' holding. The valley it sat in was a guerilla center; strife between them and the islander garrison had made many of the local peasants flee, and the men of the Duchy were working their fields. Looking out from between the branches of an almond grove, the tribune thought they were doing a good job of it, too.

There was no signal. When he judged the moment ripe, Pakhymer sent a few dozen horsemen riding hell-for-leather into the valley. They trampled through the rich green fields, slashing the growing grain with their sabers to leave as wide a track of destruction as they could. Some carried smoking torches, which they hurled here and there. Others darted toward the small flock of sheep grazing just outside the motte and started driving them into the hills.

From a quarter mile away, Marcus could hear the roars of outrage in the fort, could see men running about on the wall and shooting a few useless arrows at the pillagers outside. Then a wooden gangboard thudded down over the deep moat. Knights stormed over it, their horses' hooves echoing thunderously. Peering through the leaves, the tribune counted them as they came. Thirty-eight, thirty-nine . . . his spies' best guess was that the castle held fifty or so.

While panicked sheep ran every which way, the Khatrishers regrouped to meet the threat, using their ponies' quickness and agility for all they were worth. They peppered their heavily armored foes with arrows; Scaurus saw an islander clap his hands to his face and slide back over his horse's tail. Two of Pakhymer's men rushed toward a Namdalener who had gotten separated from his mates, one to either side. Watching from concealment, the tribune bit his lip. What would it take to convince the Khatrishers they could not stand up against islanders in close combat? Covering his left side with his shield, the Namdalener chopped the man on his right from the saddle, then used a clever backhanded stroke to send the other reeling away with a gashed forearm. The rest of the islanders shouted to applaud the feat of arms.

As if their morale was broken, the raiding party sped toward the hills, the men of the Duchy pounding after them. Now the Khatrishers' light horses were not putting out quite their best speed; they seemed unable to pull away from the islanders' ponderous chargers. Yelling and brandishing their lances, the Namdaleni held hotly to the pursuit.

Scaurus watched the gap between islanders and fortress increase. He turned to the maniple which had spent an uncomfortable night with him under the almonds. "All right, lads, at the trot!" he shouted. They burst from concealment and rushed toward the castle, carrying hurdles and bundles of brush to fill the moat.

They were almost halfway there before any of the Namdaleni spied them approaching from the side; the riders were intent on the chase, while the handful still inside the fortress had no eyes for anything but their comrades. Then one of the men on the earthwork wall let out a horrified bellow. The tribune was close enough to see mouths drop open in dismay. Islanders darted toward the gangboard, to drag it up before the legionaries reached it. Scaurus bared his teeth in a grin; he had not counted on that much luck.

The thick oak planks were heavy, and the passage of horses and mail-clad knights had driven the wooden bridge deep into the soft earth of the rampart. Marcus heard the islanders grunting and swearing with effort, but the outer edge of the gangboard had hardly moved when his *caligae* thudded onto it.

He dashed forward, doing his best not to think of the moat that yawned below. An islander, his nails broken and hands black with dirt, gave up the futile effort to shift the bridge and stepped out onto it, drawing his sword as he did. Marcus' own Gallic longsword was already in his hand. "Horatius, is it?" he panted. But unlike the span the legendary Roman hero had held against the Etruscans, this one was wide enough for three or four men to fight abreast. Before more Namdaleni could join the first quick-thinking one, Scaurus assailed him from the front, Minucius from the left, and another Roman from the right. He defended himself bravely, but three against one was a fight that could only last seconds. The soldier toppled, bleeding at throat, groin, and thigh. Cheering, the legionaries trampled over his corpse and swarmed into the castle's bailey. A couple of Namdaleni tried to fight; most threw down their arms in despair.

By then the knights chasing the Khatrishers realized the snare they had fallen into. They spun their horses and came galloping back toward the fort, spurring desperately. But the Khatrishers turned round, too, and became pursuers rather than pursued. The islanders, with more at stake than the raiders, ignored their arrows as best they could, though one charger after another rode on riderless.

"Come on, put your backs into it!" Scaurus shouted. With many more hands than the Namdaleni had used, the legionaries strained at the gangboard. They yelled as it pulled free of the clinging earth and went tumbling into the moat. It was well made; the tribune did not hear timbers crack as it hit.

Outside the castle, the islanders milled round in confusion, shut out of their own fortress and at a loss what to do next. The Khatrishers' archery suggested that lingering was not the wisest course. Looking glumly back over their shoulders, they trotted north, presumably to join their main force. Pakhymer waved to Marcus, who returned it; the assault had gone better than he had dared hope.

He spent the night in the captured fort, waiting for reports from his officers. A rider attached to Gagik Bagratouni's force came in just after sunset, to announce a success as complete and easy as the tribune's. Junius Blaesus took his target, too, but at the cost of some hard fighting. "What went wrong?" Marcus asked.

"Started his charge too damned soon," the Khatrisher scout answered, not shy about criticizing someone else's officer. "The Namdaleni managed to reverse themselves and hit him before he made it to the castle. He's brave enough, though—ducked a lance and speared one right off his horse, he did." The Katrisher tugged his ear, trying to remember something. "Ah, that's it—your friend Apokavkos lost the little finger on his right hand."

"Pity," Scaurus said. "How is he taking it?"

"Him? He's angry at himself—told me to tell you he cut instead of thrusting, and the last time he'll make that mistake, thank you very much."

That left only Gaius Philippus unaccounted for. Marcus was not much worried; the senior centurion's target was farthest from his own. But early next morning a rider came in to report flat failure. He was vague about what had happened; Scaurus did not hear the full story until he saw Gaius Philippus back at the Roman camp a few days later. He had pulled the legionaries out of the captured forts, leaving Videssians behind instead, a mixture of nobles' retainers and irregulars—troops plenty good for garrison duty.

"One of those things," the senior centurion shrugged. "The Khatrishers went whooping into the fields fine as you please, but the whoresons inside had a couple of stone-throwers in their castle, which we didn't know about till they opened up. Good aimers, too. They squashed two horses and took the head off a rider neat as you please. That discouraged the rest considerably, and what was supposed to be a fake skedaddle turned real mighty fast." He spooned up some mutton stew. "Can't say I blame 'em much. We sat under some peaches till it was dark again, then left. Some of my men have taken a flux from eating green ones, the twits."

Despite the veteran's misfortune, Scaurus knew he had gained a solid success. His mouth watered at the prospect of getting down into the plain; a full summer in the hills would leave them picked bare and his troops starving. True, all Drax' forces together could crush the legionaries, but Drax had problems of his own.

Senpat Sviodo made as if to throw his pandoura away in disgust after producing a chord even Scaurus' insensitive ear recognized as spectacularly unmusical. "I wish we were back in the highlands," he said. "It's too muggy down here; there's no way to keep gut strings in tune with all this humidity. Ah, my sweet," he crooned, holding the pandoura as he might Nevrat, "you deserve strings of finest silver. And," he added, laughing, "if I lavished money on you thus, perhaps you'd not betray me, fickle hussy."

With an enthusiast's zeal, he went on to explain the advantages and disadvantages of different kinds of stringing. Marcus fought to hide boredom; not even Senpat's easy charm could make him find music interesting, and the day's march had left him worn.

He was glad of the excuse to break away when Lucius Vorenus came up. "What now?" he asked. "What's Pullo done that you don't care for?"

"Eh?" Vorenus blinked. "Oh, nothing, sir. That valley scuffle's made fast friends of us. In fact, we're on sentry go together, over at the east gate. And just rode up, sir, is a Yezda who'd have speech with you."

"A what?" It was Scaurus' turn to gape. Senpat's Latin was enough to catch the name of his people's foes; he struck a jangling discord that had nothing to do with whether his strings were in tune. The tribune felt his mouth tighten. "What would a Yezda have to say to me?"

"I wouldn't know, sir. He's out there with a white rag tied to his bow; he doesn't carry a spear, or have a helmet to put on it, for that matter. Dirty-looking beggar," Vorenus added virtuously.

Marcus exchanged glances with Senpat. The Vaspurakaner's face showed an odd mixture of puzzlement and hostility; Scaurus felt much the same. "Bring him in," he said at last. Vorenus saluted and trotted off.

Despite the legionary's unflattering description, Marcus expected a more impressive figure than the Yezda cut—some high officer, perhaps, with Makurani blood in his veins along with the infusion from the steppe—tall, thin, handsome, with delicate hands and mournful liquid eyes, like the captain who had defended Khliat against Mavrikios Gavras. But only a scruffy nomad on a pony followed Vorenus, looking for all the world like any of the Khamorth in imperial service. Not a soldier gave him a second look. Yet his presence here, not far from Kyzikos, was a knife at Videssos' throat.

The Yezda, for his part, seemed no more happy to be in his enemies' camp than Marcus was to have him there. He turned his head nervously this way and that, as if looking for escape routes. "You Scaurus, leader of this peoples?" he asked, his Videssian labored but understandable.

"Aye," the tribune said stonily. "What would you?"

"I Sevabarak, cousin to Yavlak, who is leaders of clans of Menteshe. He send me to you to ask how much money you gots. You need plenties, I think."

"And why is that, pray?" Marcus asked, still not caring to have anything to do with Yezda.

Sevabarak was not offended; indeed, he seemed amused. "Because we—how you say?—whale stuffings out of oh-so-tough knightboys last week. Damn sight more than pissworthy Empire can do," he said. Then, ticking off names on his fingers, he went on, "We gots Drax, we gots Bailli, we gots what's-his-name Videssian thinks he's Empire—"

"Emperor," Scaurus corrected mechanically. Beside him, Senpat Sviodo's eyes were round and staring. So, for that matter, were his own.

Sevabarak waved the interruption aside. "Whatever. We gots. We gots Turgot, we gots Soteric, we gots Clozart—no, I take back, him dead, two days gone. Anyway, we gots shitpot full Namdalenis. You wants, you buy back, plenty monies. Otherwise," and his eyes grew cruel and eager, "we see how long we stretch them lives out. Some last weeks, I bet."

But Marcus paid no attention to the threat. Here was a broken rebellion handed to him on a golden plate—and if the legionaries moved quickly, they still might keep the Yezda off the coastal plain. And thinking of gold . . . "Pakhymer!" he shouted. This might cost more than the legionaries had, and he was ready to swallow all the Khatrisher's "I-told-you-so's" to get it.

VIII

THE GREAT WAIN CREAKED, MOVING ACROSS THE GENTLY rolling steppe on wheels tall as a man. Gorgidas sat cross-legged on the polychrome rug of goats' hair, paring away at his stylus' point with the edge of his sword; not what Gaius Philippus had hoped he'd use the weapon for, he thought, chuckling. He tested the point on the ball of his thumb. It would do. He opened a three-leafed tablet, frowned when he saw how poorly he'd smoothed the wax after transcribing his last set of jottings onto parchment.

He tugged on his left ear as he thought. His stylus hurried across the tablet, tiny wax curls spiraling up from it. "In sweep of territory, neither Videssos nor Yezd compares favorably with the nomads to the north. Indeed, should those nomads somehow unite under a single leader, no nation could stand against them. They do not, however, govern themselves with great wisdom or make the best use of the vast resources available to them."

He studied what he had written—not bad, something of a Thucydidean flavor to it. His script was small and very neat. As if that mattered, he said to himself with a snort. In all this world, only he read Greek. No, not quite: Scaurus could stumble through it after a fashion. But Scaurus was in Videssos, which seemed unimaginably far away from this wandering train of Arshaum wagons.

Beside him, Goudeles was making notes of his own for an oration he intended to give to Arigh's father Arghun, the khagan of the Gray Horse clan, when at last they reached the chieftain. It would not be long now, a couple of days at most. Lankinos Skylitzes, well padded with fat cushions, was sound asleep, ignoring the occasional jounce of a wheel bumping over a rock. He snored.

Gorgidas set the stylus moving again. "It is not surprising, then, that the Arshaum should have succeeded in driving the Khamorth to the eastern portion of the steppe, which extends further west than any man's knowledge of it; the former folk has adapted itself more completely to the nomadic way of life than the latter. The very tents of the Arshaum, 'yurts,' in their dialect, are set upon large wheeled carts. Thus no time is wasted pitching or breaking camp. They followed their flocks forever, like dolphins in a school of tunny."

The comparison pleased him. He translated it into Videssian for Goudeles. The pen-pusher rolled his eyes. "'Sharks' might be better," he said, and followed that with a muttered, "Barbarians!"

Gorgidas chose to think that remark was meant to apply to the Arshaum and not to him. He resumed his scribbling: "Because the plainsfolk do not act as a single nation, both Videssos and Yezd try to win them over clan by clan. By attracting such prominent khagans as Arghun to their side, they hope to influence less important leaders to join the faction that looks to be a winner." He put his stylus down, asked Goudeles, "What do you suppose this Bogoraz is up to?"

Skylitzes opened one eye. "No good for us, I'm sure," he said, and went back to sleep.

"I fear he's right," Goudeles said, sighing. The Yezda ambassador had also come to woo Arghun. Until their khagan chose one side or the other, the Arshaum were carefully keeping Bogoraz and his retainers separate from the Videssian party.

Inspiration failing him, Gorgidas stowed tablet and stylus

and stuck his head out the flap of the yurt. Agathias Psoes, riding beside the felt tent on wheels, nodded a greeting; he kept his squad on alert, not relying on the nomads to keep Bogoraz and his handful of retainers from mischief.

The Greek turned to the young plainsman guiding the yurt's team of horses. "May your herds increase," he said in polite greeting, using up a good deal of what he had learned of the sibilant Arshaum tongue.

"May your animals be fat," the nomad replied. Like most of his people, he was short and lean, with a wiry strength to him. He was flat-faced, swarthy, and almost without a beard; a fold of skin at the corner of each eye gave them a slanted look. When he smiled, his teeth were very white.

Suede fringes and brightly dyed tassels of wool ornamented his sheepskin trousers and leather coat. He wore a curved sword and dagger and a quiver on his back; his bow was beside him on the wooden seat. He smelled strongly of the stale butter he used to oil his straight, coarse black hair.

It was later than Gorgidas had thought. The sun was sliding down the sky toward a low range of hills that barely serrated the western horizon. They were the first blemishes on the skyline he had seen for weeks. Beyond them was only more steppe.

Two riders came out of the west, one straight for the Videssian embassy's yurt, the other peeling off toward that of Bogoraz. Yezd's banner, a leaping panther on a field of brownish red, fluttered above it. It was a nice touch; Gorgidas wished the Empire had been as forethoughtful.

The messenger said something in his own language to the Greek, who tossed his head to show he did not understand. The nomad shrugged, tried again in bad Khamorth; only a few Ashaum knew Videssian. Gorgidas ducked inside the tent and shook Skylitzes awake; the officer spoke the local tongue fluently.

Grumbling, Skylitzes went out and talked with the messenger for a few minutes. "We're to meet the clan's shamans tonight," he reported to his companions. "They'll purge us of any evil spirits before we're taken to the khagan." Though he had experience with the customs of the steppe peoples, his unsmiling features were more dour than usual. "Pagans," he said under his breath, and made the sign of Phos' sun on his breast. Goudeles, by contrast, did not seem unduly perturbed at the prospect of going through a foreign ritual.

Outside, the messenger was still talking with the yurt driver, who clucked to his horses. The ungreased axles screeched as the wagon swung southward. Gorgidas looked a question at Skylitzes, who said, "He's taking us to where the shamans are."

An hour or so later the yurt rumbled down into a broad valley. Looking out, the Greek saw that Bogoraz's wain was a couple of hundred yards behind. Twoscore Arshaum horsemen rode between the yurts, making sure Psoes' troopers did not mix it with the Yezda soldiers who guarded Bogoraz. The rest of the wagons with which both parties had been traveling had gone on ahead to Arghun.

A lone tent on wheels stood in the valley, its horses grazing around it. A man got down from it, torch in hand; Gorgidas was too far away to see more than that his costume was strange. Then the yurt-driver said something to the Greek. "Come inside," Skylitzes said. "He says it ruins the magic if we see the sacred fires lit." Gorgidas obeyed with poor grace; how could he learn if he was not allowed to observe?

The yurt drove up close enough for him to hear the crackle of flames; he heard Bogoraz' rolling into place beside it. The driver called out to someone. The reply came back in a reedy tenor, an old man's voice. "We can go out now," Skylitzes said. He turned to stare at Goudeles. "Phos' name, are you still working on that rubbish you spew?"

"Just finding the proper antithesis to balance this clause here," the bureaucrat replied, unruffled. He ostentatiously jotted another note, watching Skylitzes fume. "This will have to suffice," he said at last. "So much is wasted in translation, in any case. Well, come along, Lankinos—it's not I who's keeping them waiting now." And sure enough, the pen-pusher was out the tent flap first.

Bogoraz was alighting from his yurt as well, but Gorgidas hardly noticed him; his attention was riveted on the shamans of the Arshaum. There were three of them, two straight and vigorous, the third stooped with age—he must have answered the Videssian party's driver. They were dressed in ankle-length robes of suede, covered with so many long shaggy fringes sewn on that they seemed more beasts than men. All three wore snarling devil-masks of wood and leather painted in hideous greens, purples, and yellows, adding to their inhuman aspect. Silhouetted against the fires they had set, they capered about, calling out to each other now and then. Their voices echoed, hollow, inside their masks.

Gorgidas watched the display with interest, Skylitzes with active suspicion. But Pikridios Goudeles bowed to the eldest shaman with the same deep respect he might have shown Balsamon, the patriarch of Videssos. The old Arshaum bowed creakily in return and said something.

"Well done, Pikridios," Skylitzes said grudgingly. "The geezer said he didn't know whether to take us or the Yezda first, but your good manners made up his mind for him."

Goudeles bowed again, as deeply as his plump form would allow. The pen-pusher was self-indulgent and bombastic, Gorgidas thought, but he was a diplomat, too.

So, in his way, was Bogoraz. He saw at once he would not be able to change the shaman's decision and so did not try, folding his arms over his chest as if the entire matter was beneath his notice.

Again, Gorgidas watched him out of the corner of his eye. The shamans were busy at their fire, chanting incantations and throwing fragrant frankincense into the flames. The old man rang a bronze bell while his two assistants kept chanting. "Driving away demons," Skylitzes reported.

Then the elder drew out a small packet from beneath his long coat, tossed its contents over the fire. The flames flared up in pure white heat, dazzling Gorgidas' sight and making sweat start on his brow. A blot of darkness against the glare, the shaman approached the Videssian party and spoke. "What?" Skylitzes barked in Videssian. Collecting himself, he spoke in the Arshaum tongue. The shaman repeated himself, gesturing as if to say, "It's all quite simple, you know."

"Well?" Goudeles demanded.

"If I understand him, and I'm afraid I do," Skylitzes said, "he wants us to prove we mean Arghun no harm by walking through the bonfire there. If our intentions are good, he says, nothing will happen. If not—" the officer hesitated, finished, "the fire does what fire does."

"Suddenly being first is an honor I would willingly forego," Goudeles said. Skylitzes, unshakable in the face of physical danger, seemed close to panic at the idea of trusting his safety to a heathen wizard's spell. Gorgidas, who did his best to disbelieve in anything he could not see or feel, wondered why he was not similarly afraid himself. He realized he had been watching the old shaman as closely as if he were a patient; the man glowed with a confidence as bright as the blaze he had called up.

"It will be all right, I think," he said, and was rewarded with matched unhappy looks from Goudeles and Skylitzes, the first time they had agreed with each other in days. Then the old Arashaum grasped at last that the Videssian group had doubts. Waving to reassure them, he took half a dozen backward strides—and was engulfed by flames. They did not burn him. He danced a few clumsy steps in the heart of the fire, while Goudeles' party—and Bogoraz, off to one side—stared at him. When he emerged, not a fringe on his fantastic costume was singed. He waved again, now in invitation.

Goudeles had his own peculiar form of courage. Visibly pulling himself together, he said to no one in particular, "I did not fall off the edge of the map to work an injury on a nomad." He walked briskly up to the edge of the flames. The old shaman patted him on the back, then took his hand and escorted him into the bonfire. The blaze leaped up around them.

Lankinos Skylitzes was biting his lip when Goudeles' voice, full of relief and jubilation, rose above the crackle of the fire. "Quite whole, thank you, and no worse than medium rare," he called. Skylitzes set his jaw and stepped forward. Unnervingly, the old shaman appeared from out of the flames. The officer made Phos' sun-sign over his heart once more, then reached to take the shaman's outstretched hand.

"Here," Skylitzes called a few moments later, laconic as usual. Then the shaman was beckoning to Gorgidas. For all his confidence, the Greek felt a qualm as he came up to the bonfire. He narrowed his eyes to slits against the glare and wondered how long it would be before Goudeles' feeble joke turned true.

The old Arshaum's hand, though, was cool in his, gently urging him into the flames. And as soon as he stepped into the fire, the sensation of heat vanished; it might have been any summer's evening. He was not even sweating. He opened his eyes. The white light surrounded him, but no longer blinded. He looked down at the coals over which he walked and saw they were undisturbed by his passage. Beside him the shaman hummed tunelessly.

Darkness ahead, total after the brilliance that had bathed him. A sudden blast of heat at his back told him he was past the spell. He stumbled away from the fire. Goudeles caught and steadied him. As he regained his vision, he saw Skylitzes gazing back at the blaze like a man entranced. "All light," the officer murmured, awe-struck. "Phos' heaven must be thus."

Goudeles was more practical. "If it has anything to do with Phos, it'll fry that rascal of a Bogoraz to a crackling and do the Empire a great service."

Gorgidas had nursed that same hope, but a few minutes later the shaman came through the fire with the Yezda envoy in hand. At last the Greek had to pay him attention. If he had hoped Wulghash, the khagan of Yezd, would send out some half-barbarous chieflet, he saw at once he was to be disappointed.

Bogoraz was plainly of the old stock of Makuran, the state that had treated with Videssos as an equal for centuries until the Yezda swarmed down from the steppe to conquer it. In his late middle years, he stood tall and spare. He turned for a moment to look at the old shaman; outlined against the flames, a strong hooked nose gave him the brooding profile of a hawk.

His sight clearing, Wulghash's ambassador noticed the Arshaum party and came up to them with a mocking half bow. "An interesting experience, that," he remarked; he spoke the imperial tongue with old-fashioned phrasing but only the faintest hint of his native accent. "Who would have thought these barbarians had such mages among them?"

His eyes were hooded, again like a hawk's; Gorgidas could make out nothing in their black depths. The rest of his face had a lean power in it that was in good accord with his build. His chin was strong and jutting, his cheekbones sharply carved. A thick graying beard, tightly curled like his hair, covered his jaw and cheeks; he let his mustaches grow long enough to hide most of his upper lip. It was a good mouth to keep concealed, wide, with full lips that could easily wear either harshness or sensuality.

The Yezda's presence roused Skylitzes from his golden dream. He touched the hilt of his sword, growling, "I should take care of what the fire bungled."

Bogoraz met him glare for glare, unafraid. The envoy of Yezd carried no weapons; he toyed with the bright brass—or were they gold?—buttons on his coat of brown wool, cut longer behind than before. Under the coat he wore a caftan of some light fabric, striped vertically in muted colors. "Why do you think me less pure of heart than yourself?" he asked, gesturing in sardonic amusement. Gorgidas was struck by his hands, which were slim and elegant, with long tapering fingers—a surgeon's hands, the Greek thought.

"Because you bloody well are," Skylitzes said, ignoring subtleties.

"Softly, my friend." Goudeles laid a hand on the officer's arm. "The truth must be that this is a wizard himself, though shy of admitting it, with spells to defeat the flames." Though he still spoke to Skylitzes, he watched Bogoraz for any telltale response to his probe.

But Bogoraz would not rise for it. "What need have I of magic?" he asked, his smile showing no more of his thoughts than a shaman's mask might. "Truly I wish this Arghun no harm—so long as he does what he should." The mask slipped a trifle, to show the predator behind it.

Viridovix sipped from the skin of kavass. Beside him Targitaus, who had passed it to him, belched loudly and patted his belly. "That is a well-made tipple," he said, "smooth and strong at the same time, like the hindquarters of a mule."

"A mule, you say?" Viridovix needed Lipoxais' translations less each day; he was beginning to understand the Khamorth tongue fairly well, though he still answered in Videssian when he could. "Sure and it tastes like a mule's hind end. I miss my wine."

Some of the plainsmen chuckled, others frowned to hear their traditional drink maligned. "What did he say?" asked Targitus' wife Borane; like most of the women, she had no Videssian. The nomad chieftain explained. Borane rolled her eyes, then winked at the Celt. She was a heavy-featured woman, losing her looks and figure to middle age; as if to turn aside the advancing years, she affected a kittenishness that went poorly with her girth.

Her daughter Seirem showed her one-time beauty like a mirror reflecting an image twenty years gone. "If our blood-cousin does not care for kavass," Seirem said to Targitaus, "maybe he would enjoy the felt tent."

"What was that last?" Viridovix asked Lipoxais; he had caught the words, but not the meaning behind them.

"'The felt tent,'" the *enaree* translated obligingly. He took the phrase too much for granted to think it needed explaining.

"By my prize bull's pizzle," Targitaus said, "he doesn't know the felt tent!" He turned to his servants. "Kelemerish! Tarim! Fetch the hangings, the cauldron, and the seeds."

The servants rummaged with alacrity in the leather sacks on the northern side of the tent. Tarim, the younger of the two, brought Targitaus a two-eared round cauldron of bronze, full almost to the top with large flat stones. Targitaus sat it in the cookfire to heat. Kelermish gave his chieftain a fist-sized leather bag with a drawstring top. He opened it and poured a nondescript lot of greenish-brown stems, seeds, and crushed leaves into the palm of his hand.

Seeing Viridovix' bewilderment, he said. "It's hemp, of course."

"Will your honor be making rope, then?" The Gaul wished Gorgidas were with him, to wring sense from this fiddle-faddle. Targitaus only snorted. Tarim and Kelermish were closing in the space round the fire with felt blankets hung from the ceiling of the pavilion, making a tent within a tent.

The Khamorth chief looked into the cauldron; the stones were beginning to glow red. He grunted in satisfaction, fished the bronze pot out of the fire by one ear with a long-shanked fork. As he carefully set it in front of Viridovix, his household crowded closer to the Gaul. "You shall have the fine seat tonight."

"Shall I now? And what'll I do with all these rocks? A hot stone's all very well wrapped in flannel for a cold winter's bed, but not for much else I can see. Sure and I can't eat the kettleful of 'em for you."

Had Targitaus been a Videssian, he would have responded

to Viridovix' raillery with some elaborate persiflage of his own. As it was, he dumped the handful of leafy rubbish he was holding onto the red-hot stones. A thick cloud of smoke puffed out. It did not smell like the burning grass Viridovix had expected. The odor was thicker, sweeter, almost spicy; of themselves, the Gaul's nostrils twitched.

"What are you waiting for?" Targitaus said. "Don't waste the fine seat; bend down and take a deep breath."

Lured by that intriguing scent, Viridovix leaned over the cauldron until he was close enough to feel the heat radiating up into his face. He sucked in a great lungful of smoke—and then choked and coughed desperately as he tried to blow it out. His chest and windpipe felt as if he had swallowed olive coals. Tears ran down his cheeks. "Och, my puir scorched thrapple," he wheezed, voice a ragged ghost of his usual smooth baritone.

The plainsmen found his splutters funny, which only made things worse. "It's one way to blow the smoke around," Targitaus chuckled, inhaling a less concentrated draft and holding it in his lungs until the Gaul wondered that he did not burst. Other nomads were doing the same and smiling beatifically.

"He's new to it, father. I think you did that on purpose," Seirem accused. "Let him have another chance."

The chieftain's bushy eyebrows and bent nose made it impossible for him to look innocent, whether he was or not. He threw more seeds and leaves on the hot stones; a fresh cloud of fumes rose from them. He waved an invitation to Viridovix.

This time the Celt breathed more cautiously. He could not help making a wry face; however inviting the stuff smelled, it tasted like charred weeds. He coughed again but, gritting his teeth, held most of the smoke down. When he finally let it out, he saw his breath come forth, as he might on a cold winter morning.

That was interesting. He thought about it for a few seconds. They seemed to stretch endlessly. That was interesting, too. He looked at Targitaus through the murky air, which got murkier as the chieftain kept adding dried hemp to the cauldron. "Whisht! A rare potent smoke y'have there."

Targitaus was holding his breath again and did not answer.

Viridovix was not put out. He inhaled deeply himself, felt the fumes' soft heaviness behind his eyes.

The sensation was very different from too much wine. The Gaul made a rowdy drunk, always ready for a song or a fight. Now he simply felt insulated from the world in a pleasant sort of way. He knew he could get up and do anything at need, but did not see the need. Even thinking was getting to be more trouble than it was worth.

He gave it up, leaning back on his elbows and watching the nomads around him. Some were sprawled out, limp as he was. Others stalked, low-voiced. Lipoxais was playing a lively song on a white bone flute. The notes seemed to glitter in the air and pull Viridovix after them.

His eyes found Seirem's. A slow smile spread over his face; here was an exercise he would not be too lazy to enjoy. But this was no village of serfs, worse luck, and Seirem no peasant wench to be rumpled at a whim. "Och, the waste of it," he said in his own tongue.

Borane did not miss the lickerish look the Gaul sent her daughter. She said something to Seirem, too fast for Viridovix to follow. They both laughed uproariously; the nomads were an earthy folk. Seirem hid her face in her hands, peeped at the Celt through interlaced fingers, a coyness that was pure affectation. His grin was wider.

"What was she after telling you?" he asked.

The two women were laughing again. Borane made a hand gesture that showed she did not mind. Still giggling, Seirem answered him: "Something Azarmi said about you—that you were as tall as you were tall."

In a strange language, with his wits fuzzy with fumes, it took Viridovix a little while to work that through. When he did, he chuckled himself. "Did she now?" he said, and sat a bit straighter, the better to display one sort of height, at least.

Hoofbeats thundered in the night outside the tent; Targitaus' sentries exchanged shouts with the riders, then one of them peered through the entranceway and called for his master. Simply making himself sit had been no small feat for Viridovix, but Targitaus, swallowing an oath, stood at once and pushed his way through the crowd of nomads and out past the felt hangings round the fire. Some cool, fresh air got in as he left; the Celt gulped it gratefully.

He heard a man yelling something at the Khamorth chieftain. There was a moment of silence before Targitaus bellowed furiously. He stormed back into the tent. "Up, you lazy sons of lizards! We've had a herd hit!"

The plainsmen scrambled to their feet, shouting curses and questions. The hangings came down with magical speed; the Khamorth clambered for their bows and swords, their corselets of boiled leather. A few clapped on iron caps, but most kept their usual fur headgear.

Broad face dark with anger, Targitaus glared at Viridovix for his slowness. "Come on, outlander—I want you with us. This stinks of Varatesh's work."

"Well, well," Goudeles said in surprised admiration. "Who would have thought the barbarians had such a sense of style?"

The comment was made *sotto voce* as the Videssian embassy approached the Gray Horse clan's ceremonial yurt, where Arghun awaited them. Gorgidas had to agree with the pen-pusher. The Arshaum ceremony was not much less impressive than the one with which the Videssian *hypasteos* Rhadenos Vourtzes had tried to overawe the Romans at Imbros when they were first swept into the Empire.

Here, instead of parasol bearers as a sign of rank, a stalwart nomad stood spear in hand in front of the khagan's yurt. Others, not part of the ritual but real guards, flanked it on either side with drawn bows. Just below the standard-bearer's glittering spearhead dangled three horsetails, symbols of the clan. The warrior was so still he might have been cast in bronze.

So, too, was the single horse that drew the ceremonial yurt. Though only a steppe pony, its coat, which was gray, had been curried till it shone, and its shaggy mane and tail combed and tied with ribbons of orange and gold. It was splendidly caparisoned, with cheekpieces of carved wood and golden harness-ornaments in the shape of griffins' heads. To impress the eye further, it bore a magnificent orange felt saddlecloth, held in place by straps of gilded leather at chest, belly, and tail. On the sides of the cloth, applique-work griffins attacked goats, which were shown cowering away from the fierce mythical beasts.

The yurt itself was silent and closed atop its two-wheeled

cart. Unlike all the others Gorgidas had seen, it was the only half-round, with a black wool curtain screening its flattened front. Three more horsetails hung on a slim standard above it.

The standard-bearer could move after all; he spun on his heel and called out to that blank forbidding curtain. Gorgidas caught the phrase "embassy from Videssos"; he had heard it often enough since crossing the Shaum.

There was a moment in which he wondered whether anyone was behind the curtain, but then it was pulled aside, the pause plainly a dramatic effect. Black felt lined the interior of the yurt, to make the figure of Arghun himself, seated on a high-backed chair covered with shining gold leaf, all the more imposing.

Arghun was a more weatherbeaten version of his son Arigh, who stood at the right hand of the throne and smiled in greeting as the Videssians came up. The khagan's hair and straggling chin whiskers were iron-gray rather than black and his face carried deeper lines than his son's, but it was easy to see what the years would do to Arigh. Arghun wore the same furs and fringed hides as the rest of his people, of fine cut but not extraordinarily so. The only sign of his rank Gorgidas could see on his person was the gray horsetail of his clan that he worc at his belt.

To the khagan's left stood a tall, lithe young man of perhaps eighteen, who bore a family resemblance to him and Arigh both, but was far handsomer than either. He was very much aware of it, too; his eye was disdainful as he surveyed the approaching diplomats. With high cheekbones, clear golden skin, and nostrils that arched like gullwings from his slim nose, his presence struck Gorgidas like a blow. Nor did his raiment detract from it: he wore a golden belt, tunic and trousers almost as elaborately fringed as a shaman's, and fine leather shoes embroidered with silver thread.

Goudeles, as head of the mission, stepped forward and went to one knee before the khagan; not the full proskynesis the Avtokrator of the Videssians would receive, but only a step away from it. He bowed low to Arigh and the unknown prince at Arghun's left. Skylitzes, who would serve as translator, followed suit.

"Your majesty Arghun, mighty khagan, your highness prince Arigh—" the titles rolled smoothly off Goudeles' tongue. Then he hesitated in urbane embarrassment. "Your highness prince, ah—"

Arigh spoke across the throne. The young man favored Goudeles with a smile, half-charming, half-scornful. He answered with a single short sentence; his voice was tenor, sweet and self-assured. "His name is Dizabul; he is Arghun's son," Skylitzes interpreted.

"*Younger* son," Arigh emended pointedly, eyeing Dizabul with scant liking. With the sublime arrogance perfect beauty can give, his brother pretended he did not exist.

Ignoring the byplay—or seeming to; the pen-pusher missed very little—Goudeles presented the members of his embassy to Arghun and his sons. Gorgidas surprised himself with the depth of the bow he gave Dizabul; to look at, truly the most striking youth he had seen in years, if rather petulant.

While the khagan greeted the ambassadors, the rest of the clan of the Gray Horse watched from their yurts, which had been drawn discreetly away from their ruler's. More heads appeared at tent flaps and wicker-barred windows when Skylitzes rendered Goudeles' next words into the Arshaum tongue: "His Imperial Majesty Thorisin Gavras has sent the khagan gifts."

Several of Agathias Psoes' troopers stepped forward to present the Emperor's gifts; the underofficer had impressed the solemnity of the occasion on them with a profane bluntness that reminded Gorgidas of Gaius Philippus. Now they played their roles perfectly, advancing one by one to set their presents in front of Arghun's yurt, then withdrawing once more.

"His Imperial Majesty offers gold in token of our future friendship." A small but heavy sack of leather clinked musically as a soldier laid it on the thick, low grass.

Arigh spoke to his father. Skylitzes' mouth twitched in an almost-smile as he translated, "All old coins; I saw to it myself." Arigh was canny enough to insist on best value; the turmoil in Videssos' recent decades had forced the Empire to cheapen its goldpieces with lesser metals. Arghun's smile said he knew that, too. Dizabul looked elaborately bored.

Goudeles was thrown off stride for a moment, but recovered smoothly. "Silver for the khagan!" Prevalis Haravash's son brought up a larger sack to set beside the first. The jingle was higher-pitched than that of gold, but still sweet.

"Jewels for the khagan's treasury, or for his ladies: rubies, topazes, opals like fire, pearls like moonlight!" When the next trooper set his gift down, Goudeles opened the sack and displayed a glowing pearl in the palm of his hand. Gorgidas gave him high marks for shrewdness; living so far from the sea, Arghun might never have seen a pearl. The khagan leaned forward to examine it, nodded, sat back once more.

"Fine vestments for your majesty." Some of the robes were cloth-of-gold, others of samite or snowy linen, heavily brocaded, bejeweled, and shot through with gold and silver thread. Here at last was stuff to rouse Dizabul's interest, but his father seemed indifferent in the finery.

"Last, as a mark of honor, the Avtokrator presents you with boots striped in the imperial scarlet." Only the Videssian Emperor wore footgear all of scarlet; for him to share the color even in this way was a signal act of deference. Duke Tomond of Namdalen did not presume to wear red boots.

Speaking through Arigh, Arghun said, "These are fine gifts. Are there words to go with them?"

"Will a cock crow? Will a crow caw?" Skylitzes murmured in Videssian as Goudeles visibly gathered himself for a flight of rhetoric. Arigh snickered but, being pro-Videssian, did not explain the ridicule to his father.

Goudeles himself could only glower at his comrade out of the corner of his eye. He began the opening address he had been toying with for days: "O valiant Arghun, our great Emperor—" He had a bureaucrat's revenge on Skylitzes there, loading that "great" with so much stress as to make the word a travesty. "—using me as his messenger, indicates that fortune should always be auspicious for you, as you take pleasure in treating with the Empire of Videssos, and also as you show kindness to us its legates. May you always conquer your enemies and despoil your foes. May there be no malice between us, as far as is possible; such exists only to cleave asunder the establishment of friendship."

"Slow down, curse you," Skylitzes whispered frantically. "If I don't know what you're talking about, how do you expect them to?"

"They don't need to, really," Goudeles answered under

cover of a dramatic gesture. "I'm saying what has to be said at a time like this, that's all." He bowed once more to Arghun, and finished, "The people of the clan of the Gray Horse and however many subjects they may have are dear to us; may you not hold our affairs otherwise." He stepped back a pace to show the oration was done.

"Very pretty," Arigh said; his years in Videssos let him appreciate Goudeles' performance more readily than his father or brother could. "I—" The khagan interrupted him. He nodded, abashed; in Arghun's presence he was no hotspur, but an obedient son. He said, "My father would like to reply through me. No offense to you, Lankinos, you speak very well, but—"

"Of course," Skylitzes said quickly.

"We are honored to hear the khagan's remarks," Goudeles added.

Gorgidas braced himself for another high-flown speech. Instead, Arghun fell silent after two sentences. His son translated: "My thanks for the presents. As for your embassy, I will decide what to do when I have also heard the man from Yezd."

Goudeles frankly gaped. "That's all?" he squeaked, surprised out of elaborate syntax. He looked as if he had been stabbed, then slowly led the Videssian party to one side. "'My thanks for the presents,'" he muttered. "Bah!" He swore with unbureaucratic imagination.

"You spoke well, but the nomads' style is different from yours," Gorgidas told him. "They admire Videssian rhetoric, though—remember Olbiop? And Arghun strikes me as a prudent leader. Would you expect him to say yes or no without listening to both sides?"

Slightly consoled, Goudeles shook his head. "I wish he would," Skylitzes said. But Bogoraz of Yezd was already coming up to the khagan's yurt. Skylitzes' stare was as intense as if they were meeting on the battlefield.

The Yezda envoy, like Goudeles, went to one knee before Arghun; the dignity of his salute was marred when the black felt skullcap he wore fell to the ground as he dipped his head. But he quickly regained the advantage when he spoke to the khagan in the Arshaum tongue.

"A plague!" Gorgidas and Goudeles said together. The

Greek went on, "That can't help influencing Arghun, whether he realizes it or not."

"Hush!" said Skylitzes, and after listening for a moment, "Less than you'd think. The soundrel has a mushy Khamorth accent, good for making any Arshaum look down his flat nose."

"What's he saying?" Goudeles asked; he had no more of Arghun's language than did Gorgidas.

"Same garbage you were putting out, Pikridios. No, wait, here's something new. He says Wulghash—Skotos freeze him!—knows what a great warrior Arghun is, and sends him presents fit for a warrior."

At Bogoraz's imperious wave, one of his guardsmen laid a scabbard of enamel-decorated polished bronze before the khagan. With a placating glance at the Arshaum bowmen, the ambassador drew the curved sword to display it to Arghun. It was a rich and perfect product of the swordsmith's art, from hilt wrapped in gold wire to gleaming blade. After a ceremonial flourish, Bogoraz sheathed it again and presented it to the khagan.

Arghun drew it himself to test the balance, smiled with genuine pleasure, and buckled it to his belt. Smiling, too, Bogoraz gave similar blades to his sons; they differed only in that their hilts were wrapped with silver rather than gold. Dizabul fairly licked his lips as he took his weapon from the Yezda; even Arigh unhesitatingly wore his.

For the moment all but forgotten, the Videssian party watched their reaction in dismay. Skylitzes ground his teeth. "We should have thought of that."

"Aye," Goudeles agreed mournfully. "These plains barbarians are fierce folk; they take more kindly to edged metal than robes of state, where our own people, I think, would esteem them equally."

Trying as he usually did to find general rules from the examples life offered him, Gorgidas said, "It's wrong to judge others by one's own standards. We Greeks burn our dead, while the Indians—" He stopped, reddening, as the others turned to stare; India—Greece, too!—meant nothing here.

Bogoraz's parade of costly weaponry continued: daggers with hunting scenes picked out on their blades with gold leaf;

double-curved bows reinforced with horn, buffed and waxed till they sparkled; arrows of fragrant cedar fletched with iridescent peacock plumes, in quivers of snakeskin; spiked helmets ornamented with jewels.

Dizabul chose to wear every item the Yezda gave him; by the time Bogoraz was done, he looked like a walking armory. Caressing the hilt of the new sword, he turned and spoke to his father. His voice carried; plainly he meant it to. Bogoraz gave the Videssian embassy a satisfied smirk.

Skylitzes, on the other hand, worked his jaws harder than ever. He grated, "The pup is all for throwing us out now, or filling us full of holes with his new toys. He's calling us 'the worthless hucksters Arigh brought.'"

Arghun's elder son bristled at that and began a hot response. The khagan snarled at him and Dizabul both. Dizabul started to say something more, but subsided when Arghun half rose from his throne.

Collecting himself, Arghun turned back to Bogoraz, who had affected to notice nothing. But some of the Yezda's toploftiness fell away when Arghun dismissed him as abruptly as he had Goudeles. "The gifts are splendid, he says," Skylitzes reported, "but any alliance needs more thought." The Videssian officer seemed almost unbelieving.

"He *is* a clever leader," Gorgidas said.

"Indeed he is; he milks both sides impartially," Goudeles said. He sounded as relieved as Skylitzes. "Well, good for him. The game's still even."

Viridovix dismounted without grace, but with a great groan of relief. Three hard days in the saddle had left him sore and stiff to the point of anguish. As he had before, he marveled at the endurance of the plainsmen; once mounted, they seemed made into—what was the Greek word for beings half man, half horse? Unable to remember, he mumbled a curse.

The air did not lend itself to such musings; it was thick with the sickly-sweet stench of death. And Targitaus was watching, grim-faced, as the Gaul paced about trying to stomp blood back into his calves and feet. "Another ride like that and I'll be as bowlegged as you Khamorth laddies." Not knowing the word for "bowlegged," he illustrated with gestures.

He failed to amuse the nomad chieftain, who said, "Save

your jokes for the women. Nothing to laugh at here." Viridovix flushed. Targitaus did not notice; he had already turned back to the carnage spread before him.

It must have been worse a week before, when his herders found it, still fresh. Yet even after the scavengers had feasted, what was left was quite bad enough. Half a hundred cattle had been lured away from the herd, and then—what? "Slaughtered" was too gentle a word for the massacre here.

The ground was still dark from the blood that had soaked into it when the cows' throats were cut. The killing alone would have been enough to make this no ordinary raid. Cattle were for herding and for stealing, not liquidation. The steppe was too harsh to let a tradition of wanton killing grow; even in war, winners simply took herds and flocks from their defeated foes—herds and flocks were war's object, not its target.

But not here, not now. These beasts sprawled in death were more pitiful than warriors fallen on a battlefield; beasts have no choice in their fate and no chance to avert it. And that fate had been cruel, viciously so. Great cuts had been made in the carcasses, and filth smeared into them to spoil the meat. The hides were not only gashed, but also rubbed with some potent caustic that made them worthless, too. Targitaus' clan could have salvaged nothing from the animals even if they had been discovered the hour after they died.

The chief's son Batbaian paced from one mutilated cow to the next, shaking his head and tugging at his beard as he tried without success to understand what he saw. He turned helplessly to his father. "They must be mad, as dogs are, to do this!" he burst out.

The clan leader said sadly, "I wish you were right, boy. This is Varatesh's way of trying to make me afraid and make me sorry for sheltering the outlander here." He bobbed his head, so like Batbaian's, at Viridovix.

To the Gaul, though, the savagery he saw here called up another memory, of a body outside the walls of Videssos the city, when the legionaries were helping Thorisin Gavras lay siege to the Sphrantzai within. Along with other torments, poor Doukitzes' outraged corpse had borne a name sliced into its forehead: Rhavas. As soon came clear, that needed but a rearrangement of letters to reveal the killer.

"It's Avshar's sport I make this," he said. "I've tried to tell you of him till the now and made no headway at it—the which I canna blame you for, as you'd not seen the way of him. But hark, an you will." In the Khamorth speech as best he could, in Videssian when it failed him, he spoke of Doukitzes and much else: of the wizard-prince's duel with Scaurus when the Romans first came to Videssos the city; of Maragha and afterward, and Mavrikios Gavras' head flung into the legionary camp; of the Grand Courtroom in the capital, and Avshar's sorcery for making the worst of his rogues invulnerable to steel.

The obscenity and cruelty of that last tale shook the plainsmen. "He made his magic with a woman, you say?" Targitaus demanded, as if he thought his ears were tricking him.

"Aye, and with her unborn wean ripped from her," the Celt replied. The plainsman shuddered. Where the slaughter of his beasts left him coldly furious, here was malice worse than he had dreamed possible.

With youth's temerity, Batbaian cried, "Let's be rid of him, then—burn his tent over his head and all who follow him, too!" Looking at their cattle, with Viridovix' words still hanging over them, the Khamorth shouted, "Aye!"

And, "Aye," said Targitaus as well, but softly. Where his clansmen had only caught the horror in the Gaul's tale, he also saw what it revealed of Avshar's power. "Aye," he said again, and added, "if we can."

He looked at Viridovix, not happily. "I see it is time to gather the clans against Varatesh and this Avshar of yours."

"Past time," Viridovix said at once, and Batbaian gave a vigorous nod. Despite Targitaus' ringing promises of war on the outlaw chief, weeks had dragged by without much happening.

The chief looked uncomfortable. "You come from Videssos, outlander, where the khag—er, the Emperor, tells his men, 'Do this,' and they do it or lose their heads. It is not like that on the plains. If I go to Ariapith of the Oglos River clan, or Anakhar of the Spotted Cats, or Krobyz of the Leaping Goats and tell them we should clean out Varatesh together, the first thing they will say is, 'Who leads?' What do I answer?

Me? They will say I try to set my Wolfskins up as Royal Clan, and have nothing to do with me."

"Royal Clan?" the Celt echoed.

"Sometimes a clan will get the better of all the ones around it and rule the steppe for a while, even for a man's life, until they get free and pull it down." Ambition glowed in Targitaus' eyes. "Every khagan dreams of founding a Royal Clan and has nightmares his neighbor will do it first. So each watches the next, and no one gets too strong."

"So that's the way of it, eh?" Suddenly Viridovix found himself on familiar ground. In Gaul before the Romans came, the tribes were constantly jockeying for position, squabbling and intriguing for all they were worth. The Aedui had held pride of place until the Sequani allied with the Ubii from over the Rhine and usurped their dominant position. In the process, though, they had made Ariovistus the German the most powerful man in Gaul. . . .

The Celt's eyes sparked green; he whooped with glee and clapped his hands together. "How's this?" he said to Targitaus, who had swung round in surprise, half drawing his sword. "Suppose you're after telling old Crowbait o' the Spotted Hamsters, or whatever his fool name is, that Varatesh is aiming to make his piratical spalpeens Royal Clan, the which is nothing less than true. Sure and he'd piss himself or ever he let that happen, now wouldn't he?"

He could all but hear the wheels spinning inside the nomad chief's head. Targitaus looked at Batbaian, who was staring at Viridovix with awe on his face; the young are easily impressed on hearing things they have not thought of for themselves. "Hmm," said Targitaus, and the Gaul knew he had won.

Batbaian exclaimed, "Guide your herds right in this, father, and it'd be you who'd be Royal Clan khagan!"

"Me? Nonsense, boy," Targitaus said gruffly, but Viridovix saw the thought had struck him before his son voiced it. He chuckled to himself.

Dizabul stabbed the last strip of broiled rabbit from the boiled-leather bowl he held in his lap, chewed noisily with the good manners of the steppe. He leaned forward; the cook lifted more sizzling meat from the griddle with a pair of wooden tongs, refilled his bowl. He sat back with a smile of thanks. Turning to his left, he murmured something to Bogoraz and flourished the elegant dagger the Yezda envoy had given him. That dazzling smile flashed again.

Slurping kavass from a golden goblet, Gorgidas covertly admired the young man, whose beauty stirred a pleasant pain in him. In the nomad way, Arghun had provided women for the Videssian embassy, but though Gorgidas was finding he could perform with them for necessity's sake, they did not satisfy him. After each coupling he felt as a sailor might who turned at sea to a shipmate to relieve his lusts although caring nothing for love of men ashore.

With a stab of pain and loss, he remembered Quintus Glabrio's slim, quiet, intent face, remembered the mixed amusement and distaste with which the junior centurion had spoken of his time with a Videssian girl. "Damaris deserved something different from me, I suppose," he'd said once, adding with a wry laugh, "*She* certainly thought so after a while." That liaison had broken up in spectacular style, along with much crockery.

Thinking of Glabrio helped put Dizabul in perspective. The Roman had been a man, a partner, while the Arshaum princeling showed every sign of being no more than a much-coddled younger son, with spiteful temper to match. Moreover, Gorgidas had learned, he had a son and two daughters of his own by slaves and serving girls.

The Greek drank again. Still, no denying he was lovely.

In his musings over Dizabul, Gorgidas had given scant attention to the great banquet tent. That did it less than justice; it was as important to the Arshaum as the Imperial Palace was to Videssos and had proportional splendor lavished on it. The yurt was the largest he had seen on the plains, easily forty feet across and drawn by a team of twenty-two horses.

Outside, its thick, felt panels had been chalked white to make it stand out against the drab steppe. Now the Greek noticed the silk hangings that lined the stick framework within, work as splendid as any the Empire could boast. The shimmering fabric was dyed saffron and green; the embroidered horses galloping across it were executed with the barbaric vigor that characterized nomad art.

Arghun, his sons, and the rival embassies sat round the

cookfire on rugs of thick, soft wool. The clan's elders made a couple of larger circles around them. The Arshaum sat cross-legged, with either boot hiked onto the opposite thigh. Their guests sprawled every which way—unless practiced from birth, the nomad posture was fiendishly uncomfortable.

At his father's right, Arigh twisted himself into the position for a while, then gave it up with a rueful headshake and a loud creak from his knees. "You've been in Videssos too long," Skylitzes told him.

The look Dizabul gave his brother said he would have liked it better had Arigh stayed there longer still.

"Until we got here, I didn't know you had a brother," Goudeles said to Arigh; Gorgidas was not the only one who'd seen that poisonous stare.

"I'd almost forgotten him myself," Arigh said, dismissing Dizabul with a wave of his hand. "He was just a brat underfoot when I left for the Empire seven or eight years ago—hasn't changed much, looks like." He spoke Videssian so his brother would not understand, but Gorgidas frowned when Bogoraz whispered behind his hand to Dizabul. A flush climbed the young man's high cheekbones, and the scowl he sent Arigh's way made his earlier glower seem loving by comparison.

Servants scurried back and forth, filling goblets from silver pitchers of kavass and fetching food for the Arshaum not within arm's length of the cook. Along with the rabbit Dizabul enjoyed, there was an enormous roasted bird. "Eh? It's a crane," Arigh said in reply to Gorgidas' question. "Good, too—haven't eaten one in years." With that nomad way he had no trouble; his strong white teeth ripped meat away from a legbone. The Greek controlled his enthusiasm. The bird was tasty, but tough as leather.

The mutton and tripes were better, as were the cheeses, both hard and soft; some of the last had sweet berries stirred through them. As well as the kavass, there was fresh milk from cows, goats, and horses, none of which tempted Gorgidas. He would have paid a pretty price for real wine or a handful of salted olives.

When he remarked on that, Arigh shook his head with a grimace of disgust. "Wine is a good thing, but in all the time I was in Videssos I never got used to olives. They taste funny, and the imperials put them in everything. And the oil stinks." Arshaum lamps burned butter, which to the Greek's nose had its own pervasive, greasily unpleasant smell.

Conversation in the banquet tent was halting, and not only because of the language barrier. Arigh had warned the Videssian embassy that Arshaum custom did not allow serious business to be discussed at feasts. It let Gorgidas enjoy his food more, but left him bored with the few snatches of talk he could follow.

Bogoraz, who had a gift for rousing trouble without seeming to mean to, skated close to the edge of what custom permitted. Without ever mentioning his reasons for coming onto the steppe, he bragged of Yezd's might and the glory of his overlord the khagan Wulghash. Skylitzes kept translating his boasts and grew angrier by the minute. Satisfaction and sardonic amusement in his eyes, Bogoraz stayed on his course, never saying anything against Videssos in so many words, but hurting its cause with every urbane sentence.

After a while, Skylitzes' knuckles grew white on the stem of his goblet. The clan councilors were beginning to chuckle among themselves at the fury he had to hold in. "I'll tell that sleazy liar something!" he growled.

"No!" Arigh and Goudeles said together. The pen-pusher went on, "Don't you see, he'll have you in the wrong if you answer him."

"Is this better, to be nibbled to death with his sly words?"

Surprised at his own daring, Gorgidas said, "I know a story that might put him in his place."

Skylitzes, Goudeles, and Arigh all stared at the Greek. To the Videssians he was almost as much a barbarian as the Arshaum, not to be taken seriously; Arigh tolerated him largely because he was Viridovix' friend. "You won't break custom?" he warned.

Gorgidas tossed his head. "No, it's just a story." Goudeles and Skylitzes looked at each other, shrugged, and nodded, at a loss for any better idea.

Bogoraz, whose Videssian was certainly better than the Greek's, had listened to this exchange with amiable disdain, seeing that Gorgidas' companions did not put much faith in him. His heavy-lidded eyes screened his contempt as Gorgidas dipped his head to Arghun and, with Arigh translating, said,

"Khagan, this man from Yezd is a fine speaker, no doubt of it. His words remind me of a tale of my own people."

Beyond what was required for politeness, the Arshaum chieftain had not paid Gorgidas much attention either. Now he looked at him with fresh interest; in a folk that did not read, a tale-teller was someone to be respected. "Let us hear it," he said, and the elders fell quiet to listen.

Pleased Arghun had swallowed the hook, Gorgidas plunged in: "A long time ago, in a country called Egypt, there was a great king named Sesostris." He saw men's lips moving, fixing the strange names in their memories. "Now this Sesostris was a mighty warrior and conqueror, just as our friend Bogoraz says his master Wulghash is." The smile slipped on the Yezda's face; the sarcasm he relished was not so enjoyable coming back at him.

"Sesostris conquered many countries, and took their princes and kings as his slaves to show how powerful he was. He even put them in harness and made them pull his, er, yurt." As the Greek had heard the story, it was a chariot; he made the quick switch to suit his audience.

"One day he noticed that one of the princes kept looking back over his shoulder at the yurt's wheels. He asked the fellow what he was doing.

"And the prince answered, 'I'm just watching how the wheels go round and round, and how what was once at the bottom is now on top, and what used to be high is brought low.' Then he turned round again and put his shoulder into his work.

"But Sesostris understood him, and they say that, for all his pride, he stopped using princes to haul his yurt."

The strange sounding mutter of conversation in a foreign tongue picked up again as the Arshaum considered the tale, talked about it among themselves. One or two of them sent amused glances toward Bogoraz, thinking back to his boasts. As befit his station, Arghun held his face expressionless. He said a few words to his elder son, who turned to Gorgidas. "He thanks you for an, ah, enjoyable story."

"I understood him." Repeating his half bow to the khagan, the Greek tried to say that in the Arshaum speech. Arghun did smile, then, and corrected his grammar.

Bogoraz, too, wore a diplomat's mask, set so hard it might have been carved from granite. He aimed his hooded eyes at Gorgidas like a snake charming a bird. The Greek was not one to be put in fear by such ploys, but knew he had made an enemy.

IX

GARSAVRA, ONCE REACHED, MADE ALL THE FACTIONAL strife Marcus had seen in Videssos seem as nothing. On the march west the legionaries had captured and sent back to the capital upwards of a thousand Namdaleni, fleeing their defeat at the hands of the Yezda in the small, disordered bands any beaten army breaks into. A hundred or so still held the motte-and-bailey outside Garsavra, defying Roman and Yezda alike. The tribune did not try to force them out; they were more useful against the nomads nosing down from the plateau than dangerous to his own men.

There were already Yezda in Garsavra when the legionaries got there. The town was not under their control; before Scaurus' troops arrived, it was under no one's control—which meant no one kept them out, either. Attacking them hardly seemed politic while haggling with their chief, so the tribune pretended not to notice them.

The nomads caused little trouble, going through the town like tourists and marveling at the huge buildings. Compared to Videssos the city or Rome, it was a sleepy provincial capital, but to men who lived their lives in tents it was strange and exotic beyond belief. The Yezda traded in the marketplace for civilization's luxuries and fripperies. Marcus saw one of them proudly wearing a white-glazed chamberpot on his head in place of the ubiquitous nomad fur cap. He would have told the nomad what he had, but the fellow's comrades were so admiring he did not have the heart. Quite a few local Videssians saw it, too; it gave the Yezda a new nickname, which might make trouble later.

That was the least of the tribune's problems with the locals. Faced as they were with the threat of attack from the central highlands, he had expected them to join together in receiving the legionaries favorably. Moreover, he needed them to do so. Even with Pakhymer's contribution, he was still eight thousand gold pieces short of the twenty thousand Yavlak demanded for his important captives. He had dispatched messages to the capital, but had no confidence they would bring the quick results he needed. With Thorisin Gavras fighting in the east, no one in Videssos had the driving will to hurry the imperial bureaucracy along. Scaurus knew that bureaucracy too well; he planned to raise the money he needed from the people of Garsavra and repay them when the penpushers finally got around to shipping gold west.

Expecting any large number of Videssians to agree about anything, however, as he should have remembered, was so much wishful thinking. True, many Garsavrans favored Thorisin—or said so, loudly, while the Emperor's troops held their city. But almost as many still held to the lost cause of Baanes Onomagoulos; the rebellious noble Drax had crushed before revolting in his turn had held huge estates not far south of Garsavra. Dead, especially dead at foreign hands, no one remembered his faults. The arrogant, liverish, treacherous little man was magically transformed into a martyr.

By contrast, a third party was sorry to see the Namdaleni beaten and imperial rule restored. Antakinos had warned Marcus the islanders were popular in the cities they had taken, and his warning was true. Drax had a smaller state to run than the Empire and so did not tax his towns as heavily as the imperials had. From novelty if nothing else, that was enough to gain him a good-sized following.

As subject people will, some of the Garsavrans had gone over to their conquerors' ways, even to the extent of worshiping at the temple Drax had converted to the Namdalener rite for his own men to use. The idea infuriated Styppes, who got into a shouting match with a Namdalener priest he happened to run into in the city marketplace.

Scaurus, who had been dickering with a tremor over the price of a new belt, looked up in alarm at the bellow of, "Seducer! Greaser of the skid to Skotos' ice!" Face crimson with rage, fists clenched in righteous wrath, the healer-priest shouldered his way toward the man of the Duchy, who held a fat mallard under each arm.

"By the Wager, conceited Cocksure, yours is the path to hell, not mine!" the islander yelled back, facing up to him. His priestly robe was a grayer shade of blue than Styppes'; he did not shave his head, as Videssian priests did. But his faith in his own righteousness was as strong as any imperial's.

"Excuse me," Marcus whispered to the leather seller. At a trot, as if heading into battle, he hurried toward the two priests, who were swearing at each other like a couple of cattle drovers. If he could get Styppes away before argument turned to riot . . . Too late. A crowd was already gathering. But they were crying, "Debate! Debate! Come hear the debate!" This was a diversion they had enjoyed before, with local clerics against the Namdaleni. Now they came running to hear what the new priest had to offer.

Styppes glared about as if not believing his ears. Scaurus was equally surprised, but much happier. They might get away without bloodshed after all. The tribune winced as Styppes clapped a dramatic hand to his forehead and declared, "Misbelief is to be rooted out, not discussed."

"Heh! I'll talk to *you*," the Namdalener said. He was about forty, with tough, square, dogged features that seemed better suited to an infantry underofficer than a priest. Almost as heavy as Styppes, he bore his weight better, more like an athlete gone to seed than a simple glutton. He gave an ironic bow. "Gerungus of Tupper, at your service."

Styppes coughed and fumed, but the crowd, to Marcus' relief, kept shouting for a debate. With poor grace, the healer-priest told Gerungus his name. "As you are the heretic, I shall begin," the Videssian said, "and leave you to defend your false doctrines as best you can."

Gerungus muttered something unpleasant under his breath,

but shrugged massive shoulders and said, "One of us has to." His Videssian was only slightly accented.

"Then I shall commence by asking how you islanders come to pervert Phos' creed by appending to it the clause 'on this we stake our very souls.' What authority have you for this addition? What synod sanctioned it, and when? As handed down from our learned and holy forefathers, the creed was perfect, as it stood, and should receive no valueless codicils." Marcus raised his eyebrows. Here in his area of expertise, Styppes showed more eloquence than the tribune had thought in him. Cries of approval rang from the crowd.

But every Videssian priest who disputed with Gerungus challenged him so. His answer was prompt: "Your ancient scholars lived in a fool's paradise, when the Empire ruled all the way to the Haloga country and Skotos' evil seemed far away. But you Videssians were sinners, and Skotos gained the chance to show his power. That is how the barbarians came to wrest Khatrish and Thatagush from you, aye, and Kubrat that was. For Skotos inspired the wild Khamorth from the steppe and corrupted you so you could not resist. And it grew plain Skotos' power is all too real, all too strong. Who knows whether Phos will prevail in the end? It could turn out otherwise."

Now Styppes was white, not red. "A Balancer!" he exclaimed, and the crowd growled menacingly. To the imperials, Khatrish's belief in the evenness of the struggle between good and evil was a worse heresy than the one the Namdaleni professed.

"Not so, if you give me leave to finish," Gerungus returned steadily. "Neither you nor I will be here to see the last battle between Phos and Skotos. How can we know the outcome? But we must act as if we were sure good will triumph, or face the eternal ice. I take the gamble proudly—'on this I stake my very soul.'" He stared round, defying the crowd. Marcus looked, too, and saw the Videssians unwontedly quiet. Gerungus' oratory was not as florid as Styppes', but effective all the same.

The tribune saw Nevrat Sviodo standing behind Gerungus, her thick black hair curling down over her shoulders. She smiled when their eyes met. She made a slight motion of her hand to indicate the intent crowd, then pointed toward Scaurus and nodded, as if including the two of them but no one else. He nodded back, understanding perfectly. As a Vaspurakaner, she had her own version of Phos' faith, while the Roman stood outside it altogether. Neither could grow heated over this debate.

Styppes was blowing and puffing like a beached whale, gathering his wits for the next sally. "Very pretty," he grunted, "but Phos does not throw dice with Skotos over the universe—the twin ones of 'the suns' for peace and order against the double six of 'the demons' for famine and strife. That would put chaos at Phos' heart, which cannot be.

"No, my friend," the healer-priest went on, "it is not so simple; there is more knowledge in Phos' plan than that. Nor does Skotos have need of dice to work his ends, with such as you to lead men toward falsehood from the truth. The dark god's demons record each sin of yours in their ledgers, aye, and the day and hour it was committed, and the witnesses to it. Only true repentance and genuine belief in Phos' true faith can rub out such an entry. Each blasphemy you utter sets you one step closer to the ice!"

Styppes' passion was unmistakable, though Scaurus thought his logic poor. As the healer-priest and his Namdalener counterpart argued on, the tribune's attention wandered. It stuck him that, with a few words changed, Styppes' account of the demons in hell and their sin ledgers could have been a description of the imperial tax agents' account books. He did not think the resemblance coincidental and wondered whether the Videssians had noticed it for themselves.

A wisp of stale, stinking smoke made the tribune cough as he trod up the steps of the Garsavran provincial governor's hall, a red brick building with columns of white marble flanking the entrance way. Heavily armed squads of legionaries stood prominently in the marketplace and prowled the town's main streets, making sure riot would not break out afresh. Had the one just quelled erupted a few days earlier, he would have blamed it on tension from the theological debate. As it was, he suspected the rich merchants and local nobles waiting for him inside, the men who would have to pay to help buy Drax and his comrades from the Yezda. If they could drive the

Romans out of Garsavra, their purses would be safe—and too many of them were pro-Namdalener to begin with.

He was glad of his own officers at his back. They all wore their most imposing gear, with crested helms, short capes of rank, and mail shirts burnished bright, the better to overawe the Garsavrans. A buccinator followed, carrying his horn as he might a sword.

Scaurus ran memorized phrases from his address over and over in his mind. Styppes, grumbling as usual, had helped him work on it. His own Videssian was fine for casual conversation, but in formal settings the imperials demanded formal oratory, which was nearly a different language from the ordinary speech. The Gavrai now and then got away with bluntness, but that was partly because everyone assumed they had the high style at their disposal. The tribune's unadorned words would merely mark him as a barbarian, and today he needed to seem a representative of the imperial government, not some extortionate brigand. Styppes still thought the speech too plain, but it was as ornate as the Roman could stand.

He turned to Gaius Philippus, who had listened to him rehearse. "What would Cicero think?"

"That fat windbag? Who cares? Caesar's worth five of him on the rostrum; he says what he means—and with all due respect, I think Caesar'd puke right down the front of his toga."

"Can't say I'd blame him. I feel like Ortaias Sphrantzes."

"Oh, it's not as bad as *that*, sir!" Gaius Philippus said hastily. They both laughed. Ortaias never used one word when ten would do—especially if eight of them were obscure.

Marcus motioned the buccinator forward; he preceded the legionary party into the governor's audience chamber. The tribune got his first glimpse of the locals, a score or so of men who sat talking amiably with each other and fanning themselves against the late summer's humid heat.

The sharp note of the trumpet cut through their chatter. Some of them jumped; all craned their necks toward the doorway through which Scaurus was coming. He looked neither right nor left as he took his seat in the governor's high chair and rested his arms on the exquisite rosewood table in front of it. A lot of fundaments had been in that seat lately, he thought:

a legitimate governor or two, Onomagoulos, Drax, Zigabenos perhaps, and now himself—and better him than Yavlak.

His officers stood behind him: Gaius Philippus, Junius Blaesus, and Sextus Minucius frozen to attention; Sittas Zonaras lending a Videssian touch to the party; Gagik Bagratouni a powerful physical presence in Vaspurakaner armor; and Laon Pakhymer half-amused, looking as if he were playing at charades.

He rose, looking over his audience. They stared back, some as impressed as he had hoped, others bored—most of those had the sleek look of merchants—two or three openly hostile. Not a bad mix, really, no worse than he had faced in the town senate of Mediolanum—how long ago it seemed!

He took a deep breath. For a frightening moment he thought his address had fled, but it came back to him when he began to speak: "Gentlemen, you were chosen by me today for this council; pay heed now to my words. You know how the Namdalener wickedly subdued the cities of the west; he collected tribute from you, ravaged your villages and towns in his illegal rebellion, and treated men's bodies evilly, subjecting them to unbearable exaction of their few resources. Therefore it is amazing to me, gentlemen of Garsavra, how easily you are deceived by those who have outwitted you and seek your help at the cost of your blood. They are the very ones who have done you the greatest harm, for what sort of benefit did you gain from this rebellion, other than murders and mutilations and the amputation of limbs?"

He almost laughed at the pop-eyed expression on the face of the fat man in the second row, who was in the wine trade. Likely the fellow had never heard an outlander say anything more complex than, "Gimme another mug."

Relishing his speech for the first time, the tribune continued: "Now those who would help the Namdalener have stirred you to anger and strife, yet contrived to keep their own property undamaged." Let them be suspicious of each other, Marcus thought. "At the same time, however, they still claim protection of the Empire and seek to cast the blame for their actions on the innocent. Is it expedient for you, gentlemen, to allow those who fawn on the rebel to wring advantage from you thus?

"For by Phos' assent," Marcus continued, with a phrase

Styppes had suggested, and one Scaurus would not have thought of otherwise, "you see that the Namdalener is a prisoner. Now that we are delivered from his wickedness, we must ensure that he does not escape, like smoke from the oven. And he who captured him now asks his price."

Seeing he was getting to the meat of the matter, his listeners leaned forward in anticipation. "If the Emperor were not campaigning far away, or if the barbarian holding the Namdalener allowed a delay, I would hurry to Videssos to collect that price. As you see, however, this is impossible, nor do I myself have the necessary money. Therefore it will be necessary for each of you to contribute according to his ability, lest the Yezda decide to ravage your land while awaiting his payment. I declare to you that this is the situation as it exists and pledge that, as much as you pay, it shall be restored to you by the Emperor."

He sat down, waiting for their response; they looked as pleased with the prospect of parting with their gold as he had expected. The fat wine merchant spoke for them all when he said, "Pay us back? Aye, no doubt, just as the shearer gives the sheep back their wool."

Privately, Marcus would have admitted he had a point; like any state, Videssos was happier to gather money than to spend it. What he said, though, was, "I have some influence at the capital, and I do not let the folk who help me be forgotten." They understood that; the patron-client relationship was less formal in Videssos than in Rome, but no less real. But hereabouts they were the powerful men, unused to depending on anyone else, let alone a foreign mercenary.

Zonaras spoke up. "This one has a strange habit; when he says he'll do something, he does it." He told how the legionaries had held the Namdaleni out of the hills and organized the irregulars to carry the war to them in the lowlands. "And all that," he said, "seemed a lot less likely than collecting from the treasury."

"Nothing is less likely than collecting from the treasury," the fat man insisted, drawing a short laugh. But he and his companions had listened attentively; because Zonaras was a Videssian, they were more inclined to believe him than the tribune.

One of the local nobles, a lean, nearly bald man whose

back was bent with age, struggled to his feet, leaning on a stick. He stabbed a gnarled finger at Scaurus. "It was you, then, taught our farmers to be brigands, was it?" he shrilled. With his jutting nose and thin ruff of white hair, he looked like an old, angry vulture. "Two of my wells fouled, stock run off or killed, my steward kidnapped and branded. You brought this down on me?" He stood straighter in his outrage, brandishing the stick like a sword.

But from the back of the chamber someone called, "Oh, stifle it, Skepides. If you'd shown your tenants any fairness the past fifty years, you'd have nothing to moan about."

"Eh? What was that?" Not catching the jibe, Skepides turned back to Scaurus. "I tell you this, sir, I'd sooner deal with the Namdaleni than a seditionary like yourself, Skotos take me if I wouldn't. And I'll have no more to do with this scheme of yours." Slowly and painfully he made his way to the aisle. He hobbled out. Two or three of the Videssians followed him.

"Try to talk them round," Marcus urged. "The more who share the cost, the less it falls on each of you."

"And what will you do if none of us goes along?" another merchant asked. "Take our gold by force?"

The tribune had waited for that question. "By no means," he said promptly. "In fact, if in your wisdom you choose not to help me, I intend to do nothing at all."

His audience broke into confused babble, all but ignoring him. "He won't compel us?" "Ha! What trick is this?" "To the ice with him! Let him buy his barbarians with his own money!" That last sentiment, or variations of it, had wide support. It was the plump winedealer who had the wit to ask the Roman, "What do you mean, you'd do nothing at all?"

"Why, just that." Marcus was innocence itself. "I would simply take my troops back to the imperial city, as my job would be done here, or so it seems to me."

That produced worse commotion among the Videssians than his first announcement had. "Then who'd save us from the Yezda?" someone yelled.

"Why should I care about that?"

"By Phos," the man blustered, "you've used enough wind showing what a fine imperial you are." Behind Scaurus, Gaius Philippus chuckled quietly. "Now when it comes down to protecting imperial citizens, you'd rather run away." Merchants and nobles shouted agreement—all but the wine seller, who was looking at the tribune with the grudging respect one sharper sometimes gives another.

"If you are citizens, act like it," Marcus growled, slamming his fist down on the table. "Your precious Empire has kept you fat and safe and prosperous for more years than any of you can reckon, and I doubt you have any complaint over that. But when trouble comes and it needs your help, what do you do? Bawl like so many calves looking for their mothers. By your Phos, gentlemen, if you aren't willing to give aid, why should you get it? I tell you this—if I am one single goldpiece short ten days from now, I *will* pull out, and you can make your own bargain with Yavlak. And a very good day to you all."

His officers trailing, he strode out of the audience chamber, leaving dead silence behind.

"Me, I would you thrash for so talking," Gagik Bagratouni remarked as they came out into the late afternoon sun. "But as you say, these fat so very long. They pay, I think."

"I wouldn't have had to browbeat you into it," Marcus said. "Vaspurakan is frontier country, and borderers know what has to be done." He sighed. "If I admire the Empire for keeping its people secure, I suppose I shouldn't blame them for being selfish as well. They've never had not to be."

He caught motion out of the corner of his eye, swung round on Gaius Philippus. "And what in the name of the gods are you up to?"

The senior centurion gave a guilty start and jerked his hands away from his dagger. The thin keen blade stayed where he had wedged it—between the drums of one of the columns by the entranceway of the governor's hall. "I've wanted to do that for years," he said defensively. "How many times have you heard toffs going on and on about columns so perfectly made you couldn't get a knife blade between the drums? I always thought it was so much rubbish, and here I've proved it." He retrieved the dagger.

Marcus rolled his eyes. "It's a good thing Viridovix isn't here to see you, or you'd never hear the last of it. Columns, now!" He smiled to himself all the way back to the legionary camp.

The next morning a very respectful Garsavran delegation appeared to announce they were having difficulty in allotting payments proportional to wealth. The stall was so blatant Marcus almost laughed in their faces. "Come along, my friends," he said, and returned to the governor's residence. After a winter's struggle with the intricacies of the whole Empire's tax structure at Videssos the city, the local receipts were child's play. An hour and a half later he emerged from the records office and handed the nervously waiting Garsavrans a list of amounts due, down to the fraction of a goldpiece. Defeat in their eyes, they took it and slipped away.

He had all the payments within two days.

With the constant strain and motion of campaigning, he knew he had not given Helvis much time or attention the past couple of months. Sometimes he thought that pleased her just as well. If they were not together much, they could not quarrel, and she still bitterly resented his loyalty to the Empire. And as her pregnancy progressed, her desire for him faded. The same thing had happened when she was carrying Dosti; he bore it as best he could.

Once they set down a long-term camp outside Garsavra, however, they could not keep ignoring each other—and Soteric's captivity gave Helvis a new and urgent worry. The evening after Scaurus sent a heavily armed party to buy the Namdalener prisoners from Yavlak, she asked him, "What do you plan to do with them once you have them?"

She held her voice tight-reined, but he could hear the fear that rode it. Still, she urged no action on him, having learned that the easiest way to turn him against an idea was to push for it too strongly. In the lamplight her deep blue eyes were enormous as she waited for his reply.

"Nothing at once, past holding them and sending word to Thorisin. That choice is for him to make, not me."

He braced for an explosion, but was startled when her eyes swam with tears, and she scrambled clumsily to her feet to embrace him, saying brokenly, "Thank you, oh, thank you!"

"Here, what's this about?" he said, taking her shoulders and holding her at arm's length so he could see her face. "Did you think I'd kill them out of hand?"

"How was I to know? After what you said in camp after the

battle where—" She could not put a pleasant face on that, so she drew back quickly. "After the battle, I feared you might."

Her gaze went to the image of the holy Nestorios atop her little traveling shrine. "Thank you," she whispered to the saint, "for saving Soteric."

Marcus stroked her hair. "I said that in the heat of rage. That does not excuse it; I'm not proud of it. But I haven't the stomach for butchery. I thought you knew me better."

"I thought I did, too." She moved close to him, smiled when her belly touched him at the same time as her breasts. But her face grew sober again as she looked up and tried to read his. "Still, even after so long I think sometimes I don't know you at all."

His arms tightened around her. He often felt the same toward her and realized their recent isolation had done nothing to help that. Even so, he did not tell her what was in his mind—that Thorisin Gavras, Avtokrator of the Videssians, was not apt to view captured rebel chiefs kindly. The holy Nestorios notwithstanding, Soteric was a long way from saved.

The note was in Latin, and ambiguous to boot: "We have your packages. Coming in three days." Marcus read it twice before he noticed the Roman "d" was replaced by its Videssian equivalent. Little by little the Empire wore away at them all.

On the morning of the third day a Khatrisher messenger told the tribune the company he had sent out was within a couple of hours of Garsavra. "Very good," he breathed, full of relief. So Yavlak had kept his bargain after all—one hurdle overleaped.

To intimidate the islanders still holed up in their fortress outside the town, Marcus paraded almost his entire army past the castle, leaving behind only enough men to hold the legionary camp against a sally. The men of the Duchy watched him from their walls of heaped-up earth. They would be getting hungry in there soon, he thought; time enough to deal with them then.

Even so short a distance west of Garsavra, the land began to slope sharply upwards toward the central plateau. The Arandos, slow and placid in the lowlands, bumped down over cataracts to reach them. The great boulders were almost lost in seething white foam. Its greatest tributary, the Eriza, flowed down from the north to meet it; Garsavra sat at their junction.

Scaurus' guide clung to the southern bank of the Arandos, which surprised him not at all. On the plateau the rivers were the only sure source of water in summer.

He saw dust ahead, low, widespread cloud that meant men on foot—the light cavalry of the Yezda would have kicked it up in high, straight columns. He exchanged grins with the Khatrisher scout, who gave the thumbs-up gesture Pakhymer's hand had picked up from the Romans.

Then Marcus spied the marching square of legionaries, flanked by a thin cordon of Khatrisher archers to hold off any raiders that might appear—and to round up any Namdalener who somehow broke out of that hollow square.

Junius Blaesus saluted the tribune with the air of a man glad to lay down a heavy burden. "Here they are, sir, all the ones Yavlak had alive: three hundred and—let me see—seventeen. I set out with, ah, twenty-one who died on the march—they were badly wounded to start with, and I couldn't see much the Yezda had done for 'em. I didn't want to leave them behind, though," he finished anxiously.

"You did right," Marcus assured him, and watched his broad peasant face glow with pleasure. Earnest though Blaesus was, responsibility frightened him.

The tribune turned from the junior centurions to the Namdaleni in his charge. The islanders were a far cry from the proud, confident troops who had set out to wrest Videssos' westlands from the Empire. Patchy beards straggled up their gaunt cheeks. Most walked with a forward list, as if drawing themselves up straight took more vigor than they had. Almost every man limped, some from wounds, the rest because the Yezda had stolen their boots and left them only cloths with which to wrap their feet. They wore tattered rags of surcoats and trousers; like the boots, their mail shirts were the nomads' spoils. Their eyes were hollow and uncaring as they plodded along.

So this was victory, Scaurus thought. He felt like a captain of one of Crassus' fire brigades back at Rome, turning a profit from the misfortune of others by buying burning property on the cheap.

Here and there a face, an attitude stood out from the general run of prisoners. Mertikes Zigabenos' luxuriant black whiskers made him easy to pick out in the throng of new, scraggly beards. So did his expression of absolute despair, painful to see even among so much misery. He would not lift his head when Marcus called his name. Beside him walked Drax, whose short beard was startlingly red. The great count's left arm in a filthy sling. He was not ashamed to meet Scaurus' eye, but his own steady gaze was as unfathomable as ever.

Not all the Namdaleni had forgotten they were men. The veteran Fayard, who had been a member of Hemond's squadron when Marcus arrived at Videssos the city, marched where the troopers around him shambled. He threw the tribune a sharp salute, followed it with a shrug, as if to say he had thought they would meet again, but not like this. Somehow he had kept himself fit, making the best of whatever came his way.

Soteric, too, was straight as a plumb bob. That stubborn erectness was what first made Marcus know him; beard and haggardness added years to his looks, so he seemed older than the tribune when in fact he was not thirty. A half-healed, puckered scar seamed his forehead. He glared at his brother-in-law like a trapped wolf. With little sympathy in him, he expected none.

"Traitor!" Soteric shouted, and the tribune did not doubt he meant it. A strange word, he thought, after the fight at the Sangarios. But Helvis' brother was so full of the righteousness of his cause that he was blind to any other. Some of that was in Helvis, too. Not as much, Marcus thought thankfully.

He turned to Styppes, saying, "Do what you can for their hurts." Not all of those, he saw, had come in battle; some islanders carried the mark of the lash or worse.

The healer-priest had scant relish for his task. "You ask too much of me," he said, sounding for once very much like Gorgidas. "Many I will not cure, for they have had long to fester. And these are heretics and enemies as well."

"They fought for the Empire once," Marcus pointed out, "and many will again, with your help." Styppes scowled at him. Scaurus started to argue further, but found he was talking to the priest's back. Styppes was pushing past Blaesus' men to reach the wounded Namdaleni.

Gaius Philippus was trying not to smile. "What is it with that one? Does he always have to growl a while before he goes to work?"

"You're a fine one to talk. The gods help any legionary in your way after something goes wrong," Scaurus said. The veteran did grin then, acknowledging the hit.

It was drawing toward evening when the legionaries and their captives reached Garsavra. Scaurus led them past the Namdalener-held fortress once more, an implied threat that the men of the Duchy in his hands might become hostages for the castle's surrender. The ploy worked less well than he had hoped. The haler prisoners raised a cheer to see the motte-and-bailey still holding out, a cheer the knights on its rampart echoed.

Soteric gave Marcus a look filled with ironic triumph.

Nettled, the tribune paraded his army and the captured Namdaleni down Garsavra's chief street to the town market-place as a spectacle for the people. That was not quite a success, either. The Garsavrans were less fond of such shows than their jaded cousins in the capital. The verge of the road-way was embarrassingly empty as the legionaries tramped between the baths and the local prelate's residence, a domed building of yellow stucco every bit as large and important as the governor's hall. The clatter of hobnailed *caligae* on cobblestones all but drowned the spatters of applause the few spectators did dole out. Most of the townsfolk ignored the parade, preferring to go about their business.

But that did not mean the Garsavrans paid no attention to the arrival of the Namdalener prisoners. The town began to heave like a man after a stiff dose of hellebore, and street fights broke out fresh. One faction wanted to lynch the islanders out of hand. To his dismay, Scaurus found this group including not only those who hated the Namdaleni, but also some who had collaborated with them while they held Garsavra and now wanted to make sure details of their collusion never came forth.

"They'd be as glad to work for Yavlak," he said, disgusted.

"Aye, well, it's for us to see they never have the chance,"

Gaius Philippus answered calmly, too cynical to be much upset by another proof of man's capacity for meanness.

But for every man ready to roast the islanders over a slow fire, another wanted to free them and start the rebellion all over again. Marcus began to wish he had settled down to besiege the men of the Duchy in their motte-and-bailey, however wasteful of troops and time that was. He was sure they slipped into town from time to time; with Garsavra wall-less, it was impossible to keep them out. And their presence was a constant reminder to the Garsavrans of their brief rule. Every third housefront, it seemed, had "Drax the Protector" scrawled on it in charcoal or whitewash.

The tribune did his best to get his captives fit for travel east, thinking that once the bulk of them were out of Garsavra the turmoil would die down. He also wanted to show the townsfolk that the islanders themselves had to recognize the Empire's superiority. The ceremony he worked out borrowed from both Roman and Videssian practices.

In the center of the marketplace he drove two *pila* butt-first into the ground, then lashed a third across them, a little below head height; he set a portrait of Thorisin Gavras atop the crosspiece. Then he gathered the Namdalener prisoners—all save Drax, his leading officers, and the luckless Martikes Zigabenos—in front of his creation in groups of ten. Legionaries with bared swords and Khatrisher archers stood between them and the watching Garsavrans.

"As you bend your necks to pass under this yoke," Scaurus said to the prisoners—and to the crowd, "so do you yield yourselves up to the rightful Avtokrator of the Videssians, Thorisin Gavras."

Group by group, the islanders subjugated themselves, stooping beneath the Roman spear and the image of the Videssian Emperor. As they emerged on the far side, Styppes swore each group to a frightful oath calling down curses on themselves, their families, and their clans if ever they warred against the Empire, or even sat silent while others spoke of such war. And group by group the Namdaleni swore, "On this we stake our very souls." The healer-priest glowered at the form their oath took, but Marcus was well pleased. The men of the Duchy were more likely to obey an oath that followed their own usage than one imposed on them by the imperials.

The ritual of surrender went perfectly through about two-thirds of the Namdaleni. Then Styppes, in the middle of swearing yet another group to loyalty, swayed and collapsed. As he had been gulping from a large wineskin all through the ceremony, Marcus was more annoyed than concerned. There was a brief delay as a couple of Romans dragged him to one side and another pair hurried off to fetch the prelate of Garsavra, a white-bearded, affable man named Lavros.

Marcus rescued the written-out oath from where it had fallen by Styppes. Lavros quickly read it to himself, then nodded and started to administer it from the beginning to the waiting Namdaleni, who had been laughing and joking among themselves. Fayard, who happened to be in the group being sworn, called out, "Here now, your honor, we've done that bit already!"

"I doubt you'll suffer any lasting harm from doing it again," Lavros said, unruffled, and kept right on with the whole oath. The men of the Duchy made their pledge, and the ceremony went on.

Thirty Khatrishers accompanied the Namdalener prisoners Scaurus sent back to Videssos the city. They were as much to protect the islanders from Ras Simokattes' irregulars as to keep them from escaping; Namdaleni who traveled through the countryside unarmed or in small parties took their lives in their hands.

Every so often the tribune worried about Bailli's angry outburst at the edge of the southeastern hills. The men of the Duchy were beaten, but the guerillas showed no sign of shutting up shop. One problem at a time, Scaurus told himself, echoing Laon Pakhymer.

Bailli and his fellow officers were a problem in themselves. Marcus had not sent them east with the common soldiers, not caring to risk their getting away on the journey—they were too dangerous to run loose. He kept them shut up in the governor's residence, waiting for an order from Thorisin on their fate. That solution was not ideal either, for as soon as the Garsavrans realized they were there the town broke out in new turmoil—or rather the same old one.

They had quarrels within their ranks as well; Mertikes Zigabenos sent Scaurus a request to be quartered apart from the

Namdaleni who had made an unwilling Emperor of him. The tribune complied—he was much more sympathetic to Zigabenos' plight than that of, say, Drax or Soteric. The only Namdalener marshal who roused his pity was Turgot of Sotevag, who was nearly out of his mind with worry over his mistress Mavia. Scaurus remembered her from the capital, a startlingly blonde girl less than half Turgot's age. With the rest of the islanders' women, she had stayed in Garsavra when they rode west against the Yezda and, Marcus thought, likely fled when news came of their defeat. That, he had seen after Maragha, was part of a mercenary's life, too. But Turgot would not hear it, swearing she had promised to wait for him.

After a week of this, Drax' patience wore thin. "And what's a promise worth?" he snapped. When he heard of it, Marcus thought the remark showed more of the great count's nature than he usually let through his self-possessed facade.

Imprisonment was not a usual Roman penalty, its place being taken by corporal punishment, fines, or sentence of exile. Inexperienced jailers, the legionaries paid for learning the trade. One morning a shaking guardsman woke Scaurus to report Mertikes Zigabenos' cell empty.

"A pox!" the tribune said, leaping off his sleeping-mat. Helvis murmured drowsily as he threw a mantle over his shoulders, then leaped up in alarm when he shouted for the buccinators to sound the alarm. By the time Dosti's first frightened wail rang out, Marcus was already out in the *via principalis* setting up search teams.

Going through Garsavra house by house, he was gloomily aware, was a task that had been beaten before he began. And yet when the legionaries quickly found their fugitive, the news was no great delight. Zigabenos was on his knees at the altar of Garsavra's main temple to Phos, which was set behind the city prelate's home. Clinging to the holy table with hands pale-knuckled from the force of his grip, the reluctant Avtokrator cried, "Sanctuary!" over and over, as loud as he could.

The tribune found a Roman squad standing uncertainly outside the temple doorway. A body of locals was gathering, too, plainly not willing to see Zigabenos dragged from the shrine by force. Nor did the legionaries seem eager to go in after him. Some of them had taken to Phos themselves since coming to the Empire, and temples were refuge-places in the Roman world as well.

Rubbing sleep from his eyes, Lavros the prelate arrived at the same time Marcus did. He placed himself in the entrance to block the tribune's path. Making Phos' sun-sign on his breast, he said loudly, "You shall not take this man away against his will. He has claimed sanctuary with the good god." The swelling crowd shouted in support, pressing forward despite the Romans' armor, swords, and spears.

"May I go in alone and speak with him, at least?" Scaurus asked.

His mild reply took Lavros by surprise. The senior priest considered, running the palm of his hand across his shaven skull. "Will you put aside your weapons?" he asked.

Marcus hesitated; he did not like the idea of parting with his potent Gallic blade. At last he said, "I will," and stripped off sword and dagger. He handed them to his squad leader, a solid trooper named Aulus Florus. "Take care of these," he said. Florus nodded.

As Lavros stood aside to let the tribune pass, he whispered, "And what's all this in aid of?" Marcus shrugged; he heard the ghost of a laugh behind him as he stepped into the temple.

It was laid out like all of Phos' shrines, with the altar in the middle under the dome, and seats radiating out in the four cardinal directions. The mosaic in the dome was a poor copy of the one that graced the High Temple in the capital. This Phos was stern in judgment, but not the awesome, spiritually potent figure that made any man unsure of his own worthiness.

A prickle of unease ran through the Roman as he came down the aisle. If Zigabenos had somehow armed himself . . . but the Videssian guards officer tightened his grasp on the altar still further and kept up his cry of, "Sanctuary! In Phos' name, I claim sanctuary!"

"There's but the one of me, Mertikes," Marcus said. He spread his hands to show they were empty. "Can we talk?"

In the flickering candlelight Zigabenos' eyes were haunted. "Shall I say aye, then, when you haul me off to the headsmen? Why should I ease your conscience for you?" A veteran of imperial politics, he knew the usual fate of failed rebels.

Marcus only waited, saying nothing. A painful sigh

escaped Zigabenos. His shoulders sagged as the tribune's silence let him realize how hopeless his position was. "Damn you, outlander," he said at last, voice old and beaten. "What use to this farce, after all? Thirst or hunger will drive me out soon enough. Here; you have me, for what joy it brings you." He let go the altar; Scaurus saw sweat beaded on the polished wood where his hands had been.

Seeing the clever Zigabenos succumbing thus to fate wrenched at the tribune. He blurted, "But you must have had some plan when you fled here!"

"So I did," the Videssian said. His smile was bitter. "I would have yielded up my hair and turned monk. Even an emperor thinks three times before he sends the knives after a man sworn to Phos. But I was too quick—the shrine was dark and empty when I got here, with no priest to give my vow to. Wretched slugabeds! And now it's you here instead. I always thought you a good soldier, Scaurus; I could wish I was wrong."

Marcus hardly heard the compliment; he was shouting for Lavros. The prelate hurried toward him, concern overriding his usual good nature. "I hope you'll not try to cozen me into believing this suppliant has changed his mind—"

"But I have, reverend sir," Zigabenos began.

"No indeed," Scaurus said. "Let it be just as he wishes. Fetch all the people in and let them see the man who was forced to play the role of Avtokrator now make amends for what he was compelled to do, by assuming the garments of your monks."

Lavros and Mertikes Zigabenos both stared at him, the one in delight, the other in blank amazement. The priest bowed deeply to Scaurus and bustled up the aisle, calling to the crowd outside. "You'll let me?" Zigabenos whispered, still unbelieving.

"Why not? What better way to get you out of the political life for good?"

"Thorisin won't thank you for it."

"Then let him look to himself. If he put Ortaias Sphrantzes in a blue robe after getting nothing but ill from him, he shouldn't grudge you your life. You served him well until your luck tossed sixes at you." Marcus felt an absurd pleasure at remembering the losing Videssian throw and being able to bring it out naturally.

"I threw my own 'demons,' trusting the Namdaleni too far."

"So did Thorisin," the tribune pointed out, and Zigabenos really smiled for the first time since Scaurus had reclaimed him from the Yezda.

They had little more chance for talk; the temple was filling fast with chattering Garsavrans. Scaurus took a seat in the first row of benches, leaving Zigabenos alone by the altar. In his shabby cloak, he was a poor match for its silver-plated magnificence.

Lavros had disappeared for a few minutes. He returned bearing a large pair of scissors and a razor with a glittering edge. A second priest followed him, a swarthy, stocky man who carried an unadorned blue robe and bore a copy of Phos' sacred writings, bound in rich red leather, under his arm. The townsfolk grew quiet as they strode toward the holy table in the center of the shrine.

Zigabenos lowered his head toward Lavros. The scissors snipped, shearing away his thick black hair. Once there was only stubble on his pate, Lavros wielded the razor. Zigabenos' scalp gleamed pale, and seemed all the whiter when compared to his sun-weathered face.

The short, swarthy priest held out the leather-bound volume to the officer, saying formally, "Behold the law under which you shall live if you choose. If in your heart you feel you can observe it, enter the monastic life; if not, speak now."

Head still bent, Zigabenos murmured, "I will observe it." The priest asked him twice more; his voice gained strength with each affirmation. After the last repetition, the priest bowed in turn to Zigabenos, handed his book to Lavros, and invested the new monk with his monastic garb. Again following ritual, he said, "As the garment of Phos' blue covers your naked body, so may his righteousness enfold your heart and preserve it from all evil."

"So may it be," Zigabenos whispered; the Garsavrans echoed his words.

Lavros prayed silently for a few moments, then said, "Brother Mertikes, would it please you to lead this gathering in Phos' creed?"

"May I?" said Zigabenos—no, Mertikes, Scaurus thought, for Videssian monks yielded up their surnames. His voice was truly grateful; the tribune had yet to meet a Videssian who took his faith lightly. Mertikes was a strange sight, standing by the rich altar in his severely plain robe, a little trickle of blood on the side of his newly shaved head where the razor had cut too close. But even Scaurus the unbeliever was oddly moved as he led the worshipers in the splendid archaic language of their creed, "We bless thee, Phos, Lord with the great and good mind, by thy grace our protector, watchful beforehand that the great test of life may be decided in our favor."

"Amen," the Garsavrans finished, and Marcus found himself repeating it with them. Lavros said, "This service is completed." The crowd began to stream away. Mertikes came up to squeeze Scaurus' hand with his own strong clasp. Then Lavros said gently, "Come with me, brother, and I will take you to the monastery and introduce you to your fellow servants of Phos." Head up now, not looking back, the new monk followed him.

That crisis solved itself neatly, but was only peripheral to the greater problem of the captive Namdalener lords. A week after Zigabenos became Brother Mertikes, a mob tried to storm the provincial governor's hall and free Drax and his comrades. The legionaries had to use steel to drive the rioters back, leaving a score of them dead and many more wounded. They lost two of their own as well, and after that the Romans could only walk Garsavra's streets by squads. Three nights later the townsmen tried again. This time Marcus was ready for them. Khatrisher archers on the roof of the hall broke the mob's charge before it was well begun, and none of the tribune's men was hurt.

He knew, though, that he did not have the troops to hold down sedition forever, not and watch Yavlak, too. And so he met with the Namdaleni in their confinement. Soteric gave a sardonic bow. "You honor us, brother-in-law. I've seen my sister a few times, but you never deigned visit before."

And Bailli sneered. "Still sweating, are you? I hope they wring all the water from your carcass." Drax' lieutenant was far from forgetting the peasant irregulars.

The great count himself sat quiet, along with Turgot.

Marcus guessed that Turgot did not care what he was about to say; Drax' silence was likelier from policy.

The tribune nodded to Bailli. "Yes, I'm still sweating. I don't fancy going through another night like the couple just past and I don't intend to, either. And so, gentlemen—" He looked from one islander to the next. "—something will have to be done about you. Easiest would be to strike off your heads and put them on pikes in the marketplace."

"Whoreson," Soteric said.

Drax leaned forward, alert now. "You'd not say that if it was your plan."

"I'll do it if I have to," Marcus answered, but he admired the great count's quickness all the same. "Truly, I'd sooner not—it's Thorisin's place to judge what you deserve. But I won't chance the townsfolk freeing you. You're too dangerous to the Empire for that." Drax bowed slightly, as if acknowledging praise.

"What do you leave us with, then?" Soteric demanded scornfully.

"Your bare lives, if you want them. Do you?" The tribune waited. As the Namdaleni saw he meant the question, they slowly nodded, Turgot last of all. "Very well, then . . ."

"You're getting good at these spectacles," Gaius Philippus said out of the corner of his mouth. "The locals'll think twice before they get gay." A hollow square of legionaries in full battle dress stood at attention in the center of the Garsavran marketplace, *pila* grounded, staring stolidly out at the hostile Videssians around them. A raw northerly breeze whipped their cloaks back from their shoulders.

"I'm glad the weather's holding off," Marcus said. When the wind came from the north, rain and then snow were bound to follow. The tribune was happy to be next to the small fire in the center of the Romans' square—until a blown spark stung his calf behind his greave. He cursed and rubbed.

The buccinators' horns brayed; heads turned toward the maniple tramping into the marketplace, its swords drawn and menacing. Taller than their Roman captors, Drax and Bailli, Soteric and Turgot were easy to recognize in the center of the column.

Marcus glanced toward Ansfrit, the captain of the Namdalener castle, to whom he had granted a safe-conduct to his drama. Ansfrit looked as though he wanted to try a rescue on the spot, but the fearsome aspect of Scaurus' troopers was enough to intimidate the Garsavrans.

The maniple merged with the hollow square. Legionaries frog-marched their prisoners up to the tribune, two to each islander. In front of them strode Zeprin the Red. The enormous Haloga cut an awesome figure in the gleaming gilded cuirass of Imperial Guards—freshly regilded for the occasion, in fact. He saluted Scaurus Roman-style, shooting right fist out and up. "Behold the traitors!" he cried, bass thundering through the open market.

Barefoot, shivering in the wind in thin gray linen tunics, fists clenched tight with tension, the men of the Duchy awaited judgment. The silence stretched. Then the crowd of Garsavrans around the square of the legionaries parted as if fearing disease, to let a single figure through. Like Spartan hoplites of the world Scaurus had known, Videssian executioners wore red to make the stains of their calling less evident. Only the man's black buskins were not the color of blood.

There were Yezda in the crowd; the tribune saw them staring admiringly at the tall, angular, masked shape of the executioner. Here was pomp and ceremony to suit them, he thought with distaste.

No help for that—he was bound to go on with what he had devised. "Hear me, people of Garsavra," he said; Styppes had been glad to help with *this* speech. "As traitors and rebels against his Imperial Majesty Thorisin Gavras, Avtokrator of the Videssians, these wretches deserve no less than death. Only my mercy spares them that." But as his listeners began to brighten, he went on inexorably, "Yet as a mark of the outrage they have worked on the Empire, and as fit warning to any others who might be mad enough to contemplate revolt, let the sight of their eyes be extinguished and let them know Skotos' darkness forevermore!" By Videssian reckoning, that constituted mercy, for it avoided capital punishment.

But a moan rose from the crowd, overtopped by Ansfrit's bellow of anguish. The Garsavrans started to surge forward, but Roman *pila* snapped out in bristling hedgehog array to hold them off.

Inside the hollow square, the four Namdaleni jerked as if stung. "Blinded?" Drax howled. "I'd sooner die!" The islanders wrenched against their captors' grip and, with panic strength, managed to tear free for an instant. But for all their struggles, the legionaries wrestled them to the ground and held them there, pulling away the hands with which they vainly tried to shield their eyes.

Tunelessly humming a hymn to Phos, the executioner put the tip of a thin pointed iron in the fire. He lifted it every so often to gauge its color; his thick gloves of crimson leather protected him from the heat. Finally he grunted in satisfaction and turned to Scaurus. "Which of 'em first?"

"As you wish."

"You, then." Bailli happened to be closest to the executioner, who went on, not unkindly, "Try to hold as steady as you can; 'twill be easier for you so."

"Easier," Bailli mocked through clenched teeth; sweat poured down his face. Then the iron came down, once, twice. Tight-jawed no longer, the snub-nosed Namdalener screamed and screamed. The scent of charring meat filled the air.

Pausing between victims to reheat his iron, the executioner moved on to Turgot and Drax, and then at last to Soteric. Helvis' brother's cries were all curses aimed Marcus' way. He stood unmoved over the fallen Namdaleni and answered only, "You brought this upon yourselves." The burned-meat smell was very strong now, as if someone had forgotten a roasting joint of pork.

The legionaries helped their groaning, sobbing prisoners sit, pulling thick black veils over their eyes to hide the hot iron's work. "Show them to the people," Scaurus commanded. "Let them see what they earn by defying their rightful sovereign." The troopers who formed the hollow square opened lanes to let the crowd look on the Namdaleni.

"Now take them away," the tribune said. No one raised a hand to stop the islanders from being guided back to their captivity in the governor's hall. They stumbled against each other as they staggered between their Roman guards.

"Ansfrit," Marcus called. The Namdalener captain approached, fear and rage struggling on his pale face. Scaurus gave him no time to compose himself: "Surrender your castle to me within the day, or when we take it—and you know we can—everyone of your men will suffer the same fate as these turncoats. Yield now, and I guarantee their safety."

"I thought you above these Videssian butcheries, but it seems the dog apes his master."

"That's as may be," the tribune shrugged, implacable. "Will you yield, or shall I have this fellow—" He jerked his head toward the red-clad executioner. "—keep his irons hot?" Under his shiny leather mask, the man's mouth shaped a smile at Ansfrit.

The Namdalener flinched, recovered, glared helplessly at Scaurus. "Aye, damn you, aye," he choked out, and spun on his heel, almost running back toward the motte-and-bailey. Behind his retreating back, Gaius Philippus nodded knowingly. Marcus smiled himself. Another pair of troubles solved, he thought.

The druids' marks on his blade flared into golden life, scenting wizardry, but it was scabbarded, and he did not see.

Far to the north, Avshar laid aside the black-armored image of Skotos he used to focus his scrying powers. A greater seer than any *enaree*, he cast forth his vision to overleap steppe and sea, as a man might cast a fishing line into a stream. The power in Scaurus' sword was his guide; if it warded the hated outlander from his spells, it also proclaimed the Roman's whereabouts and let Avshar spy. Though he could not see the tribune himself, all around him was clear enough.

The wizard-prince leaned back against a horsehair-filled cushion of felt. Even for him, scrying at such a distance was no easy feat. "A lovely jest, mine enemy," he whispered, though no one was there to hear him. "Oh yes, a lovely jest. Yet perhaps I shall find a better one."

News somehow travels faster than men. When Scaurus got back to the legionary camp, Helvis met him with a shriek. "Animal! Worse than animal—foul, wretched, atrocious brute!" Her face was dead white, save for a spot of color high on each cheek.

Legionaries and their women pretended not to hear—a privilege of rank, Marcus thought. They would have gathered round to listen to any common trooper scrapping with his leman.

He took Helvis by the elbow, tried to steer her back toward their tent. "Don't flare at me," he warned. "I left them alive, and more than they deserved, too."

She whirled away from him. "Alive? What sort of life is it, to sit in a corner of the marketplace with a chipped cup in your lap, begging for coppers? My brother—"

She dissolved in tears. The tribune managed to guide her into the tent, away from the camp's watching eyes. Malric, he guessed, was out playing; Dosti, napping in his crib, woke and started to cry when his mother came in sobbing. Marcus tried to comfort her, saying, "There's no need for that, darling. Here, I've brought a present for you."

Helvis stared at him, wild-eyed. "So I'm your slut now, to be bought with trinkets?"

He felt himself reddening and damned his clumsy words; the Videssian oratory was turgid, but at least it could be rehearsed. This, now— "See for yourself," he said brusquely, and tossed her a small leather pouch.

She caught it automatically, tugged the drawstring open. "This is a gift?" she stuttered, confusion routing fury for a moment. "Chunks of half-burned fat?"

"I hoped you might think so," Scaurus said, "since each of your precious islanders—aye, your honey-mouthed brother, too—clapped them over his eyes as my troopers fought 'em in the dirt."

Her mouth moved without sound, something the tribune had heard of but never seen. At last she whispered, "They're not blind?"

"Not a bit of it," Marcus said smugly, "though Turgot flinched and got an eyebrow seared off, the poor mournful twit. A pretty joke, don't you think?" he went on, unaware he all but echoed his deadliest foe. "All the riots and plots in town have collapsed like a popped bladder, and Ansfrit's panicked into giving up lest he earn what Drax got."

But Helvis was not listening to him any more. "They're not bl—" she started to scream, and then bit the palm of his hand as he clapped it over her mouth.

"You don't know that," he said, stern again. "You've never heard that. Apart from the legionaries who wrestled them down and a few others close enough to see what happened, the only one who knows is that butcher in his suit of blood, and he's well paid to keep quiet. D'you understand me?" he asked, cautiously taking his hand away.

"Yes," she said in so small a voice they both laughed. "I'd pretend anything, anything, to keep Soteric safe. Oh, hush, you," she added to Dosti, plucking him out of the crib. "Everything is all right."

"All right?" Dosti said doubtfully, and followed it with a hiccup. Marcus scratched his head; every time he looked at his son, it seemed, Dosti had something newly learned to show him.

"All right," Helvis said.

THE SIEGE TOWER RUMBLED ACROSS THE BOARD. "GUARD your Emperor, now!" Viridovix said, scooping up a captured foot soldier—no telling when he might be useful, coming back into play on the Gaul's side.

Seirem twisted her mouth in annoyance, blocked the threat with a silverpiece. He pulled the siege tower back out of danger. She advanced her other silverpiece a square, reaching the seventh rank of the nine-by-nine board. With a smile, she turned the flat piece over to reveal the new, jeweled character on its reverse. "Promote to gold," she said.

"Dinna remind me," he said mournfully; as a more powerful goldpiece, the counter attacked his prelate and a horseman at the same time. The prelate was worth more to him; he moved it. Seirem took the horseman. It was like the Videssians, Viridovix thought, to have money fight for them in their board game—and to grow more valuable deep in enemy territory.

He wondered how long the board and men had wandered with the nomads, an unplayed curiosity. No doubt some plainsman had brought the set back with him from Prista, taken by the rich grain of the oaken game board, by the inset lines of mother-of-pearl that separated square from square, and by the ivory pieces and the characters on them, made from emeralds and turquoise and garnets. In Videssos the Gaul had learned the game on a stiff leather board, with counters crudely hacked from pine. He admired it tremendously, most of all because luck played no part in it.

In the Empire he had only been a fair player; here he was teaching the game, and still ahead of his pupils. Seirem, though, was catching on fast. "Too fast by half," he muttered in his own Celtic speech; she had turned the captured horseman against him, with wicked effect.

It took a sharp struggle before he finally subdued her, trapping her emperor in a corner with his siege tower, prelate, and a goldpiece. She frowned, more thoughtfully than in anger. "Yes, I see," she said. "It was a mistake to weaken the protection around him to throw that attack at you. You held me off, and there I was in the open with no help around to save me." Her fingers reset the board. "Shall we try again? You take first move this time; my defense needs work."

"Och, lass, for the wee bit you've played, you make a brave show of it." He advanced the foot soldier covering a silverpiece's file, opening the long diagonal for his prelate. Seirem frowned again as she considered a reply.

Watching her concentrate, he thought how different she was from Komitta Rhangavve. Once he had managed to steal a whole day with Thorisin Gavras' volcanic mistress; the gameboard was a pleasant diversion between rounds. Or it should have been, but the Celt had never learned the courtier's art of graceful losing. One game Komitta beat him fairly; the next he managed to win. She'd screeched curses and hurled the board, pieces and all, against a wall. He never did find one of the spearmen.

Here was Seirem, by contrast, paying the price of trouncings to learn the game, her fine dark eyes full of thought while she waited for his next move. She also had a sweet, low voice and was equally skilled with the pipes and the light women's bow. Yet Komitta, with her passion for rank, would have called her barbarian, or worse. "Honh!" the Celt snorted, again in his own language. "The bigger fool her, the vicious trull!"

"Will you be all night?" Seirem asked pointedly.

"Begging your pardon, lass; my wits were wandering." He

moved a foot soldier and promptly regretted it. He tugged at his mustaches. "Sure and that was a rude thing to do!"

From the fireside where she was gossiping with a couple of other women, Borane glanced over at the game-players. She recognized the tone Viridovix used toward her daughter, perhaps better than he did; after so many casual amours, he was not ready to admit to himself that he might feel something more for Seirem. But for those with ears to hear, his voice gave him away.

Targitaus stamped into the tent, face like thunder. He, too, was bright enough to see how Seirem had become the outlander's favorite partner at the gameboard. But when he growled, "Put your toys away!" and followed that with an oath that made Borane's friends giggle, the Gaul was not panic-stricken; he had seen this fury before.

"Who's said us nay the now?" he asked.

"Krobyz, the wind spirits blow sleet up his arse! May his ewes be barren and his cows' udders dry. What did you call his clan, V'rid'rish, the Hamsters? You were right, for he has the soul of a hamster turd in him." He spat into the fire in absolute disgust.

"What excuse did he offer?" Seirem asked, trying to pierce her father's anger.

"Eh? Not even a tiny one, the shameless son of a snake and a goat." Targitaus was not appeased. "Just a no, and from what Rambehisht says, he counts himself lucky not to come back with a hole in him for his troubles."

Viridovix grimaced as he helped Seirem put the pieces away, hardly noticing that their hands brushed more than once. "That's not good at all. Every one o' these spalpeens should be seeing the need to put the fornicating bandits down, and too many dinna for me to think the lot of 'em fools. A pox on Varatesh, anyhow; the omadhaun's too clever by half. Belike he's got his hooks into some o' the nay-sayers."

"You have it, I think," Targitaus said heavily. "The rider I sent to Anakhar said the whole clan was shaking in their boots to move against the outlaws. I doubt we'll see help from them, any more than from Krobyz. We have better luck with the clans east of the Oglos, where fear of the whoreson doesn't reach. That Oitoshyr, of the White Foxes, fell all over himself promising help."

"Easy enough to promise," the Gaul said. "What he does'll count for more. He's far enough away to say, 'Och, the pity of it. We didna hear o' the shindy till too late,' and have no one to make him out a liar."

Targitaus scaled his wolfskin cap across the tent, grunted in somber satisfaction when it landed on the leather sack nearest the pile of bedding. "A point. Should I thank you for it?"

Lipoxais the *enaree*, who had been quietly grinding herbs with a brass mortar and pestle, spoke up now. "Think of the animal's tail as well as its head." A Videssian would have said, "Look at the other side of the coin," Viridovix mused. The *enaree* went on, "Oitoshyr runs less risk of you dominating him if you win than your neighbors do, because he is far away. That should make him more likely to join us."

"Do you say that as a seer?" Targitaus asked eagerly.

"No, only as one who's seen a good deal," Lipoxais answered, smiling at the distinction with as much pleasure as an imperial might have taken over such wordplay.

"Still not bad," Viridovix said. He had gained a great deal of respect for the *enaree*'s shrewdness in the weeks since he came to Targitaus' clan. He was still not sure whether Lipoxais was a whole man—unlike most of the Khamorth, he kept his modesty, even in the cramped conditions of nomadic life. Whole or not, nothing was lacking from his wits.

A pessimist by nature, Targitaus had no trouble finding new worries. "For all the allies we may bring in, what good will they do us, V'rid'rish, if your Avshar is as strong as you say? Will he not help Varatesh's renegades ride over us no matter what we do?"

The Celt chewed at his lower lip; he lived with that fear, too. But he answered, "It's a tricksy thing, battle magic, indeed and it is. Even himself may have it turn and bite him." Lipoxais nodded vigorously, his chins bobbling. Sorcery frayed all too often in the heat of combat.

A fresh thought struck Viridovix. "Sure and it was a braw scheme, for all the Romans thought of it," he exclaimed, and then remembered: "Nay, they said 'twas first used against 'em." He reddened when he realized that, of course, his listeners had no idea what he was talking about. Targitaus was standing with folded arms, impatiently drumming his fingers on his elbows.

The Gaul explained how the legionaries had frightened a band of Yezda out of a valley one night by tying fagots to the horns of a herd of cattle, then lighting the sticks and stampeding the crazed beasts at the nomads. He did not make light of his own role either, for he had ridden at the head of the herd and sworded down one Yezda who did not panic. "But the rest o' the kerns were running for their lives, shrieking like so many banshees," he finished happily. "They must have thought it was a flock o' demons after 'em—and likely so would Varatesh's rogues."

All of the Khamorth, though, even Seirem, even Borane's gossip partners, looked at him in horror. When Targitaus made as if to draw his sword, Viridovix saw how badly he had blundered, but did not know why. Lipoxais reminded his chief, "He is not of us by blood and does not know our ways."

Muscle by muscle, the khagan relaxed. "That is so," he said at last, and then to Viridovix, "You fit well with us; I forget how foreign you are in truth." Viridovix bowed at the implied compliment, but Targitaus was speaking to him now as to a child. "Here on the plains, we do not let fire run wild." The nomad's wave encompassed the vast, featureless sea of grass all around. "Once started, how would it ever stop again?"

Coming as he did from damp, verdant Gaul, Viridovix had not thought of that. He hung his head, muttering, "Begging your pardon, I'm sorry." But he had the quick wits to see that the ploy might still be used, or something like it. "How would this be, now?" he said, and gave them his new idea.

Targitaus ran his hand through his beard as he thought. "I've heard worse," he said—highest praise.

Seirem nodded in brisk satisfaction, as if she had expected no less.

His sons flanking him, councilors grouped around him, Arghun found the key question and asked it directly of the rival embassies: "Why should my people take service with one of you instead of the other?"

Perhaps Goudeles had expected some polite conversation before getting down to business, for he did not have his answer instantly ready. When he hesitated, Bogoraz of Yezd seized the chance to speak first. Forehead furrowed in annoyance, Goudeles—and Gorgidas with him—listened to Skylitzes' whispered translation: "Because Videssos is a cow too tired and old to stay on its legs. When a beast in your own herds—may they increase—cannot keep up, do you rope another to it to help it along for its last few days? No, you slaughter it at once, while it still has flesh on its bones. We invite you to help with the butchering and share the meat."

Against his will, Gorgidas found himself respecting Bogoraz' talents. His argument was nicely couched in terms familiar to the Arshaum and doubly effective because of it.

Yet Goudeles, though robbed of the initiative, thought quickly on his feet. "Having seen his own Makuran collapse at the first shout, Bogoraz may perhaps be forgiven for his delusion that such decay has befallen us as well. He ministers to his new masters well."

Arigh interpreted for his father and the elders. "Your pun didn't translate," Skylitzes muttered when the plainsman's version was through.

"Never mind. I meant it for Bogoraz," the bureaucrat answered. The shot went home, too; the Yezda envoy gave him a fierce glower. Goudeles was not bad at finding weaknesses himself, Gorgidas thought. Serving overlords only a generation off the steppe had to be humiliating for Bogoraz, who was as much a man of culture as the Videssian.

"I give Wulghash all my loyalty," the ambassador said, rather loudly, as if to convince himself. He must have succeeded, for he returned to the attack: "Yezd is now a young, strong land, filled with the vigor fresh blood brings. Its time is come, while Videssos falls into shadows."

Proud in the full power of his strength, Dizabul threw back his head. As Bogoraz doubtless intended, he identified Yezd's situation with his own. But Gorgidas wondered if the envoy had not outsmarted himself. There were few young men among Arghun's councilors.

One of the oldest of them, a man with a scant few snowy locks combed across his skull, slowly rose and tottered toward Bogoraz. The diplomat frowned, then yelped in outrage as the Arshaum reached out and plucked a hair from his beard. Holding it at arm's length, he peered at it with rheumy eyes. "Fresh blood?" he said, slow and clear enough so even Gorgidas and

Goudeles could understand. "This is as white as mine." He threw it on the rug.

"Sit down, Onogon," Arghun said, but as much in amusement as reproof. Onogon obeyed, as deliberately as he had risen. Several of the elders were chuckling among themselves; Bogoraz barely hid his fury. Abuse would have been easier for him to bear than mockery.

Gorgidas, for his part, started when he heard the old man speak. The devil-mask had distorted the chief shaman's voice, but the Greek still knew it when he heard it again—a powerful ally to have, if ally he was. Gorgidas reached forward to tap Goudeles on the shoulder, but the pen-pusher was speaking again.

"Our presence here gives the lie to the Yezda's foolish effrontery," he said. "As it always has, Videssos stands."

Bogoraz bared his teeth in a shark's smile. "Khagan, the senile Empire has no bigger liar than this man, and he proves it out of his own mouth. I will show you the state Videssos is in. This Goudeles, when he offered you his desperate tribute, paid you in old coin, not so?"

"Oh, oh," Skylitzes said under his breath as Arghun nodded.

"See, then, what the Empire mints these days and tell me if it stands as it always has." And Bogoraz reached into his wallet, drew forth a coin, and cast it at the khagan's feet.

Even from several paces way, Gorgidas could see what it was—a "goldpiece" of Ortaias Sphrantzes, small, thin, poorly shaped, and so adulterated with copper that it was more nearly red than honest yellow.

Bogoraz retrieved the coin. "I would not cheapen myself by offering you so shabby a gift," he said to Arghun.

The dramatic flourish hurt as badly as the damning money itself. It grew very quiet in the banquet tent, which now served another function; all the Arshaum watched Goudeles to see what response he had.

He stood a long time silent, thinking. Finally he said, "That was the coin of a usurper, a rebel who has been put down; it is not a fair standard to judge by." All true, though he did not tell the Arshaum he had followed Ortaias until Thorisin Gavras took Videssos. Just as if he had served Gavras all his life, he went on, warming to his theme, "Now we have an

Emperor who is strong-willed and to be feared, well able to do that which is necessary in administering the state, both in war and in the collection of public revenues."

"Sophistry," Bogoraz fleered in Videssian. The Arshaum tongue lacked the concept, so he was blunter: "Lies! And your precious Emperor had best be skilled at war, for it is not merely Yezd he fights; his paid soldiers from Namdalen have revolted against him, and in the east he wars with the Duchy itself. His forces are divided, spread among many fronts; since we are fighting no one but Videssos, it is plain victory will soon be ours."

Gorgidas, Skylitzes, and Goudeles exchanged glances of consternation. Isolated on the plains for months, they knew nothing of events in the Empire; it was only too likely Bogoraz had fresher news than theirs. The very set of his body, the enjoyment he took from his revelation, argued for its belief.

The Greek had to admire Goudeles then. Rocked as he was by Bogoraz' announcement, the seal-stamper laughed and bowed toward the Yezda envoy as if he had brought good news. "What nonsense is this?" Bogoraz said suspiciously.

"None at all, sir, none at all." Goudeles bowed again. "May all be well for you, in fact, for though born a man of Yezd, you have testified to the courage of Videssos and not hidden the truth out of fear."

"You have gone mad."

"No, indeed. For unless the Videssian power was distracted, as you said, and was extending its army against various foes, do you think the Yezda could stand against it in battle? Were we facing Yezd alone, even its name would be destroyed along with its army."

It was a brave try, but Bogoraz cut through words with a reminder of real events. "We fared better than that at Maragha. And now we and Namdalen grind Videssos to power between us." He made a twisting motion with his hands, as though wringing a fowl's neck.

The Arshaum murmured back and forth; Goudeles, at last with the look of a beast at bay, had no ready answer. Beside him Skylitzes was as grim. In desperation, Gorgidas spoke to Arghun: "Surely Yezd is a more dangerous friend for you than

Videssos. The Empire is far away, but Yezd shares a border with your people."

If he expected the same success the tale of Sesostris had brought him, he did not gain it. When his words were interpreted, the khagan laughed at him. "We Arshaum do not fear the Yezda. Why should we? We whipped them off the steppe into Yezd; they would not dare come back."

That reply hardly pleased Bogoraz more than the Greek; he might have mixed feelings toward his overlords, but he did not care to hear them scorned.

And Skylitzes seized on Arghun's words as a drowning man would grab a line. "Translate for me, Arigh," he said tensely. "I must not be misunderstood." Arigh nodded; he had watched Bogoraz take control of the debate with as much anxiety as the Videssians. If their cause went down to defeat, his as their sponsor suffered, too—and Dizabul's grew brighter, for backing the right side.

"Tell your father and the clan enders, then, that Gorgidas here is right, and Yezd menaces your people even now."

Understanding the officer's Videssian, Bogoraz shouted angry protest. "More twaddle from these talksmiths! If words were soldiers, they would rule the world."

"More than words, Yezda! Tell the khagan, tell his elders why Yezd is making cats'-paws of the Khamorth outlaws by the Shaum, if not to use them against the Arshaum. Then who would be between whom?" With wicked precision, Skylitzes imitated Bogoraz's neck-twisting gesture. The Videssian officer might lack Goudeles' flair for high-flown oratory, but with a soldiers' instinct he knew where a stroke would hurt.

The clan leaders' eyes swung back to Bogoraz, sudden hard suspicion in them. "Utterly absurd, your majesty," he said to Arghun. "Another load of fantastic trumpery, no better than this suet-bag's here." The broad sleeve of his coat flapped as he pointed at Goudeles. He sounded as sure of himself as he had when wounding the Videssians with word of Drax' revolt.

But Skylitzes still had his opening and pounded through it, "How is it that Varatesh and his bandits struck west over the Shaum this past winter, the first time in years even outlaws dared act so?"

The Gray Horse clan was far enough from Shaumkiil's

eastern marches that Arghun had not heard of the raid. He snapped a question at the elders. Onogon answered him. Triumph spread over Skylitzes' saturnine face. "He knows about it! Learned from another shaman, he says."

Bogoraz remained unshaken. "Well, what if these renegades, or whatever they are, came cattle-stealing where they don't belong? They have nothing to do with Yezd."

"No?" Gorgidas had never heard so much sarcasm packed into a single syllable. "Then how is it," Skylitzes asked, "that Avshar rides with these renegades? If Avshar is not second in Yezd after Wulghash, it's only because he may be first."

Now the Yezda envoy stared in dismay and disbelief. "I know nothing of this," he said weakly.

"It's true, though." That was not Skylitzes, but Arigh "This is what I spoke of, father, when I rode ahead of the embassy." Skylitzes interpreted for Gorgidas and Goudeles as Arigh told the elders of Viridovix' kidnapping on the Pardrayan steppe, and of the part Avshar's magic had played in it.

"You see he did not scruple to attack an embassy," Goudeles put in, "contrary to the law of all nations, who recognize envoys' persons as sacrosanct."

"What have you to say?" Arghun asked Bogoraz. As usual, the khagan kept his face impassive, but his voice was stern.

"That I know nothing about it," the Yezda ambassador repeated, this time with more conviction. "This Avshar has not been seen in the court at Mashiz for two years and more, since he took up the army that won glory for Wulghash at Maragha." An eyebrow quirked, a courtier's grimace. "There are those who would say Wulghash has not missed him. Whatever he may or may not have done after he last left Mashiz should not be held to Yezd's account, only to his own."

"Khagan!" That was Skylitzes, shouting in protest; Goudeles clapped a dramatic hand to his forehead. The officer cried out, "If your men go to tend a herd five days away from your yurt, they still ride under your orders."

Several of the councilors behind Arghun nodded in agreement. "Well said!" came Onogon's thin voice. But others, unable to take seriously a threat from the despised Khamorth, still seemed to think Bogoraz' arguments carried more weight, nor did Dizabul pull away from the man whose cause he backed. The deadlock held.

The khagan gestured to both embassies in dismissal. "It is time for us to talk among ourselves on what we've heard," he said. His own eyebrow lifted in mild irony. "There is a bit to think about." Bogoraz and the Videssian party ignored each other as they left the banquet tent; the driver whistled his horses to a brief halt so they could alight.

Once back in their own yurt, Goudeles threw himself down on the rug with a great sigh of relief. "Scratch one robe," he said. "I've sweated clean through it." A serving girl, understanding tone if not words, offered him a skin of kavass. "Phos' blessings on you, my sweet," he exclaimed, and half emptied it in one great draught.

"Save some," Skylitzes ordered. After he had drunk, he slapped the bureaucrat on the back. Ignoring Goudeles' yelp, he said, "Pikridios, I never thought I'd see the day when you disowned the Sphrantzai and spoke up for Thorisin—aye, and sounded like you meant it."

"Professional pride compelled," the bureaucrat said. "Should I let a mere Makuraner get the better of me, how could I show my face in the chancery again? And as for your precious Gavras, my hardheaded friend, if he had given me my just deserts, I would still be comfortably ensconced there."

"If he had given you your just deserts," Skylitzes retorted, "you'd be short a head, for your embassy to him during the civil war."

"Such details are best forgotten," Goudeles said with an airy wave. The pen-pusher went on, "The shock of my sensibilities here on the barren steppe is punishment enough, I assure you. So far from being the safe center of the cosmos, Videssos seems an island in a barbarous sea, quite small, lonely, and surrounded by deadly foes."

Now Skylitzes was staring at him. "Well, Phos be praised! You really have learned something."

"If the two of you can hold off singing each other's praises for a bit," Gorgidas said pointedly, "you might send that skin this way."

"Sorry." Skylitzes passed it to him. As the Greek drained it, the Videssian officer said, "We might find you a line or two while we're singing. You gave me the idea to warn the Arshaum of Avshar's games."

"Aye, aye, aye." After the tension in the banquet tent, the

kavass was hitting Goudeles hard; his round cheeks were red, and his eyes a little glassy. He nodded as if his head were on springs, bobble, bobble, bobble. "And that parable about what's-his-name, your king with the funny name. That took Bogoraz' high-necked pretensions down a peg, yes it did." He giggled.

"Glad to help," Gorgidas said, warming to their praise. He remembered something he had caught in the arguments before the khagan and spoke it before he could lose it again: "Did you notice how Bogoraz slighted Avshar? Are there splits among the Yezda?"

"Never a court without 'em," Goudeles declared loudly.

"Even if there are, what use can we make of it here?" Skylitzes asked, and the Greek had to admit he did not know.

"Not to worry about that, my dears," Goudeles said. His elegant syntax was going fast, but his wits still worked. "Now we got—*have*—an idea of where the clan elders stand, we throw gold around. Works pretty good, most times." He giggled again. "Wonderful stuff, gold."

"It would be even more so if Bogoraz didn't have it, too," Gorgidas said. Goudeles snapped his fingers to show what he thought of that.

The pony's muscles flexed between Viridovix' thighs as the beast trotted over the plain. The Celt held the reins in his left hand; the right was on the hilt of his sword. He tried to look in every direction at once. Riding to war, even in a scouting party such as this, was new to him; he was used to fighting on foot.

The steppe's broad, flat reaches also oppressed him. He turned to Batbaian beside him. "What's the good of being a general, now, with the whole country looking all the same and not a place to lay an ambush in the lot of it?"

"A gully, a swell of land to hide behind—you use what you have. There's plenty, when you know where to look." The khagan's son eyed him with amusement. "A good thing you aren't leading us. You'd get yourself killed and break my sister's heart."

"Sure and that'd be a black shame, now wouldn't it?" Viridovix whistled a few bars of a Videssian love song. His soldier's alertness softened as he thought of Seirem. After so many women, finding love in place of simple rutting was an unexpected delight. As is often true of those whose luck comes late, he had fallen twice as hard, as if to make up for squandered years. "Och, she's a pearl, a flower, a duckling—"

Batbaian, who could remember his sister as a squalling tot, made a rude noise. Viridovix ignored him. "At least you have nothing to fear for her sake," the young Khamorth said. "With so many clans sending men to fight Varatesh, the camp has never been so large."

"Many, yes, but not enough." That was Rambehisht, who led the patrol. As sparing of words as usual, the harsh-featured plainsman pierced to the heart of the matter. Targitaus' army grew day by day, but many clans chose not to take sides, and some few ranged themselves with Varatesh, whether from fear of Targitaus or a different kind of fear of the outlaw chief and Avshar.

The scouting party's point rider came galloping back toward his mates, swinging his cap in the air and shouting, "Horsemen!" Viridovix' blade rasped free of its scabbard; the plainsmen he rode with unslung their bows and set arrows to sinew bowstrings. On this stretch of steppe other horsemen could only be Varatesh's.

A few minutes after the outrider appeared, the patrol spied dust on the northwestern horizon. Rambehisht narrowed his eyes, taking the cloud's measure. "Fifteen," he said. "Twenty at the outside, depending on remounts." The numbers were close to even, then.

The opposing commander must have been making a similar calculation from what he saw, for suddenly, before his men came into view, he swung them round sharply and retreated as fast as he could go. Batbaian let out a yowl of glee and punched Viridovix in the shoulder. "It works!" he shouted.

"And why not, lad?" the Celt said grandly, swelling with pride as he accepted congratulations from the plainsmen. Even Rambehisht unbent far enough to give him a frosty smile. That truly pleased Viridovix, to have the man he had beaten come to respect him.

Behind them, the six or eight cattle that accompanied the patrol took advantage of the halt to snatch a few mouthfuls of grass. Each of the beasts had a large chunk of brush tied behind it and threw as much dust into the air as a couple of dozen men. "The polluted kerns'll be after thinking it's whole armies chasin' 'em," Viridovix chuckled.

"Yes, and tell their captains as much," Rambehisht said. He was a thoughtful enough warrior to see the use of confusing his foes.

"And we must have a double handful of patrols out," Batbaian said. "They'll be running from so many shadows they won't know when we really move on them." He gazed at Viridovix with something close to hero worship.

Feeling pleased with themselves, the scouts camped by a small stream. To celebrate outfoxing the enemy, Rambehisht slit the throat of one of the cattle. "Tonight we have a good feed of meat," he said.

Viridovix scratched his head. "I'm as fond o' beef as any man here, but how will you cook him? There's no wood for a fire, nor a pot to seethe him in, either."

"He'll cook himself," the plainsman answered.

"Och, aye, indeed and he will," Viridovix scoffed, sure he was the butt of a joke. "And belike come morning the corp of him'll grow feathers and fly off tweeting wi' the burdies."

After Rambehisht opened the cow's belly, a couple of nomads dug out the entrails and tossed them into the stream. It turned to silvery turmoil as fish of all sizes swarmed to the unexpected feast. A couple of large, brown-shelled turtles splashed off rocks to steal their share. Another was staring straight at Viridovix. It blinked deliberately, once, twice.

Rambehisht proved as good as his word. Arms gory to the elbows, he stripped hunks of flesh from the beast's bones and made a good-sized heap of the latter. To the Celt's surprise, he proceeded to light them; with the marrow inside and the fat still clinging to them, they burned well. The resourceful Khamorth then threw enough meat to feed the patrol into a bag made of the cow's raw hide, dipped up water from the stream and added it to the meat, and hung the makeshift cauldron over the fire with a javelin. Before long boiled beef's mouth-watering scent filled the air, mixing with the harsher smell of the burning bones.

Most of the nomads stuck strips of raw meat under their saddles, to rough-cure as they rode along. There the Celt declined to imitate them. "I'd sooner have salt on mine, or mustard, thanking you all the same. Horse sweat doesna ha' the same savor."

What Rambehisht had cooked, though, was delicious. "My hat's off to you," Viridovix said, and so it was—with the coming of night he had laid aside the bronze-studded leather cap he wore. He belched magnificently. As any plainsman would, Rambehisht took it for a compliment and dipped his head in reply.

Patting his belly, the Gaul rose and ambled over to the creek, well upstream from the offal in it—a precaution the Romans had taught him. The water was cool and sweet. He dried his mustaches on his sleeve and saw that same fat turtle still sitting on its boulder. He flapped his arms, screeched, "Yaaah!" Horrified, the little animal flapped its legs insanely, trying to swim before it was in the water. After a moment it collected the few wits it had and dove into the stream.

"Och, what a terror I am," Viridovix laughed. He remembered Arigh's joke with the frogs at Prista, looked in vain for the turtle. "Puir beastie! If you were but a puddock, now, you could take revenge on the lot of us wi' a single peep."

Varatesh listened in consternation as the scout babbled, "It's a horde, I tell you. From the dust, there must be hundreds of 'em coming this way. You'd best believe we didn't stick around for a closer look, or I wouldn't be here to warn you."

The outlaw chief bit his lip, wondering how Targitaus had conjured up such an army. Seven patrols, now, had sighted big forces moving on his camp. Even discounting their reports by half, as any sensible leader did, his enemies were showing more vigor than they ever had before. If they kept pushing forward, they would drive him back toward the Shaum—or over it. He weighed the risks, wondering whether Targitaus could be as dangerous as the Arshaum. A raid was one thing, a fine piece of bravado, but to try to establish himself in Shaumkhiil . . .

White robes swirling around him, heavy boots clumping in the dirt, Avshar emerged from his tent and strode toward the outlaw chief. Varatesh could not help flinching; the scout, who knew far less than he, cringed away from the wizard-prince. "What lies is this coward grizzling out?" Avshar demanded, cruelly disdainful.

Varatesh glanced up at the veiled face, not sorry he could not meet those masked eyes. He repeated the rider's news, adding out of his own concern, "Where are they getting the men?"

Avshar rubbed mailed hands together, a tigerish gesture of thought. He swung round on the scout. "Whose patrol are you with?"

"Savak's." The renegade kept his answer as short as he could.

"Savak's, eh? Then you *are* a coward." As the scout began to protest, Avshar's booted foot lashed out and caught him in the belly. He spun away and fell, retching, to the ground. In showy contempt, the wizard-prince turned his back on him. The rider would have tried to kill any outlaw, even Varatesh himself. From Avsahr he crept away.

The sorcerer turned back to Varatesh, deigning to explain. "Your escaped swordsman rides with the 'army' Savak's putrid carrion fled from, which makes it easier for me to track them with my scrying. Shall I tell you how they grow their soldiers?"

"Yes." Varatesh's hands had balled into fists at Avshar's viciousness and scorn. At mention of Viridovix they tightened further. He was not glad to be reminded of how the Celt had bested him. Nothing had gone right since that red-whiskered rogue appeared on the plains.

When the wizard-prince was done, Varatesh stood rigid with fury at the trick. The gall of it all but choked him. "Cattle?" he whispered. "Brush?" Realization burst in him. "All their bands must be so!" His voice rose to a roar, summoning the camp. "Ho, you wolves—!"

"Here's that lad back again," Viridovix said. His comrades sat their horses calmly as the point rider came toward them. After days of frightening off Varatesh's patrols without fighting, they looked forward to doing it again.

When Rambehisht saw the cloud of dust behind the scout, though, his sneer became a worried frown. "Lots of them, this time," he said, and unshipped his bow. The rest of the Khamorth did the same.

"Is it a brawl, now?" the Gaul asked eagerly.

Rambehisht spared him one sentence: "They aren't here to

trade tunics with us." Then the plainsman was shouting, "Spread out, there! Quick, while there's time! Oktamas, fall back with the remounts. And kick those cattle in the arse, somebody; they're no good to us any more."

Horsemen grew visible through the dust, trotting forward at a good clip. Rambehisht's "spread out" order confused Viridovix for a moment. Used to infantry fights, his natural inclination would have been to gather his forces for a charge. Then the first arrow whizzed past his head, and he understood. A headlong rush would have been pincushioned in seconds.

Nomads were darting every which way, or so it seemed, snapping off shots at what looked like impossible ranges. Yet men screamed when they were hit, and horses, limbs suddenly unstrung, went crashing to the steppe. It was deadly and confusing, and the Gaul, an indifferent rider with a weapon whose reach was only arm's length, was of little use to himself or his comrades.

His ignorance of the plains' fluid way of fighting almost got him killed or captured in the first moments of the skirmish. Varatesh's men outnumbered Rambehisht's patrol, which promptly gave ground before them. For Viridovix, retreat and defeat were as one word. He held his ground, roaring defiance at the outlaws, until Batbaian shouted, "Fall back, fool! Do you want to see Seirem again?"

That brought the Celt to his senses as nothing else could have. It was nearly too late. Already one of the outlaws was past him and twisting in the saddle to fire. Viridovix slammed his heels into his horse's flanks. It sprang forward, and the arrow flew behind him.

"Try that again, you black-hearted omadhaun!" Viridovix yelled, spurring straight at the nomad. Without time to nock another shaft, the plainsman danced his mount aside. The Gaul thundered by. He rode hard, bent low over his horse's neck. An arrow point scraped the bronze at the very crown of his protective cap, sending a shiver through him. He could feel his back muscles tightening against a blow.

But quivers were emptying, and shamshirs came out of scabbards as the fight moved to closer quarters. Even then engagements were hit-and-run as horses carried riders past each other; a slash, a chop, and then wheel round for the next pass. Suddenly Viridovix, with his long, straight sword, owned the advantage.

Then he heard an enemy horseman cry his name. His head whipped round—he knew that voice. Varatesh drove his horse forward, shouting, "No tricks between us now and no truce either!"

"Sure and Avshar's pup has slipped his leash!" the Celt retorted. Varatesh's swarthily handsome features twisted with rage. He struck, savage as a hunting hawk. Viridovix turned the blow, but it jolted his arm to the shoulder. His own answering slash was slow and wide.

Varatesh spun his horse faster than Viridovix could. The Gaul was quickly finding he did not care for mounted fighting. Afoot, he had no doubt he could cut Varatesh to pieces, for all the outlaw chief's speed and ferocity. But a horse was as much a weapon as a sword, and one at which the plainsman was a master.

With a deft flick of the reins, the renegade drove his mount to Viridovix' shield side, cutting across his body at the Celt. A Khamorth might have died from the unexpected stroke. Viridovix, though, was used to handling a far heavier shield than the boiled-leather target he bore and got it in front of the slash. But his roundhouse reply was a poor thing which just missed cutting off his own horse's ear.

Though Varatesh's blow had failed, the Gaul realized he could not let the outlaw keep the initiative—he was too dangerous by half for that. "Get round there, fly-bait!" he roared, jerking his horse's head brutally to the left. The beast neighed in protest, but turned.

This time Viridovix was as quick as his foe. Varatesh's eyes went wide with surprise as the Celt bore down on him. His shamshir came up fast enough to save his head, but Viridovix' stroke smashed it from his fingers. The renegade gasped an oath, wondering if his hand was broken. He drew his dagger and threw it at the Celt, but the cast was wild—he had no feeling above his wrist.

In plainsman style, Varatesh was not ashamed to flee then. "Come back, you spineless coistril!" Viridovix cried. He started to gallop after him, then glanced round, looking for comrades to join him in the chase. "Well, where are they all gone to?" Most of Rambehisht's men were a quarter-mile south and still retreating in the face of the outlaws' superior numbers.

The Gaul paused, of two minds. There was Varatesh ahead, disarmed and temptingly close. If Viridovix had the faster horse, he could overhaul him and strike him down, but he would surely cut himself off from his mates in the doing. Then his choice was made for him, for two of the outlaw chief's men were riding to his rescue, one with a bow.

The little battle had only increased Viridovix' respect for the potent nomad weapon. He wheeled his horse away from the threat. The Khamorth fired twice in quick succession, his last two arrows. One of the shafts darted over the Celt's shoulder. Of the other he saw nothing. Short, he thought, and turned back to shake his fist at the bowman.

An arrow was sticking in the high cantle of his saddle. He blinked; the archer was tiny in the distance. "Fetch the executioner!" he exclaimed. He tugged the shaft out, wondering how long it had been there. "Did you fly all this way, or were you riding?" The arrow gave no answers. He threw it to the ground.

It took another hour of skirmishing to shake free of Varatesh's followers. At last they gave up. Their horses were not as fresh as those of Rambehisht's patrol, and Varatesh was too canny to let his men be caught on tired animals. Having accomplished his main purpose—turning his enemies' advance—he drew back.

"The grandest sport of all!" Viridovix shouted to his comrades as they reformed. The Gaul was still exhilarated from the fighting. It was not the hand-to-hand he was used to, but all the more exciting for its strangeness. Not until he brushed a sweaty arm over his cheek did he discover he was cut, whether from a sword or an unnoticed arrow-graze he never knew.

Several Khamorth were wounded, but even a plainsman with an arrow through his thigh grinned through clenched teeth at the Gaul's words. Like him, the nomads enjoyed war for its own sake. They had every reason to be proud, Viridovix thought. Badly outnumbered, they had only lost one man—the corpse was slung over a remount—and given Varatesh's hard-bitten bandits all they wanted.

Even gloomy Rambehisht seemed satisfied as the patrol

made camp under lowering skies. "They paid for everything today," he said, gnawing on the flattened chunk of meat he had carried under his saddle.

"Yes, and dearly!" Batbaian said. He was tending to an arrow wound in his horse's hock. His voice cracked with excitement; combat was still new to him, and he swelled with pride on facing it successfully.

Viridovix smiled at his enthusiasm. "A pity the spalpeens twigged to the kine," he said.

"Any trick is only good till the other fellow figures it out." Rambehisht shrugged. "We got farther than we would have without 'em, pushed the outlaws back and our own camp forward." He looked up at the gathering clouds. "Rain soon anyway, and then no dust to raise."

The death of Onogon the shaman delayed whatever choice of allies the Arshaum were going to make. The clanswomen bewailed his passing, while the men mourned in silence, gashing their cheeks with knives to mark their grief.

"As for me, I'd just as soon cut my throat," Pikridios Goudeles remarked, knowing Onogon's loss hurt the cause of Videssos.

Arigh visited the imperial embassy's yurt the next day, his self-inflicted wounds beginning to scab. He glumly sipped kavass, shaking his head in disbelief. "He's really gone," the Arshaum said, half to himself. "Somewhere down inside me, I didn't think he could ever die. All my life he's been just the same—he must've been born old. He looked as if a breeze would blow him over, but he was the wisest, kindest man I ever knew." Perhaps it was his years in Videssos, perhaps his deep grief, but, nomad custom notwithstanding, Arigh was close to tears.

"There will be no mourning in Bogoraz's tent," Goudeles said, still thinking of the Empire's interest.

"That's so," Arigh said indifferently. His private sorrow dimmed such concerns.

More sensitive to the plainsman's mood than was Goudeles, Skylitzes said, "I hope his passing was easy."

"Oh, yes. I was there—we were arguing over you folk, as a matter of fact." Arigh gave Goudeles a tired, mocking smile. "He finished a skin, stepped outside to piddle. When he got back, he said his legs were heavy. Dizabul, curse him, laughed—said it was no wonder, the way he guzzled. Well, to be fair, Onogon took a chuckle from that.

"But he kept getting worse. The heaviness crept up his thighs, and he could not feel his feet, not even with a hard pinch. He lay down on his back, and after a bit his belly grew cold and numb, too. He covered up his face then, knowing he was going, I suppose. A few minutes later he gave a sort of a jerk, and when we uncovered him his eyes were set. He showed no pain—that old heart just finally stopped, is all."

"A pity," Skylitzes said, shaking his head—as much tribute as the pious officer could render to a heathen shaman.

Gorgidas had all he could do to keep from crying out. Suddenly the historian's cloaking he had assumed sloughed away, to reveal the physician beneath. To a doctor, Onogon's death screamed of poisoning, and he could name the very drug—hemlock. Arigh's account described its effects perfectly; especially in the old, it would seem a natural death to those who did not know them.

When the plainsman finally left, the Greek told his comrades what he guessed. Skylitzes grunted. "I can see it," he said judiciously.

"Oh, indeed, Bogoraz has it in him to kill," Goudeles said. "No doubt of that. But what good does knowing do us? If we put it about, who would believe us? We would but seem to be slanderers and do ourselves no good. Unless, of course," he added hopefully to Gorgidas, "you have a supply of this drug with which to demonstrate? On an animal, perhaps."

"Now there's a fine idea, Pikridios," Skylitzes said. "He shows the stuff off, and they think we blew out the old bastard's light. Just what we need."

"I have none in any case," Gorgidas said. "When I became a physician I swore an oath to have nothing to do with deadly drugs, and was never tempted to break it." He sat unhappily, head in his hands. It ached in him that Goudeles should be right. He hated poisons, the more so because physicians had such feeble countermeasures. Most so-called antidotes, he knew, came from old wives' tales and were good for nothing.

The women Arghun had bestowed on the embassy knew no Videssian, but Gorgidas', a tiny, exquisite creature named

Hoelun, had no trouble understanding his dismay. She gently touched his slumped shoulder, ready to knead away his trouble. He shrugged her away. When she withdrew, silent and obedient as always, he felt ashamed, but only for a moment. Revenges on Bogoraz kept spinning through his mind; Onogon deserved better than to be murdered for the sake of a war hundreds of miles away.

He laughed without humor at one particularly bloodthirsty vengeance. Viridovix, he thought, would be proud of him—a fine irony there.

The shaman's funeral occupied the next several days. He was buried rather than burned, common custom on the firewary steppe. A sleeping-mat was set in the center of a great square pit, and Onogon's body, dressed in his wildly fringed shaman's garb, laid on it. A roof of woven brush set atop poles formed a chamber over the corpse; the Arshaum buried gold cups with it, while Tolui, the shaman who had succeeded Onogon as the clan's chief seer, sacrificed a horse over the grave. The blood spurted halfway across the brush roof below.

"A good omen," Arigh said as the horse was tipped into the pit. "He will ride far in the world to come." Almost all the clan elders were at the graveside, watching servants begin spading earth into the tomb. Gorgidas watched them in turn, trying to gauge what they were thinking. It was next to impossible; mourning overlay their features, and in any case they were as impenetrable a group of men as he had seen.

The Greek's own short temper rose to watch Bogoraz make his way among them, exuding clouds of sincere-sounding sorrow—like a squid shooting out ink, he thought. Dizabul was at the Yezda's side; Arshaum heads turned to hear him laugh at some remark Bogoraz made.

Wulghash's legate and Goudeles played out their game of bribe and counterbribe, promise and bigger promise. "Insatiable," the Videssian groaned. "Three times now, I think, I've paid this Guyuk to say aye, and if Bogoraz has been at him four for a no, then all the gold's for nothing."

"Terrible, when you can't trust a man to stay bought," Gorgidas murmured, drawing a crude gesture from Goudeles and a rare smile from Skylitzes.

Whether they finally concluded there was nothing left to milk or they came to a genuine decision, the Gray Horse Arshaum sent riders out to the neighboring clans, inviting them to send envoys to a feast at which the choice would be announced. "Clever of Arghun," said Skylitzes, who had a better feel for Arshaum usages than his comrades. "He can make clear which side he favors at the start of things, and by their custom the other won't be able to complain."

The envoys came quicker than Gorgidas had expected; he still found it hard to grasp how much ground the nomads could cover when they needed to. Two of them promptly reached for their blades when they saw each other and had to be pulled apart. Arghun ordered them kept under watch, just as he had the rival embassies from the powers to the south.

Even the banquet yurt was too small to hold all the feasters. After carefully clearing a stretch of earth, the Arshaum dug three firepits: a small central one for Arghun, his sons, and the ambassadors, with larger ones on either side for the khagan's councilors and the envoys from other clans. The nomads unrolled rugs around each fire, initiating the layout of a tent as closely as they could.

"One way or the other, it will be over soon now, and there's some relief," Goudeles said, trying to get the creases out of a brocaded robe that had been folded in a saddlebag for several weeks. He was not having much luck.

"Unless they choose against us, and offer us up to Skotos to seal their foul bargain," Skylitzes said. He patted his sword. "I'll not go alone."

Changing into his own meager finery, Gorgidas reflected on the inconsistencies that could dwell in a man. Skylitzes got on well with the Arshaum, liked them better than he did Goudeles, some ways. But in anything touching religion, he kept all the aggressive intolerance that characterized Videssians. The pen-pusher was far more broad-minded there, though to him the plainsmen were so many savages.

"Well, let's be off," Goudeles said with forced lightness. The suave calm he cultivated was frayed.

Gorgidas felt himself the center of all eyes as the Videssian party walked toward the feast. Agathias Psoes and his men anxiously watched the embassy, while the Arshaum themselves seemed as curious as its members about whether they would be friends or foes.

The evening was cool, with a smell of rain in the air. As

well, the Greek thought, that the Arshaum had made their choice at last; another week or so and the fall storms would begin in earnest—and good luck to an outdoor feast then!

The leaping flames in the fire pits gave an inviting promise of warmth. Goudeles might have been reading Gorgidas' mind, for he said, "Tonight I almost would not mind tramping through the coals." He pulled his robe more tightly about him. After months in tunic and trousers, Videssian ceremonial costume was drafty.

The Greek scowled when he saw Bogoraz climb down from his yurt. Wulghash's emissary, urbane as always, waved and hailed his rivals. "Wait for me, if you would. We shall learn our fate together." A smile was on his full lips as he came up. It did not reach his eyes, but that meant nothing. It never did.

The Yezda diplomat's small talk, though, was its usual polished self. "See what an eminent audience we shall perform before tonight," he said, and the sneer in his voice was delicate enough to make Goudeles lift an envious eyebrow.

Most of the Arshaum were already in their places; some had begun to eat, and the skins of kavass were traveling among them. They grew quiet as they spied the two embassies approaching out of the twilight. With a nod to his sons to follow him, Arghun rose to meet them.

Gorgidas looked from one face to the next, trying to find his answer before the khagan gave it. Arghun was unreadable and seemed faintly amused, as if savoring the suspense he was creating. Nor was anything to be gleaned from Arigh, who stood impassive, yielding the moment to his father. But when the Greek saw Dizabul's ill-concealed pout, he began to hope.

Arghun stepped forward, embraced Goudeles, Skylitzes, and Gorgidas in turn. "My good friends," he said. He greeted the Yezda envoy with a nod, civil but small. "Bogoraz." He paused for a moment to make sure he was understood, then said, "Come. The food is waiting."

Behind the Videssian embassy, Psoes whooped with joy. "All you can drink tonight, lads!" he shouted, and then it was his men's turn to cheer. Bogoraz' guards, wherever they were, were silent.

The Yezda envoy managed a courteous bob of the head for Goudeles. "I would have won, without so clever an opponent," he said. Beaming, the Videssian bowed in return. He would have had equally insincere compliments for his rival had their places been reversed, and they both knew it.

When Dizabul started to say something, Bogoraz hushed him. "I know you did all you could for our cause, gracious prince. Now let us enjoy the fare your father offers. This custom your people have of not speaking of important matters at meals is wise, I think." Taking the arm of Arghun's younger son, he sat by the fire and fell to with good appetite.

Sitting in turn, Gorgidas gave him a slit-eyed look. He was still only catching about one word in three of the Arshaum speech, but tone was something else. Bogoraz did not sound like a defeated man.

"Aye, no doubt he has front," Skylitzes allowed, dipping a strip of roast mutton into dark-yellow mustard. The Videssian officer's eyes went wide when he tasted it. "Kavass," he wheezed, and gulped to put out the fire.

Warned just in time, the Greek offered his own similarly anointed hunk of meat to Arigh, who said, "Thanks," and devoured it. "Too hot for you, eh?" he chuckled. "Well, I never got used to that vile Videssian fish sauce, either." Gorgidas, who was fond of liquamen, nodded, taking his point.

The kavass was flowing fast; their decision made, the Arshaum saw no reason to hold back. Gorgidas did not feel like waking up to a pounding head come morning. In Greek style, he was used to watering his wine when he wanted to stay close to sober. The serving girl looked at him as if he was mad, but fetched him a pitcher and a mixing cup anyway. The fermented mares' milk was not improved for being diluted to half strength.

"A useful trick, that," said Goudeles, who did not miss much. "You give the look of drinking twice as much as you really do." His eyes sparkled with triumph. "Tonight, though, I don't care how much I put down."

On Arghun's left, Bogoraz was eating and drinking with a fine show of unconcern. Dizabul matched him draught for draught and, being young, soon grew drunk. "Things would have been different if *I* had been khagan," he said loudly.

"You're not, nor likely to be," Arigh snarled.

"Quiet, both of you," Arghun said, scandalized. "Have you no respect for custom?" His sons obeyed, glaring at each other, Arigh suspicious of Dizabul for threatening his position, Dizabul hating Arigh—whose existence he had almost forgotten—for returning and destroying his. Strife fit for a tragedian, Gorgidas thought—Euripides, perhaps, for there was no easy right and wrong here.

Despite Arghun's warning to his sons, the feast bent Arshaum propriety to the breaking point. It was, after all, the occasion for announcing an alliance, and one by one the envoys from the neighboring clans found their way over to the central firepit to meet the Videssian ambassadors. Some spoke to Bogoraz as well, but most seemed ready to follow Arghun's lead; the Gray Horse clan held the widest pastures and was thus the most influential on the plains of Shaumkhiil.

The succession of tipsy barbarians soon bored Gorgidas, who did not envy his companions for having to be cordial toward each of them in turn. Sometimes being unimportant had advantages.

The only nomad who briefly managed to rouse the Greek's interest was the envoy of the Black Sheep clan, the most powerful next to Arghun's. His name was Irnek; tall and, for an Arshaum, heavily bearded, he carried himself with an air of sardonic intelligence. Gorgidas feared he might favor Bogoraz simply from ill will between his clan and that of the Gray Horse, but Irnek, after a long, cool, measuring stare, ignored the Yezda diplomat.

That slight and others like it seemed to reach Bogoraz at last. Where before he had kept his wits about him at all times, tonight he drank himself clumsy. After almost emptying a skin of kavass with one long draught, he dropped it and had to fumble about before he was able to pick it up and pass it on to Arghun. "My apologies," he said.

"No need for them." The khagan drained it, smacked his lips thoughtfully. "Tangy." He called for another.

Gorgidas was gnawing meat from a partridge wing when Arghun uncoiled from his cross-legged seat and stomped in annoyance. "My cursed foot's fallen asleep."

Arigh laughed at him. "If I'd said that, you'd say I was still soft from Videssos."

"Maybe so." But the khagan stamped again. "A plague! It's both of them now." He tried to stand and had trouble.

"What's wrong?" Gorgidas asked, not following the Arsham speech.

"Oh, nothing." Arigh was still chuckling. "His feet are asleep." Arghun rubbed the back of one calf, his face puzzled.

Gorgidas' eye swept to Bogoraz, who had opened his coat and was wiping his forehead as he talked with Dizabul. Suspicion exploded in the Greek. If he was wrong he would have much to answer for, but if not— he seized the dish of mustard in front of Arigh, poured in water till it made a thin, pasty soup, and pressed the bowl into the Arshaum prince's hands.

"Quick!" he cried. "Give this to your father to drink, for his life!"

Arigh stared. "What?"

"Poison, you fool!" In his urgency, politeness was beyond Gorgidas; it was all he could do to speak Videssian instead of Greek. "Bogoraz has poisoned him, just as he did Onogon!"

The Yezda ambassador leaped to his feet, fists clenched, face red and running with sweat. He bellowed, "You lie, you vile, pox-ridden—" and then stopped, utter horror on his features. The expression lasted but a moment, and haunted Gorgidas the rest of his life.

Then everyone was crying out, for Bogoraz burst into blinding white flame, brighter by far than the bonfire by him. His scream cut off almost before it began. He seemed to burn from the inside out, a blaze more furious with every passing second. And yet, as he kicked and writhed and tried to run from the fate he had called down on himself, his flaming body gave off no heat, nor was there any stench of burning. Onogon's magic and the protective oath he had extracted from Bogoraz had not been enough to save himself, but they served his khagan still.

"Oath-breaker!" cried Tolui, the new shaman, from among the clan elders. "See the oath-breaker pay his price!"

Mouth working in terror, Dizabul scrambled away from the charring ruins of what had been his friend.

Arghun stood transfixed, gaping at the appalling spectacle. Gorgidas had no time for it. He seized the mustard from Arigh once more, thrust it on the khagan. "Drink!" he shouted, by a miracle remembering the Arshaum word. Automatically, Arghun obeyed. He suddenly bent double as the emetic took hold, spewed up kavass and food.

Under the sour smell of vomit was another, sharper, odor, the telltale scent of hemlock. Gorgidas barely noted it; Bogoraz' hideous end had banished any doubts he might have had.

After vomiting, Arghun went to his knees and stayed there. He touched his thighs as if he had no feeling in them. Gorgidas' lips tightened. If the poison reached the khagan's heart he would die, no matter that he had thrown most of it up. "Keep him sitting!" the Greek barked at Arigh, who jumped to support his father with arm and shoulder.

The physician shouted for Tolui, who came at the run, a short, middle-aged nomad with a surprisingly deep voice. Through Arigh, Gorgidas demanded, "Have you any potions to strengthen a man's heart?"

He almost cried out for joy when the shaman answered, "Yes, a tea made from foxgloves."

"The very thing! Brew some quick and fetch it!"

Tolui darted away. Gorgidas thrust a hand under Arghun's tunic; the skin at the khagan's groin was starting to grow cool. The Greek swore under his breath. Arghun, bemused a moment before, was turning angry; hemlock left the victim's mind clear to the end.

Dizabul hesitantly approached his father, knelt to take his hand. Against every Arshaum custom, there were tears in his eyes. "I was wrong, father. Forgive me, I beg," he said. Arigh snarled something short and angry at his brother, but Gorgidas could guess how much that admission had cost the proud young prince.

Before Arghun could reply, a handful of concubines rushed toward him, shrieking. He shouted them away with something close to his healthy vigor, grumbling to Arigh, "The last thing I need is a pack of women wailing around me."

"Will he pull through?" Goudeles asked Gorgidas. He was suddenly full of respect; they were in the Greek's province now, not his.

The physician was feeling for Arghun's pulse and did not answer. His fingers read a disquieting story; the khagan's heartbeat was strong, but slow and getting slower. "Tolui! Hurry, you son of a mangy goat!" the Greek shouted. To get more speed, he would have called the shaman worse, had he known how.

Tolui came trotting up, holding a steaming two-eared cup in both hands. "Give that to me!" Gorgidas exclaimed, snatching it away from him. The shaman did not protest. A healer himself, he knew another when he saw one.

"Bitter," Arghun said when the Greek pressed the cup to his lips, but he drank it down. He sighed as the warm brew filled his stomach. Gorgidas seized his wrist again. The foxglove tea was as potent in this world as in his own; the khagan's heartbeat steadied, then began to pick up.

"Feel how far the coldness has spread," Gorgidas ordered Tolui.

The shaman obeyed without question. "Here," he said, pointing. It was still below Arghun's navel—an advance, but a tiny one.

"If he dies," Arigh said, voice chill with menace, "it will not be a horse sacrificed over his tomb, Dizabul; it will be you. But for you, this cursed Bogoraz would have been run out long since." Sunk in misery, Dizabul only shook his head.

Arghun cuffed at his elder son. "I don't plan on dying for a while yet, boy." He turned to Gorgidas. "How am I doing?" The physician palpated his belly. The hemlock had moved no further. He told the khagan so.

"I can feel that for myself," Arghun said. "You seem to know this filthy poison—what does it mean? Will I get my legs back?" The khagan's eyebrows shot up. "By the wind spirits! Will I get my prick back? I don't use it as much as I used to, but I'd miss it."

The Greek could only toss his head in ignorance. Men who puked up hemlock were not common enough for him to risk predictions. As yet he was far from sure Arghun would survive; he had not thought past that.

Lankinos Skylitzes held a wool coat, a long light robe, and a black felt skullcap in front of him. "What is this, a rummage sale?" Gorgidas snapped. "Don't bother me with such trash."

"Sorry," the Videssian officer said, and sounded as if he meant it; like Goudeles, he was taking a new look at the physician. "I thought you might be interested. It's all that's left of Bogoraz."

"Oh."

Gorgidas felt Arghun's pulse again. The khagan's heart was still beating steadily. "Get me more of that foxglove tea, if you would," the Greek said to Tolui. Arigh smiled as he translated. He knew Gorgidas well enough to realize his return to courtesy was a good sign. The physician added, "And bring back some blankets, too; we should keep the poisoned parts as warm as we can."

Gorgidas stayed by Arghun through the night. Not until after midnight was he sure he had won. Then at last the chill of the hemlock began, ever so slowly, to retreat. As the sky grew light in the east, the khagan had feeling halfway down his thighs, though his legs would not yet answer him.

"Sleep," Arghun told the Greek. "I don't think you can do much more for me now—and if you prod me one more time I may wring your neck." The twinkle in his eye gave the lie to his threatening words.

The physician yawned until his jaw cracked; his eyes felt full of grit. He started to protest, but realized Arghun was right. His judgment would start slipping if he stayed awake much longer. "You rout me out if anything goes wrong," he warned Tolui. The shaman nodded solemnly.

Waking Skylitzes and Goudeles, who had dozed off by the fire, Gorgidas headed back with them toward the Videssian embassy's yurt. "I'm very glad indeed old Arghun chose us over the Yezda," the pen-pusher said.

"I should hope so," Skylitzes said. "What of it?"

Goudeles looked round carefully to make sure no one who understood Videssian was in earshot. "I was just thinking that if he had not, I might have been foolish enough to essay something drastic to change his mind." The plump bureaucrat patted his paunch. "Somehow I don't think I would have burned so neatly as Bogoraz. Too much fat to fry, you might say. Rrrr!" He shuddered at the very notion.

XI

"A MESSENGER?" SCAURUS REPEATED. PHOSTIS APOkavkos nodded. The tribune muttered to himself in annoyance, then burst out, "I don't want to see any bloody messenger; they only come with bad news. If he's not from Phos himself, I tell you, I'll eat him without salt. If some tin-pot noble wants to complain that my men have lifted a couple of sheep, let him do it himself."

Apokavkos grinned self-consciously at the near-sacrilege. "Next best thing to Phos, sir," he said in careful Latin; though he clung to the Empire's religion, he acted as Roman as he could, having got a better shake from the legionaries than his own folk ever gave him. He rubbed his long, shaven chin, continuing, "From the Emperor, he is."

"From Thorisin?" Marcus perked up. "I'd almost given up on getting word from him. Go on, fetch the fellow." Apokavkos saluted and hurried out of what had been the provincial governor's suite of offices. Raindrops skittered down the windowpane behind the tribune.

The messenger squelched in a few minutes later. Despite his wide-brimmed leather traveling hat, his hair and beard were soaked; there was mud halfway up his knee-high boots. He smelled of wet horse.

"This is a bad storm, for so early in the season," Marcus remarked sympathetically. "Care for some hot wine?" At the man's grateful nod, the Roman used a taper to light the olive oil in the small brazier that sat at a corner of his desk. He set a copper ewer of wine atop the yellow flame, wrapped his hand in a protective scrap of cloth when he was ready to pick it up and pour.

The imperial messenger held his cup to his face, savoring the fragrant steam. He drank it off at a gulp, to put something warm in his stomach. "Have another," Marcus said, sipping his own. "This one you'll be able to enjoy."

"I do thank you. If you'll let me have that rag—ah, thanks again." The Videssian poured, drank again, this time more slowly. "Ah, yes, much better now. I only wish my poor horse could do the same."

Scaurus waited until the courier set this cup down empty, then said, "You have something for me?"

"So I do." The man handed him a tube of oiled silk, closed at either end with a wooden plug and sealed with the imperial sunburst. "Waterproof, you see?"

"Yes." Marcus broke the seal and unrolled the parchment inside it. He set it on the polished marble desktop with his cup at one end and the corner of an abacus at the other to keep it from spiraling up again.

The script was plain and forceful; Scaurus recognized the Emperor's writing at once. The note had Gavras' straightforward phrasing, too, with none of Drax' rhetorical flourishes added. "Thorisin Gavras, Avtokrator, to his captain Marcus Aemilius Scaurus: I greet you. Thanks to some pen-pusher's idiocy, your latest letter did not get out of the city till I came here, so I have it only now. I say well-done to you; you have served me better than I could have hoped. I have sent some of your islander prisoners to enjoy the winter in garrison duty on the Astris and will exchange the rest for my own men whom the brigands captured. That will take time, as I drove them off the mainland at Opsikion with much loss, though I fear pirate raids still continue all along our coasts. As soon as possible, I will send the Garsavrans gold to repay what you took from them—I trust you have receipts." The tribune smiled at the sly reference to his brief bureaucratic career. He read on: "Bring Drax and the remaining rebel leaders here at once, with as small a detachment as may be counted on to prevent their escape—do not weaken Garsavra's garrison more than you must. Head the detachment yourself, that I may reward you as you deserve; your lieutenant has enough wit to hold his own in your absence. Done at Videssos the city, nineteen days after the autumn equinox."

Marcus thought rapidly, then looked up at the messenger. "Six days, eh? You made good time, riding through such slop."

"Thank you, sir. Is there any reply?"

"Not much point to one. You'll only beat me to the capital by a few days. Tell his Majesty I'm carrying out his orders—that should be enough."

"I'll do it. Can I trouble you for some dry clothes?"

"Aye, it should be easy enough duty," Gaius Philippus said. "The Yezda won't be doing much in this weather, not unless they teach their little ponies to swim." Sardonic amusement lit his face. "And come to that, you'll have a jolly little tramp through the bog, won't you?"

"Don't remind me," Marcus said. He longed for a good Roman road, wide, raised on a embankment to keep it free of mud and snow, solidly paved with flat square stones set in concrete. Each fall and spring, with the rains, Videssos' dirt tracks turned into bottomless quagmires. That they were easier on horses' hooves than paving stones did not, to the tribune's way of thinking, make up for their being useless several months out of the year.

"Will two dozen men be enough?" the senior centurion asked.

"To keep four from getting loose? They'd better be. And with women and children and what-have-you, the party will look plenty big to discourage bandits—not that the bandits won't be chin-deep in slime themselves. Besides, I have my orders, and there's no doubt Thorisin's right—you'll have more need of troops here than I will. I'm sorry I'm stealing Blaesus from you."

"Don't be. Most of your men are from his maniple, and he knows them. And while he's gone," Gaius Philippus continued with his usual practicality, "I get the chance to bump Minucius up a grade for a while. He'll do well."

"You're right. He has the makings of a centurion in him, that one." Scaurus grinned at the veteran. "You're bumping up a grade yourself."

"Aye, so I am, aren't I? I hadn't thought of that, but I'll remember when the time comes to deal out the pay, I promise."

"Go howl," the tribune laughed.

The rain pelted down, whipped into almost horizontal sheets by a fierce north wind. Thus, while the Namdalener prisoners' departure from Garsavra made a little procession, few townsfolk watched it. Senpat and Nevrat Sviodo rode ahead of the main body of legionaries as scouts. In the midst of the Romans came the four islanders, at Scaurus' command still wearing their veiling. Baggage-mules and donkeys for the soldiers' families followed, while Junius Blaesus led the five-man rear guard.

The legionaries were plodding past the graveyard just outside Garsavra when the tribune looked back through the storm and saw a lone figure riding after them. "Who is it?" he yelled back to Blaesus. The howling wind swept away the junior centurion's answer. Uselessly wiping at his face, Marcus filled his lungs to shout again.

Before he could, Styppes came splashing up to him, astride a scrawny, unhappy-looking donkey that made heavy going of his bulk. The rain had soaked the healer-priest's blue robe almost black. Looking down at Scaurus afoot, he announced, "I shall accompany you back to the city. I have been away from my monastery too long, and there are perfectly capable healers at Garsavra to tend to your soldiers there."

As it often did, his peremptory tone grated on the tribune. "Please yourself," he said shortly, but in truth he was not sorry to have Styppes' company this once—not with Helvis carefully riding sidesaddle a hundred feet behind and due in less than three months. He had tried to persuade her to stay at Garsavra, but when she refused he yielded. After all, he thought, she was not likely to see her brother again.

Styppes' donkey stepped into a particularly deep patch of mire—what had been a rut in the road in drier times—and almost stumbled. The healer-priest pulled sharply on the reins. The beast recovered, but gave him a reproachful look.

Scaurus' sympathies lay with the donkey. Marching during the rainy season was an exercise suited to Sisyphos, save that the tribune's burden, instead of rolling down a hillside in the underworld to be hauled up anew, only grew heavier. Every step was hard work. The mud clung to his *caligae* and made a soft sucking sound of protest every time he pulled his leg free. In some stretches, he could not lift his legs at all, but had to slog forward pushing a mucky wake ahead of himself. He began to envy his prisoners, burdened by neither armor nor packs.

As eagerly as he looked forward to camping at the end of the day, the halt proved hardly better. Camp was a slapdash affair; he did not have the men to dig in with, and the weather foredoomed that anyhow. It was impossible to start a fire in the open. The Romans and their companions made miserable meals half-heated over braziers or olive-oil lamps, in their tents.

"Are you all right?" the tribune asked Helvis as he clashed flint and steel over tinder that was not as dry as it should have been. *Click, click!* The metal and gray-yellow stone seemed to laugh at him.

Helvis toweled at her hair. "Stiff, tired, drowned—otherwise not bad," she said, smiling wryly. While on donkeyback she had worn a thick, belted, woolen cloak, now cast aside, but her yellow linen shift had got wet enough to mold itself to her belly and swelling breasts. She toweled again, harder. "I must look like that monster your people have, the one whose head is all over snakes."

"The Medusa?" Marcus said, still clicking away. "No, not really. When I look at you, only one part of me turns to stone." She snorted. He paid no attention, bending over the little pile of tinder to blow gently on the orange spark that had caught at last. As it burst into flame, he sighed in relief. "There, that's done; now we can close the tent flap."

Helvis did, while the tribune lit lamps. When he started to ask, "Is the baby—" she cut him off firmly.

"The baby," she declared, "is better than I am, I'm sure. And why not? He's out of the cold and damp. He gave me such a kick when I got down from that mangy hard-backed beast that I thought he was this one." She nodded at Malric, who was rolling a giggling Dosti over and over on the sleeping mat. Bored from having ridden all day, he had energy to spare. Helvis gave a little shriek. "Not into the mud!" She sprang forward, too late.

Later, after both boys had finally fallen asleep, she took Marcus' hand, guided it to her belly. Her skin was warm and smooth as velvet, taut from pregnancy. The tribune smiled to feel the irregular thumps and surges as the baby moved within her. "You're right," he said. "He's lively."

She stayed quiet so long he wondered if she'd heard him. When she finally spoke, he heard unshed tears in her voice. "If it is a boy," she said, "shall we call him Soteric?"

He was silent himself after that, then touched her cheek. "If you like," he said, as gently as he could.

"I remember marching from Videssos to Garsavra in a week's time," Marcus said to Senpat Sviodo. "Why is it so much farther from Garsavra back to Videssos?"

"Ah, but the land knows you and loves you now, my friend," Senpat answered, cheery despite his bedraggled state. The brightly dyed streamers that hung from his three-pointed Vaspurakaner hat were running in the rain, putting splotches of contrasting colors on the back of his cloak; his precious pandoura was safe inside a leather bag behind him. Grinning, he went on, "After all, did it not love you, why would it embrace you so? It fairly cries out for you to stay with it forever."

"You can laugh, up there on your horse," Scaurus growled, but Senpat's foolishness pleased him, even so.

As for the rich black loam of the Empire's coastal lowlands, he was ready to consign it to the Namdaleni, the Yezda, or Skotos' demons for that matter. The soil grew progressively more fertile and quaggier, too, as the sea drew closer. Traveling across it when it was wet was like trying to wade through cold, overcooked porridge. The tribune's party was almost alone on the road. He had no trouble understanding that—only mad men or desperate ones would go journeying in the fall rains.

"And in which of those classes do you fit?" Senpat asked when he said that aloud.

"You're here with me—judge for yourself," Marcus came back. Something else occurred to him. "I begin to see why the symbol of Videssian royalty is the umbrella."

Early the next morning Styppes' donkey fell again, throwing him into the ooze. He came up spluttering and cursing in most unpriestly fashion, face, beard, and robe plastered with mud. The donkey did not rise; it had broken a foreleg. It brayed piteously when Bailli, who knew more of horseleeching than any of the Romans, touched the shattered bone. "I doubt you'll trust me with a knife, so cut its throat yourself," he said to Marcus. Turning to Styppes, he went on, "As for you, fatty, you'll use your own hooves from here on out."

"Skotos' ice is waiting for you, insolent heretic," Styppes said, trying to wipe the muck from his face but only spreading it about. From the glare he gave Bailli, it was plain he did not like the idea of marching for several days.

The donkey squealed again, a sound that tore at Scaurus' nerves. He said, "Why not heal it, Styppes?"

The Videssian priest purpled under his coat of mud. He shouted, "The ice take you, too, ignorant heathen! My talent lies in serving men, not brute beasts. Do you want me to prostitute myself? I have no idea how the worthless creature is made inside and no interest in learning, either."

"I was but looking to help," the tribune began, but Styppes, insulted and petulant, was in full spate and trampled the interruption. He railed at Marcus for every remembered slight since the day they met, dredging up things the Roman had long forgotten.

The entire party came to a halt to listen to his tirade, or try not to. A couple of legionaries knelt in the mud to tighten the ankle-straps on their *caligae*; Helvis, as she often did, urged her donkey forward so she could talk to her brother and the other islanders. The Romans paid no attention to her, understanding why she had come with them. Turgot reached out to touch Dosti's fair hair. He shook his head in pain as he remembered his lost Mavia.

Scaurus bent and put the donkey out of its pain. It kicked once or twice and was still. Styppes railed on.

"Be quiet, you bloated, bilious fool," Drax said at last. "Are you a four-year-old bawling over your broken toy?" He did not raise his voice, but the flash of cold contempt in his eyes brought Styppes up short, mouth opening and closing like a fresh-caught fish.

Drax bowed slightly to Marcus. "Shall we get on with it?" he said, as courteously as if they were on their way to a feast or celebration. The tribune nodded, admiring his style. He called out an order. The company lurched forward.

"By the gods, sir, there were times I thought we'd never make it," Junius Blaesus said to Scaurus as the dirty gray of the afternoon's rainy sky darkened toward night, "but it's getting close now, isn't it?"

"So it is," the tribune said, brushing back a loose lock of hair that crawled like a wet worm down his cheek. "A day and a half, maybe, to the Cattle-Crossing. In decent weather it'd be half a day."

A six-man mounted party splashed west past them, kicking up muck and earning curses from the legionaries. Here among the suburbs of the capital, there was a good deal of local traffic. It made the roads worse, something Marcus had not thought possible. He had his prisoners resume their black veils full-time; in the less crowded country further west he had only made them clap on the veiling once or twice a day when someone approached. This was safely imperial territory and the charade was probably unneeded, but where Drax was concerned he took few chances.

More splashing from up ahead, and another rider loomed out of the rain—Nevrat. Her head turned as she searched for Scaurus in the gloom. She smiled when she saw him, teeth flashing against her dark skin. "I've found us a campsite," she said, "a farm with a good stone horse barn to keep our, ah, guests warm and safe. I looked it over. It has little slit windows—" She held her hands a palm's breadth apart to show him. "—and a door that bars from the outside."

"Perfect," Marcus exclaimed. "The great count won't break out of that." He had made Junius Blaesus virtually ring the prisoners' tent with sentries each night. Behind stone and wood, though, they'd be safe enough. A single sentry each watch should do, giving his troopers a much-needed rest.

The farmer on whose land the barn stood was a toplofty little man whose prosperity was made plain enough by the very fact that he owned several horses. He tried to bluster when the tribune asked to use the barn, naming two or three minor court officials who, he declared, "will not be pleased to hear of my being mistreated in this way!"

Annoyed, Marcus dug out Thorisin Gavras' letter and wordlessly handed it to the man, who went red and then white as he saw the imperial signature. "Anything you desire, of course," he said rapidly, and shouted for his farmhands. "Vardas! Ioustos! Come quick, you lazy wretches, and drive the horses into the field!"

The two men emerged from a little cottage set to one side of the main farmhouse, one of them still chewing at a mouthful of supper. Having won his point, the tribune could afford to be gracious. He waved them back. "Let the beasts be. The men inside will have no fire, and the animals' heat will help keep them warm."

Vardas and Iuostos looked toward their master, whose name Scaurus did not know. "As he pleases," the farmer said; they went back to their interrupted meal. Now ingratiating, the short tubby man said to the Roman, "You will honor me by joining me for supper?"

"Thank you, no." An hour of nervous chatter from this fellow, arrogant and servile by turns, was not to Marcus' taste. He gave an excuse that let the man save face. "I have to see to setting up camp."

"Ah." The farmer nodded wisely, as if understanding what a great labor that was. He bobbed a stiff bow, turned, and fled back into his house. Marcus laughed silently at his retreating back.

The legionaries, whose tents were going up nicely without any supervision, greeted his orders with barely muffled cheers. They did whoop out loud when Blaesus volunteered to take a turn at the barn door himself. Grinning with pleasure at their response, the junior centurion said, "Why not? It's easier than sleeping, almost."

"You'd better not sleep, Junius," the tribune said, driving a tent peg into the muddy ground—at last, something the rain made easier. His tone was bantering, and Blaesus still smiled, but not as widely as he had. The *fustuarium* waited for sentries who dozed at their posts.

Once the tent was up, Scaurus dried himself as best he could. Malric and Dosti fell deeply asleep as soon as their dinner was done. "What did you do, beg a potion from Styppes?" the tribune whispered to Helvis as she covered the two boys. "They've been hellions since we set out."

"Not far wrong," she said, rising. She tossed him a half-empty wineskin. "I gave them each a good nip while you were busy."

"Did you? Whatever for?"

She gave him a slow sidelong look. "For us," she said, her voice thick and sweet as the unwatered wine in the skin.

He scarcely had time to set it down before she stepped smiling into his arms. He kissed her in glad surprise; her desire turned fickle when she was carrying a child.

Her fingers toying with him, she undid his sword belt, pulled down his metal-studded military kilt. "Such complications," she murmured. Scaurus kissed her eyes and then her ear, having already tugged her simple shift over her head. He blew out the lamps. Together, they slipped to the sleeping mat.

After a while she turned her back on him; he slid into her from behind. The posture, made for slow, lazy love, was easy on them both, her for her pregnancy and him for his weariness after days of pushing through mud. She sighed and wriggled closer.

When he was spent, he rolled lazily onto his back, whistling up into the darkness. Malric stirred, muttering something. "Hush, dear," Helvis said softly. Marcus was not sure which of them she was talking to until she groped for the wineskin, found it, and gave her son a long swallow. He smacked his lips, then turned over and went back to sleep.

"There," Helvis said to the tribune. "Tonight, no interruptions." She pressed herself against him, her hand busy once more.

"Easy there," he said. "I'm fine."

"I think you're fine," she said, mischief in her voice, and did not stop.

"I'm not sure anything will happen." But as he spoke, he felt himself rising to her touch. His arms tightened around her.

"You are the noisiest man," she grumbled, kindly, a bit later, pushing him away from her; his gasps had wakened Dosti. Every pore content, he did not answer. She quieted the baby the same way she had Malric, then returned to the tribune's side.

After a while, she touched him again. He looked at her, bemused, but there was not enough light to read her expression. "You're asking too much, you know," he said sleepily.

She laughed at him. "Times I've said that to you, you sulked for days. See how it feels to be mouse instead of cat, sir? But I want you, and I'll have you."

He stroked her hair, damp now with sweat as well as rain. So was his own. "There is a difference, though. If I can't, I can't."

"There are ways," she said, and used one. It took a while, but he discovered she was right. Amazement gave way to delight. Drowned in her flesh, he sank into as profound a sleep as he had ever known.

Helvis waited for what seemed an endless time, listening to Scaurus' slow, steady breathing and the beat of the rain on the tent. He did not stir when she moved away from him and got to her feet; her mouth twisted in vexation as his seed dribbled down her thigh. She was glad he had not been able to see her face.

She dressed quickly, pinning her heavy cloak closed over her shift. She found the wineskin with her fingers and slipped it into a deep pocket. Then she felt the ground until she came upon his sword belt.

The broad-bladed dagger slid free of its sheath with a tiny scrape of metal against metal. It was heavier in her hand than she had expected. She looked down at the sleeping tribune, hardly more than a deeper shadow in the darkness. Her grip tightened on the hilt. . . . She bit her lip till she tasted blood, shook her head violently. She could not. The knife went with the wineskin.

Malric whimpered as she picked him up, but did not wake. Dosti made no complaint at all, snoring and breathing wine fumes into her face. She held both of them under her outspread cloak so the raindrops would not wake them when she went outside, and thanked Phos that Marcus had pitched his tent just to one side of the horse barn. She did not think she could carry Malric far.

She wished she were not pregnant. It made her slow-moving and clumsy, and what would be necessary would be all the more dangerous.

The chilly rain beat against her face as she shouldered the tent flap open and stepped out into the night. She did not look back at Marcus, but around to take her bearings. There was the barn, with the sentry in front of it. She wondered who he was.

Most of the legionaries' tents were behind her; she could see lamplight under a couple of flaps. Snatches of pandoura music came sweet through the storm, Senpat Sviodo whiling away the time. Closer by she heard Titus Pullo laugh at a joke Vorenus told. Relief seeped through her; it would have been impossibly difficult with either of them on guard. They were too alert by half. All these Romans, she knew too well, were fine soldiers, but the ex-rivals surpassed the rest.

She wondered how long the watchman had been on duty. Was his turn just starting or almost done? She could not gauge the time, not with moon and stars swaddled in clouds. Gamble, then—her lips thinned in a humorless smile as she realized the Videssians' scornful nickname for her people, like most caricatures, fit somewhat.

And Marcus did not believe at all.

She squashed carefully through the mud, as if toward the latrines dug behind the horsebarn. If anyone was there, she could still withdraw in safety—and leave her brother and the other Namdaleni to the judgment of the Avtokrator of the Videssians. It did not bear thinking of.

No one squatted over the noisome slit trenches. She breathed a prayer of thanks to Phos for his protection; confidence soared in her. As soon as the barn's wall screened her from the view of the Roman sentry, she stepped under the shelter of its broad, overhanging eaves. She dug her face into the hollow of her shoulder, wiping the rain from her eyes. Then she stooped and set her sleeping children in the small dry space by the gray stone wall.

"Back soon, my dears," she breathed, though the wine in them meant they did not hear. The sight of Dosti tore at her. She felt whore and deceiver both, to have used his father so. But blood, faith, and folk were ties older and stronger than two and a half years of what was sometimes love with Scaurus.

She straightened, found the tribune's knife, and held it concealed in the flowing sleeve of her cloak. Her heart pounded, her breath came short and fast, not in the passion she had counterfeited but from fear. Recognizing it helped steady her. She turned the corner of the barn and came up to the man on guard.

She was sure she would have no chance of sneaking up on him—she had never seen a Roman sentry woolgathering on watch. So she came openly, splashing and complaining in a loud voice about the dreadful weather.

"Who—?" the Roman said, tensing as he peered through the rain and dark. "Oh, it's you." He relaxed, gave a rueful chuckle. "Aye, it's hideous, isn't it? And to think I was chuckleheaded enough to volunteer to stand out in it. Here, come under the eaves; it's a little drier, though not much, not with this cursed north wind."

"Thank you, Blaesus."

"What can I do for you, my lady?" the junior centurion asked, an open, friendly man with no suspicion in him. He knew Helvis was a Namdalener, in the same way he knew Senpat Sviodo was a Vaspurakaner or Styppes a Videssian. It meant little to him—as well find danger in Scaurus himself as in his woman.

"I have some sweetmeats here Marcus thought you might like," she said, stepping closer. Her hands, Blaesus saw, were sensibly hidden against the cold and wet in her mantle's broad sleeves. He felt his face flush with gladness. Truly the tribune was an officer in ten thousand, to think of sharing tidbits with a sentry.

The knife was in the Roman's neck before he saw it glitter. He tried to scream, but blood gushed into his mouth, tasting of iron and salt. He knew a moment's chagrin—he should have been more careful. Scaurus had spoken to him about that before.

The thought was dizzy, distant as he fought in vain to breathe through the fire and flood in his throat. His knees gave way. He fell face-down in the muck.

A legionary stuck his head into Marcus' tent and shouted, "Sir!"

"Hmm? Wuzzat?" The tribune rolled over, grunted at the contact between the cold sleeping mat and his backside.

The trooper—it was Lucius Vorenus, he realized—blasted sleep from him. "Blaesus is murdered, sir, and the islanders fled!"

"What? Ordure!" Scaurus sprang to his feet, groping for clothes. Suddenly wakened with such news, it took him a few seconds to notice that Dosti and Malric had not begun to howl, that Helvis was not beside him. At the jakes, he thought.

But his sword belt hefted wrongly when he seized it. His fingers found the empty sheath. "Murdered?" he barked tensely at Vorenus. "How?"

The legionary's voice was grim. "Stabbed through the throat like a pig, sir."

"No," Scaurus whispered, half prayer, half moan, finding a horrid pattern in the night's events. Bare-chested and barefoot, he burst past Vorenus and ran for the horse barn. The trooper splashed after him, making heavier going through the mud in his mail shirt and *caligae*. "Is Helvis back of the barn with the children?" Marcus flung over his shoulder.

"At the latrines? I don't think so, sir. Why?" Vorenus said, puzzled and panting.

"Because they're not in my tent either," the tribune grated, tasting the cup of desperation and betrayal, "and my dagger is missing."

Vorenus' jaw shut with an audible click.

Still looking surprised, Blaesus' corpse leaned against the wall of the barn, by the opened door. Vorenus said, "When I came to relieve him, I thought he'd been taken ill until I shifted him and spied—that." A second mouth gaped in the junior centurion's neck. The trooper went on, "The door was shut when I got here, I suppose so anyone looking from camp would see nought amiss. But there's not a Namdalener in there now, or a horse either."

"There wouldn't be," Scaurus agreed. "Do Nevrat and Senpat still have theirs?"

"I don't know, sir. I came to you first, and their tent's some way from yours."

"Go find out; if they do, we'll need them. Rouse the camp, send out searchers—" Not that they'll find anyone, he jeered to himself, not with them afoot and the islanders mounted and with the gods knew how long a start. But maybe by some miracle Helvis was nearby after all, wondering what the commotion was about. He winced at the unlikelihood. As Vorenus started to dash away, the tribune added, "And fetch me Styppes."

Vorenus saluted and was gone. Marcus looked down at Blaesus' body, saw both his scabbards gaping wide as his throat. A *gladius* and a couple of daggers for the Namdaleni, then, he thought—not much. His mind, numbed by disbelief, chewed doggedly on trivia to keep from working at the empty tent a hundred feet away. The real pain would come soon enough.

Vorenus' yells tumbled the legionaries from their tents in alarm. Scaurus heard him switch from sonorous Latin to Videssian. Nevrat Sviodo's clear contralto pierced the rain: "Yes, we have them." The islanders had not risked entering the camp; Marcus doubted he would have himself.

A black shadow stumped toward the horse barn—Styppes, from its angry forward lean and its width. As he drew near, the tribune heard him muttering to himself. The healer-priest grunted in surprise when he saw Scaurus half-naked by the doorway. "If you called me to cure your chest fever," he said with heavy sarcasm, "I cannot until you catch it. But you will."

Reminded of the rain and cold, Marcus began to shiver; he had not noticed them. As baldly as he could, he told Styppes what had happened. Save for what had passed inside his tent, he held back nothing, knowing it would have been useless. He finished, "You know something of magic—can you learn where they fled? We may catch them yet. They cannot travel quickly, not with a pregnant woman."

"That heretic slut—" Styppes growled. He got no further; Scaurus knocked him down.

The priest slowly got to his feet, dripping and filthy. Marcus expected him to storm off in fury. Instead he groveled, saying, "Your pardon, master!" The tribune blinked, but he had not seen the murder in his own eyes. Styppes went on, "I know a spell of searching, but whether it will work I cannot say—that skill is not mine. Would you set a silversmith at an anvil and have him beat out swords?"

"Try it."

"I will need something belonging to one of the fugitives."

"I'll bring it to your tent," the tribune told him. "Wait for me there." He went back to his own at a gluey trot. Something belonging to one of the fugitives would be easy to get there.

Mounted and armed, Senpat and Nevrat Sviodo loomed over him. "What do you want of us?" Senpat asked, his voice carefully neutral. Surely the whole camp knew by now, and waited to see what Marcus would do.

"Take half a dozen men with you, ride back to the last big farm, and commandeer however many horses they have," he said. "We're going after them, and when I dogged Ortaias Sphrantzes after Maragha I learned it's no use chasing riders on foot."

The young Vaspurakaner nodded and started to ride away, shouting for Romans to join him. Nevrat leaned down from her saddle, close enough for Scaurus to read the compassion on her face. "I'm sorry," she said quietly. "The fault is partly mine. Had I not found this place, you would have gone on as you had been doing, and none of this would have happened."

He shook his head. "As well blame the pompous little man who built the barn. I set the guard as I did, and I—" He could not go on.

Nevrat understood, as she often seemed to. She said, "Do not blame her too much. She did not act out of wickedness, or, I think, from hatred of you."

"I know," the tribune said bleakly. "That makes it harder to bear, not easier." He shook free of the comforting hand Nevrat held out. She stared after him for a long moment, then rode to join her husband.

Back at his tent, Marcus threw his tribune's cape over his wet shoulders. Helvis' traveling chest was where she had left it, off to one side of the sleeping mat. He flipped up the latch and fumbled in the chest. Near the top, under an embroidered tunic, he came across a small, flat square of wood—the icon he had given her a few months before. His eyes squeezed shut in pain; he pounded a fist down onto his thigh. As if to give himself a further twist of the knife, he picked up the image and carried it to Styppes.

"A good choice," the healer priest said, taking it from him. "Phos' holiness aids any spell cast in a good cause, and the holy Nestorios, as you know, has a special affinity for the Namdaleni."

"Just get on with it." Scaurus' voice was harsh.

"Remember, I have not tried this in many years," Styppes warned. The ritual seemed not much different from one Nepos had used to seek a lost tax-document for the tribune at the capital. After prostrating himself before the icon, Styppes held it over his head in his right hand. He began chanting in the same ancient dialect of Videssian Phos' liturgy used. His left hand made swift passes over a cup of wine, in which floated a long sliver of pale wood. One end of the sliver had been dipped in blue paint that matched his priestly robes.

His chant ended not with a strong word of command, as Nepos' had, but imploringly; his hand opened in supplication over the cup. "Bless the Lord of the great and good mind!" Styppes breathed, for the chip of wood was swinging like a nail drawn toward a lodestone. "Southeast," the healer-priest said, studying the blue-tipped end.

"Toward the coast, then," Marcus said, almost to himself. Then, to Styppes once more, "You'll ride with us, priest, and cast your spell every couple of hours, to keep us on the trail."

Styppes looked daggers at him, but did not dare say no.

The pursuit party rode out near dawn, mounted on a strange assortment of animals: a couple of real saddle horses beside Senpat's and Nevrat's; half a dozen packhorses, two of which were really too old for this kind of work; and three brawny, great-hoofed plow horses. "A miserable lot," Senpat said to Marcus, "but I had to scour four farms round to get 'em. Most folk use oxen or donkeys."

"The islanders aren't on racers either," the tribune answered. The turmoil in the Roman camp had roused the farmer whose beasts were gone, and Scaurus' ears were still ringing from his howls of outrage. Mixed with the curses, though, was a good deal of description; even with the inevitable exaggeration of his horses' quality, Marcus doubted they would tempt the Videssian cavalry much.

The rain died away into fitful showers and finally stopped, though the stiff north wind kept whipping bank after bank of ugly gray-black clouds across the sky. Styppes, who had brought a goodly supply of wine with which to work his magic, nipped at it every so often to stay warm. It did nothing for his horsemanship; he swayed atop his plow horse like a ship on a stormy sea.

Marcus, taller and heavier than his men, also rode one of the ponderous work animals. Feeling its great muscles surge under him, he reflected that he was at last beginning to react like a Videssian. Styppes' spell of finding was but another tool to grasp, like a chisel or a saw, not something to make a man gasp in lumpish terror. And for traveling quickly, a horse was better than shank's mare.

Other thoughts bubbled just below the surface of his mind. He fought the anguish with his stoic training, reminding himself over and over that nothing befell a man which nature had not already made him fit to bear, that there was no point to being the puppet of any passion, that no soul should forfeit self-control of its own accord. The number of times he had to repeat the maxims marked how little they helped.

Whenever the legionaries rode past a herdsman or orchard keeper, the tribune asked if he had seen the fugitives. "Aye, ridin' hard, they was, soon after dawn," a shepherd said at mid-morning. "They done somethin'?" His weather-narrowed eyes flashed interest from under a wool cap pulled low on his forehead.

"I'm not out for the exercise," Scaurus retorted. Even as the herder gave a wry chuckle, he was booting his horse forward.

"We're gaining," Senpat Sviodo said. Marcus nodded.

"What will you do with Helvis when we catch them?" Nevrat asked him.

He tightened his jaws until his teeth ached, but did not answer.

A little later Styppes repeated his spell. The chip of wood moved at once, to point more nearly east than south. "There is the way," the healer-priest said, sounding pleased with himself for having made the magic work twice in a row. He took a healthy swig from the wineskin as reward for his success.

As the coast grew near, the ground firmed under the horses' hooves, with sand supplanting the lowlands' thick, black, clinging soil. Terns soared overhead, screeching as they rode with wild breeze. The horses trotted past scrubby beach plums loaded with purple fruit, trampled spiky saltwort and marram grass under their feet.

The sea, gray and threatening as the sky, leaped frothing up the beach; Scaurus licked his lips and tasted salt. No tracks marred the coarse yellow sand. "Which way now?" he called to Styppes, raising his voice above the booming of the surf.

"We will see, won't we?" Styppes said, blinking owlishly. Marcus' heart sank as he watched the priest's lurching dismount. The wineskin flapped at his side like a crone's empty dug. He managed to pour the last few drops into his cup, but a fuddled smile appeared on his face as he tried to remember his magic. He held the icon of the holy Nestorios over his head and gabbled something in the archaic Videssian dialect, but even the tribune heard how he staggered through, fluffing half a dozen times. His passes, too, were slow and fumbling. The sliver of wood in the wine cup remained a mere sliver.

"You worthless sot," Scaurus said, too on edge to hold his temper. Muttering something that might have been apology, Styppes tried again, but only succeeded in upsetting the cup. The thirsty sand drank up the wine. The tribune cursed him with the weary rage of hopelessness.

Titus Pullo gestured southward. "Smoke that way, sir, I think!" Marcus followed his pointing finger. Sure enough, a windblown column was rising into the sky.

"We should have spied that sooner," Senpat Sviodo said angrily. "A pox on these clouds; they're hardly lighter than the smoke themselves."

"Come on," Marcus said, swinging himself back into the saddle. He thumped his heels against the plow horse's ribs. With a snort of complaint, it broke into a jarring canter. The tribune turned his head at a shout; Styppes was still struggling to climb aboard his horse. "Leave him!" Scaurus said curtly. Sand flying, the pursuit party rode south.

They rounded a headland and saw the bonfire blazing on the beach less than a mile away. Marcus' pulse leaped. There were horses round that fire, and others walking free not far away, grazing on whatever shore plants they could find. Senpat whooped. "Gallop!" he shouted, and spurred his horse forward. The others followed.

Jouncing up and down, his eyes tearing from the wind of his passage, Scaurus had all he could do to hold his seat. The legionary Florus could not, and went rolling in the sand while his horse thundered away. Vorenus jeered as he rode by the helpless trooper, then almost joined him when his packhorse stumbled.

Because the Romans had to give all their attention to their horsemanship, Nevrat Sviodo was first to spot the warship lying offshore. Its broad, square sail was tightly furled in the stiff breeze; small triangular topsail and foresail held it steady in the water. Its sides and decking were painted sea green, to make it as near invisible as could be.

The color reminded Marcus of Drax' tokens. He knew with sudden sick certainty that this was no imperial craft, but one of the Namdalener corsairs hunting in Videssian waters.

A moment after Nevrat cried out, the tribune spied the longboat rowing out to meet its parent vessel. He saw the wind catch a woman's hair and blow it in black waves round her face. A smaller shape sat to either side of her. She was looking toward the beach and pointed back at the oncoming legionaries. She called out something at the same time; though he could not hear the words, Scaurus knew that sweet contralto. The rowers picked up their stroke.

The boat was hardly two hundred yards from shore. Fitting an arrow to his bow, Senpat Sviodo rode out till his horse was belly-deep in the sea. He drew the shaft to his ear, let fly. Marcus muttered a prayer, and did not know himself whether or not he asked for Senpat's aim to be true.

He saw the arrow splash a few feet to one side of the longboat. The rowers pulled like men possessed. Senpat nocked another shaft, then swore vilely as his bowstring snapped when he drew it back. Nevrat rushed forward to hand him her bow, but it was a lighter one that did not quite have the other's range. Senpat fired; the arrow fell far short of its mark. He shot again, to prove to himself the first had been no fluke, then shook his head and gave Nevrat back her bow. Knowing they were safe, the oarsmen eased up.

Scaurus' cheeks were wet. He thought the rain had started again, then realized he was weeping. Mortified, he tried to stop and could not. He stared at the sand at his feet, his eyes stinging.

Once the longboat and its occupants were recovered, the islanders unreefed their mainsail. It seized the breeze like a live thing. When the tribune raised his head again, there was a white wake under the ship's bow. The steersmen at the stern leaned hard against their twin steering oars. The corsair heeled sharply away from land, driving east with the wind at its beam. No one on deck looked back.

Afterward, Marcus remembered little of the next two days; perhaps mercifully, grief, loss, and betrayal left them blurred. He must have returned the horses, both stolen and appropriated, for he was afoot when he entered the capital's chief suburb on the western shore of the Cattle-Crossing, the town the Videssians simply called "Across."

What stuck in his mind most, oddly, should have been least likely to remain. Senpat and Nevrat, trying to free him from his black desperation, bought a huge amphora of wine and, carrying it together, hauled it up the stairs to the cubicle he had rented over a perfumer's shop. "Here," Senpat said, producing a mug. "Drink." His brisk tenor permitted no argument.

Scaurus drank. Normally moderate, this night he welcomed oblivion. He poured the wine down at a pace that would have left Styppes gasping. Though they did not match him cup for cup, his Vaspurakaner friends soon sat slack-jointed on the floor of the bare little room, arms round each other's shoulders and foolish smiles on their faces. Yet he could not reach the stupor he sought; his mind still burned with terrible clarity.

The wine did loose deep-seated memories he had thought buried forever. As the returning rain pattered on the slates of the roof and slid through shutter slats to form a puddle by his bed, he paced up and down declaiming great stretches of the *Medea* of Euripides, a play he had learned when studying Greek and hardly thought of since.

When he first read the *Medea*, his sympathies were with the heroine of the play, as its author intended. Now, though, he had committed Jason's hubris—maybe the worst a man can fall into, taking a woman lightly—and found himself in Jason's role. He found, too, as was often the case in Euripides' work, that misery was meted out equally to both sides.

Senpat and Nevrat listened to the Greek verses in mixed admiration and bewilderment. "That is poetry, truly," Senpat said, responding to sound and meter with a musician's ear, "but in what tongue? Not the one you Romans use among yourselves, I'm sure." While he and his wife knew only a little Latin, they could recognize it when they heard it.

The tribune did not answer; instead he took another long pull at the wine, still trying to blot out the reflections that would not cease. The cup shook in his hand. He spilled sticky purple wine on his leg, but never noticed. Even Medea, he thought, had not seduced Jason before she worked her murders and fled in her dragon-drawn chariot.

"Was any man ever worse used by woman?" he cried.

He expected no answer to that shout of despair, but Nevrat stirred in her husband's arms. "As for man by woman, I could not say," she said, looking up at him, "but turn it round, if you will, and look at Alypia Gavra."

Marcus stopped, staring, in mid-stride. He hurled the half-empty wine cup against a wall, abruptly ashamed of his self-pity. The ordeal Mavrikios Gavras' daughter had endured outshone his as the sun did the moon. After Ortaias Sphrantzes' cowardice cost her father his life at Maragha, Ortaias—whom flight had saved—claimed the throne when he made his way back to the capital; the Sphrantzai, the bureaucratic family supreme, had produced Emperors before. And to cement his claim, Alypia, whose house opposed everything his stood for, had been forced into marriage with him.

But Ortaias Sphrantzes, a foolish, trivial young man with more bombast than sense, was only a pawn in the hands of his uncle Vardanes. And Vardanes, whose malignance was neither mediocre nor trivial, had coveted Alypia for years. Dispossessing his feckless nephew of her, he kept her as slave to his lusts throughout Ortaias' brief, unhappy reign. When the Sphrantzai fell, Scaurus had seen her thus and seen her spirit unbroken despite the submission forced from her body.

Turning his back on the spattered wall, he knelt clumsily beside Nevrat Sviodo and touched her hand in gratitude. When he tried to speak his thanks, his throat clogged and he wept instead, but it was a clean weeping, with the beginning of healing in it. Then at last the wine reached him; he did not hear Nevrat and her husband when they rose and tiptoed from the room.

* * *

It was cold in the Hall of the Nineteen Couches, and the tribune felt very much alone as he made his report to Thorisin Gavras. The Sviodos had crossed with him to the capital, and Styppes—for whatever his company was worth—but Marcus had sent his Romans back to Gaius Philippus at Garsavra. Without the Namdaleni to guard, there was no point keeping them; Gaius Philippus could use them, and in Garsavra they did not risk the Avtokrator's wrath.

He told the truth, as much of it, at least, as had happened outside his tent. Thorisin was silent when he finished, studying him stony-faced over steepled fingers. When I first met him, Marcus thought, he would have worn his feelings on his sleeve. But he was learning the emperor's art of never revealing too much; his eyes were perfectly opaque.

Then the imperial façade cracked across and showed the man behind it. "Damn you, Scaurus," he said heavily, the words ripped from him one by one, "why must I always love you and hate you at the same bloody time?"

The officers who sat in council with him stirred. The Roman did not know many of them well, nor they him. They were most of them younger men, come to prominence under the Emperor's eye this past campaigning season while the tribune was far away in the westlands; so many of the marshals who had served with Scaurus under Mavrikios Gavras were dead or in disgrace as rebels—or both.

"Your Highness, you cannot credit this tale, can you?" protested one of the new men, a cavalry officer named Provhos Mourtzouphlos. The disbelief on his handsome, whiskery face—like several other soldiers round the council table, he imitated Thorisin's carelessness about hair and beard—was manifest. Heads bobbed in agreement with him.

"I can," the Emperor replied. He kept on examining Scaurus, as if wondering whether the tribune had left something out. "I haven't said I do, yet."

"Well, you ought to," Taron Leimmokheir told him abruptly. His, at least, was a familiar face and voice; as always, the drungarios of the fleet's raspy bass, used to roaring out commands at sea, sounded too big for any enclosed space, even one the size of the Hall of the Nineteen Couches. Smiling at Marcus, he went on, "Anyone with the courage to come back to you after such misfortunes deserves honor, not blame. And what if the fornicating Gamblers got away in the end? There's no New Namdalen over the Cattle-Crossing, and for that you have only the outlander here to thank."

Mourtzouphlos sent an aristocrat's sneer toward the gray-bearded admiral, who had risen from the ranks by dint of courage, strength, and—rare among Videssians—unswerving, outspoken honesty. The cavalryman said, "No wonder Leimmokheir speaks up for the foreigner. He owes him enough."

"So I do, and proud to own it, by Phos," the drungarios said.

The Emperor, though, frowned, remembering how Leimmokheir had sworn loyalty to Ortaias before he knew Thorisin had survived Maragha—and how, with his stubborn loyalty, he refused to go back on that oath. He also remembered the assassination attempt he had blamed on the admiral, and the months Leimmokheir had spent in prison until Scaurus proved him guiltless—and touched off Baanes Onomagoulos' revolt by showing him to be the man behind the plot.

Thorisin passed a weary hand in front of his eyes, then scratched his left temple. The dark brown hair there was thinner than it had been when Marcus and the legionaries came to Videssos, and more streaked with gray as well. At last he said, "I think I do believe you, Roman. Not for what Taron here says, though there's truth in that, too. But I know you have the wit to make a better lie than the yarn you spun, so it's most likely true. Aye, most likely," he repeated, half to himself. Then, straightening abruptly on his gilded chair, he finished, "Stay in the city a while; you needn't hurry back to Garsavra. That lieutenant of yours is plenty able to hold the town when winter slows everyone to a crawl, Yezda and us alike."

"As you wish, of course, sir," Marcus said, saluting. The Emperor was right; if anything, Gaius Philippus was a better tactician than Scaurus. But the order was strange enough to make the tribune ask, "What would you have me do here?"

The question seemed to catch Thorisin Gavras by surprise. He scratched his head again, thinking. After a few seconds he answered, "For one thing, I want a full report in writing from you, covering what you've told me today in more detail. The Namdaleni are demons to fight; anything I can learn from what you did to them will be useful. And, oh yes," he went on, struck by a happy afterthought, "you can ride herd on the plague-taken pen-pushers as you did last winter."

Marcus bowed, but he was somber as he took his seat. Although Thorisin professed believing him, he did not expect he would be trusted to command again any time soon.

The Emperor had already dismissed him from his mind. He looked round the hall. "Now for the next piece of good news," he said. He unrolled a square sheet of parchment, elaborately sealed and written in a large, gorgeous hand. Gavras held it as if it gave off a bad smell. "This little missive is from our dear friend Zemarkhos," he announced sardonically, and began to read aloud.

Stripped of the fanatic priest's turgid phrasing, the proclamation declared Amorion and the westlands surrounding that city the rightful principality of Phos on earth and hurled venomous anathemas at Thorisin and Balsamon the patriarch of Videssos. "By which the madman means we've no taste for massacring Vaspurakaners," the emperor growled. He tore the parchment in half, threw it behind him. "What do we do about such tripe?"

The council threw out a few suggestions, but they were all halfhearted, suicidal, or both. The plain truth was that, since a wide stretch of territory held by the Yezda—whom Zemarkhos hated almost as much as he did heretics within his own faith—separated Amorion from imperial troops, Thorisin could not do much but fume.

He glared at his advisors for being as unable to get around that as he was himself. "No more brilliant schemes, the lot of you?" he asked at last. Silence answered. He shook his head in disgust. "No? Go on, then. This council is dismissed."

Servants swung back the Hall of the Nineteen Couches' mirror-bright bronze doors. Videssos' officers trooped out. Marcus wrapped himself in his cape to ward off the icy breeze. At least, he thought, the bureaucrats kept their offices warm.

Videssian troops occupied two of the four barracks halls the legionaries had used in the palace complex; a company of Halogai, newly come from their cold northern home, was quartered in the third. The last stood empty, but Scaurus had no desire to rattle around in it like a pebble inside a huge Yezda drum. Instead, he took up residence in an empty second-floor room of the bureaucrats' wing of the compound that held the Grand Courtroom. The seal-stampers greeted him with wary politeness, recalling his meddling in business they considered theirs alone.

He worked in a desultory way on the report the Emperor had requested, but it seemed stale and flat even as he wrote it. He could not attach any importance to it; in trying to numb himself to the shock of Helvis' leaving him as she had, he pulled away from the rest of the world as well. He moved in a gray haze that had nothing to do with the weather.

He did his best to disregard the knock on his door—which he kept closed most of the time—but it went on and on. Sighing, he rose from a low chair by the window and lifted the latch.

Waiting outside, beringed hands on hips, was a plump, smooth-cheeked man of uncertain age, clad in a robe of saffron silk shot through with green embroidery—one of the eunuchs who served the Videssian Emperors as chamberlains. "Took you long enough," he sniffed, giving Marcus the smallest bow protocol allowed. He went on, "You are bidden to attend his Imperial Majesty this evening in his private chambers at the beginning of the second hour of the night." The Videssians, like the Romans, divided day and night into twelve hours each, beginning respectively at dawn and sunset.

Marcus started; Thorisin had ignored him in the week since the officers' council. He asked the chamberlain, "Does he expect my account of the western campaign? I'm afraid it's not quite done." Only he knew how much an understatement that was.

The eunuch's shrug set his puddingy jowls shaking. "I know nothing of such things, only that an attendant will come to lead you thither at the hour I named. And I hope," he added, putting Scaurus in his place, "you will be prompter in greeting him than you were for me." He turned his back on the tribune and waddled away.

The attendant proved to be another eunuch, somewhat less splendidly robed than his predecessor. He started shivering as soon as he stepped from the well-heated wing of the Grand Courtroom into the keen night breeze. Scaurus knew a moment of sympathy. He himself wore trousers, as most Videssians did when not performing some ceremonial function. He did not miss his Roman toga; the Empire's winters demanded warmth.

The cherry trees surrounding the imperial family's personal quarters sent bare branches reaching skeletal fingers into the sky—no fragrant blooms at this season of the year. A squad of Halogai stood guard at the doorway, their two-handed axes at the ready. In fur robes of otter and white bear and fox and snow leopard over gilded cuirasses, the big blond men seemed perfectly at ease. And why not, the tribune thought—they were used to worse weather than this. They eyed him curiously; he looked as much like one of them as like an imperial. They discussed him in their own guttural language as the chamberlain led him by; he caught the word "Namdalen" spoken in a questioning tone.

The entrance hall still showed scars from the fighting this past spring, when Baanes Onomagoulos had slipped a murder-squad into the city to try to do away with Thorisin. The legionaries, opportunely returning from a practice march, had foiled that. Scaurus glanced at a portrait of the great conquering Emperor Laskaris, now seven and a half centuries dead. As always, the tribune thought Laskaris looked more like a veteran underofficer than Avtokrator of the Videssians, but now a bloodstain marred the lower left quadrant of his image, and sword strokes had chipped at the hunting scenes of the floor mosaics over which the tribune walked.

The chamberlain paused. "Wait here. I will announce you."

"Of course." As the eunuch bustled down the passage, Marcus leaned against a wall and studied the alabaster ceiling panels. They were dark now, of course, but the translucent stones were cut so thin that during the day they lit the hall with a pale, shifting, pearly light.

The imperial servitor vanished round a corner, but he did not go far. Scaurus heard his own name spoken, heard Thorisin's impatient reply: "Well, fetch him." The eunuch reappeared, beckoned Marcus on.

The Emperor was leaning forward in his chair, as if willing the Roman into the room. On a couch beside him sat his niece; Marcus' heart gave a painful thump to see her. As was often true, especially since her torment at the hands of Vardanes Sphrantzes, Alypia's face wore an abstracted expression, but warmth came into her fine green eyes as Marcus entered.

Remembering his etiquette, the tribune bowed first to Thorisin, then to the princess. "Your Majesty. Your Highness." The eunuch frowned when he did not prostrate himself, but Thorisin, like Mavrikios before him, had always tolerated that bit of republican Roman stubbornness.

Now, though, his finger darted forward. "Seize him!" Two Halogai sprang out from behind the chamber's double doors to lock Scaurus' arms back of him in an unbreakable grip. Struggle would have been useless; the burly warriors overtopped even the tribune's inches by half a head. Like some of the sentries outside, they wore their hair in thick braids that hung down to the small of their backs, but there was nothing effeminate about them. Their hands were big as shovels, hard as horn.

Surprise and alarm drove discretion from the tribune. "This is no way to get a proskynesis," he blurted.

A smile flickered on Alypia's face, but Thorisin's remained hard. "Be silent," he said, and then turned to the other occupant of the room. "Nepos, is that hell-brew of yours ready yet?"

First seeing Alypia and then being collared by the Haloga giants, Marcus had hardly noticed the tubby little priest, who was busily grinding gray, green, and yellow powders together. "Very nearly, your Majesty," Nepos replied. He beamed at the Roman. "Hello, outlander. It's good to see you again."

"Is it?" Scaurus said. He did not like the sound of "hell-brew." Nepos was mage as well as priest, and a master at his craft, master to the point of teaching theoretical thaumaturgy at the Videssian Academy. The tribune wondered if he was so expendable as to be only an experimental animal. He had no relish for life since Helvis had forsaken him, but there were ends and ends. Nepos, cheerfully oblivious, poured his mixed powders into a golden goblet of wine, stirred it with a short glass rod.

"Can't use wood or brass for this, you know," he said, perhaps to Thorisin, perhaps to Marcus, perhaps only because he was used to lecturing. "They'd not be the better afterward." The Roman gulped despite himself.

The Emperor fixed him with the same searching glance he had brought to bear in the Hall of the Nineteen Couches. "After you let the islanders loose, outlander, my first thought was to put you on the shelf and leave you there till the dust covered you up. You've always been too thick with the Namdaleni for me to really trust you." The irony of that almost jerked laughter from Scaurus, but Thorisin was going on, not altogether happily, "Still and all, there are those who think you truly are loyal, and so we'll find out tonight." Alypia Gavra would not meet the tribune's eye.

Nepos raised the goblet by its graceful stem. "Do you remember Avshar's puppet," he asked Marcus, "the Khamorth who attacked you with the spell-wound knife after you bested Avshar at swords?" The tribune nodded. "Well, this is the same drug that wrung the truth from him."

"And he died when you were done questioning him, too," Scaurus said harshly.

The priest gestured in abhorrence. "That was Avshar's sorcery, not mine."

"Give it to me, then," the tribune said. "Let's be done with it."

At Thorisin's nod, the Haloga who pinioned Scaurus' right arm let go. The Avtokrator warned, "Spilling it will do you no good. There'll just be another batch, and a funnel down your throat."

But when the goblet was in his hand, Marcus asked Nepos, "Is there only just enough, or a bit more?"

"A bit more, perhaps. Why?"

The tribune sloshed a few drops of wine onto the floor. "Here's to that fine fellow Thorisin, then," he said. The Videssians frowned, not understanding; he heard one of the Halogai behind him grunt in confusion. It was the toast of Theramenes the Athenian to Kritias when forced to take poison in the time of the Thirty Tyrants after the Peloponnesian War.

He swallowed the wine at a single draught. Beneath the sweetness he could taste Nepos' drugs, tart on his tongue, but also numbing. He waited, wondering if he would start to gibber, or thrash about on the floor like a poisoned dog.

"Well?" Thorisin Gavras growled at Nepos.

"The effects vary from case to case, from person to person," the priest replied. "Some take longer to respond than others." Scaurus heard him as if from very far away; the whole of his mind was suffused with a golden glow. Of all the things he had expected, this godlike feeling was the last. It was like an orgasm that went on and on, but with all the pleasure gone and only transcendence left.

Someone—it was the Emperor, but that did not matter to him—was asking him something. He heard himself answering. Why not? Whatever the question was, it could only be trivial next to the immanence in which he drifted. He heard Thorisin swear; that was not important either. "What drivel is he mouthing?" the Avtokrator said. "I can't follow a word of it."

Alypia Gavra said quietly, "It's his birth-speech."

"Well, he should use ours, then."

Marcus obeyed, untroubled; one language was as good as another. The questions came faster: why had he let Mertikes Zigabenos take refuge in a monastery? "I thought that if you could do as much for Ortaias Sphrantzes, who deserved worse, then I could for Mertikes, who deserved better."

A grunt from Thorisin. "Is he truly under, priest?"

Nepos peeled back one of Scaurus' eyelids, waved a hand an inch in front of his face. The tribune neither flinched nor blinked. "Truly, your Majesty."

Gavras laughed ruefully. "Well, I suppose I had that coming. Still, Zigabenos hadn't a tenth the political muscle the Sphrantzai carry, and only fear of that saved Ortaias' scrawny neck." Alypia made a sound in the back of her throat that might have meant anything or nothing.

Why had the tribune only pretended to blind the Namdalener marshals at Garsavra?

"I wanted to do nothing that could not be undone later. You might have had some use for them that I did not know." Thorisin grunted again, this time in satisfaction, but Marcus went on, "And Soteric was Helvis' brother, and I was sure she would leave me if I harmed him. I did not want her to leave me."

The Roman, who had not bothered to close his eye after Nepos pulled it open, saw but did not notice the look of triumphant suspicion Gavras shot his niece. "Now we come down to it," the Emperor said. "So you did not want the doxy gone, eh?"

"No."

"Tell me, then, how it happened she escaped, and the whole nest of snakes with her. Tell me *everything* about that: what she did, what you think she did, what you did, what you thought while you were doing it. Damn you, Scaurus, I'll know your soul for once."

Drugged as he was, the tribune stood silent a long time. The grief Thorisin was probing could touch the tranquility of a god. "Answer me!" the Emperor shouted, and Scaurus, his will overborne by the other's, began again. While one part of him listened and bled, the rest told exactly how Helvis had worn him down into drowsiness. The worst of it was knowing he would remember everything after Nepos' potion no longer held him.

As he droned on, Nepos reddened in embarrassment. The Haloga guardsmen muttered back and forth in their own tongue. And Alypia Gavra turned on her uncle, saying angrily, "In Phos' name, stop this! Or why not flay the skin from him while you're about it?"

At the word "stop," Marcus obediently did. But Thorisin's voice was cold as he told Alypia, "This was your idea, to have the truth from him. Now have the stomach to sit and hear it, or else get out."

"I would not stay to see anyone stripped naked against his will." Her face was pale as she whispered, "I know the taste of that too well." She stepped past Marcus and was gone.

"Bah!" Thorisin seemed to notice Scaurus was not talking. "Go on, you!" he roared. The tribune told him of the pursuit; of the beacon fire that had drawn the Namdalener corsair; of Helvis, her sons, and the rest of the islanders escaping the beach in the raiders' longboat. "And what did you do then?" the Emperor asked, but quietly; Marcus' account of that desperate, futile chase had left him without his hectoring tone.

"I cried."

Thorisin winced. "To the ice with me if I blame you for it," he said to himself. "Alypia had the right of it after all; I've raped an honest man." Very gently then, to Scaurus, "And what then, and why?"

The tribune shrugged; the Halogai were still at his back,

but no longer restrained him. "Then I came to the city here, to you. There was nothing else for me to do. How could I flee to a monastery, when I do not follow your god? And if Drax was wrong to turn rebel, so would I have been. Besides, I would have lost."

Thorisin gave him a very odd look. "I wonder. I do wonder."

XII

SEIREM PRESSED HER LIPS AGAINST VIRIDOVIX'; HE HUGGED her to him. "You're *too* tall," she said. "My neck gets stiff when I kiss you."

"Make yourself used to it, girleen, for you'll be doing a lot of it after we're back from the squashing o' that flea of a Varatesh," the Gaul answered. A measure of his fancy for her was that he passed up the obvious bawdy comeback to her words. Between them there was no need for such artificial warmers; they were pleased enough with each other as they were.

She hugged him. "You be after comin' back, hear?" she said, mimicking his brogue so perfectly they both laughed.

"Mount up, you lazy groundling!" came Targitaus' gruff bellow. "You think we have time to waste on your mooning about?" But the khagan was fighting a smile, and next to him Batbaian grinned openly.

"Och, the corbies take you," Viridovix said, but after a last squeeze he let Seirem go and swung up into the saddle. As it often did, his steppe pony snorted a complaint; he was heavier than most Khamorth.

Targitaus looked over to Lipoxais. "You promised ten days

of decent weather," he said, half-threateningly. It was no small matter. The first autumn rains had already fallen, and war among the nomads depended on clear skies. Wet bowstrings made a mockery of their chief fighting skill.

The *enaree* shrugged, flesh bobbling inside his yellow wool robe. "I saw what I saw."

"I wish you'd seen who would win," Targitaus grumbled, but not in real complaint. The passion that surrounded battle clouded foretelling. "We'll have to find out, then," the chieftain said. He raised his voice to a shout. "We ride!" Batbaian raised the wolf standard of the clan, and the Khamorth clucked their horses into motion. Scouts trotted ahead, with flank guards out to either side.

"You, too, wretched beast," Viridovix said, snapping the reins and digging his boots into the pony's sides. He turned to wave a last good-bye to Seirem and was almost pitched off the horses's back when it shied at a blowing scrap of cloth. He clutched its mane, feeling a fool.

Perhaps over the last few years he had grown more used to Roman discipline than he suspected, for the army Targitaus led seemed a very disorderly thing. Indeed, he could be said to lead it only because more plainsmen rode round his standard than any other. But no one could make the other clanchiefs follow his orders if they did not care to. They fought Varatesh for their own reasons, not his.

A dozen separate bands of nomads, then, rode north and west against the outlaws. They ranged in size from the double handful in white fox caps who followed Oitoshyr to the several hundred with Anakhar of the Spotted Cats, a contingent second in size only to Targitaus'. Anakhar's wavering had abruptly stopped when he discovered that Krobyz, his hated neighbor on the steppe, favored Varatesh. "If that goat's arse is for him, there's reason enough to smack him down," he had declared, and joined Targitaus forthwith.

Beyond finding Varatesh and then fighting him, they had no plan of action. When Viridovix suggested working one out, Targitaus and the rest of the clan leaders looked at him as if he had fallen from the moon. The Celt had to laugh when he thought of it. "As if I'd have listened to a Roman spouting such balderdash," he said to himself. Even so, he worried a little.

"One thing," Batbaian said, "the rains have laid the dust to rest."

"They have that, and not sorry I am for it," Viridovix agreed. Going to fight without choking on the grit his comrades kicked up was a pleasure he had not known since Gaul. Clouds covered the sun every few minutes, sending shadows racing over the plains. The day was cool, the air crisp and clean. Sometimes, tramping across Videssos' dry plateau, he'd thought the whole country made of dust.

After a moment, he said, "But outen the dust, how are the scouts to be spotting the kerns we're after?" Batbaian blinked; he had not thought of that. Viridovix worked up a fair-sized anger—was nothing without its drawbacks?

Targitaus stretched his mouth in what was not quite a smile. "For one thing, they have the same problem with us. For another, scouts who don't pay attention to what's ahead of them end up dead, and that keeps 'em lively."

"Well, you have the right of it there," the Gaul allowed.

The nomad army seemed larger than it was, thanks to the string of remounts behind each plainsman. The rumble of hooves on damp ground reminded Viridovix of the constant murmur of the sea. "But it doesna make me want to gi' back my breakfast," he said happily.

He thought of Arigh's jibe about horsesickness and was glad there was nothing to it. Though he still could not stomach the half-raw beef the Khamorth used for iron rations, he munched on wheatcakes and curded cheese, washed them down with kavass. He wished for something sweet, wine or fruit or berries. When Rambehisht passed him a chunk of honeycomb and the heady tang of wild clover filled his mouth, he was content with the world. "A braw lass, a good scrap to go to, and e'en a bit o' honey when you need it most," he said to no one in particular. "Who could want for more?"

After the Khamorth camped that night they went from fire to fire, trading news, telling tales, and gambling with a bizarre assortment of money, some of it so worn Viridovix could not tell whether it had been minted in Videssos or Yezd. There were also square silver coins stamped with dragons or axes, whose like he had not seen. "Halugh," a nomad explained.

The Gaul won several goldpieces and one of the Haloga coins, which he pocketed for luck.

The next day's travel was much like the one before. The steppe seemed endless, and the plainsmen with whom Viridovix rode the only men on it. But when the evening fires went up, there was a faint answering glow against the northern horizon. Men checked harness and gear; here a nomad tightened a girth, there another filed arrow-points to razor sharpness, while two more practiced sword-strokes on horseback, making ready for what would come tomorrow.

Viridovix woke before dawn, shivering from the cold. In Gaul the trees would have been gorgeous with autumn's colors; the only change the steppe grass showed was from green to grayish yellow. "Sure and it's bleak enough, for all its size," he mumbled around a mouthful of cheese.

The Khamorth teased the handful of older men left behind to guard the remounts. The latter gave back good as they got: "When you're done beating the bastards, drive 'em this way. We'll show you what we can do!"

Clan by clan, the plainsmen mounted. As they rode north they shook themselves out into a rough battle line. Targitaus' band held the right wing. Eyeing the gaps between clans and the ragged front, Viridovix consoled himself by thinking that Varatesh's bandits would keep no better ranks.

Moving dots against the steely sky, the outlaws appeared. A murmur ran down the line; men nocked arrows and freed swords in scabbards. Varatesh's men drew closer with a speed that Viridovix, still used to foot campaigns, found dismaying. He waved his sword, howling out a wild Celtic war cry that startled his comrades; what it did to the foe was harder to tell.

Skirmishers traded arrows in the shrinking no-man's-land between the armies. A pair of nomads dueled with sabers. When the outlaw slid from his saddle, a cheer rang out from his foes.

It clogged in Viridovix' throat when he spied in the center of the enemy line a white-robed figure riding a black horse half again the size of the steppe ponies around it. "Well, you didna think himself'd stay away," he muttered. "Och, would he had, though." The Gaul thought his side outnumbered the bandits, but who knew how many men Avshar was worth?

No time for thought after that—the two main bodies were

shooting at each other now. The arrows flew, bitter as the sleet that could be only days away. Useless in the long-range fight, the Celt watched over the edge of his small, light shield. The deadly rhythm had a fascination to it: right hand over left shoulder to pull a shaft from the quiver, nock, draw, a quick glance for a target, shoot, and over the shoulder again. The plainsmen methodically emptied their quivers. Now and again the measured cadence would break down: a curse, a grunt, or a scream as a man was hit, or a wild scramble to leap free of a foundering horse before it crushed its rider.

Varatesh watched in astonishment as Avshar wielded his great black bow. It was built to the same double-curved pattern as any nomad bow, but not even the burliest outlaw could bend it. Yet the wizard-prince used it as Varatesh might a child's weapon, killing with his wickedly barbed shafts at ranges the outlaw chief would not have believed a man could reach. His skill was chillingly matter-of-fact. He gave no cry of triumph when another shot struck home, nor even a satisfied nod, but was already choosing his next victim.

An arrow whined past Varatesh's cheek. He ducked behind his horse's neck—futile, of course, if the shaft had been truly aimed. He fired back, saw a rider topple. He wondered if it was the man who had shot at him. "No," Avshar said, reading his thought. The wizard-prince's voice held scornful mirth. "Why should you care, though? He would have been glad enough to kill you." That was true, but even truth from Avshar left a sour taste.

The wizard's eye traveled the enemy line for new targets. He wheeled his horse leftward, steadying it with his knees. He drew the black bow back to his ear, but as he shot Varatesh reached out and knocked his wrist aside. The arrow flew harmlessly into the air.

The wizard-prince seemed to grow taller in the saddle, glaring down at Varatesh like an angry god. "What are you playing at, fool?" he rasped, a whisper more menacing than any other man's roar of rage.

The outlaw chief quailed as Avshar's wrath fell on him, but his own anger sustained him. "The red-haired one is mine," he said. "You may not have him."

"You speak to me of 'may not,' grub? Remember who I am."

That memory would stay with Varatesh forever. But he summoned all that was left of his own pride and flung it back at Avshar: "And you, sorcerer, remember who *I* am." Afterwards, he thought it the bravest thing he had ever done.

The wizard-prince measured him with that terrible unseen stare. "So," he said at last, "another tool turns and bites me, does it? Well, for all that your mother was a cur, you make a better one than that scrannel Vardanes, who thought only of his prick in the end." He spread his hands in ironic generosity. "Take the red-haired one, then, if you can. I make you a present of him."

"He is not yours to give," Varatesh said, but only to himself.

As fighters on both sides began running out of arrows, the battle lines drew closer. Shamshirs flashed in the autumn sun; a nomad near Viridovix gaped at the spouting blood where two fingers of his left hand had been sheared away. "Tie 'em up!" Targitaus shouted. The rider came out of his stupor. Cursing furiously, he wrapped a strip of wool over the wound and tied it tight with a leather thong.

An outlaw rode straight for the Gaul; Viridovix booted his horse on to meet him. Straight sword rang off curved one. With the lighter weapon, the Khamorth slashed again before Viridovix had recovered. He leaned away from the stroke, turned the next one with his shield. His own cut laid the nomad's leg open. The rider cursed and dropped his guard. Viridovix brought his blade round in a backhand swipe. It crunched into the renegade's cheek. Blood spattered; the Khamorth's fur cap flew from his head. Dead or unconscious, he fell from the saddle, to be trampled by his own horse.

Rambehisht had cannily saved his arrows till the fighting came to close quarters. At point-blank range his bow, reinforced with horn, could drive a shaft right through a man, or pin him to his horse. Then his own animal toppled, shot just below the eye. Lithe as a cat, he kicked free of the stirrups before it fell, and faced an oncoming bandit sword in hand.

Mounted man against one afoot, though, was a contest with an ending likely grim. Viridovix, who was not far away, howled out a wild Gallic war cry. It froze the outlaw for the moment the Celt needed to draw close. Rambehisht ran forward, too. Suddenly it was two against one; the horseman tried to flee, but in the press he could not. Seizing his left calf, Rambehisht pitched him off his beast. Viridovix leaned down to finish him off. Rambehisht leaped onto the steppe pony before it got away. He drew, fired, and hit a nomad riding up behind the Gaul.

Viridovix jerked his head round at the bandit's cry of pain. "Thank you, Khamorth darling. That one I hadna seen."

"Debts are for paying," the dour plainsman answered. Viridovix frowned, wondering if Rambehisht intended to pay back his beating one day as well.

No time to fret over might-be's. Three brigands spotted Viridovix at once. By luck, one of Targitaus' men took the closest out of the fight with a well-cast javelin. The other two bored in on the Gaul. He let out another ululating shriek, but it did not daunt them. Thinking fast, he spurred toward one, then clapped his bronze-studded leather cap from his head and hurled it in the other's face. He wheeled his horse with a skill he hardly knew he had, smashed his sword down on the head of the distracted renegade's beast. The luckless horse dropped, stone dead. Viridovix never knew what happened to its rider. He was already whirling back to face the other bandit, but the outlaw fled before him.

He laughed gigantically. "Back to your mother, you skulking omadhaun! Think twice or ever you play a man's game again!" Blood flew from his sword as he brandished it overhead. This was what the battlefield was for, he thought—bending the foe to your mastery, whether by steel or force of will alone. Intoxicating as strong kavass, the power tingled in his veins.

He brushed his long hair back from his eyes, looked round to see how the bigger fight was going. It was hard to be sure. These cavalry battles took up an ungodly lot of room and ebbed and flowed like quicksilver. Worse, he had trouble telling his own side from the outlaws at any distance.

There was, he saw, a battle within a battle in the center of the field, with Anakhar's Spotted Cats in a wild melee with Krobyz' Leaping Goats. Most of Varatesh's nonoutlaw allies seemed to be bunched there, from the standards waving over them. They might fight along with his blank black banner, but were not eager to join too closely with the renegades who followed it.

As a result, Anakhar's men were outnumbered and hard-pressed. Targitaus waved to his son to ride to their rescue. Batbaian led a company leftward. Unlike Viridovix, he knew friend from foe at a glance. His horsemen plugged what had been a growing gap, making the enemy give ground. Heartened, the Spotted Cats fought with fresh vigor.

Targitaus took the rest of his men on a flanking move round the outlaws' left. Avshar met them head-on, leading half a hundred of Varatesh's hardest brigands, scarred rogues who knew every trick of fighting, fair and foul. They were steeped in evil but far from cowards, giving no quarter and asking none.

On his huge stallion, Avshar stood out from the Khamorth around him like a war galley among rowboats. His fearsome bow was slung over his shoulder; he swung a long straight sword with deadly effect. "Another oaf!" he cried as one of Targitaus' riders drove at him. The blade hissed as it cleaved air and bit into the plainsman's neck. "That for your stupidity, then, and Skotos eat your soul forever!"

Viridovix raised his voice to carry through the battle clamor: "Avshar!" The wizard-prince's head came up, like a dog taking a scent. "Here, you kern!" the Celt yelled. "You wanted Scaurus, but I'll stand for him the now!"

"And fall, as well!" Avshar spurred past one of his own men. "Out of my way, ravens' meat!" He brought his sword up in mock salute as he neared the Gaul. "You will make Varatesh angry, gifting me with your life so."

Viridovix barely beat the wizard's first stroke aside, turning the flat of the blade with his shield—the edge would have torn through it. The heavy horse Avshar rode let him carry the full panoply he always wore beneath his robes—his shield was a kite-shaped one, faced with metal, on the Namdalener pattern. The gear made the Gaul's boiled leather seem flimsy as linen.

You'll not beat this one on strength, the Gaul thought as he turned his horse for the next pass, nor on fear either. That left wit. He remembered the lesson he had learned in his fight with Varatesh: a horse was as important as a sword. It was doubly true of Avshar's huge charger, which reared to dash the brains from a dismounted nomad with its iron-shod hooves.

The wizard-prince brought it down and sent it charging at Viridovix, who dug spurs into his own mount. When they met, his slash was aimed not at Avshar in his mail, but at the stallion. He had intended to deliver the same crushing blow he had used against the outlaw's mount, but misjudged the speed the charger could deliver. Instead of crashing down between the beast's eyes, the sword tore a great flap of skin from the side of its neck.

That served nearly as well as the stroke he had intended, for the wounded animal screamed in shock and pain and bucked frantically, almost throwing Avshar. Bellowing in rage, the wizard-prince had to clutch its mane to keep from going over its tail. And even though he held his seat, the wounded animal would not answer the reins; it ran off at full gallop, carrying him out of the fight.

"Come back, ye blackguard!" Viridovix howled gleefully. "It's only just begun that I have."

Avshar spun in his saddle, shouting a curse. For a moment the battlefield swayed and darkened before the Gaul's eyes. Then the druids' marks on his blade flashed golden as they turned aside the spell. His vision cleared. He squeezed the sword hilt gratefully, as if it were a comrade's hand.

The battle hung, undecided, for some endless time, with no lull long enough to let the fighters do much more than sob in a few quick breaths or swig at skins of water or kavass. The sun had passed west of south before Viridovix fully realized he was moving forward more often than back.

"Press 'em, press 'em!" Targitaus shouted. "They're going to break."

But as his horsemen gathered themselves for the charge that would finish the outlaws, yells of alarm came from the center and left, the most dreaded cry on the steppe: "Fire!" Clouds of thick black smoke leaped into the air, obscuring the renegades. Targitaus' face purpled with rage. "Filthy cowards! Better to die like men than cover a retreat that way."

Then Viridovix heard Avshar's gloating laughter and knew all his hopes were undone, for the flames spread faster than any natural fire, and at the direction of a malignant will. Horses shrieked and men screamed as the advancing walls of fire swept over them. But they were merely caught by accident in the web of the wizard-prince's design. He used his blaze to net his foes as a hunter would drive hares into his meshes, trapping them in small pockets between fiery sheets that raced between and behind horses faster than any beast could hope to run.

As the main body of their enemies was caught, Varatesh's brigands took fresh heart, while the clans that rode with them saw Avshar's prowess with mingled awe and terror. They drove against the untrapped remnants of Targitaus' army with redoubled force. Now all the weight of numbers was on their side. There was no checking them. The retreat that followed was close to rout.

Viridovix tried to stem it singlehanded, slashing his way through the enemy ranks toward Avshar. The wizard-prince was afoot, having dismounted from his wounded charger the better to direct his sorcery. The Gaul's desperation burned bright as the wizard's flames; few outlaws dared stand against him.

Varatesh and a band of outlaws rode to Avshar's rescue, but the wizard needed no protection. He gave Viridovix a quick glance, gestured, sent a tongue of flame licking his way through the grass. The Celt spurred toward it regardless, confident his sword would carry him past the magic. The druids' marks on the blade glowed as he thundered toward the fire.

But his mount knew nothing of sorcery and shied at the flames ahead, its eyes rolling with panic. For all his roweling, it would go no further. He cried out to Epona, but the Celtic horse-goddess held no power in this world. Avshar's image wavered through the flames, tauntingly out of reach.

"All right, then, I'll go my ain self," the Celt growled, fighting to steady the beast enough to let him climb down. But Varatesh chose that moment to loose a hoarded arrow at him. It missed, but sank deep into his horse's rump. The beast squealed and leaped into the air, almost throwing him. It bolted away, out of control. That was, perhaps, as well for Viridovix; goaded by pain, the steppe pony outran the bandits pursuing it. Avshar's vengeful laughter burned in the Gaul's ears.

When he finally made his horse obey him, he could only join the fragments of Targitaus' shattered army in their retreat.

The renegades and their allies let them go. They were hovering like carrion flies round Avshar's prisoning walls of fire, which burned on, fierce as ever, long after the grass that should have been their only fuel was gone.

Black as despair, smoke filled all the autumn sky.

Krobyz bowed low in the saddle as Varatesh rode by. Exhausted as he was, the outlaw chief flushed with pleasure at the acknowledgement of his prowess from a legitimate khagan. This, he told himself, was what he had been reaching toward for so many years. At last he had earned the place which belonged to him by right, and that despite the foes he did not deserve. His lip curled—they had seen his might today.

The crackling flames ahead reminded him the triumph had not been entirely his. As if to reinforce that reminder, Avshar came up beside him. But the wizard-prince only waved toward the warriors trapped in his blazing cells. "What is your pleasure with them?"

Varatesh was ready to be magnanimous in victory. "Let them surrender, if they will."

Shrugging, Avshar called to the plainsmen in the nearest fiery box. "Yield yourselves to Varatesh, grand khagan of the Royal Clan of Pardraya!" The unexpected title made the outlaw chieftain blink. Why, so I am, he thought proudly.

The box held Oitoshyr and his three or four surviving clansmen, their white fox caps dark with dust and soot. Oitoshyr was wounded, but not ready to quit. "Bugger Varatesh, the grand pimp of the plains," he shouted, "aye, and you, too, you hulking turd!"

The wizard-prince looked a question to Varatesh. Furious at the rebuff, he spat in the dirt. Avshar took that as answer and gestured with his left hand. One wall of flame holding the White Foxes turned transparent, then died. Varatesh waved a hundred bandits in. Grinning, they set about the butchery they had been waiting for. Oitoshyr took a long time to die.

After that, surrenders came one on the other. Varatesh was staggered by the victory he had won. No bard sang of, no *enaree* remembered, a battle with so many prisoners taken. There must have been a thousand in all; as each flame pocket opened, his men swarmed over them like locusts, taking weapons, armor, and horses as spoils of war. He wondered how long he could feed them.

"Why should you?" Avshar said. "Give them back to their own worthless clans."

"And have them take up arms against me again the next day? I did not think you such a trusting soul."

The sorcerer laughed, deep in his throat. "Well said! But if you could get them off your hands, and at the same time prove your supremacy to every petty chief on the steppe?" He paused, waiting for Varatesh's response.

"Go on," the plainsman urged, intrigued.

Avshar laughed again and did.

"I thank you, but no," Gorgidas told Arghun for what must have been the twentieth time. "When the imperial embassy goes back to Videssos, I intend to go with it. I am a man made for cities, just as you belong here on the plain. I could no more be happy following the flocks than you could in the Empire."

"We will speak of this again," the khagan said, as he did each time Gorgidas declined to stay with the Arshaum. Arghun leaned back against a pile of cushions in the Videssian embassy's yurt and stretched a blanket of rabbit fur over his legs. Feeling had returned to them, but not full use. The khagan needed two sticks to walk and still could not sit a horse.

His gratitude for his life, though, knew no bounds. He had showered the Greek with presents: a knee-length coat of marten's fur so soft it almost did not register to the fingers; a string of fine horses; a falcon with blood-colored eyes—no hawker, Gorgidas had been able to decline that in good conscience; a splendid bow and twenty arrows in a quiver covered in gold leaf, which he discreetly passed on to Skylitzes, who could use it; and, perhaps at Tolui's urging, a supply of all the herbs the nomads reckoned medicinal, each in a little bone jar with a stopper carved from horn.

"You are starting to speak our language well," Arghun went on.

"My thanks," Gorgidas said, rather insincerely. Like most Greeks, he thought his own supple, subtle tongue the one proper speech for a civilized man. Learning Latin had been a concession to serving in the Roman army, Videssian a necessity in this new world. In a generous moment, he might have admitted each had a few virtues. But the Arshaum speech was fit only for barbarians. As he had written, "It is a tongue with more words for the state of a cow's hoof than for that of a man's soul. No more need be said."

Thunder rumbled in the distance; Arghun curled his fingers in a protective sign. Rain pounded against the yurt's tight-stretched felt. In a normal year, the plainsmen would have been moving toward their winter pastures. This fall, though, the flocks went south with boys and graybeards, while warriors gathered to avenge the attack on the Gray Horse khagan.

A pony splashed up to the yurt, which slowed to let the rider swing himself up onto it. Dripping, Arigh slithered through the tent flap. He sketched a salute to his father. "The standard is ready," he reported.

Goudeles cocked a sly eyebrow at Gorgidas."Here's something for your history, now; you can style this the War of Bogoraz' Coat."

The Greek rubbed his chin; he hardly noticed the feel of his whiskers any more. "You know, I like that," he said. He rummaged in his kit for tablet and stylus, then scribbled a note in the wax. To unite the Arshaum clans, they had chosen to fight, not behind any tribal banner, but under the symbol of their reason for going to war.

The exchange had been in Videssian, but Arghun, catching the Yezda's name, asked to have it translated. When Arigh rendered it into the plains speech, his father let out a short, grim laugh. "Ha! If any more of him was left, that would go up on a lance instead of his coat."

"And rightly so," Lankinos Skylitzes said. He hesitated, then went on carefully, "You are building a potent army here, khagan."

"Yes," Arghun said, pride in his voice. "Are you not glad to have friends so strong?"

The imperial officer looked uncomfortable. "Er, of course. Yet traveling to Prista in such force might alarm the Pardrayan Khamorth—"

"As if that mattered," Arigh snorted. He drew a finger across his throat and made a ghastly gurgling noise. "This to them if they dare turn on us. I hope they try."

Skylitzes nodded, but he was a dogged man and plowed on

with his chain of thought. "And should such an army reach Prista, it would be hard to find shipping enough to transport it easily to Videssos."

Angry and baffled, Arigh said, "What's chewing on you, Lankinos? You come all this way for men and now you have them and don't want them."

But Arghun was eyeing Skylitzes with new respect. "Ride lightly on him there, son."

"Why should I?" Arigh looked resentfully at the Videssian.

"Because he knows his business." Seeing his son still mutinous, Arghun began to explain: "He came to us for soldiers for his own khagan."

"Well, of course," Arigh broke in. "What of it?"

"This army here is *mine*, as he sees. He has the right to wonder how I will use it, and if it might be more dangerous to him than the enemies he already has."

"Ahh," said Arigh, taking the point. Goudeles seemed chagrined at missing it himself, while Gorgidas dipped his head, admiring Skylitzes' subtlety.

The officer saluted Arghun, plainly relieved he was not annoyed. "If I may ask straight out, then, how will you use it?"

"I will hurt Yezd as much as I can," Arghun said flatly. "Arigh is right, I think; the Khamorth will stand aside for us when they see we mean them no harm—or, if not, the worse for them. But the easiest way to Mashiz is through Pardraya, and that is the way I aim to take." He bowed to the envoys from Videssos. "You will ride with us, of course."

"An honor," Skylitzes said.

Goudeles, on the other hand, looked like a man who had just been stabbed. Even more than Gorgidas, he longed for a return to the city and now saw it snatched away from him at the whim of this barbarian chief. "An honor," he choked out at last.

"Back to sword practice, Pikridios," Skylitzes chuckled, understanding him perfectly. The pen-pusher did not quite stifle a groan.

"This yurt will have to go, too," Arigh said, grinning as he rubbed salt in Goudeles' wounds. "Just a good string of horses, maybe a light shelter tent to keep the snow off at night."

"Snow?" Goudeles said faintly.

"Speak my tongue, please," Arghun grumbled; his son had dropped into Videssian to talk to the imperials. When he had caught up with the conversation, the khagan nodded in sympathy with Goudeles. "Yes, I know the snow is a nuisance. It will slow us up badly. But if we leave as soon as the clans have gathered, we should be nearing Yezd come spring."

"That's not precisely what I was worrying about," the bureaucrat said. He buried his face in his hands.

The nomads rode through steppe winters every year, following their herds. Knowing it could be done did not make the prospect appetizing. Gorgidas said the first thing that came to his mind. "Arigh, I'll need a fur cap like yours, one with—" He gestured, unsure of the word. "—ear flaps, by choice."

The plainsman understood him. "You'll have it," he promised. "That's a good job of thinking ahead, too; I knew a man who froze his ears in a blizzard and broke one clean off without ever knowing it till they thawed."

"How delightful," Goudeles muttered, almost inaudibly.

Gorgidas remembered something else. "Avshar is still loose in Pardraya."

That sobered his Videssian colleagues, and even Arigh, but Arghun said, as others had before, "A wizard. We have wizards of our own."

"Keep them moving, curse it!" Valash shouted. Viridovix nodded; he stood tall in the saddle, flapped his arms, and howled Gallic oaths. The flock of sheep picked up its pace by some meaningless fraction. Snug in their thick coats of greasy wool, they were more comfortable in the cold fall rain than the men who herded them.

The storms had come back two days ago, as Lipoxais foresaw, and made the nomads' retreat that much worse. There were not enough men to drive the herds as fast as they could go, either. That Targitaus had put a lubber like Viridovix to work was a measure of his desperation. Women were riding drover, too, and boys hardly old enough to have their feet reach the stirrups.

The Celt bullied a knot of sheep back into the main flock. He was glad Targitaus had any duty for him at all. It would have been easy to pile blame for the disaster on the foreigner —the more so as Batbaian had not returned with his father. Dead or captured, no one knew.

But Targitaus said only, "Not your fault, you fought well." If he did not want to see much of Viridovix after the fight, the Gaul found that easy to understand and kept his distance as best he could. It meant he could not spend much time with Seirem, but that would have been so anyhow. Targitaus drove his family no less than the rest of the clan; his daughter's hands were chafed and blistered from riding with the animals.

"*Get* along there, you gangling fuzz-covered idiot pile o' vulture puke!" Viridovix roared at a ewe that kept trying to go off on its own. The black-faced beast bleated indignantly, as if it knew what he was calling it.

Valash darted away from the Celt to keep more sheep in line. The young Khamorth's face was drawn with fatigue as he rode back. "This job is too big for two," he said. He shook his head; rainwater flew from his beard.

"Aye, well, maybe not much longer to it, I'm thinking," Viridovix said. "Sure and that son of a serpent Varatesh couldna be finding us the now, not with the rain and all to cover our trail." There had been no serious pursuit after the battle, none of the harrying the Celt had dreaded. For what it was worth, Targitaus had brought off his retreat masterfully.

Valash looked hopeful at the Gaul's words, but as they left his mouth Viridovix cursed himself for a fool. Avshar could track him by his sword as easily as a man following a torch through the night. For a moment he thought of throwing it into the muck to break the trail. But before his hand touched the sword hilt he jerked it away and spat in defiance. "If the whoreson wants it, let him earn it."

Darkness came swiftly these fall nights, thick clouds drinking up the light almost before the sun they hid was set. The Khamorth traveled as long as they could see the way ahead, then ran up their tents, largely by feel. The camp was cheerless—so many men missing or dead, others wounded, and all, men and women alike, exhausted.

Wrapped in a thick wool blanket, Viridovix huddled close to the cookfire in Targitaus' tent. The khagan's greeting was a grunt. He ate in gloomy silence, new lines of grief scored into his cheeks.

The Gaul made a cold supper of cheese and smoked mutton sausage, declined the blackberries candied in honey that Seirem offered him. "Another time, lass, when I'm more gladsome than now. The sweet of 'em'd be wasted on me, I'm thinking."

Lipoxais the *enaree* ate greedily; the thick juice ran sticky down his chin. "How can you pig it so?" Viridovix asked him. "Does it not fair gag you, wi' your folk in sic straits?"

"I take the pleasures I can," Lipoxais said shortly, his high voice expressionless, his jowly, beardless face a mask. Viridovix took a large bite of sausage and looked away, his own cheeks reddening. He had his answer about the *enaree*'s nature and found he did not want it.

"I wasna after the shaming of you," he muttered.

The *enaree* surprised him by laying a pudgy hand on his arm. "I suspect I should be honored," he said, a hint of a twinkle in his fathomless dark eyes. "How many times have you apologized for a clumsy tongue?"

"Not often enough, likely." Viridovix thought about it. "And I wonder whyever not? There's no harm to me and maybe some good to the spalpeen I'm after slanging."

Lipoxais glanced over to Seirem. "You're civilizing him."

"Honh!" Viridovix said, offended. "Am I a Roman, now? Who wants to be civilized?" After a while he realized the *enaree* had borrowed the Videssian word; it did not exist in the Khamorth speech. "Shows what he knows," the Gaul said to himself, and felt better.

"All right, I made a mistake!" Dizabul said, slamming his fist against the floor of the yurt. It hurt; he stared at it as if it had turned on him, too. He went on, "Is that any reason for everyone to treat me like a bald sheep? Is it?"

Yes, Gorgidas thought, but he did not say so. Dizabul was at an age where yesterday receded into the mist and tomorrow was impossibly far away. It seemed monstrously unfair to him still to be held accountable for his choices after their results became clear. But the elders remembered, and treated him as they would anyone who backed the wrong side. It stung; he was used to acclaim, not snubs.

He was, in fact, desperate enough to talk with the Greek, whom he had ignored before. Gorgidas did not suffer fools gladly, but Dizabul sometimes got off the subject of his own mistreatment and would answer questions about the history and customs of his clan. He was not stupid, only spoiled, and knew a surprising amount of lore. And his beauty helped the Greek tolerate his arrogance.

He was, indeed, so striking a creature that Gorgidas found himself tempted to play up to him with exaggerated sympathy. That made him angry at himself, and in reaction so short with Dizabul that the boy finally glared at him and shouted, "You're as bad as the rest of them!" He stomped off into the rain, leaving Gorgidas to reflect on the uses of self-control.

The Greek and Goudeles went into serious training for war. The pen-pusher never made even an ordinary swordsman, but Gorgidas surprised the Arshaum with his work with the *gladius*—at least on foot. "For the nomads," he recorded, "accustomed as they are to cutting at their foes from horseback, employ a like style when not mounted and are thus confounded facing an opponent who uses the point rather than the edge."

He hung a merciful veil of silence over his own efforts with the saber and the slashing stroke.

Even so, his progress satisfied Skylitzes. "No one would mistake you for a real soldier, true, but you've learned enough so you won't be butchered like a sheep. . . ." The officer rounded on Goudeles, who was rubbing a knee he had twisted trying to spin away from the plainsman with whom he had been practicing. Skylitzes rolled his eyes. "Unlike this one, who might as well tattoo 'rack of mutton' on his forehead and have done."

"Hrmmp," the bureaucrat said, still sitting in the mud. "I daresay I do better on the field than one of these barbarians would in the chancery. And what do you want from me? I never claimed a warrior's skills."

"Neither did the Hellene," Skylitzes retorted, startling Gorgidas, who had not realized the Videssian knew what his people called themselves.

The officer's praise did not altogether please him. He loathed war with the deep and sincere loathing of one who had seen too much of it too closely. At the same time, he was driven to do whatever he tried as well as he could. Having decided he needed the rudiments of the soldier's trade, he set about acquiring them as conscientiously as he had his medical lore, if not with the same burning interest.

He blinked, suddenly understanding how Gaius Philippus could see soldiering as just another trade, like carpentry or leatherworking. He would never like that perspective, but it was no longer alien to him.

He had to laugh at himself. Who would have thought insight could come from learning butchery? He remembered what Socrates had told the Athenians: "For a human being, an unexamined life is not worth living." And Socrates had fought in the phalanx when his *polis* needed him.

He must have murmured the Greek aloud, for Goudeles asked, "What's that?"

He translated it into Videssian. "Not bad," the pen-pusher said. "He was a secret agent, this Socrates?" Gorgidas threw his hands in the air.

When they got back to the yurt, Gorgidas carefully scraped the dirt from his horsehide boots before going in. Goudeles and Skylitzes followed suit, having learned he was much easier to live with if they went along. As a result, the yurt was undoubtedly cleaner than it had been when it housed plainsmen.

Goudeles cocked an eyebrow at the Greek. "What will you do when we move east, and it'll be a tent over bare mud?"

"The best I can," Gorgidas snapped. He did not think he had to apologize for his fastidiousness. He had long since noticed that wounds healed better when kept clean and sick patients recovered faster in clean surroundings. He had taken that as a general rule and applied it all through his way of living, reasoning that what aided against ill health might also help prevent it.

"Don't mock him over this one, Pikridios," Skylitzes said. He stretched full length on the rug with a grunt of pleasure. "Nothing wrong with coming back to something that's dry and isn't brown."

"Oh, no doubt, no doubt," Goudeles allowed. "But I'll never forget Tolui's face when our friend here called him a filthy ball of horse droppings for tracking mud on the carpet." Gorgidas had the grace to look shamefaced, the more so as the shaman had come to talk about the medicinal plants Arghun had given him.

"Well, still and all, I think the yurt's a more comfortable place now that he's taken charge of it than it was when our wenches were still here," Skylitzes said.

"Have it any way you like." The bureaucrat was working at his knee again and rolling up his sheepskin trousers for a look at it. It was already turning purple. Even so, he managed a leer. "You must admit, they had an advantage he lacks."

"First time I've heard it called that," Skylitzes snorted.

Gorgidas laughed, too, and not very self-consciously. With no other choice available, he had been more successful with women than he would have imagined possible. Hoelun had helped that immensely; her desire to please was so obvious it would have been difficult—to say nothing of churlish—not to respond in kind. He found himself missing her now she was gone. But he missed acting according to his own nature more.

"Are you a crazy man, to come riding into our camp this way?" Targitaus demanded, glowering at the outlaw. "Put that fool white shield away—why should I care about your truce sign?" His hand twitched eagerly toward his sword.

Varatesh's rider matched the chieftain stare for disdainful stare. He was about forty, with a proud, hard face that might have been handsome but for his eyes, which were set too close together and, with their slitted lids, showed only cruelty. His horse and gear were of the finest, probably loot from the recent battle. He did not offer his name, but answered with a jeer, "Go ahead, kill me, and see what happens to your precious clansmen and their friends then."

The spirit seemed to go out of Targitaus. His shoulders sagged; Viridovix, watching, would have sworn his cheeks slumped, too. "Say on," he said, and his voice suddenly quavered like an old man's.

"Thought you'd see sense," the outlaw said. He was enjoying his mission; he rubbed his hands together as he got down to business. "Now that we've seen a new Royal Clan come to be, it's time the rest of the steppe recognized what's what—starting with you and yours."

As nothing else could have, that stung Targitaus back to life. His face purpled with fury. He roared, "You bastard, you cheese-faced crock of goat piss, you frog!" It was the deadliest Khamorth insult, and the outlaw's lips skinned back from his teeth in anger. Targitaus paid no attention, storming on, "You go tell Varatesh he can lick my arse, for I'll not lick his!" The clansmen around him shouted their approval.

The tumult gave Varatesh's man the time he needed to recover his temper; the renegade chief had not chosen foolishly. As the yells died down to mutters, the outlaw spread his hands in conciliation and spoke as mildly as he could. "Who spoke of licking arses? You know Varatesh is stronger than you. He could crush you as a boy squeezes a newt in his fist." Viridovix scowled at the heartless comparison, which let him see into the outlaw's soul, soft words or no. "But he does not. Why should he? One way or another, you will be his subjects. Why not willingly?"

"And put the Wolf under your bandits' black flag? Never."

"All right, then," the outlaw said, with the air of a man beaten down by hard bargaining. "He will even make you a present."

Targitaus spat in contempt. "What gift would I take from him?"

"He will give you back all the prisoners he holds and ask no ransom for them."

"You toy with me," Targitaus said. But he saw the terrible, haunted hope on the faces of his people, and when he repeated, "Toy," doubt was in his voice.

"By my sword, I do not," Varatesh's man said. The nomads fell silent and looked at each other, for among their warrior folk the worst renegade would think three times before he broke that oath.

Unable to check himself, Targitiaus burst out, "Is Batbaian among them?"

"Aye, and luckier than most. By my sword I swear it."

Dismay filled Viridovix as he heard Targitaus heeding the bandit. He cried, "Sure and your honor canna take the omadhaun's lies for truth, can you now? What's the word of a Varatesh worth, or an Avshar?" A few heads bobbed in agreement, but not many.

With his son in Varatesh's hands and a straw to grasp, the nomad chief answered, "V'rid'rish, I followed your path once, and see what it gained me." The Gaul's jaw fell at the reversal, and at the unfairness of it, but Targitaus went on with worse: "So where do you find the brass to urge a course on me now?"

"But—"

Targitaus overrode him with a slashing gesture. "Be grateful your neck is not the price asked for, for I would trade you for Batbaian and my clansmen." The Celt bowed his head; he had no reply to that.

Having decided to treat with his foes, Targitaus dickered with all his skill and wrung the most from his wretched bargaining position. He argued concession after concession from Varatesh's man, making the renegade agree that, as he took the risk of halting his clan, none of Varatesh's men should be allowed to approach the camp with the column of prisoners.

"You understand the captives will be unarmed and afoot," the outlaw warned.

"Aye, aye," the chieftain said impatiently. "Had we won, we'd have plundered you." Once his mind was made up, he moved ahead at full speed. He exchanged oaths with the outlaw, calling on the spirits to avenge any transgressions in the terms agreed upon.

Viridovix watched morosely from the edge of the crowd of Khamorth. Few of them would speak to him; for the first time in weeks he felt himself once more an alien among them. Seirem's smile said she had not forgotten him, but he wondered how long he would enjoy it now that her father had turned against him. In a way, the couple of sentences Rambehisht ostentatiously gave him cheered him more. "Maybe it's not me that's crazy after all," he said to himself, tugging at his mustache.

The agreement went forward regardless. "Ride hard," Targitaus told Varatesh's man. "Truce or no truce, we will not stay here long."

The renegade nodded. He kicked his shaggy dun pony into a trot, lifted his shield of truce on his lance so none of Targitaus' patrolling pickets would attack him on his return to his master. A stray breeze brought back his laughter as he rode out of camp.

"Ah, we can set them free after all," Avshar said. "How noble for us." He sipped kavass with a hollow reed that went through a slit in his visored helm. Somehow he still managed the proper nomad slurp.

Varatesh had been drinking hard for days. He wished he had never given the orders that went with the prisoner release. Far too late for regrets or turning back now, he thought. "Yes, let them go," he said. The thing was done, and he had to live with it. His hand shook as he lifted the skin to his mouth; he gulped without tasting what he drank.

"They're coming!" the rider called as he rode into camp. The Khamorth cheered; everyone was milling about among the tents, the men armed, the women in holiday best, wearing their finest bughtaqs and long flounced festival shirts of wool dyed in horizontal bands of bright color. The day cooperated with their celebration. It was cold but clear, the last storm having blown itself out the night before.

Tension and fear mingled with the joy. Wives, daughters, brothers of missing men, all hoped their loved ones were prisoners and knew some of those hopes would be broken.

"The bastards tied them together, it looks like," Targitaus' scout was reporting. "They're in lines of twenty or so, one bunch next to the other."

There was an angry rumble from the nomads, but Targitaus quelled it. "So long as they're coming," he said. "Ropes come off, aye, and other bonds as well." His clansmen growled eagerly at that, like the wolves that were their token.

From beside Viridovix, Seirem called, "How do they look?" Her hand held the Gaul's tight enough to hurt. He knew how much she wanted to ask for word of Batbaian, and admired her for holding back to keep the scout from being deluged in similar questions. He squeezed back; she accepted the pressure gratefully.

"I didn't ride close, I fear," the plainsman said "As soon as I saw them, I turned round and came here to bring word." Seirem bit her lip, but nodded in understanding.

"Let's go out to meet them!" someone shouted. The Khamorth started to surge forward, but Targitaus checked them, saying, "The agreement was to receive them here, and we shall. For now we are weak; we cannot afford to break any part of it. Yet . . ." he added, and the nomads nodded, anticipating the day.

Waiting stretched. Then a great cry went up as the first heads appeared over a low swell of ground a few hundred yards from the camp. Heedless of the khagan now, his people pelted toward them. He trotted with them, not trying to hold them back any longer. Still hand in hand, Viridovix and Seirem were somewhere near the center of the crowd. He could have been at the front, but slowed to match her shorter strides.

More and more freed captives stumbled into view, roped together as the scout had said. Viridovix whistled in surprise as he saw their numbers. "Dinna tell me the blackguard's after keeping his promise," he muttered. Seirem looked up at him curiously; he realized he had spoken Gaulish. "Never you mind, love," he said in the plains speech. "Seems your father had the right of it, and glad I am for it."

"So am I," she said, and then, with a little gasp, "Look, it's Batbaian, there at the front of a line!" They were still too far away for Viridovix to recognize him, but Seirem had no doubts. She called her brother's name and waved frantically. Batbaian's head jerked up. He spotted Viridovix, if not his sister, and wagged his head to show he had heard; with his hands tied behind him, he could not wave back.

As they hurried closer, Seirem suddenly flinched, as if struck. "His eye—" she faltered. Her own filled with pain; there was only an inflamed empty socket under Batbaian's left brow, the lid flapping uselessly over it.

"Och, lass, it happens, it happens," Viridovix said gently. "The gods be praised he has the other, and home again to heal, too." Seirem's hand was cold in his, but she managed a nod. She had seen enough of war's aftermath to know how grim it could be.

The returning captives only added more proof of that as they shambled forward. Many limped from half-healed wounds; more than one had only a single hand to be roped behind his back.

Seirem was recognizing more plainsmen now. "There's Ellak, heading up another column. The spirits be kind to him; he's lost an eye, too. And Bumin over there—you can always tell him because he's so bowlegged—oh, no, so has he. And so has Zabergan, and that tall man from the Spotted Cats, and Nerseh there—" She looked up at Viridovix, fear on her face.

It congealed in him, too, like a lump of ice under his heart. He recalled what sort of gifts Avshar gave.

The rush from the camp reached the prisoners, and welcoming shouts turned to cries of horror. Women screamed and wailed and fainted, and men with them. Others reeled away to spew up their guts on the muddy ground. One man drew his saber, cut his brother from a file of captives, then cut him down. Before anyone could stop him, he drew the blade across his own throat and fell, spouting blood.

For what Seirem had seen at the columns' heads was such mercy as Avshar and Varatesh had shown. The file leaders had been left with an eye apiece, to guide their lines over the steppe. Every man behind them was blinded totally; their ruined eyes dripped pus or thick yellow serum in place of the tears they would never shed again. It took time for the atrocity to sink in: a thousand men, with half a hundred eyes among them.

Lipoxais, his usually pink face dead pale, went from column to column, pressing soothing herbs on the most cruelly mutilated nomads and, perhaps as important, offering a kindly voice in their darkness. But the hopeless magnitude of the task exhausted the *enaree*'s medicines and overwhelmed his spirit. He went to his knees in the mud, weeping with the deep, racking spasms of a man not used to tears. "Fifty eyes! I foretold it and knew not what I saw!" he cried bitterly. "I foretold it!"

The short hairs on the back of Viridovix' neck prickled up as he remembered the *enaree*'s mantic trance. What else had Lipoxais seen? A mountain doorway and a pair of swords. The Gaul shivered. He spat to avert the omens, wanting no part of the rest of Lipoxais' prophecies.

Targitaus was staring about like a man who knew he was awake but found himself trapped in nightmare all the same. "My son!" he groaned. "My clan! My—" He groaned again, surprise and pain together, and clutched at his head—or tried to, for his left arm would not answer his will. He swayed like an old tree in a storm, then toppled, face down.

Seirem shrieked and rushed to his side, Viridovix close behind. Borane was already there, gently wiping mud from Targitaus' cheeks and beard with the sleeve of her festive blouse. And Lipoxais, torn from his private grief, came at the run.

"Cut me loose, curse it!" Batbaian shouted. Someone slashed through the rope that held him to his fellow captives. Deprived of their one sighted comrade, they froze in place, afraid to move. Batbaian, his hands still tied behind him, pushed through the crowd and clumsily knelt beside his father.

The right side of Targitaus' face was still screwed up in anguish, the left slack and loose as if made from half-melted wax. One pupil was tiny, while the other filled its iris. The chieftain's breath rattled in his throat. While his family, the rest of the Khamorth, and Viridovix watched and listened helplessly, it came slower and slower till it stopped. Lipoxais closed his staring eyes. With a moan, Borane clutched at Targitaus, trying to squeeze life into him once more and trying in vain.

XIII

ALTHOUGH MARCUS PASSED THE ORDEAL OF THE DRUG, THE Emperor did not summon him again. Thorisin lacked the front of a Vardanes Sphrantzes, to savor dealing with a man he had shamed. The tribune was as pleased to be left alone. Eventually he finished his report and sent it to the Avtokrator by messenger. A scrawled acknowledgement returned the same way.

Gaius Philippus kept Garsavra under control. Yavlak's Yezda tried raiding farms near the town not long after Scaurus reached the capital. The report the senior centurion sent him was a model of terseness: "They came. We smashed 'em."

The tribune was glad to hear of the victory, but less so than he would have imagined possible a few weeks before. The constant murmurous shuffle of parchment insulated the bureaucrats' wing of the Grand Courtroom from such struggles. And knowing the Romans had done well without him only made Marcus feel more useless.

He stayed at his desk or in his room most of the time, narrowing his world as much as he could. There were few people in Videssos he wanted to see. Once, rounding a corner, he found one of Alypia's servants knocking at his door. He ducked back out of sight. The servant left, grumbling. Scaurus shrank from facing the princess after revealing himself to her under Nepos' elixir, all his private griefs private no more.

Without Senpat and Nevrat Sviodo, he would have been altogether reclusive. And the first time they came calling, he did not intend to answer. "I know you're there, Scaurus," Senpat called through the door. "Let's see if I can pound longer than you can stand." Aided by his wife, he beat out such a tattoo that the tribune, his ears ringing, had to give in.

"Took you long enough," Nevrat said. "I thought we'd have to stand here and drip all night." The finery the two Vaspurakaners were wearing was rather the worse for rain.

"Sorry," Marcus mumbled untruthfully. "Come in; dry off."

"No, you come out with us," Senpat said. "I think I've found a tavern with wine dry enough to suit you. Or if not, drink enough and you won't care."

"I soak up enough wine by myself, thanks, dry or sweet," Marcus said, still trying to decline. Along with the patter of raindrops against his window, the grape eased him toward such rest as he got.

But Nevrat took his arm. "Drinking by yourself is not the same," she declared. "Now come along." Left with only the choice of breaking away by force, the tribune came.

The tavern was not far from the palace compound. Scaurus gulped down a cup of wine, grimaced, and glowered at Senpat Sviodo. "Only a Vaspurakaner would call this syrup dry," he accused. The "princes" favored even sweeter, thicker vintages than the Videssians drank. "How is it different from any other wine hereabouts?"

"As far as I can tell, it isn't," Senpat said breezily. While Scaurus stared, he went on, "But the lure of it pried you out of your nest, not so?"

"I think your wife laying hold of me had more to do with it."

"You dare imply she has charms I lack?" Senpat mimed being cut to the quick.

"Oh, hush," Nevrat told him. She turned to Marcus. "What's the use of having friends, if they don't help in time of trouble?"

"I thank you," the tribune said. He reached out to touch her hand, let go of it reluctantly—any small kindness could move him these days. Her smile was warm.

"Another thing friends are good for is noticing when friends' mugs are empty," Senpat said. He waved to the tapman.

Scaurus found Nevrat was right. When he holed up in his cubicle with a bottle, all he got was stuporous and sad. With Senpat and Nevrat, though, wine let him receive the sympathy he would have rejected sober. He even tried to join in when one of the men at the bar started a round of drinking songs, and laughed at the face Senpat made to warn him his ear and voice were no truer than usual.

"We must do this again," he heard himself saying while he stood, a little unsteadily, outside his doorway.

"So long as you promise not to sing," Senpat said.

"Harumph." With drunken expansiveness, Marcus embraced both Vaspurakaners. "You are good friends indeed."

"Then as good friends should, we will let you rest," Nevrat said. The tribune sadly watched them go. They, too, were swaying as they made their way down the corridor toward the stairs. Senpat's arm slid round his wife's waist. Marcus bit his lip and hurried into his room.

That small sting at the end did not badly mar the evening. Scaurus' sleep was deep and restful, not the sodden oblivion that was the most he dared hope for since Helvis left him. The headache he woke with seemed a small price to pay. When he went up to the office where he worked, he nodded to the bureaucrats he was overseeing, the first friendly gesture he had given them.

He found the pen-pushers easier to supervise than they had been the year before. None had Pikridios Goudeles' talent for number-shuffling, and they all knew Marcus had managed a draw with their wily chief. They did not have the nerve to try sneaking much past him.

Going through page after page, scroll after scroll of tax accounts without finding a silver bit out of place was encouraging in a way, but also dull. The tribune worked away with mechanical competence; he was not after excitement.

Seeing Scaurus in a mood rather less dour than he had shown before, one of the bureaucrats came up to his desk.

"What is it, Iatzoulinos?" the tribune asked, looking up from his counting board. Even without his eyes to guide them, his fingers flicked through an addition with blurring speed; long practice with the beads had made him adept as any clerk.

"This has the possibility of providing you with some amusement, sir," Iatzoulinos said, holding out a scroll. The pen-pusher was a lean, sallow man of indeterminate age. He spoke the jargon of the chancery even on matters that had nothing to do with finance; he probably used it when he made love, Marcus thought scornfully.

He wondered what so bloodless a man would find funny. "Show me."

"With pleasure, sir." Iatzoulinos unrolled the strip of parchment. "You will note first that all required seals have been affixed; to all initial appearances, it is a proper document. Yet note the inexpert hand in which it is written and the childishly simple syntax. Finally, it purports to be a demand on the capital for funds from a provincial town—" Iatzoulinos actually laughed out loud; he saw the joke there as too obvious to need spelling out.

Scaurus studied the document. Suddenly he, too, began to laugh. Iatzoulinos looked gratified, then grew nervous as the tribune did not stop. At last the pen-pusher said, "I pray your pardon, sir, but you appear to have discovered more risibility here than I had anticipated. Do you care to impart to me the source of your mirth?"

Marcus still could not speak. Instead, he pointed to the signature at the bottom of the parchment.

Iatzoulinos' eyes followed his finger. The color slowly faded from his narrow cheeks. "That is your name there," he said in a tiny voice. He glanced fearfully at Scaurus' sword—he was not used to overtly deadly weapons in the chancery, which dealt with the subtler snares of pen and ink.

"So it is." The tribune finally had control of himself. He continued, "If you check the file, you'll also find an imperial rescript endorsing my request here. The citizens of Garsavra did the Empire a great service in contributing their own funds to obtain the Namdalener prisoners from Yavlak. Simple justice required repayment."

"Of course, of course. I shall bend every effort toward the facilitation of the reimbursement process." In his dismay, Iatzoulinos was practically babbling. "Illustrious sir, you will, I hope, grasp that I intended no offense in any remarks that may perhaps have appeared at first hearing somewhat slighting."

"Don't worry about it." Scaurus got up and patted the unfortunate bureaucrat on the shoulder. There was no way to explain he actually felt grateful to Iatzoulinos; not even with Senpat and Nevrat had he laughed so hard.

"I shall draft the memorandum authorizing the dispatch of funds posthaste," Iatzoulinos said, glad of an excuse to edge away from the Roman.

"Yes, do," Marcus called after him. "Gaius Philippus, who heads the Garsavra garrison these days, lacks my forbearance." Iatzoulinos' sidling withdrawal turned into a trot.

Shaking his head, the tribune sat again. Even the relief his laughter brought was mixed with misery. He would rather have been at Garsavra himself, with his countrymen, than lonely and under a cloud at the capital. And thinking of how he had acquired the men of the Duchy only reminded him how he lost them afterward.

A few days later, the chamber was rocking with merriment when he came in the door. He caught snatches of the bad jokes the pen-pushers were throwing back and forth: ". . . knows which side his bread is buttered on, all right." "Buttered-Bun would be a better name for him." "No, you fool, for her—"

Silence fell as the bureaucrats saw him. After Iatzoulinos' disaster, they did not include him in their glee. He walked past clerks who avoided his eyes, listened to their conversation abruptly turn to business.

Stung, he sat down, opened a ledger, and began adding a long column of figures. This once, he wished he needed conscious thought to work the abacus. It would have taken his mind away from the hurt he felt.

"Play some more tunes, Vaspurakaner!" someone called through shouted applause. A score of throats took up the cry, until the tavern rang with it.

Senpat Sviodo let his pandoura rest in his lap for a moment, flexed his hands to loosen them. He sent a comic look of dismay toward the corner table where Marcus and Nevrat were sitting.

Nevrat called something to him in their own language. He

nodded ruefully and rolled his eyes. "I'm sorry," she said to Scaurus, dropping back into Videssian. "I told him he could have been here drinking with us if he'd left the lute at home."

"He enjoys playing," the tribune said.

Nevrat raised an eyebrow. 'Oh, indeed, and I enjoy sugarplums, but I'd burst if I tried eating a bushel basket full."

"All right." Marcus yielded the point. Senpat had only intended playing a song or two, more for his own amusement than anyone else's. But he found a wildly enthusiastic audience, not least among them the taverner, who had all but dragged him to his current seat atop the bar. His Vaspurakaner cap lay beside him, upside down. He had been singing a couple of hours now, with the crowd around him too thick and too keen to let him go.

They cheered all over again at the first chords of a familiar tune and roared out the chorus: "The wine gets drunk, but you get drunker!"

"He should spin that one out as long as he can," Marcus said. "Maybe they'll all pass out and give him a chance to get away."

The taverner might have been thinking along with him. Two barmaids labored to keep the mugs of the throng round Senpat filled; two more, carrying large jugs of wine on their hips, went from table to table.

Nevrat held out her cup for a refill. Scaurus declined; his was still half full. Nevrat noticed. "You're stinting tonight."

"You should understand that, you and your sugarplums."

She smiled. "Fair enough." Then she grew serious, studying him like a theologian pondering a difficult text. She held her voice neutral as she remarked, "You have been drinking deep lately, haven't you?"

"Too deep, maybe."

Her face cleared. "I thought as much myself, but I doubted it was my place to say so. Although," she added quickly, anxious that he take no offense, "no one could blame you, considering—"

"Aye, considering," he finished for her. "Still and all, you can only look at the world from the inside of a bottle so long. After that, you just see the bottle."

Remembering why he drank, he looked downcast enough

for Nevrat's dark brows to come together in concern. She reached out to touch his hand. "Is it still so bad?"

"I'm sorry." He needed a deliberate effort to come back to himself. "I didn't think it showed so much."

"Oh, someone who passed you in the street might not notice," she said, "but we've known each other some years now, you and I."

"So we have." Thinking about it, he realized he knew Nevrat and Senpat about as well as he did any non-Romans, knew Nevrat better than any woman in this world save Helvis—thinking of her made him grimace again, though he did not know it—and Alypia Gavra. And no imperial ceremonial hedged in Nevrat.

Before he quite realized it had, his hand tightened on hers. It was strange to feel a woman's hand callused from the sword hilt, like his own; reins and the bow had also hardened Nevrat's palm and fingers. She looked at him in surprise, but did not draw away.

Just then, Senpat finished his song. He scrambled down from the bar in spite of fresh shouts for more, saying, "No, no! Enough, my friends, enough!" The sound of his voice, unaccompanied by pandoura, made Marcus jerk back as if Nevrat's hand had burst into flame.

"Well, well, how do we fare here?" Senpat said after he finally fought his way through the crush to the corner table. "What have you two been plotting while they held me hostage? Up to no good, I don't doubt."

The tribune was glad he still had wine in his cup. He drained it, which let him avoid answering.

After a tiny pause, Nevrat said, "No reason for you to doubt it." She used the same noncommittal tone she had with Scaurus a few minutes before.

He winced. It must have been his conscience nipping at him, for Senpat noticed nothing amiss. He hefted his cap, which jingled with the copper and silver his audience had tossed in. "You see?" he said. "I should have been a minstrel after all."

Nevrat's snort told what she thought of that. "Put the money in your belt-pouch," she said. "You'll need your hat—the rain's started again."

"When does it ever stop, these days?" Senpat upended the

cap; a couple of coins rolled off the table onto the floor. "Let be," he said when Nevrat started to pick them up. "Something to make the sweepers happy." He stowed his pandoura in a soft leather sack, then glanced at Marcus. "It'll be dryer than you are, without a hat."

"Dryer than any of us." The reply sounded lame in the tribune's ears, but it served well enough. Sometimes a laconic way had its advantages.

"Sometimes I think you take better care of your toy than you do of me," Nevrat said, bantering much as she usually did.

"Why not?" Senpat came back. "You can take care of yourself."

"I'm glad you think so."

Nevrat's answer was tart enough that Marcus half turned toward her, wondering if she might have meant it for him as well. Senpat only chuckled, saying, "Truly a viper's tongue tonight." He thrashed about, as if bitten by a snake. Nevrat mimed throwing a plate at him, but she was laughing, too. Marcus' lips twitched; Senpat was incorrigible.

He slung his pandoura over his shoulder, jammed his Vaspurakaner cap down as far as it would go on his head. He made for the door, Nevrat close behind him. Scaurus followed more slowly. He thought for a moment of staying until the rain let up, but that might take days. Besides, as he had said to Nevrat, after a while drinking grew to be for its own sake alone. He knew himself too well to pretend to be blind to that.

A Videssian tried to pull Nevrat into his arms. She swung away, plucked the wine cup from his hand, and, smiling sweetly, poured it over his head. "Never mind," she said to Senpat, who had spun round, his hand darting to his knife. "I *can* take care of myself."

"So I see." He stayed wary, wondering if anyone would take it further. Marcus shouldered through the crowd to help at need.

The imperial was coughing and swearing, but the fellow next to him growled, "Stifle it, you fool. You had that coming, for fooling about with someone else's woman." The drenched man looked round for support and found none. With his music, Senpat was everyone's hero tonight, even if he and his wife were outlanders.

Marcus gasped at the cold rain and briefly regretted deciding to leave. He turned up the collar of his coat to give the back of his head what protection he could, and looked down at the puddles growing between the cobblestones. That did not do much to keep the raindrops off his face.

Senpat and Nevrat splashed along beside him. Their heads were down, too. Scaurus' eyes kept returning to Nevrat. He swore at himself under his breath and reflected that the man in the tavern who had upbraided the other Videssian might as well have been talking to him instead.

On the other hand, Nevrat had not upended a cup of wine on him, either. He dimly realized the state he was in, when so small a thing could be a reason for optimism.

The rain turned to sleet. A dripping courier brought a message to the tribune at his office in the Grand Courtroom. "Fancier digs than you had at Garsavra," he said, handing Scaurus the parchment.

"Hmm? Oh, yes." Marcus had not noticed it was the same man who had delivered Thorisin's dispatch ordering him to the capital.

He broke the seal, felt mixed loneliness and pleasure at seeing angular Latin letters rather than the snaky Videssian script. As always, Gaius Philippus' note was to the point; he found writing too hard to waste words. The scrawled message said, "The locals are paid off, them as didn't die of shock. Now where's *our* back wages?"

The tribune scribbled a reminder to himself. When he looked up, the courier was still there. "Yes?"

The fellow shifted his feet; water squelched. "Last time I saw you, you fed me hot wine," he said pointedly.

"I'm sorry." Marcus reddened. He took care of the rider, apologizing again for his discourtesy. It was not even that he resented the man for starting him on his disastrous journey; he had simply been thoughtless. In a way, that was worse.

Mollified at last, the courier gave him a salute before going off to deliver the rest of his dispatches. Scaurus, his conscience somewhat assuaged, decided not to let another chance to show good manners pass by.

"I've just had word you sent the Garsavrans the money the

fisc owed them," he said to Iatzoulinos. "I want to thank you for attending to it promptly."

"Once you pointed out the urgency, I did my best to implement your request," the bureaucrat said. What else was I going to do, with you looking over my shoulder? his eyes added silently, faint contempt in them. Marcus pursed his lips, annoyed that civility could be taken as a sign of weakness.

His voice hardened. "I trust you will also be punctual in seeing that the pay for the garrison at Garsavra—the garrison of my countrymen—does not fall into arrears."

"Accounts for military expenditures are maintained in an entirely different ledger," Iatzoulinos warned. "The policies of the present government have occasioned so many transfers of funds that I have difficulty being certain if this request can be expedited so readily as the last."

The tribune's tours in the chancery, especially this latest one, had made him understand how, to the pen-pushers who spent all their time here, ledgers became more real than the men whose deeds and needs they recorded. Gaius Philippus would have another opinion about that, he thought.

He said, "Garsavra is important in holding the Yezda at bay. The Emperor would not care to hear of disaffection among the troops there. And, as I told you, I am one of them, and I know them. Their current commander is not a man to make an enemy of."

" I will exert every effort," Iatzoulinos said sulkily.

"A fine idea. If you work as hard to pay the Romans as you did for the people of Garsavra, I'm sure their wages will reach them very soon."

Marcus gave the bureaucrat a friendly nod and returned to his desk. Iatzoulinos actually permitted a smile to touch his thin face for a moment, which let the tribune hope the warning had sunk home without stinging too much.

In spite of his gloom, he suddenly smiled himself. Iatzoulinos might think him a nuisance, but the pen-pusher would run shrieking from a meeting with Gaius Philippus.

"Three pieces of silver?" The leatherworker's stare was scornful. "This is a fine belt, outlander. See the tooling? See the fine tanning? See how strong it is?" He tugged at it.

"It doesn't come apart in your hands," Scaurus observed

dryly. "If it did, someone would have lynched you long since, and you would not be standing here trying to cheat me. Still, perhaps if I offered you four, you might be so ashamed at your ill-gotten gains that you would keep quiet and leave off letting the whole plaza of Palamas know what a thief you are."

"I, a thief? Here you try to rob me without even drawing sword. Why, after the price I had to pay for the cowhide, after the hard labor I lavished on it, I would be stealing from my own children to let it go for seven."

They eventually settled on six silver coins, a quarter of a goldpiece. Marcus was vaguely displeased; had his heart been in the haggle, likely he could have got the belt for five. He shrugged. He could not really make himself care. These days, there was not much he did care about.

At least he had the belt. The one he was wearing was old and frayed. He unbuckled it, slid off his sword and dagger, and leaned them against his leg. Holding up his trousers with one hand, he began threading the new belt through the loops.

He was fumbling for the one behind his back when a cheery voice said, "Aye, that's the hard one; I remember from the days when I wore breeches."

"Nepos!" The tribune started, then had to make a quick grab to keep from losing his trousers—and his dignity. He whirled to face the priest, and his weapons fell clattering to the flagstones. His face scarlet, he stooped to retrieve them, and almost lost his pants again.

"Here, let me help you." Nepos lifted Scaurus' knife and sword out of the slush on the pavement. He waited until the tribune had the belt on, then handed them back to him.

"Thank you," Marcus said stiffly. He did not want to have anything to do with Nepos, not after he had drugged him and then listened with Thorisin and Alypia as he bared his soul.

If Nepos sensed that, he did not show it. "Good to see you," he said. "You've been as hard to catch as a cockroach lately. Do you just scuttle along the edges of the walls, or have you actually figured out a way to disappear into the wainscoting?"

"I haven't had much use for people," Marcus said lamely.

"Well, considering what you've been through, one could hardly blame you." Seeing the Roman's face freeze, Nepos realized the blunder he had made. "Oh, my dear fellow, your pardon, I pray you."

"You will excuse me, I hope." Voice as expressionless as his features, Scaurus turned to go.

"Wait! In Phos' name, I beg you."

Reluctantly, Marcus stopped. Nepos was not the sort of priest who kept his god's name on his lips every moment of the day. When he called on Phos, he had important reason, or so he thought.

"What do you want with me?" The tribune could not contain his bitterness. "Haven't you seen enough to glut you already?"

"My friend—if I may still call you such . . ." Nepos waited for some sign from Scaurus, but the tribune might have been carved from stone. Sighing, the priest went on, "Let me tell you how deeply I regret how that entire affair turned out . . . as does the Emperor himself, I might add."

"Why? It didn't hurt *him* any."

Nepos frowned at the harsh way Marcus spoke of Thorisin, but continued earnestly, "But it did, in reducing you. His Majesty had the right to ensure you were involved in no sedition against him, but when it came to probing in such, uh, intimate detail into your private affairs . . ." Nepos hesitated again, casting about for some way to go on without doing more damage. Finding none, he finished, "He should have stopped his questions sooner."

"He didn't," Marcus said flatly.

"No, and as I told you, he is sorry for it. But he is also stubborn—think back to the case of Taron Leimmokheir if you doubt that. And so he is slow in admitting any error, even to himself. Nevertheless, please note he has you in the same important post you held last year."

"It's not as important as the command at Garsavra," the tribune said, still unwilling to believe.

"No, but fill it well, raise no further suspicions, and I daresay you will have your old rank back again come summer, when campaigning season is here again."

"Easier for you to say than for Thorisin to do."

Nepos sighed again. "You are a stubborn man, Scaurus—in gloom as in other things, I see. I leave you with a last bit of advice, then: judge by the event, not before it."

Marcus blinked. Nepos' admonition might have come from the lips of a Stoic philosopher. The priest bent his plump frame into a half-bow and departed. The wan winter sun gleamed off his naked pate.

Scaurus frowned, watching him go. Nepos might think him somber, but the priest was lighthearted himself, which probably made him double any good things Thorisin had said and halve the bad. If the Emperor really wanted him back in meaningful service, he could have restored him by now. No, the tribune thought, he was still out of favor with Thorisin—and that, as Nepos had recommended, was judging by the event.

He shook his head. The motion made him catch sight of another familiar face. Like Scaurus, Provhos Mourtzouphlos was taller than most imperials and so stood out from the crowd that filled the plaza of Palamas.

The handsome aristocrat was also frowning. He was—Marcus stiffened, his long-dormant soldier's alertness suddenly waking—he was watching Nepos. The priest's robe and shaven pate were easy to spot as he walked through the square.

Then Mourtzouphlos' gaze swung back to the tribune. Marcus caught his eye, nodded deliberately. Mourtzouphlos grimaced, turned, and began haggling with a man who carried a brazier and a wicker basket full of shrimp.

Interesting, Scaurus thought, most interesting indeed. He started toward the palace complex. After half a minute or so, he turned back, as if he had forgotten something. Mourtzouphlos might be holding a roasted shrimp by the tail, but he was also definitely keeping an eye on the tribune. In fact, he had come a few paces after him. Seeing that Scaurus realized what he was about, he stopped in confusion and chagrin.

At first the Roman was furious, certain Thorisin Gavras had set Mourtzouphlos on him. So much for Nepos' optimism, he thought. But then he decided the Emperor had no need to put such an inept spy on his trail. If he wanted someone to watch Scaurus secretly, the tribune would never know it.

What, then? The only thing he could think of was that Mourtzouphlos was suspicious of his influence with Thorisin, and that seeing him talking to Nepos—who certainly did have the Emperor's ear—had alarmed the aristocrat. But Mourtzouphlos was in Thorisin's good graces himself. If he thought Scaurus was a rival, perhaps it was so.

Gardeners raked the last withered autumn leaves from the broad lawns that surrounded the buildings of the palace quarter. They nodded respectfully as the tribune walked past. He returned their salutes automatically. They meant nothing; the gardeners were too low in the hierachy to risk offending even someone out of favor. Mourtzouphlos' jealousy, though, was the first good news Marcus had had in some weeks.

He spun on his heel. A bowshot behind him, Provhos Mourtzouphlos abruptly found a bare-branched tree fascinating. He did not acknowledge or seem to notice the cheerful wave Scaurus sent him.

A grin felt strange on the tribune's face, but good.

Marcus' pleased mood lasted through the afternoon. He lured an answering smile out of Iatzoulinos, no small accomplishment. The bureaucrat even unbent far enough to tell him a joke. He was astonished; he had not realized Iatzoulinos knew any. He did not tell it well, but the effort deserved notice.

Dinner also seemed uncommonly enjoyable. The roast lamb really was lamb, not gamy mutton; the peas and pearl onions were cooked just right; enough snow had fallen for the taverner to offer ice and sweet syrup for dessert. And so, when Scaurus went back to his chamber a little past sunset, he felt it was the best day he'd had since coming to Videssos the city.

Darkness came quickly in late fall; the tribune was not ready to sleep. He lit several lamps, rummaged about till he found Gorgidas' history, and began to read. He wondered how the Greek and Viridovix were faring on the steppe. With a guilty start, he knew he had hardly thought about them since —his mind searched for a painless way to say it—since things went wrong.

He was trying to unravel an elaborate passage when the knock on the door came. For a moment, he did not notice it. Then it was only an unwelcome distraction, and he did his best to ignore it. He found Greek hard enough giving it his full attention.

"Must you always pretend you're not in? I can see the light under the door."

He sprang to his feet, rolled the book up as fast as he could. "Sorry, Nevrat, I didn't expect you and Senpat tonight." He hurried to the door and pulled it open. "Come in."

"I thank you." Nevrat stepped past him. "Always good to visit you; the pen-pushers heat their digs well." She undid the heavy wool scarf she was wearing in place of the bright silk one she preferred, let her fleecy coat fall open.

Marcus hardly noticed her making herself comfortable; he was still eyeing the empty corridor outside his room. "Where's Senpat?" he blurted.

"Singing—and drinking, I imagine—at the wine shop we've all been visiting. I chose not to go along."

"Ah," Scaurus said, more a polite noise than anything else. He hesitated, then asked, "Does he know you're here?"

"No."

The word seemed to hang in the air between them. Marcus started to shut the door, paused again. "Would you rather I left it open?"

"It's all right; close it." Nevrat sounded amused. She looked round the tribune's rather bare quarters. Her eye fell on the book he had so hastily set down. She opened it, frowned at the alien script—the Greek alphabet looked nothing like Videssian or her native Vaspurakaner. Helvis had reacted the same way, Marcus recalled; he bit his lip at the unbidden memory.

To cover the stab of hurt, he waved Nevrat to the room's only chair. "Wine?" he asked. At her nod, he pulled a bottle and cup from the top drawer of the pine chest next to his bed. He poured for her, then sat on the bed, leaning back against the wall.

She raised any eyebrow. "Aren't you having any? You said you'd gone moderate, not teetotal."

"Perish the thought!" he exclaimed. "But, you see, I have just the one cup."

Her laughter filled the little room. She drank, then sat forward to pass him the cup. "We must share, then."

His fingers brushed hers as he took it. "Thank you. I hadn't planned to do much entertaining here."

"So I see," she said. "Certainly it's not the lair a practiced seducer would have."

"As is only fitting, because I'm not." He filled the cup again, offered it to her.

She took it but did not drink at once, instead holding it and contemplating it with an expression so ironic that Scaurus found himself flushing. "I didn't mean it like that," he protested.

"I know you didn't." Nevrat raised the cup to her lips to prove it. She passed it to him, went on, "Marcus, I have cared for you as long as we've known each other."

"And I for you, very much," he nodded. "Aside from everything else, without you these past weeks would have been . . . well, even worse than they are. I owe you so much for that."

She waved that aside. "Don't speak foolishly. Senpat and I are happy to do whatever we can for you."

He frowned; she had not mentioned her husband since she sat down. But as they talked on, Senpat's name did not come up again, and the tribune found his hopes rising. He remembered the joke he had heard from Iatzoulinos. Judging by Nevrat's laughter, he told it better than the seal-stamper had.

"Oh, a fine story," she said. "'What in Skotos' name was that?'" Repeating the punch line set her chuckling again. Her black eyes glowed; her grin was wide and happy. She was, Scaurus thought, one of those uncommon women whose features grew more beautiful with animation.

A lamp went out. The tribune got up. He took out a little bottle of oil, filled the lamp, and relit the wick with one of the others. He had to pass close by Nevrat to get back to his seat on the bed. As he did, he reached out to stroke her dark, curly hair. It was coarser under his fingers than he had imagined.

She rose, too, and turned to face him. He stepped forward to embrace her.

"Marcus," she said.

Had she spoken his name another way, he would have gone on to take her in his arms. As it was, she might have held up Medusa's head, to turn him to stone in his tracks. He searched her face, found regret and compassion there, but not eagerness to match his own.

"It's no good, is it?" he asked dully, already sure of the answer.

"No," she said. "I'm sorry, but it's not." She started to put a hand on his shoulder, then arrested the gesture. That was worse than her words.

"I should have known." He had to look away from her to continue. "But you were always so caring, so sympathetic, that I hoped—I thought—I let myself think . . ."

"Something more might be there," she finished for him.

He nodded, still avoiding her eyes.

"I saw that," she said. "I did not know what to do, but finally I decided we had to speak of it. Truly I do not want any man but Senpat."

"The two of you are very lucky," Marcus said. "I've thought so many times." Holding his voice steady was rather like fighting after taking a wound.

"I know we are," she said quietly. "And so I came tonight to say what I had to say—and instead we ended up chatting like the friends we've always been. That silly story of yours about the rich man who wanted to be an actor—" Thinking of it, she smiled again, but only for a moment. "I suppose I just thought I could let things go on as they had. But then—"

"Then I had to make a mess of it," he said bitterly.

"No!" For the first time, Nevrat sounded angry. "I don't blame you for it. How could I? After what happened to you, of course you hope to find again the happiness you once knew. But—I am as I am, and I cannot be the one to give it to you. I'm sorry, Marcus, and sorrier that now I've hurt you, too, when that is the last thing I ever wanted."

"It doesn't matter," Scaurus said. "I brought it on myself."

"It matters very much," Nevrat insisted. "Can we go on now as friends?" She must have sensed his thoughts, for she said quickly, "Think now, before you say no. How do we—either of us—explain to Senpat what went wrong?"

The tribune found himself promising to keep the friendship going. To his surprise, he also found himself meaning it. Not being an outgoing sort, he had too few friendships to throw any casually away. And whatever he wished was there with Nevrat, they did genuinely like and care for each other.

"Good," she said crisply. "Then we need not break our next meeting-day—three days from now, wasn't it?"

"Yes."

"I'll see you then. Truly, I will be glad to. Always believe that." Nevrat smiled—a little more cautiously than she would have before, Marcus judged, but not much—and stepped out into the hallway, closing the door behind her.

Her footsteps faded. Scaurus put the wine away. It was probably for the best, he told himself. Senpat was a good man as well as a close friend. He had no business trying to put cuckold's horns on him. Down deep, he knew that perfectly well.

He kicked the side of the cheap pine chest as hard as he could. It split. Pain shot up from his toe. He heard the jug of wine break. Swearing at fate, his damaged foot, and the wine, he used a rag to mop up the mess. By luck, the jar was almost empty, so only one tunic was ruined.

He gave a sour laugh as he blew out the lamps and crawled into bed. He should have known better than to think he was having a good day. Since Helvis left, there were no good days for him.

He was still limping as he climbed the stairs to his office two days later. His right big toe was twice its proper size and had turned purple and yellow. The day before, one of the pen-pushers had asked what happened.

"I gave the wardrobe in my room a kick." He'd shrugged, leaving the bureaucrat to assume it was an accident. Sometimes literal truth made the best lie.

Seeing him abstracted, a middling-important scribe tried to sneak some fancy bookkeeping past him. He spotted it, picked up the offending ledger, and dropped it with a crash on the luckless seal-stamper's desk.

"You piker," he said contemptuously to the appalled bureaucrat. "Last winter, Pikridios Goudeles used that same trick to get himself an emerald ring with a stone big enough to choke on, and here you are, trying to steal a miserable two and a half goldpieces. You ought to be ashamed."

"What—what will you do with me, illustrious sir?" the pen pusher quavered.

"For two and a half pieces of gold? If you need it so badly, keep it. But the next time I find even a copper out of place in your books, you'll see how you like the prison under the government offices on Middle Street. That goes for all of you, too," Marcus added for the benefit of the rest of the bureaucrats, who had been listening and watching intently without seeming to.

"Thank you, oh, thank you, merciful and gracious sir," the would-be embezzler said over and over. Marcus nodded curtly and started back to his own desk.

He remembered something as he passed Iatzoulinos. "Have you arranged to send the Romans at Garsavra their pay?" he asked.

"I would, ah, have to check my records to be certain of that," Iatzoulinos answered warily. No, Scaurus translated without effort.

He sighed. "Iatzoulinos, I've been patient with you. If you make Gaius Philippus angry, I don't think he will be. I know this man; you don't. Take it as a warning from one who means you well."

"I shall, of course, attend to it at once," Iatzoulinos said.

"See that you do." The tribune folded his arms and waited. When Iatzoulinos realized he was not going to leave, the pen-pusher set aside the project he had been working on and picked up the ledger that dealt with military expenditures in the westlands. He inked a pen and, with poor grace, began drafting a payment authorization. Satisfied for the moment, Marcus moved on.

He jumped as a hailstone rattled off the window. His sore foot made him regret it. Winter would be here in earnest soon, he thought; the storm that blew in yesterday had already covered the lawns of the palace complex with a snowy blanket. The tribune hoped the weather would stay bad awhile. Despite his promises to Nevrat, he was not ready to face her and Senpat together quite so soon as tomorrow. Maybe the snow would force them to put things off.

His office and his room were both pleasantly warm. He was glad the bureaucrats heated their wing of the Grand Courtrooms so lavishly. Then he thought of his friends on the steppe and was even gladder.

XIV

THE WIND HOWLED AND MOANED LIKE A DEEP-VOICED HOUND gone mad, driving snow into Batbaian's face and frosting Viridovix' ruddy mustaches. A thick, short beard hid his cheeks and chin; he had not shaved in weeks and did not know when he would have the chance again. He swore when a gust sneaked under his heavy fur greatcoat and chilled his back. The coat did not fit him very well. It had been made for one of Varatesh's riders, but the fellow had no use for it now.

The Gaul gave a gusty sigh. His breath puffed out white. He sighed again, remembering the felt tent and how breathing smoke had bemused him. His face hardened. Targitaus' tent was smoke now, and the tents of all his clan, and the clansmen with them.

Timing pitilessly exact, Varatesh had given the Wolves three days to thrash with caring for nearly a thousand blinded men who could do nothing to help themselves—and with the torment their coming brought. Then he struck, and shattered the clan.

Viridovix and Batbaian were herding an outlying flock of sheep when the blow fell, or they would have perished with the rest. As it was, when evening came they rode into camp and found massacre waiting for them. In his way, Varatesh was a gifted leader, to instill order into his cutthroats: they had descended on their foes, killed, raped, looted, and gone, probably all in two hours' time.

Gaul and nomad rode together through silence so thick it echoed; even the yapping little dogs that had run scavenging from tent to tent were slain. For Viridovix, shock piled on shock left an eerie calm; Batbaian's face was twisted in agony too deep for words. Every so often one of them would nod to the other when he came across the body of someone he cared for. There was dour Rambehisht, with three dead outlaws around him and an arrow in his back. If he had planned vengeance on Viridovix, he would never have it now. And Lipoxais, yellow *enaree*'s robe soaked with blood. And Azarmi the serving wench, her skirt on the ground beside her. She still wore a blood-soaked blouse; the outlaws had not bothered tearing it off before their sport, only stabbed through it when they were done.

Filled with the same dreadful surmise, Batbaian and Viridovix leaped from their horses and ran for what had been Targitaus' tent. It leaned drunkenly to one side, half its framework broken. And inside their worst fears were realized. Borane's dead fist clutched a dagger. The blade was stained—she had fought before she died. But she was fat and getting old; Varatesh's men had merely slaughtered her. By all the signs, Seirem had not been so lucky.

Viridovix cursed himself for memory; the anguish flared in him, red and agonizing as when he had first seen Seirem's corpse. He wished for the thousandth time that he had never known his few short weeks of love, or that he had died with the one who gave it to him.

"And what's a wish worth?" he said to himself. "Damn all anyway." A bitter tear ran down his cheek.

Batbaian turned at the sound of his voice. "That does no good," he said stonily. "It will only freeze to your skin." The dead khagan's son was no more the near-boy he had been till summer; he seemed to have aged ten years in as many weeks. His face was thinner, with lines of suffering carved into his forehead and at the corners of his mouth.

He had been the one who suggested firing the camp. "It will warn off any other herders who might still be alive," he had said, "and might lure Varatesh's riders back." A cold, hungry light kindled in his eye then, and he patted his bow-case. He and Viridovix found an ambush point; it would not do to give their lives away without as rich a revenge as they could take.

But the renegades had not returned, no doubt thinking the smoke came from an overturned lamp or smoldering torch that had set the encampment ablaze. When it was clear they would not, Batbaian took the patch from his ruined eye and threw it to the ground. "When I kill them, let them know what I am," he said.

His score stood at four now, one ahead of the Gaul's.

They lived as outlaws, one of the many reversals since the war against Varatesh went so disastrously awry. Now the bandit chief and his brigands lorded it over the steppe and hunted its one-time leaders like vermin. But as Varatesh himself had shown, running them to earth was no easy task. A goat here, a sentry there, two horses stolen somewhere else—the blowing winter snow covered tracks. It was the hardest life Viridovix had ever known, but it could be lived.

Hands clumsy inside thick gloves, they fought their tent into place as evening fell. Despite the windbreak of snow they piled in front of it, the raw north wind still found its way through the felt. They huddled in blankets next to the bonfire, roasting chunks of mutton over it. No problem keeping meat fresh in winter, Viridovix thought—the trick was thawing it again.

He rubbed grease from his chin and licked his fingers clean. Let the Romans try to live in this cold with their journeybread and porridges, he thought. Red meat was all that kept up a man's strength here.

Instead of wiping it away, Batbaian smeared the mutton fat over his cheeks, nose, and forehead. "Helps against frostbite," he said. He spoke seldom, these days, and always to the point.

"Next time, lad," Viridovix nodded. He drew his sword, examined it for rust. In the cold and constant wet it spread all too easily. He scoured away a tiny fleck of red, rust or dried blood. "Wouldna hurt to rub the blade wi' fat, either."

A wolf howled in the distance, a bay chill as the night. One of the horses snorted nervously.

"North again come morning?" Viridovix said.

"Oh yes." Batbaian's lips opened in a humorless smile. "Where better than down their throats? Richer pickings, too—more flocks. More men." His one eye gleamed in the sputtering firelight. The other socket was a ghastly shadow.

The Gaul nodded again, but through a smothering sense of futility. Not even killing could bring back what he had lost. "Is it any use at all, at all?" he cried. "We skulk about pretending it's some good we're about, slaying the spalpeens by ones and twos, but I swear by gods it's nobbut a sop to our prides. It no more hurts 'em than the grain a pair o' wee mice steal'll make the farmers starve."

"So what will you do? Fold up and die?" A nomad's harsh contempt rode Batbaian's voice for the comparison and for the despair as well. "We're not the only men in Pardraya who'd tie Varatesh in a rope of his own guts."

"Are we not, though? Too near it, I'm thinking. Them as'd try it did, and see what we got for it. And as for the rest, there's no more will in 'em than your sheep; they'll follow whoever leads 'em. Precious few have the ballocks to go after a winner."

"Leave if you like, then. I'll go on alone," Batbaian said. "At least I'll die as a man, doing as I should. And I say again, even without you I won't be alone forever. Pardraya is a wide land."

"Not wide enough," Viridovix came back, stung by the plainsman's dismissal and wanting to wound him in return. Then he hesitated. "Not wide enough," he repeated softly. His eyes went wide. "Tell me at once, Khamorth dear, would you ride away from Varatesh the now—och, and from Avshar, too—for a greater vengeance later, and mayhap one you might live through in the bargain?"

Batbaian's glare seized him, as if to drag his meaning out by force of will. "What does dying soon or late mean to me? But make me believe in a greater vengeance, and I will follow you off the edge of Pardraya."

"Good, for you'll need to," the Celt replied.

"A pox!" Gorgidas said, clutching too late at the top of his head. The freezing wind tore his otter-fur cap free and sent it spinning over the snowy ground. He ran cursing after it, his naked ears tingling in the cold.

The nearby Arshaum laughed and shouted bad advice. "Kill it!" "Shoot it!" "Quick, it's getting away! Stab it with that thrusting-sword of yours!"

Recapturing the flyaway headgear, the Greek whacked it against his trousers to get the snow off—and to work off his own annoyance. Then he jammed it back in place, and swore again as a last, freezing clump came loose and horrified the back of his neck.

Skylitzes' mouth was twitching; Goudeles did not try to hide a grin. "Now you see why all plainsmen, east or west of the Shaum, swear by wind spirits," he said.

He meant it as a joke, but it brought Gorgidas up short. "Why, so they do," he said. "I hadn't noticed that." He reached for the tablet on his belt—it hung at his right hip, where most men would carry a dagger. He scrawled a note, writing quickly but carefully. When he set stylus to wax in this weather, great chunks wanted to come away from the wood.

"That's nothing," Arigh said when he complained. "One winter a long time ago, a man went out riding without remounts and his horse broke a leg. He tried to yell for help, but it was so cold no one heard him till his shout thawed out next spring. That was a few months too late to do him any good, I fear."

Arigh told the story with so perfect a dead-pan air that Gorgidas wrote it down, though he added pointedly, "I have heard this, but I do not believe it." If that sort of disclaimer was enough to let Herodotos sneak a good yarn into his history when he found one, it should be good enough for him, too.

Arghun hobbled out of his tent, leaning on Dizabul. Arigh sent his brother a glance that was still full of mistrust. The khagan's elder son shouted for quiet, a shout the officers of the Gray Horse clan took up. The riders gathered round their chief. The rest of the Arshaum, attracted by the motion, also drew near, so that Arghun soon commanded the whole army's attention.

An attendant led the khagan's horse through the crowd. "See if you two can work with each other for once," Arghun said to his sons. Dizabul scowled; Arigh nodded, though his lips pursed. Together they helped their father into the saddle.

Arghun's hands curled lovingly on the reins he had not held for so long. But his legs were still all but useless. Arigh had to place his booted feet in the stirrups and then lash them there so they would not slip out. Even so, pride glowed on the khagan's face. A great cheer rang from the nomads to see him mounted once more; to them a man who could not ride was only half alive.

"Fetch the standard," Arghun said to the attendant, who hurried back with the spear that carried Bogoraz' long coat. Arghun held it high over his head so even the most distant rider could see it. "To Mashiz!" he cried.

The Arshaum host was silent for a moment, then echoed the cry, brandishing their swords, bows, and javelins. "Ma-shiz! Ma-shiz! Ma-shiz!" The noise dinned in Gorgidas' ears. Still roaring the war call, the plainsmen dashed to their horses, leaving a great trampled place in the snow to show where they had stood.

Almost as at home on horseback as an Arshaum, Skylitzes was grinning as he mounted. "I can hardly care whether this comes off or not," he called to Goudeles. "Either way we make Wulghash sweat to hold against us."

"No one could sweat in this weather," the pen-pusher said firmly, scrambling onto his own beast. "And it had best work, or my mistress will be most disappointed."

"Your mistress? What of your wife?"

"She inherits."

"Ah." Skylitzes started to say something more, but a fresh round of cheers from the nomads drowned him out. Still carrying the standard, Arghun rode east, his back straight in the high-cantled saddle, only the firm set of his mouth showing the strain he felt. As usual, his two sons flanked him; perhaps, thought Gorgidas, each was afraid to let the other have their father to himself for long. Singly and by bands, the Arshaum streamed after them.

Goudeles wanted to show the Videssian presence by riding in the van beside the khagan, but Skylitzes vetoed that. "Why wear out our horses breaking trail?" he asked with a veteran's experience. "You wait a bit, and he'll drop back to us." He soon proved right; for all Arghun's will, he could not set the pace for long.

The khagan threw questions at Skylitzes about the land east of the Shaum and especially about the mountains of Erzerum, which stretched between the Mylasa Sea and the Videssian Sea and separated Yezd from the Pardrayan steppe. The discussion on the ways and means of mountain warfare quickly bored Gorgidas. Despite Arghun's disappointed look, the Greek went searching for Tolui to talk about plant lore, something nearer his own heart.

"One of the ground roots you gave me smells like—" Gorgidas stopped, annoyed, not knowing the name in the Arshaum speech. "Orange, about so long, fatter than my thumb."

"Carrot," the shaman supplied.

"Yes, thanks. All my people do with it is eat it. What do you use it for?"

"We mix it with nightshade and wild rue in honey. It cures —" Tolui used another word Gorgidas did not know. The shaman grinned and made an unmistakable gesture.

"I understand: hemorrhoids." In a folk as much in the saddle as the Arshaum, the Greek could see how piles would be a common problem. He asked, "Is it given by mouth, or put directly where, ah, it will do the most good?"

"By mouth. For the other, we make an ointment of goose or partridge fat, egg white, fennel, and oil of wild roses, then smear it on. It soothes well."

Gorgidas dipped his head in agreement. "It should. You might also try mixing honey with that, I think. Honey is good for relieving inflammations generally."

That sort of conversation pleased the Greek much more than arguments over the best way to sniff out an ambush in a pass. After a while he guiltily remembered that he had come to the plains as historian, not physician. He asked Tolui, "Why do your people and the Khamorth differ so much from each other in your looks and in the build of your bodies?"

Tolui frowned. "Why should we be the same as the Hairies?" His voice carried as much disdain as a Greek's would, talking about barbarians.

"I'm looking to learn, not to offend you," Gorgidas said hastily. "To a foreigner like me, you and they seem to live on similar land under much the same kind of weather. So I wondered why the two folk are not the same as well." They should have been, if the doctrine Hippokrates put forward in *Airs, Waters, Places* was correct, as the Greek had always believed.

Tolui, though, operated with an entirely different set of assumptions. Mollified by Gorgidas' explanation, he said, "I will tell you. We Arshaum were the first race of men. The only reason there are Khamorth is that one of our men, many lives ago, was without a woman too long and futtered a goat. The Khamorth were the get of that union; that is why they are so disgustingly shaggy."

"I see." Gorgidas suddenly regretted his whiskers. He wrote Tolui's fable down; it was an interesting bit of lore, if nothing else. And Hippokrates was not doing so well here; he wrote that steppe nomads were stocky or plump, hairless, and of a ruddy complexion. The Khamorth met only the first criterion, the Arshaum the second, and neither people the third.

The Greek rubbed his earlobe between thumb and forefinger. "Tell me more about this goat."

Viridovix peered down into the valley of the Shaum through swirling snow. "Well, where's the other side o' the fool stream, now?" he said indignantly, as if Batbaian had hidden it on purpose.

"Oh, it's there," the Khamorth said. "All we have to do is get to it—and then persuade the devils across the river not to kill us on sight." He spoke with morbid anticipation; Viridovix' notion of begging help from the Arshaum had horrified him, fey though he was. Next to them, Avshar was a new terror; tales of the Arshaum frightened naughty children into behaving.

The Gaul pretended not to notice his gloom. "One thing at a time. Once we're after crossing the river, then we think on the folk as live there." He did not give Batbaian a chance to argue, but clucked to his horse and trotted toward the Shaum. Shaking his head, Batbaian followed.

Had Viridovix been a more experienced horseman, he would have known better than to set a fast pace downhill through snowdrifts that hid the ground below. His pony whinnied in terror as a forefoot came down in some unseen hole. It stumbled and fell, throwing the Gaul. He was lucky; he had the wind knocked out of him as he hit the ground, but the thick blanket of snow cushioned him from worse damage.

But he had heard the horse's legbone snap. As he was struggling to his feet, Batbaian dismounted and put the animal out of its pain. Blood steamed in the snow. Batbaian turned to the Gaul. "Help me butcher it," he said. "We'll take as much as we can carry." Viridovix pulled out his dagger. He did not care for the thick, gluey taste of horse, but it was better than an empty belly.

When the gory task was done, Batbaian said only, "We'll take turns on the beast that's left. It'll make a path for the man on foot." He did not waste time railing at the Gaul; Viridovix knew what his carelessness had cost them. They would be at walking pace from here on, and their one remaining animal, the Celt thought, would have to carry their gear all the time.

Once they reached the riverbank, though, Viridovix wondered if they would go any farther at all. The Shaum did not flow swiftly; it iced over in winter. But it was so wide that a stretch of a couple of hundred yards still ran free in the center of the stream, with pieces of ice crashing against each other in the current as they bobbed their way south.

The Gaul shivered, looking out toward the frigid black water. "I wouldna try to swim it," he said to Batbaian. "Three strokes and you'd be another icicle."

"Look there, though," the plainsman said, pointing downstream. A broad cake of drift ice had run against the farther edge of the ice, and a couple of smaller ones against it. Water splashed over them, but they made a bridge of sorts.

"We'd not get the pony across that," Viridovix protested.

"No, but then we wouldn't anyhow. He'd crash through where a man can crawl on his belly and spread his weight on the ice. Are you still set on this mad scheme of yours?"

"I am that."

"Well, then." Batbaian slid down from the saddle, went up to touch his horse's nose. Before Viridovix knew what he was doing, he slit the beast's throat. It gave a reproachful, dreadfully human cough as its legs buckled and it went down.

"Are you witstruck?" the Gaul cried.

"No. Think through it," Batbaian said, sounding like a Roman. "If he can't cross with us, he's more use dead than alive. Don't stand there gaping—give me a hand getting the hide off." His knife was already busy; Viridovix helped mechanically, wondering if the nomad really had lost his wits.

Batbaian had not. After another rough job of worrying chunks from the horse's flank and hock, he used the hides as a sack to hold the meat, their knocked-down tent, and his pack. "Give me yours, too," he told the Celt, who undid it from his back. Batbaian lashed the hide closed, hefted it. "Weighs less than a man," he said, satisfied. He added another length of rope. "You see? We'll haul it behind us, far enough away so it won't put extra strain on the ice."

"And aren't you the cleverest little chappie, now?" Viridovix said admiringly. In his Gallic forests he might have done as good a job of improvising, but here on the plains it took the Khamorth to see what to do with what they had.

Batbaian shrugged the praise away; it meant nothing to him. He dragged the hide downstream along the bank until he was even with the ice jam in the Shaum. Viridovix followed. At the very edge of the river the Khamorth handed him the rope. "You take this. I'll go first and scrape the snow away so we can tell how the ice is."

"And why not me for that?" the Gaul said, wanting to do something, at least, of importance.

But Batbaian replied, "Because I'm lighter," which was unanswerable. He stepped onto the ice. It held his weight, but he walked slowly and very carefully, planting each foot before he raised the other. "Wouldn't do to slip," he said with forced lightness.

"You're right there," Viridovix said. He moved as cautiously as the Khamorth.

From behind them came an excited baying and yapping, then snarls as a band of wolves fell on the Gaul's dead horse. He looked back, but they were lost in the blowing snow. He heard bones crunch. "Might you step it up a bit, Batbaian dear?"

"No." The plainsman did not turn his head. "Going through the ice is the bigger risk. They won't be after us, not with two horses to keep them happy."

"Sure and I hope you're right. If I'm eaten I'll not forgive it." The Celt made sure his blade was loose in its scabbard. The idea of facing wolves on the treacherous ice chilled him worse than the biting north wind.

He scowled when one of the beasts, driven away from the first carcass, found the second one. More came running to gorge themselves; the noise of their feasting seemed almost at his elbow. Now he could see them, back by the riverbank. He cursed and half drew his blade when one of them trotted onto the frozen river, but its feet flew out from under it, and it sprawled on its belly. With a startled yip, it fled back to land. "Ha! You like it no better here than I," Viridovix said.

"Shut up," said Batbaian. "This is getting tricky." They were almost to midstream. The Khamorth picked his way with even greater care now, for there were patches where the Shaum's water showed dark through the ice. He skirted them as long as he could, staying with the ice that was thick enough still to be white. At last, he sighed, defeated. "No help for it now," he said, and went down on his belly to wriggle forward.

Viridovix' thick coat kept the worst of the cold from him, but his knees burned to the ice's kiss. Memory floated into him, of sliding on a frozen pond in Gaul one winter when he was very small, of the squeals of glee from the other children and the sight of bare-branched trees all around. No trees here, not for miles. He squirmed faster to catch up with Batbaian.

They were side by side when they came to the edge of the ice pack. Seen close up, the tumbled slabs of ice ahead were far less promising as a way across than they had looked from the bank. Batbaian waved the Celt to a halt while he considered. "As fast as we can," he decided. "I don't know how long this first one will hold us."

"But what if we break it free?"

The Khamorth shrugged. "Then we have a raft. Maybe we can steer it to the far side."

"Honh!" Viridovix said, but Batbaian was already gathering himself for the rush. He scrambled from the pack onto the chunk of ice ahead. It groaned under his weight. With a final, frantic slither, he rolled onto the next slab.

As soon as the plainsman was off the first piece of ice, Viridovix clambered onto it, the horsehide sack bumping after him. It rocked alarmingly. The sudden, queasy motion reminded the Gaul of a pitching boat. "None o' that now," he said to himself, wrestling with his weak stomach. Freezing water soaked his trousers. He yelped and tried to move faster.

The thin ice crackled beneath him; a network of cracks

appeared, spreading fast. "Hurry!" Batbaian yelled. With a last desperate lunge, the Celt tumbled onto the next block, hauled their gear after him. Widening lines of inky-black water showed as the last chunk of ice shifted and started to break up.

Batbaian gave a sarcastic dip of his head. "I hope you didn't forget anything back there."

"Only my anvil." Viridovix managed a winded grin; the Khamorth bared his teeth in what might have been a smile. He inched ahead. This chunk of ice was thicker than the last one, but more precariously placed. It teetered and swayed as the two men crawled across it. Batbaian grunted in relief as he swarmed onto the last frozen cake. He helped pull Viridovix up after him. "My thanks," the Gaul said. "One of my hands is fair frozen."

"If the tinder isn't soaked, we'll have a fire as soon as we get to the other side," Batbaian promised. For the first time he sounded as if he thought they would make it.

There was one dreadful moment when Viridovix thrust his left arm through the ice into the frigid Shaum up to the elbow. He waited for the pack to split and drop him into the river, but it held; the weak spot proved no bigger than a man's head. He wriggled his arm out of his sleeve and pressed it against his body to try to put some tiny warmth back in it.

Then Batbaian was shouting ahead of him—there was sand and dirt under the snow, not ice. Viridovix lurched onto the land and lay gasping like a fish cast up by the stream. The Khamorth fought the horsehide sack; it had frozen nearly hard. He used the lead pommel of his dagger to hammer tent pegs an inch or two into the iron-hard ground. Viridovix gave what one-handed help he could in spreading the felt fabric of the tent over its framework of sticks. They scrambled into it together, groaning with relief to be out of the ceaseless, piercing wind.

Clumsy in his thick mittens but careful all the same, Batbaian opened the bone box that held bark and dry leaves. He looked inside. "Ah," he said. He rummaged in his kit for flint and steel. He pushed the snow to one side, found a few flat stones so he would not have to set the tinder on damp ground. After several tries he got a small fire going. He scraped fat from the inside of the roughly butchered horsehide, cut more strips from the hunks of horsemeat. The fat ran as it melted and stank foully, but it burned. "What I wouldn't give for a few handfuls of dry horsedung," Batbaian said.

Viridovix huddled close to the fire. He held his left arm over it, trying to chafe back feeling. "Hack off a couple of gobbets there and set 'em up to roast," he said through chattering teeth. "E'en horsemeat'll be good in my belly. And if you're keen to be dreaming of turds, why go ahead, and may you ha' joy of 'em. As of me, I'll think on mulled wine, and thank you just the same."

On the eastern bank of the Shaum, a wolf lifted its head in suspicion. A low growl rumbled deep in its throat; the hair stood up on its shoulders and ridged along its back. The oncoming rider did not falter. The growl turned to whine. The wolf slunk out of the horseman's path; the pack scattered before him as he trotted down to the very edge of the frozen stream.

He dismounted. His white robes, swirling in the wind, might almost have been blowing snow themselves. Hands on hips, he stared across the river. Even he could not see the tent on the far shore, but he knew it was there. This once his great size and the weight of mail on his shoulders worked against him; for one of his bulk, there was no crossing the Shaum. He felt of the ice in his mind and knew it would not hold him.

He cursed, first in the guttural Khamorth speech, then in archaic Videssian, slow and full of hate. "Winter, then, shall my work complete," he said in the same language. "Skotos will aid his servant thus, I trow." He swung himself back into the saddle, wheeled his horse, and rode east.

The wolves were a long time returning.

Tied together so they would not lose each other in the storm, Batbaian and Viridovix slogged west. Shaumkhiil was as featureless as the Pardrayan plain, but there was no danger of wandering in circles. As long as they kept the wind blowing against their right sides, they knew they could not be far wrong.

They had yet to see an Arshaum, which left Viridovix angry and frustrated and Batbaian, as far as the Gaul could tell, secretly relieved; down deep he still seemed to believe they were ten feet tall and armed with fangs.

Maybe the Arshaum ate sheep at a gulp and spat out the bones, but eat sheep they did. The Gaul and Khamorth came on a dozen or so that must have strayed from their main herd. Viridovix ate mutton until he missed the horsemeat he had had to make himself choke down. Batbaian, a skillful jackleg tailor, sewed scraped sheepskins together into cloaks the two wanderers wore over their greatcoats.

They needed the extra layer of warmth; the weather was the worst Batbaian had seen. To Viridovix it was appalling beyond belief: snow, ice, ravening wind, endless days without glimpse of sun or stars through thick black clouds. The storms on the Videssian plateau had been bitter, but they were storms, each with beginning and end. This went on and on, as if summer left the world for good.

"It's dogging us, I'm thinking," Viridovix shouted through the screaming gale.

"What's that?" Batbaian yelled back. He was only a yard in front of the Celt, but the wind flung words away.

"I say the blizzard's after dogging us, to pounce when it's worn us down." Viridovix had meant it as a figure of speech, but suddenly wondered if it were not truth. Batbaian turned round and mouthed a name. The Gaul could not hear it, but he knew what it was. His shudder, for once, had nothing to do with cold. He thought again about throwing away his sword, this time more seriously than he had before.

The storm blew harder, as though it acknowledged Avshar as its parent. The wind hurled stinging snow into Viridovix' eyes. He shielded them with his hands as best he could, stumbling ahead all but blind. The icy blast fought his every forward step; it was like trying to walk through ocean waves.

A savage gust stopped him and Batbaian in their tracks. "The tent!" the plainsman shouted. "This will kill us if we stay in it!" Viridovix cursed as he tried to drive the pegs; the ground had frozen so hard it did not want to take them. Somehow he and Batbaian forced the felt over its framework. Like animals darting into a nest, they scrambled for shelter.

The raging wind seemed to scream louder once they were out of it. Viridovix rubbed at his legs, stamped his feet; his boots were thick and lined with several layers of felt, but his toes turned to ice each day regardless. "Sure and I understand the now why you were mooning over horseapples back there," he said. "A sheepshit fire's better than none."

"This is the last of it, worse luck," Batbaian said. Fat caught more easily, but once alight the uncured dung burned longer and, to the Celt's surprise, cleaner than the drippings the Khamorth always caught from his meat. Viridovix had hesitated almost a day over eating anything cooked on a dung fire, but hunger broke down his qualms.

He sighed in relief as the fire began to give off a little warmth. The snow and ice clinging to his mustaches started melting; he wiped his face on his cloak. The wool was rank and greasy, but he did not mind. "Mutton again," he grumbled.

"We're almost to the end of that, too," Batbaian said. "You'll like it better than empty, I'd bet."

"Truth that." Viridovix skewered a hunk on his dagger, held it over the flames. His belly rumbled at the smell. "Sure and my insides think so."

A poorly planted tent peg tore out of its hole. The wind smacked it against the side of the tent like a flung stone. Batbaian's head came up in alarm. "We've got to set that again," he exclaimed, "before—" The second peg came loose as he was scrambling to his feet. The gale roared in under the bottom of the tent, lifted the felt free of its framework. Viridovix clutched it for a moment. Then, with what sounded like mocking laughter, the storm ripped it from his hands and sent it flapping away over the steppe.

"After it!" Batbaian screamed. "We won't last a day without it!" He flung the last words over his shoulder as he vanished into the blowing snow.

Viridovix plunged after him. He had not gone twenty paces when he knew he was in trouble. Ahead, Batbaian might have been snatched from the face of the earth. The fire was lost behind him. He cried the Khamorth's name again and again, howled out Gallic war cries. If there was any answer, the wind blew it away.

Still shouting, he ran with the wind at his back for a while. In the blizzard, Batbaian could have been almost at his elbow, and would not have known it. He stopped, irresolute. If Batbaian had caught the runaway tent fabric, what would he do with it? Stay and wait for Viridovix or try to bring it back to what was left of the frame? "Och, a murrain take it," the Celt muttered. "Whichever way I guess'll turn out wrong."

He dug in his pouch and found the square Haloga coin he had won. He tossed it in the air, caught it with both hands. When he uncovered it, a dragon leered at him. "To the tent, then." He turned to face the bitter wind. It stung like fire against his face; he was glad of his new beard, and wished it were heavier.

He tried to follow his own footprints back, but the storm was already blowing snow over them. They grew fainter as he watched. He thought he was getting close when they finally gave out altogether. He fought panic. There had to be some way—the wind! If it had held steady, he could use it to steer his way back.

It must have shifted. After a while he knew he had gone too far. He cast about blindly then, hoping luck would serve where wit had failed. It did not. He stood shivering, pounding his hands together and wondering what to do next. No food, no fire, no shelter—he could feel the heat draining from his body and knew Batbaian had been right; the storm could kill quickly.

"If only the cursed snow'd stop so a body could use the eyes of him," he said, shaking his head like a baffled bear. It seemed ready to snow forever, though, thick gusts of white powder blowing by almost horizontally.

Realizing he had to shield himself from the ravening gale, he knelt and began pushing up a heap of snow as a windbreak. The storm swept it away about as fast as he piled it up, but at last he had a waist-high wall that blocked the worst of the wind. He crouched behind it, knowing his makeshift would do no good if the storm did not blow itself out soon.

The numbness came insidiously; he hardly noticed when he could no longer feel his nose, his feet, his forearms. In a way it was a relief, for they did not hurt any more. His mind grew numb, too, slipping into a frigid lassitude in which he knew he was dying but lacked the will to care. He had always thought he would fight death to the end, but the irresistible cold stripped his defenses one by one and left him nothing to strike back at. He did not notice closing his eyes; what was there to see, in any case?

He slept.

* * *

"Bloody ghastly," Goudeles shouted over the shrieking wind.

"What are you complaining about, Pikridios?" Skylitzes said beside him. "With your blubber you're likely warmer than any of us." The officer rode hunched over the right side of his pony's neck to gain a little protection from the blizzard.

The brute power of the plains winter chilled Gorgidas' heart as much as it did his body. A child of the sunny Mediterranean, he was ill-equipped to face miles of snow and ice; they daunted him worse than sudden death on the battlefield. No wonder the Videssians gave Skotos a frozen lair, he thought.

He turned to Arghun, asking, "Is it always so fierce?"

The khagan's face, like his own, was smeared so thick with grease that it glistened even in this murky light. "I have seen storms as bad as this, a few," he answered, "but never one that lasted so long. And it grows worse as we ride east, which is strange. Usually the fouler weather stays to the west." A gust kicked snow into his face. He coughed and bundled his robe of long-haired goatskin tighter around him. Since his poisoning he felt the cold more than his followers, and the Greek could only guess the hardship he was enduring. No complaint passed his lips, though, nor a suggestion that the Arshaum army slow its advance.

A pair of scouts came riding back through the nomads toward the khagan, one a few yards ahead of the other. The leader bobbed his head in salute, spoke with faint distaste: "We found a Hairy, sir, freezing in the snow, and some other foreigner with him."

Arghun's brows shot up. "A Khamorth? On our side of the river?"

"Outlaw?" Skylitzes rapped.

"That or a madman, or maybe both. No horse, and he's lost an eye sometime not long ago—not pretty. Just an idiot Khamorth, rolled in felt."

"Oh, a pox on him," the second scout burst out as he came abreast of his companion. He was younger than the other man, with lively, humorous eyes. "Tell them about the fire-demon."

The first picket made a rude noise. "You and your fire-demons. If he is one, this storm's put him out for good. Even money he's frozen dead by now—he didn't look to be far from it, and I shouldn't wonder, either, lying in the snow in only his coat."

"Well, I still say he's no natural breed of man," the younger Arshaum insisted. "Or will you tell me you've seen his like before, with hair and whiskers and great long mustache the color of polished bronze?"

Gorgidas, Skylitzes, and Goudeles shouted together. The scout started; Arghun's horse shied at the outcry. "Our this friend is," Gorgidas said to the khagan, losing grammar in his excitement.

Skylitzes nodded. "That could only be one man."

Gorgidas swung round on the scouts. "You left him there to freeze, you idiots?"

"And up your arse, too," the leader of the two retorted. "What do we want with foreigners on Arshaum land?" That included the Greek, his glare said.

But Arghun roared, "Hold your tongue, you! These foreigners here are our allies, and this one saved my life. If their friend dies in the snow, you'll wish you had, too." The khagan's temper was usually mild; the plainsmen quailed at his outburst.

"Take me to him," Gorgidas said. The outriders obeyed without a word. "Gallop, damn you!" the Greek shouted. The three spurred their horses forward, snow flying. Goudeles and Skylitzes in their wake, they pounded through and then past the Arshaum army.

Gorgidas wondered how the nomads knew just where to ride in this howling white wilderness. Steering by the wind, no doubt, and by landmarks they recognized but which meant nothing to his untrained eyes. His own eyes stung and watered from the headlong pace, and his nose, despite the coating of fat that covered it, felt like an icicle in the center of his face. These flat-featured nomads were better suited than he to life in a steppe winter.

"There," the younger scout said, pointing ahead through the swirling snow. The Greek spied the ponies first, then the dismounted Arshaum beside them—no, he saw as he drew near, one of the squatting figures had to be a Khamorth, from its heavy beard. He dismissed the man from Pardraya from his thoughts. If the fellow was well enough to move around like that, he was not going to freeze in the next few minutes.

"Out of my way!" Gorgidas shouted, leaping down from his horse. The three Arshaum huddled round the shape in the snow jumped to their feet, reaching for swords. The scouts who had fetched the Greek were shouting, too, explaining to their comrades who he was.

He paid them no attention, bending down over Viridovix' prone form. When he pulled him over onto his back, he thought the Celt was dead. His flesh was pale and cold; his head rolled limply on his neck. He did not seem to be breathing.

The Greek cradled Viridovix' face in his hands. Just so had he held Quintus Glabrio when an arrow killed his lover, helpless for all his skill. And now another one dear to him—true, in a different and lesser way—he could not save. Futile rage and frustration tore at him; would he never be of any use?

Then he jumped—was that a pulse in the Gaul's throat? It came again, so slow and faint he hardly dared believe he felt it.

Afterwards, he never remembered thinking what to do next. His dogged rationality had been Nepos' despair when the priest-mage tried to teach him the Videssian healing art. "Never mind how or why," Nepos had shouted once. "Know that you must—and you will." But for the Greek that was worse than no explanation, and he never did succeed.

His lover's wound could have been the trigger to free him from the grip of reasoned thought and let the healing gift burst forth, but Glabrio had died before he hit the ground. Not even the Videssian art could raise the dead. And so Gorgidas had turned his back on it in his anguish over the failure—for good, he thought.

Now, though, desperation lifted him outside himself, stripped away everything but the need to save his friend. Seeing him suddenly stiffen above Viridovix, Goudeles pushed aside an Arshaum who was about to take him by the shoulder. The nomad spun round in anger. "Shaman," the bureaucrat said, pointing to the Greek. "Let him be." The Arshaum's slanted eyes went wide. He nodded and stepped back.

Gorgidas, staring down at the Celt's white face, never noticed the byplay. He felt his will gather into a single hard point, like the sun's rays focused by a burning glass. This was where he had always fallen short, trying to force that focused will outward. But it leaped forward before he consciously tried to project it.

A conduit, a channel—he sensed Viridovix' failing body as if it were his own; sensed the ravages of cold and exposure that froze fingers and cheeks, reached deep into entrails; sensed the chilled blood in its thick, sluggish motion through the Gaul's veins.

In that first dizzying rush of perception the Greek was almost swept away, almost lost himself in the Celt's distress. But his stubborn reason would not let him be submerged; he *knew* who he truly was, no matter what sense impressions his mind was receiving. And the conduit ran both ways—in the same instant he felt Viridovix flood in on him, he was also reaching out to reverse, repair, revive.

Quicken the heart; send warmth surging into belly, streaming into arms and legs. Strengthen lungs, and speed them, too—they had barely been sipping the frigid air. More delicate work: feel the damage of frost in fingers, toes, cheeks, ears, eyelids—melt it gently, gradually, let the new flow of blood work with his power. The poor makeshift words for what he did came later. In the crisis they meant nothing. The healing went on at a level far below words.

The Celt stirred under his hands like a restless sleeper, muttered some drowsy protest in his own musical speech. His eyes, green as the Gallic forests, came open, and there was intelligence in them. Then Gorgidas truly realized what he had accomplished. Joy leaped in him, joy and as crushing a weariness as he had ever known: the price of the healer's art.

Viridovix had not thought he would wake again, surely not with this new hot tide of strength flowing through him. As he stretched and—oh, miracle!—felt all his limbs answer him, he thought for a moment he had passed to the afterworld; he could not imagine feeling so well in this one. The hands gently touching his face, then, might belong to some immortal maid, to make him glad through eternity.

But when he looked up, the face he saw was a man's, thin, tense, etched with lines of triumph and harsh fatigue. "Foosh!" he said. "No lassy you, more's the pity."

Gorgidas rolled his eyes and laughed. "No need to ask

whether you're healed. By the dog, do you think of nothing else, you satyr?"

Viridovix' sudden flinch of pain made the Greek wonder if he was in fact healed, but all the Gaul said, very quietly, was, "Aye, betimes I do." Viridovix struggled to sit. The blood roared in his ears, but he fought his dizziness down. "Batbaian!" he exclaimed. "Is he after being found?"

Hearing his name, Batbaian hurried over to the Celt, still swaddled in the thick felt fabric of the tent. He seemed glad for any excuse to sidle away from the Arshaum, who were eyeing him like a pack of wolves sizing up a stray hound. Skylitzes and Goudeles crouched by Viridovix, too; the Videssian officer steadied him with a strong right arm, while the bureaucrat pressed Gorgidas' hand in congratulation.

"Are you all right, now?" Viridovix said to Batbaian, dropping into the Khamorth speech. Gorgidas followed it with difficulty; he had not used that language in months.

"I'm well enough, thanks to this," the nomad answered, shaking snow from the felt. He looked in wonder at Viridovix. "But how is it you're here to ask me? You shouldn't be, not after being out in the blizzard with no cover."

"Truth that." There was wonder on Viridovix's face, too, but aimed at Gorgidas. "He healed me, must be." Almost accusingly, he said to the physician, "I didna think you could."

"Neither did I." Now that it was done, the Greek longed for nothing so much as the warm inside of a tent, a deep draught of kavass, and his bedroll to take him through the long winter night—and most of the next day, if he could get away with it.

But Viridovix was saying, "If it's a druid of leechcraft you are now, Gorgidas dear, have a look at Batbaian and the eye of him, and see if there's somewhat to be done for the puir lad."

The Greek sighed, a long, frosty exhalation; no doubt Viridovix was right. "I'll do what I can." He leaned toward the young Khamorth, who drew back in suspicion, still full of mistrust for anyone who had anything to do with the Arshaum. "Hold still," Gorgidas said in Videssian. Though he hardly spoke the imperial tongue, Batbaian understood it enough to obey.

Gorgidas sucked in his breath sharply when he took a good look at the nomad's ruined socket. Not having paid any real attention to Batbaian, he had assumed the Khamorth's eye lost to sword or arrow in some steppe skirmish. But the scar he saw was wrong for that: too large, too round, too neat, with the look of cautery to it. His gently probing fingers confirmed the impression. "How did you come by this?" he asked.

Voice cold as the north wind, Batbaian told him. He did not have the Videssian for all of it, but Viridovix and Skylitzes helped interpret, and his final, plunging gesture was graphic enough. Skylitzes, hardened soldier though he was, turned his head and was sick in the snow. He bent down and scooped up more to clean his mouth.

"Aye, that was the way of it," Viridovix said grimly. "A sweet fellow, Avshar." With a grunt of effort, the Celt fought his way to his feet. He stood swaying but triumphant. "And a deal to pay him back for, that there is." His face grew bleak once more, his eyes far away. "That there is," he repeated softly. He touched his sword, drawing strength from the thought of revenge.

Then he seemed to come back to himself, and asked Gorgidas, "Is anything to be done for the eye, now?"

The Greek had to toss his head in his people's no. He knew he could heal again; like a boy's first spending of his seed, the one success promised more. But that knowledge was useless here. "Time has given the wound such healing as it will have. Had I seen it when it was fresh, the best I could have done would have been to bring it to the state it is in now. The art works with what it finds; it cannot give back what is lost."

Viridovix' nod was unhappy, Batbaian's only impatient—he wore the mutilation as a reminder to himself of what he owed.

Goudeles sneezed. The sound reminded Gorgidas that the blizzard had not gone away simply because he had found Viridovix. The Gaul could freeze all over again—and so could the rest of them. The physician ran back to his horse, pulled a blanket from his saddlebag, and wrapped Viridovix in it.

The Celt accepted it absently; being alive, being warm enough to feel the snow stinging his cheeks, was enough to savor. He hardly heard Gorgidas when the Greek asked him if he could ride, but the physician's impatient growl got through. "I can that," he said, and managed the ghost of a chuckle. "Dinna fash yoursel'."

He mounted behind Gorgidas, Batbaian back of Skylitzes. The physician's pony snorted resentfully at having to carry two; Gorgidas got it moving with the rest regardless. "Your riding's better than it was," Viridovix said.

"Yes, I know. I have many useless talents these days," the Greek said, tapping the *gladius* that swung at his left hip. He paused, and added wonderingly, "And a real one, it seems."

The ride west to the Arshaum army was short; the nomads had been pushing forward at their own steady pace while Gorgidas labored over the Gaul. Outriders yelled challenges. The scout leader answered with loud praise for Gorgidas' healing talents. The physician's mouth quirked in a wry smile. Now that he had done something worth talking about, the picket was glad enough to claim a share of it.

Viridovix did not know the Arshaum language, beyond a few obscenities Arigh had taught him. But his eyes grew wide as he took in the size of the approaching force. "The lot of you've not been wasting your time, have you now?" he said to Gorgidas. The Greek tossed his head.

Then there was a shout: "V'rid'rish!" Arigh rode up at a near-gallop, clumps of snow flying under his horse's hooves. His grin as white as the landscape around them, he pounded the Gaul's back. "I wanted to kill someone when I found the scouts who came across you were gone again before I knew about it."

"Blame me for that," Gorgidas said. Like Arigh, he spoke Videssian so Viridovix could understand.

"Blame, is it?" the Celt snorted. "Pay him no mind, Arigh darling. A little later and there'd only be the frozen corp of me here, the which'd be no good for saying hello."

"You're without a horse, I see," Arigh said—the nomads' first priority. "Take a couple from my string."

"Obliged," Viridovix said. "Might you also be having one for Batbaian my friend?"

Arigh's grin disappeared as his glance slid to the Khamorth. His lip curled; for the first time, he reminded Gorgidas of Dizabul. "Your taste in friends has gone down," he said.

"Has it now?" Viridovix said. "Well, belike you have the right of it; I keep picking khagans' sons." He locked eyes with the Arshaum prince.

With his swarthy skin and the thick layer of grease on his

face, it was impossible to see whether Arigh flushed, but after a few moments he walked his horse over to Batbaian. He had learned a little of the Khamorth speech traveling across Pardraya to Prista and the Empire; now he used it to ask, "A horse—you need?"

Batbaian had stiffened as the Arshaum came up to him; he jerked in surprise to hear his own language. Then he nodded with a dignity beyond his years. "I thank you," he said. He fumbled at his belt, undid the dagger there—fine metalwork, with a leaping stag in high relief on the bronze sheath—and offered it to Arigh. "A gift for a gift."

The smile returned to Arigh's face; he accepted the knife, clapped Batbaian on the shoulder. The watching Arshaum murmured in approval. Few of them, probably, had understood Arigh when he made his gift to Batbaian, but his return gesture needed no words. "The Hairy acts as a man should," Gorgidas heard one nomad say, and his companion's reply: "Why not? He's seen a fight or two, looks like—that scar's not pretty."

Arigh said, "Skylitzes, Gorgidas, bring 'em along to my father. We can all hear what they have to say then." He rode off toward the gray horsetail standard.

Viridovix bowed to Arghun as best he could riding double. The khagan was frailer than he had expected and sat his horse with difficulty; the Gaul wondered if he had been ill. He was soft-spoken, without the blustery temper Targitaus had used to browbeat his clansmen, but the Arshaum hurried to obey when he said something. Now he studied Batbaian cautiously, Viridovix with lively curiosity. He said something in the sibilant Arshaum tongue.

"He didn't believe Arigh when he told him of your looks," Gorgidas translated, "but he sees he was telling the truth after all."

"Honh!" Viridovix said. In Latin he went on, "And I never set eyes on such a lot of slant-eyed flat-noses in all my days either, but no need to tell him that, I'm thinking. Give him top o' the day instead."

Gorgidas did. Arghun nodded at the courtesy, then said, "I'd be curious to know how the two of you happened to come here." It was phrased as a request, but was plainly a command; Gorgidas put it into Videssian for Viridovix and Skylitzes into the Khamorth language for Batbaian.

"Up to me to start, it is," Viridovix said, and began to tell of what had befallen him since Varatesh snatched him from the camp. The outlaw's name raised a growl from a few of the Arshaum by Arghun, the ones whose clans wandered closest to the Shaum. They remembered his raid over the winter the year before, and its savagery. The Gaul was soon talking faster than Gorgidas could easily interpret; Arigh helped him when he faltered.

Another horseman pushed his way through thc crowd gathering round the newcomers. What a dandified sprout, Viridovix thought; he wore furs and leather as if they were silk and cloth-of-gold, and even in the wind and snow he somehow kept his pony perfectly groomed, its mane braided with bright red ribbons.

"Father, I—" Dizabul began.

Arghun cut him off. "Whatever it is, it'll have to keep, boy. These foreigners bear important news."

The young prince's handsome face clouded as he looked Viridovix' way, the more so because of Arigh beside him. But when he spied Batbaian his jaw dropped. "Am I less than a Hairy, now?" he began angrily.

But Arghun silenced him again, this time with a gesture of dismissal. "Go on, redbeard," he said.

"Not bad, not bad," he said, laughing, when the Gaul told of the trick with the cattle he had suggested to drive Varatesh's men back. By then Viridovix and Batbaian were speaking alternately as they described the events that had led up to the attack on the outlaws and their allies.

The khagan snapped sharp questions about the battle itself. Hearing it in detail reminded Gorgidas all too much of the catastrophe at Maragha. Avshar's battle magic, whatever might be true of others', did not fail in the heat of combat. If the soldiers he led could fight on anywhere near even terms, that sorcery would be enough to spell victory for them.

And the aftermath of victory—the Arshaum prided themselves on their hardness, but more than one cried out in loathing and horror as Batbaian, his voice dispassionate as if it had all happened to some stranger, spoke of endless red-hot irons. They flinched again when Viridovix told of the winners' cruel toying with their enemies' hopes, and of Targitaus' seizure when the dreadful truth came clear. Apoplexy, thought Gorgidas, sickened but unsurprised.

After that, the story of the sack of the camp seemed almost anticlimax, though Viridovix felt the thin scabs tear open and the pain flow out like blood when he thought of Seirem. "So there it stands," Batbaian finished. "Varatesh, the spirits dung on him, has Pardraya, and Avshar him, or so it looked to me when I was in their hands. Next to them," and Batbaian looked Arghun full in the face, beyond fear now, "even you Arshaum are a good choice. So we came to beg your help, if you care to give." The Khamorth glanced at the warriors all around, said dryly, "You may not need me to persuade you to move east."

Arghun stroked his wispy beard. He turned to Gorgidas. "This is the Avshar you have spoken of, the one from Yezd?"

"Aye," said the Greek, echoed by words or nods from his friends and comrades.

The khagan said, "I had not intended to leave much of Yezd on its wheels in any case. Your wizard will be one more yurt to knock down." Arghun folded his arms with the serene confidence of a man who has not known defeat. The Arshaum who heard his declaration cheered; they, too, were sure only victory was possible when facing Khamorth and other weaklings.

Their guests, who had seen the wizard-prince's handiwork, were less sanguine, but saw little point in saying so. "As well explain music to a deaf man," Goudeles muttered. "One way or another, they'll find out."

"Or another," Gorgidas agreed gloomily. Having warned Arghun over and over of the deadly might he would face, the physician was coming to understand the nature of the curse Apollo had laid on Kassandra.

Winter's short day and the raging storm combined to force the Arshaum to an early halt. "Will you share my tent?" Gorgidas asked Viridovix as they dismounted. "I want to examine you—I can hardly believe you're alive." As nothing else could, curiosity held wariness at bay.

"I am that, thanks to you," the Celt said. He poked Gorgidas in the ribs. "I'll come wi' you, though its nobbut the carcass o' me you're hankering after."

"Bah!" From anyone but Scaurus or Viridovix, the crack would have frightened the Greek; and the tribune, he thought, would never have made it—too mannerly by half. As it was, he was obscurely pleased. He looked Viridovix up and down. "You flatter yourself."

"Do I now?" Chuckling, the Gaul helped him set up his tent. "This is better than the one I had, but mind you drive the pegs down firm."

The physician was adept with flint and steel and he soon had a dung fire going. After he and the Gaul had eaten, he seized Viridovix' wrist; the pulse was firm and steady, that of a healthy man. When the fire had warmed the cramped space inside the tent, he had his friend strip off coat and tunic and listened to his lungs. The air whistled smoothly in and out, with none of the damp, soggy sound that would have warned of chest fever. Finally, he examined the Celt's hands and feet, cheeks, nose, and ears for traces of frostbite. He tossed his head. "You're disgustingly well."

"The which is only your fault, so dinna come carping to me over it."

"Scoffer. Truly, though, had you not been a strong, healthy man, you would have been dead long before I got to you." Pride and delighted awe lit the Greek's face as the notion that he had really healed took hold.

Viridovix dressed again with some haste; it was not so warm as all that. He gulped kavass. After months on the steppe, he hardly noticed the faintly sour taste—and it, too, was warmth of a sort. He said to Gorgidas, "You're after hearing what's befallen me—tell me now how the lot o' you fared once I was raped away." The Greek obeyed, talking much of the night away as the wind howled outside. Listening, Viridovix thought the past months had been good ones for Gorgidas. His wit was still biting, but he spoke with a confidence and a sense of his own worth the Gaul had not seen in him since his lover's death—and perhaps not before.

Once the story was done, the physician seemed to change the subject. "Do you remember the argument we had a couple of years ago, not long after we came to Videssos?"

"Och, which one was that?" Viridovix said, grinning and

yawning. "There've been so many, and rare sport they are, too."

"Hmm. Well, maybe so. The one I'm thinking of had to do with war and what it was good for."

The reminiscent smile disappeared from Viridovix' face. "So that's the one you mean, is it?" he said heavily, sighing through his thick mustaches. "I'm afeared you had the right of it after all. A cold cruel thing it is, warring, and glory only a word a reeking corp'll never hear again."

Gorgidas stared at the Celt, thunderstruck as if a second head had appeared on his shoulders. This, from the barbarian who exulted in combat for its own sweet sake? "Odd you should say so, when—" the physician began, and then stopped, looking at his friend more closely. He had examined the Gaul's body; now he looked at the man, really saw for the first time the grief that sat behind his eyes and showed at the corners of his mouth and in the deepening lines of his forehead. "You lost more than a battle when you rode with the Khamorth," he blurted.

"Too canny, y'are," Viridovix said, and sighed again. "Aye, there was a lass, Batbaian's sister she was. She's dead now, though not soon enough." After a while he went on, very low, "And part o' me with her. And what was the sense in that, or the use?" he asked the Greek. "None I could see when I found her, puir broken thing, nor the now either. Blood for blood's sake, the which is why I own I was wrong and you right."

Gorgidas thought of Quintus Glabrio, face blank in death. The memory burned in him still, and from his own pain he knew the Gaul's. They sat silent for a time, words no good to them. Then the Greek said, "No little irony here."

"And what might that be?"

"Only that when I brought up that argument I intended to yield it to you."

"Go on with you." Viridovix was as startled as the physician had been before. "You, the chap who wouldna carry a sword, come to relish soldiering? Next you'll be after taking heads and nailing 'em to your gate like a proper Celt."

"Thank you, no. But—" Gorgidas slapped the *gladius* on his hip, which Viridovix had not noticed. "—I wear a blade these days, and I begin to know what to do with it. And perhaps I begin to understand your 'glory.' For is it not true," he said, falling naturally into disputational style even though he was not speaking Greek, "that the idea of winning acclaim from one's fellow will make a man more likely to resist the onslaught of the wicked?"

"Honh!" The Gaul shook his head; having once changed his mind, he held to his new view with a convert's zeal. "An omadhaun'll go after glory no less than an honest man, so where's the use of it there?"

Gorgidas leaned forward with pleasure, sleep forgotten, loving the argument for its own sake. "That's true, but the renown of a good man lives forever, while an evildoer's fame is buried in disgrace. Four hundred years ago Herodotos said of the sycophant at Delphi who carved the Spartans' name on a golden bowl they did not offer, 'I know his name, but I will not record it.' And no one knows it now."

"He did that?" the Gaul said admiringly. "Now there's a revenge for you. But listen—"

They wrangled through the night, pounding fists onto knees and shouting at each other, quite without rancor: "Thick-skulled woodsrunner!" "Hairsplitting knave of a Greek!" Fire and smelly tallow lamps guttered low, leaving them in near darkness. At last the thin murky light of winter dawn began to creep under the tent flap.

Gorgidas knuckled his eyes, suddenly feeling exhaustion catch up with him again. No help for it, not with another day in the saddle ahead. The left side of his mouth quirked up in a wry grin. "Here we sit, not knowing which of us is right and which wrong, but we go on even so."

"Aye, well, what else can we do?" Viridovix rose, stretched, jammed on his fur hat and stuck his head outside. "Come on, laddie, they're stirring out there." The swirl of cold air helped wake Gorgidas. Shivering, he belted his coat shut and followed the Gaul out into the snow.

XV

MARCUS WAS WORKING IN HIS CUBICLE LATE ONE AFTERnoon when he found he needed to go up to the records room to compare a protested assessment to the one levied the year before. He scratched his head; the place was empty. Where were the clerks hunched over registers, their ink-smudged fingers flicking beads on reckoning boards?

Only a single grizzled watchman paced the corridors, and he was making his rounds as fast as he could. When Scaurus hailed him, he looked at the tribune as at any madman. "Go on with you, sir. Who's for work on Midwinter's Day? The lot of 'em left hours ago, they did."

"Midwinter's Day?" Marcus echoed vaguely. He counted on his fingers. "Why, so it is." The watchman was gaping now, exposing a few blackened stumps of teeth. Not even foreigners forgot the chief festival of the Videssian year, the celebration to call the sun back from the winter solstice.

Chilly air bit at Scaurus' nose as he left the pen-pushers' warm den. That had been true last year, too, when he'd been dragged from his desk by Viridovix and Helvis. . . . He kicked at the snow, remembering.

Hardly anyone walked the broad ways of the palace complex; the servants, soldiers, and bureaucrats who made up the Empire's heart reveled with the rest of the city. The plaza of Palamas, just east of the palaces, was a sea of humanity. Venders cried their wares: ale, hot spiced wine, roast goat in cheese sauce, shellfish, squid fried in olive oil and dusted with breadcrumbs, perfumes, jewelry of all grades from cheap brass trash to massy gold encrusted with gems big as a man's eye, minor magic charms, images of Phos and his holy men. Strolling musicians wandered through the crowds, singing or playing pipes, lutes, horns straight or recurved, even a Vaspurakaner pandoura or two, all in the hope of enjoyably separating the frolickers from their coins.

Marcus, who had no ear for music in his best moods, gave them a wide berth. They reminded him of Helvis, who delighted in music, and of his recent fiasco with Nevrat Sviodo. Nevrat went out of her way to be friendly whenever she, Senpat, and the tribune went out, but her manner had a slight constraint that had not been there before. It was, he knew, no one's fault but his own. He growled a curse, wishing he could be free of his memories.

Monks' sober blue robes stood out from the gaudy finery most Videssians wore. Some joined the celebration around them; Scaurus would have bet a good many goldpieces that Styppes was already oblivious to the world. Others led little groups of laymen in prayer or hymns of praise to Phos, forming islets of dignity and deep faith in the jollier, more frivolous throng.

Some, though, abominated all fleshly pleasures, and in their narrow fanaticism devoted themselves only to destroying everything of which they disapproved: Zemarkhos had his spiritual brothers in the city. One such, a dour man whose robe flapped ragged round his scrawny shanks, came panting by the tribune, chasing fine singing youths in masks. Seeing he would never catch them, he shook his fist, shouting, "Your japes profane Phos' holy days! Give your souls to contemplation, not this reckless gaiety! It is a defilement, you witless fools, and Skotos' everlasting ice awaits you!" The young men were long gone. "Bah!" the monk said softly, and looked round for other evil to root out.

Marcus feared the monastic would turn on him; his shaven cheeks and light eyes and hair marked him as an outlander, and so a likely heretic or outright unbeliever. But there was better game close by. A ring of people watched a little dog, its fur dyed green, prance back and forth on its hind legs to the tap of its master's hand-drum. He had trained it to take money from their fingers and scamper back to him with the coins.

"Isn't t'at marvelous?" boomed one of the spectators, a tall Haloga mercenary whose chilly homeland offered no such diversions. His companion, a darkly beautiful whore, smiled up at him, nodding. Her velvet gown, shot through with maroon brocade, clung to her like a second skin. His arm was tight round her waist; now and again his massive hand would slide up to tease the bottom of her breast.

He let her go for a moment, went to one knee; his blond braid, tied with a cord the color of blood, almost brushed the cobbles. "Here, pup!" he called. The dog minced over to take a coin, dropped to all fours to scurry off to the man with the drum. "Gold!" he exclaimed, and bowed low to the Haloga. "A thousand thanks, my master!" The crowd cheered.

But when the mercenary rose, the Videssian monk was stabbing a long bony forefinger into his face. "Filthy, obscene revelry!" he cried. "You poor benighted heathen, you should be at prayer thanking Phos for his mercy in restoring the light for yet another year, not defiling yourself with this lewd creature here!" His glare swung to the courtesan, who returned it; her eyes had glowed at the soldier's lavishness.

The Haloga blinked in surprise at the onslaught. Perhaps he had been briefed about the dangers of inciting Videssian clerics, for his answer was mild enough: "Take your hand away, sir, if you please."

The monk did. He must have thought he had hit the mercenary's conscience, for he softened his harsh commanding tones and tried to speak persuasively. "For all that you are a foreigner, sir, you have the look of a gentleman, so think on what I say. Is your carnal pleasure worth the risk of your soul?"

"Go stifle yourself, you skin-headed vulture!" the tart shrilled. "You leave him alone!" She clutched the mercenary's arm possessively.

"Be silent, trull," the monk said. He kept looking her up and down, as if against his will. Videssian monks were celibate, but he could not tear his gaze away from her invitingly displayed flesh. His words were for the Haloga, but his eyes stayed riveted on the woman. "I grant she's a lovely thing, yet desire is but Skotos' honied bait to trap the unwary."

Marcus grimaced at the sally, though it was not meant for him.

The monk was fairly howling now: "Look at the fine round arse of her, and her narrow waist, oh, and a bosom to make any man weak, in truth—" Scaurus found him almost pitiful to hear, thinking he was condemning the sensual delights he had forsworn, but instead lingering lovingly over them all. "Sparkling eyes and full red lips; sweet as aged wine they must be." He fairly twitched with lust.

The Haloga threw back his head and laughed, a great bass roar loud enough to turn heads over half the plaza. "Bugger me with a pine cone, priest, if you don't need her worse than I do. Here." He tossed a goldpiece at the feet of the monk, who stared at it, popeyed. "Go on," the mercenary told him, "have a good frike on me. I'll find another wench, have no fear; this burgh crawls with queans."

Monk and whore screamed at him together, then at each other. The Haloga turned his broad back on both of them and tramped away. The crowd whooped behind him, loose enough this one day of the year to enjoy a cleric's comeuppance, even at the hands of a heathen.

Nor could Scaurus help smiling; no sea of sorrows was big enough for a man to drown in it altogether. As with Styppes' bilious temper and fondness for the grape, this monk's sad slaverings reminded him that under those blue robes dwelt human beings, perhaps not too different from himself. That was worth remembering. Most times, Videssos' monks roused only dread in him, for fanaticism in the cause of faith was not something a Roman was well equipped to understand.

Thinking of Styppes and his thirst, the tribune bought a cup of wine. It sat warm in his belly. When a man ran through the plaza shouting the praises of the mime troupes performing at the Amphitheater, he drifted south along with a good many others.

The Amphitheater's great oval bowl marked off the southern boundary of the plaza of Palamas. Scaurus paid his two-copper fee and passed through one of the tunnel-vaulted passageways and into the arena. Ushers herded him up ramps and stairways to the very top of the bowl; the mimes had been playing all day, and the Amphitheater was packed.

Seen from so far away, the obelisk, chryselephantine statues, and other memorials of past imperial triumphs that decked the Amphitheater's central spine was almost more impressive than they had been when the tribune stood among them. The tip of the tall granite spike was at the level of his eyes, even here. Not far away from its base bloomed the twelve bright silk parasols that marked the Avtokrator of the Videssians as the same number of lictors with their rods and axes distinguished a Roman consul.

The tribune could not make out Thorisin's features. Somehow that heartened him. He drank more wine, rough cheap stuff that snarled on his palate. Catching his grunt of distaste, the man to his right on the long stone bench said, "A rare vintage—day before yesterday, I think." He was a skinny, bright-eyed little fellow with the feral look of a cutpurse to him.

Marcus smacked his lips. "No, you're wrong. I'm sure it's last week's." The joke was feeble, but he had not made many lately.

His benchmate's reply was lost in the crowd's flurry of applause as a new set of players came out onto the track where, most days, race horses galloped. One of the actors pantomimed stepping in something distasteful and earned a guffaw.

In the Empire's small towns the citizens put on their own skits instead of having professionals entertain them, but all through Videssos the playlets had the same principle behind them. They were fast-paced, topical, and irreverent—on Midwinter's Day, anyone was fair game.

This troupe's first sketch, for instance, featured three chief characters, one of whom, by his robes of state, was obviously the Emperor. The rest of the actors kept getting in his way on various pretexts until at last he stumbled on the other two chief players, a brown-haired woman and a big man wearing a golden wig and Haloga-style furs, thrashing together under a blanket. And oh, the crockery that flew when she—he, actually; the mime troupes were all-male—was discovered! The mock-Emperor had to flee, crossing his arms in front of his face to save it from the barrage of pots and dishes the actor playing his mistress kept pulling from beneath the covers. He only subdued her with the aid of the rest of the players, who had changed into the gilded corselets of Imperial Guards. The pseudo-Haloga tried to hide under that blanket, but a boot in his upraised rump dealt with him.

And that, Marcus thought, doubtless explained why Komitta Rhangavve was not sitting by Thorisin—one lover too many at last, or one too blatant. He suddenly understood the sniggering remarks the bureaucrats had been making, things he had paid no attention to in his gloom.

He turned to his benchmate. "I've been out of the city. When did this happen?"

"A couple months ago, I guess. When the headman got back from that Opsikion place. There's a song about it, goes like this—oh, wait, they're starting up again."

The next skit bored the tribune, but the Videssians around him roared with laughter. It was a satire of some theological debate that had entertained the city this past summer. Only gradually did Scaurus realize that the leading player, a man wearing a huge gray false beard that hung down over the pillow he had stuffed under his threadbare blue robe to fatten himself, was supposed to be Balsamon, ecumenical patriarch of the Empire of Videssos. The real Balsamon was sitting on the Amphitheater's spine not far from the Emperor. He was clad quite properly in the patriarchal regalia: precious blue silk and pearl-encrusted cloth-of-gold, vestments as magnificent in their own way as Thorisin Gavras'. But Marcus—and evidently the whole city—knew he turned comfortably shabby whenever he got the chance.

Thorisin had sat unmoving as he was burlesqued, tolerating Midwinter Day license without enjoying it. Balsamon chortled along with the rest of the Amphitheater when his turn came. He held his big belly in his hands and shook when the actor lampooning him cracked a priestly opponent over the head with an ivory figurine, then ignored the thrashing victim to make sure the statuette was undamaged.

Balsamon shouted something to the mock-patriarch, who cupped a hand at his ear to hear through the noise of the crowd. Whatever it was, Balsamon repeated it. The actor nodded, bowed low in his direction—and walloped the fellow again.

"He's a pisser, that one," Scaurus' raffish neighbor said admiringly as the Amphitheater exploded with glee. Balsamon, as was his way, flowered in the applause. He was much loved in the city, and for good reason.

The mimes darted under the Amphitheater for a change of costume. The first one to re-emerge stepped forth in the furs and leathers of a nomad, with a silver circlet on his head to show he was of some rank. He prowled about fiercely, brandishing a saber and ignoring the hisses and catcalls that showered down on him. Those turned to cheers when another actor came out wearing imperial raiment. But he took no notice of the nomad, turning his back on him and staring off into the distance.

More fur-clad actors emerged, three of them pushing a covered cart over to their chief. He scowled and gnashed his teeth at it, whacking it with the flat of his blade.

There was a flourish of trumpets. Out from the runway strutted a tall man in outlandish military getup, followed by four or five more wearing less splendid versions of the same costume. Marcus frowned, wondering who these apparitions were supposed to be. Their shields were taller than they were. . . . The tribune leaned forward in his seat, feeling his face grow hot.

The pseudo-legionaries far below marched very smartly, or would have, if they had been able to move more than three paces without suddenly changing direction. After a while their leader literally stumbled over one of the mock-nomads, which produced a good deal of startlement and alarm on both sides.

The Yezda chieftain pointed to his cart, then to the figure of the Emperor, who was still aloof from it all. After some comic misunderstanding, the Roman leader paid him a gigantic bag of coins and took possession of the cart. Pantomiming falls in the mud, he and his men wrestled it over to within a few feet of the Emperor.

Marcus' heart sank anew as he watched the mock-legionaries curl up for sleep around the cart. As soon as they were motionless, the four men inside, dressed Namdalener-style in trousers and short jackets, tore the cover off, scrambled out, and danced a derisive jig on their backs. Then, kicking up their heels, they fled for the runway and disappeared.

Still with his back turned, the actor in imperial robes gave a great shrug, as if to ask what could be expected from such hopeless dubs as the ones he had to work with.

The tribune looked at Thorisin. He was laughing now. So much for Nepos' warm words, Marcus thought.

"There's more coming," the little man next to him said as the Roman rose from his seat.

"I'm for the jakes," Scaurus mumbled, sliding crabwise toward the stairs past the row of drawn-up knees. But he did not stop at the latrines. Pausing only to drain another cup of new green wine, he hurried out of the Amphitheater. The crowd's snickers burned in his ears. They would have laughed louder yet, he thought, had the mime troupe known the whole story.

It was nearly dusk; men were lighting torches round the Amphitheater. They crackled in the wind. A cheese-paring of moon sank over the palaces. Marcus started back to his room in the Grand Courtroom, but changed his mind while he was still in the plaza of Palamas. Tonight he needed more of the grape, and every tavern in the city would be open to oblige him.

Turning his back on the palace complex, Scaurus walked through the forum and east along Middle Street. The thoroughfare was nearly as crowded as the plaza. He kept one hand on his belt-pouch; there were more thieves in Videssos than the one he had been sitting by.

The granite pile that housed more government offices, the archives, and a prison took up most of a long block. As the tribune passed the massive building, he heard his name called. His head spun. Alypia Gavra waved his way as she came down the broad black marble steps toward him.

He stood frozen in the street a moment, while revelers surged round him. "Your Highness," he managed at last. Even in his own ears his voice was a startled croak.

She looked about to see if anyone in the crowd had heard him, but no one was paying any attention. "Plain Alypia will do nicely tonight, thank you," she said quietly. She was not dressed as a princess, but in a long, high-necked dress of dark green wool with rabbit fur at the sleeves and collar. If anything, she was more plainly gowned than the women around her, for she wore no jewelry at all, while most of them glittered with gold, silver, and precious stones.

"As you wish, of course," Scaurus said woodenly.

She frowned up at him; the top of her head came barely to his chin. "This ought to be a night for rejoicing," she said. A long, loud thunder of mirth came from the Amphitheater. "Maybe you should go and enjoy the farcers."

He gave a bitter laugh. "I've seen enough of the mimes already, thanks." He had not intended to say anything more, but at her questioning look found himself explaining.

Her eyes widened in sympathy. "They can be cruel," she nodded. Marcus had not seen any of the skits the year before; he suddenly wondered what might have been in them. Alypia went on, "But it's not as if the islanders' escape was all your fault."

"Was it not?" the tribune said, as much to himself as to her. Wanting to get away from that set of memories, he remarked, "To judge by your clothes, you hardly seem ready for a celebration yourself."

"No, I suppose not," she admitted with a brief smile. "I hadn't planned on one. I sent my servants off to keep the holiday early this afternoon and then came here to paw through the archives. That, I thought, would be an all-day job."

It was Scaurus' turn to nod; as an accounts auditor, he had made use of old records himself a few times. The Videssians were marvelous for keeping records, but storing the ones no longer immediately useful was something else again. Even the clerks who kept them often had no idea of what they held. "This was for your history?"

"Yes," she said, seeming pleased he remembered. "I was looking for the general Onesimos Kourkouas' report on an early brush with the Yezda in Vaspurakan, thirty-six, no, thirty-seven years ago. By some accident, it was in the second room I searched. Then again, it was only half as long as I'd thought. So here it is only twilight, and I find myself at loose ends." She studied him. "What do you intend to do the rest of the night? Can it be shared?"

"Your Highness—no, Alypia," Marcus corrected himself before she could, "all I had planned was getting thoroughly sozzled. If you don't get in the way of that, you're welcome to come along; otherwise, I'll see you another day."

He had expected his candor to drive her off, but she said briskly, "A capital idea. Where were you going to go?"

He raised an eyebrow. "I hadn't thought that far ahead. Shall we wander?"

"Why not?" They set out together down Middle Street, away from the palace complex. Around them, the city kept celebrating. Fires blazed at every street corner, and men and women jumped over them for luck. Some, laughing, wore clothes that did not match their gender; Scaurus was almost knocked down by a chubby bearded fellow prancing in skirts. "Careful, there," he growled, in anything but holiday spirit.

Alypia, who understood his pain from her own ordeal, deliberately kept the talk impersonal, not risking a closer touch. Without noticing her tact, the tribune was glad of it. He asked, "How did your Kourkouas find the Yezda?"

"He was horrified by them, by their archery and savagery both. The Vaspurakaners, at first, thought them a race of demons. Some among us thought they were a sending to punish Vaspurakan for its stubborn heresy—until, of course, they invaded Videssos, too."

"That wouldn't do much for that interpretation," the tribune agreed. He spoke with care, not quite sure how vehemently devout Alypia was. From what he had seen, though, he thought her piety more of Balsamon's genial sort than the narrow creed of a Styppes or Zemarkhos. He went on, "I might have reckoned them devils, too, from what they did in the Maragha campaign. And yet Yavlak and his Yezda near Garsavra were vicious cutthroats, aye, but not past human ken. They were happy enough to sell their islander captives back to me instead of torturing them all to death for Skotos' sake."

But thinking of that reminded Scaurus of what had come afterward. He changed the subject in some haste. "Tell me," he said, waving at the square they were entering, "why is this place called the forum of the Ox? I never did know, for all the time I've been here." It was perhaps a third the size of the plaza of Palamas, with none of the latter's imposing buildings.

"There's not much to it, I'm afraid. In ancient times, when Videssos was hardly more than a village, this was the town cattle market."

"Is that all?" he blurted.

"Every bit." Alypia looked at him in amusement. "Are you very disappointed? I could make up a pretty fable, if you like, with plots and wizards and tons of buried gold, but it would only be a fable. Sometimes what's so is a very plain thing."

"I have what I asked for, thanks." He hesitated. "Not even one wizard?"

"Not even one," she said firmly. They crossed the square, which was as full of people as the forum of Palamas. The revelers here were a more motley group than the richer citizens further west. The songs were gamier, the laughter shriller. There was a good sprinkling of town toughs, swaggering in tights and baggy-sleeved tunics; in a new fashion, some had taken to shaving the backs of their heads, Namdalener-style.

Past the forum of the Ox was the coppersmiths' district. The shops on Middle Street were closed now, hiding the ewers and bowls, plates and bells behind stout wooden shutters. The hammer's clang and the patient scratch of burin on metal were silent. Alypia said, "You have an odd way of getting drenched, Marcus. Or did you plan to hike all the way to the wall?"

The tribune flushed, partly in embarrassment and partly in pleasure that the princess still used his praenomen. She had learned enough of Roman customs to know it was reserved for warm friends, yet kept it after his debacle. He remembered the proverb: prosperity makes friends, adversity tries them.

"As you wish," he said once more, but this time in agreement, not resignation.

Save for the establishments along Middle Street, Scaurus hardly knew the coppersmiths' quarter. When he ventured off the thoroughfare, he found himself in a strange, half-foreign world. The metalworkers' trade was dominated by folk whose ancestors had come from Makuran, and they still clung to some of their western customs. Fewer luck-fires burned here than in the rest of the city; more than once Marcus saw four parallel vertical lines charcoaled on a whitewashed wall or chalked on a dark one.

Following his eye, Alypia said, "The mark of the Four Prophets of Makuran. Some follow them even now, though they dare not worship openly for fear of the monks."

Ironic, Scaurus thought, that the Makuraners faced persecution in Videssos from the worshipers of Phos, and in Makuran itself—Yezd, now—from the followers of Skotos. He asked idly, "What do you think of them?"

Alypia's reply was prompt. "Their faith is not mine, but they are not wicked because of that."

"Fair enough," he said, happy he had judged her rightly. Balsamon had said much the same thing to the Roman when he was newly came to Videssos. Most of their countrymen, smug in righteousness, would have called such tolerance blasphemy.

Alypia on his arm, he wandered the quarter's mazelike side streets for some little time, rejecting one dive because it was full of hooligans who leered out at the two of them, another because it reeked of rancid oil, and a third for its signboard, which prominently displayed the four vertical bars. He had no more desire to meet Makuraner religious enthusiasts than their Videssian counterparts.

The inn he finally chose was a neat two-story building whose sign carried no hidden meanings, religious or political, being merely a bright daub showing a jolly fat man in front of a table loaded with food and drink. The smells that came from inside were some of them unfamiliar but all mouth-watering.

The ground floor of the inn was packed tight with tables, and almost all of those packed with people. Scaurus looked round in disappointment until he spotted a small empty table set against the wall near the open kitchen. "Perfect!" he said, and shouldered his way to it through the crush, Alypia close behind. In summer the blast of heat from braziers and cookfires would have been intolerable, but on Midwinter's Day it was welcome.

Three waiters scurried from tables to kitchen and back again, but the holiday crowd made service slow. The tribune had a chance to look the patrons over: ordinary Videssians for the most part, neither rich nor poor. A few affected Makuraner style, the men, their hair and beards curled into tight ringlets, wearing coats longer behind than in front and their ladies in linen caftans brightly dyed in geometric patterns, with hairnets of silver mesh on their heads. All the talk sounded friendly and cheerful, as if the place's sign had been painted from one of the patrons.

Eventually a server came up. "Hello, stranger, my lady,"

he said, bowing to Alypia as though he recognized her as a princess. "Phos bless you on the day. What will it be?"

"Wine, for now," Marcus said; Alypia nodded. The man hurried away. Scaurus thought he had Makuraner blood; he was a touch swarthier than most Videssians, with pitch black hair and large, dark, luminous eyes.

The wine arrived with reasonable speed; the waiter poured for them. He said, "My name is Safav." That confirmed the tribune's guess. "If you want more or decide to eat, yell for me." Just then someone did. Safav dodged off toward him.

As Videssians usually did before wine or meat, Alypia Gavra raised her hands and murmured Phos' creed, then spat in the rushes on the floor in rejection of Skotos. Scaurus simply drank. Although she did not seem put out by the omission, Alypia's smile was a bit rueful. "I'm so used to thinking of you as one of us that it sometimes jolts me to remember you have your own customs," she said.

"It does me, too, sometimes," Marcus said. But the traces of his birth-speech gave his Videssian a sonorous flavor it did not have in her mouth and, as usual, he found the wine sticky-sweet on his tongue. "But never for long."

Syrupy the wine might have been, but also potent; it did as much to warm him as the fires at his back. He looked across the table at Alypia. She masked her thoughts well—not from policy, like her uncle, but from pensiveness. He remembered the quiet attraction that had grown between them and wondered whether she chose to do so, too, or as quietly to forget. Behind the cool façade it might have been either.

Was she even fair? he asked himself. Certainly her body lacked Helvis' rich curves—he frowned and cut that thought short. Her face was not as long as Thorisin's or her father's, nor as sharply sculpted; she left her cheeks pale and did nothing to play up her fine green eyes. But there was no mistaking the keen wit and spirit behind them. Conventionally beautiful or not, she was herself, something harder to attain.

A waiter—not their own, but an older man—bustled out of the kitchens past his elbow, cutting into his reverie. "Your pardon, sir," the man said, lifting a square bronze tray higher to make sure it missed the tribune. Agile as a lizard, he slid between tables toward three couples in Makuraner costume. He set enamel bowls before them, ladled soup from a copper tureen. Then, with a flourish, he took the lid from a pan, dug in with a wooden spoon, and plopped light-brown steaming chunks into the soup bowls.

The soup hissed and crackled as though hot metal was being quenched. Scaurus jumped. So, he saw, did Alypia and several of the more Videssian-looking people in the inn. Those before whom it was set, though, ate with gusto. A mystery to be explored! "Safav!"

The waiter handed a patron a plate of broiled prawns and hurried over to the tribune. Marcus asked, "What's the secret of the soup there? Hot pitch, maybe?"

"Sir?" Safav said, confused. Then his face cleared. "Oh, the sizzling rice soup? Would you care for some?"

Marcus hesitated, but at Alypia's nod he said, "Why not?" He was more suspicious than he sounded. All but unknown to the Romans, rice was not common in Videssos either. Despite sputters, the tribune foresaw something on the order of barley mush, not what he wanted for holiday fare.

But when Safav reappeared, the soup bowls he gave Scaurus and Alypia were full of a delicate golden broth rich with peas, mushrooms, and big hunks of shrimp and lobster. "In Makuran, now, this would be lamb or goat, but seafood works well enough," Safav said. Scaurus, waiting for the sizzle, was hardly listening.

With the same flourish the other waiter had shown, Safav whipped the lid from the thick iron pan on his tray and dropped a steaming spoonful into each bowl. They crackled heartily for a few seconds, then sank. "Reminds me of burning ships," the tribune muttered. He prodded the crisp chunk of rice with his spoon, still dubious.

"How is it done?" Alypia asked.

"First boil the rice, then fry it in very hot oil until the moment it starts to scorch. It has to be hot to sizzle, which is why this," Safav said, tapping at the heavy pan. He laid a finger by the side of his nose. "You never heard that from me, my lady, else my cousin the cook comes after me with a big knife. Most people I would not tell; they ask just for talk's sake. But I could see you really want to know." Someone shouted the waiter's name; he bobbed his head shyly and left them.

The tribune gave a tentative taste. The soup was splendid,

the crisp rice in it nutlike and flavorful. "What do I know?" he said, and emptied the bowl.

Tuna followed, broiled with oregano and basil; wine; greens with garlic and mint; wine; simmered squid stuffed with lentils and currants; wine; lamb stew with celery, leeks, and dates—another Makuraner dish; wine; squash and beans fried in olive oil; wine; quinces and cinnamon; wine.

Alypia had hold of the conversation without seeming to, deftly steering it to divert him but lay no demands upon him. For all her tact and skill, that game could go on only so long. As the grape mounted to Marcus' head, his responses grew steadily shorter. "Have you done what you set out to do, then?" Alypia said, her tone slyly bantering.

But the tribune was not fuddled, as she supposed. Rather the wine had left his thoughts clear and simple, stripping veils of pretense from him. Too well he remembered standing in front of her like an automaton, nakedly spewing forth his inmost, most secret self under the influence of Nepos' cordial. He stabbed at a chunk of lamb with needless violence.

Sensitive to his swing in mood, Alypia put her goblet down; she had drunk much less than he. She could be direct as well as artful and asked it straight: "What's amiss?"

"What are you doing here with me?" Marcus exclaimed. He stopped in dismay, mouth hanging foolishly open.

"I could ask the same of you," Alypia replied with some heat. But her annoyance was not for his candor, for she went on, "When you sheered off from my servant—oh yes, he saw you—I thought you were angry at me, as you have a right to be. Yet here you sit, peaceably enough. Explain yourself, if you would."

"Angry at you? No, never. I owe you a debt I cannot hope to repay, for finding a way to make your uncle believe me loyal. But—" The tribune fell silent. Alypia waited him out. At last he had to continue. "How could I have anything to do with you, when I blight everything I put my hand to?"

The furious stare she gave him said she was of the Gavras clan after all. "I did not think you would belittle yourself. Who saved my headstrong uncle from Onomagoulos' assassins? Who warned him of Drax, though he would not listen? And who beat Drax in the end? Unless I'm much mistaken, the finger points at you."

"And who let all his prisoners get free, for being, for being—" He had to take a long swallow of wine before he could get it out. "—for being too blind to see his woman was using him as a carter uses a mule? That finger points at me, too, from my own hand."

"There's no denying your Helvis had a hard knot to untie, but I thought better of her." Alypia kept her voice judicious, but her nostrils flared in indignation as she spoke Helvis' name. "But to do as she did, taking advantage of your love for a weapon against you—" She made a gesture of repugnance. "I wish I had not heard that. No wonder you blame me for urging Thorisin to try Nepos' potion."

"Blame you?" Scaurus said, echoing her again. "I just told you I did not; you were doing what you could to help me—and in fact you did. How can there be blame for that? But," he paused to gather his thoughts, "it's hard to meet you, to know what to say, to know how to act, after baring myself before you."

The touch of her fingers was gentle on his. She slowly dipped her head; her eyes were lowered to the tabletop as she reminded him, "Marcus, you have also seen me naked." Her voice was hardly more than a whisper.

The tribune remembered her, calm with Vardanes Sphrantzes' dagger against her throat, her slim body revealed by the transparent silks that were the only garments the elder Sphrantzes allowed her after taking her as plaything from Ortaias. His hand closed tightly around hers. "That was no fault of yours; the crime was Vardanes'."

"Well, did Drax and his comrades escape by your will, then?" Alypia demanded, looking up at him. "We both know the answer to that." She did not seek a reply. Her eyes were far away; she was remembering, too. "Strange," she mused, "that I should thank Avshar in his wickedness for delivering me from my tormentor."

"He gave short measure, as he always does," Marcus said. "Vardanes earned worse than the quick end he got."

She shuddered, still looking backward, but then tried to smile. "Let it lay. I'm sorry I spoke of it." Her hand stayed in his; he touched the writer's callus on her middle finger. He was afraid to say anything. He wondered if he was seeing only what he wished to see, as he had with Nevrat.

When Safav came by, he smiled to himself. Marcus hardly noticed the waiter as he set the spiced quinces on the table and slipped away. In spite of his tension, memory held him again, of Alypia in his embrace, of her lips warm on his—for a few seconds, until she took fright and pulled away. Had that only been this past spring?

"So much between," she murmured, seeming to read his thoughts as she did so often. She was silent again for some time, then drew in a long breath, as if in decision. She said, "As well nothing came of that, don't you think? I was unready to, to . . ." It was her turn to come to an awkward halt. Marcus nodded to show he understood; her eyes thanked him. She went on, "And in any case you had commitments you could not have—should not have—set aside."

"Should I not?" he said bitterly.

By luck, she paid him no attention; she was arguing with herself as much as talking to him. Her face set with resolve a warrior might have envied, she pushed ahead, a sentence at a time. "But your reasons for hesitating are gone now, aren't they? And as for me . . ." Her voice trailed away once more. At last she said, very low, "Marcus, would you see me naked again?"

"Oh, with all my heart," he said, but a moment later felt he had to add, "if you think you can."

"Truly I don't know," she answered. She blinked back tears. "But were you not one to say such a thing as that, I'm sure I could not try." In spite of her determination, her hand trembled in his. He looked at her questioningly. Her nod was short and fierce.

Almost before the tribune could wave for him, Safav appeared. He bent to whisper to Scaurus, "There is a room upstairs, should you want it."

"Damn me," the Roman said, "my head must be transparent as glass tonight." He fumbled in his belt-pouch, pressed coins into Safav's hand.

The waiter stared. "My lord," he stammered, "this is far too much—"

"Take it," Marcus said; a goldpiece more or less seemed a small thing here and now. Safav bowed almost double.

"The second door on the right from the stairs," he said. "A lamp is lit inside; there's charcoal in the brazier, and fresh straw in the mattress, and clean fleeces, too—we made ready for the day."

"Good." Marcus stood with Alypia. She came round the table to him; that his arm went round her shoulder struck him as the most natural thing in the world. Safav bowed again, only to be jerked upright as someone shouted his name. He shrugged comically and scurried away.

One of the men in Makuraner costume gave a sodden cheer as Scaurus and Alypia climbed the stairs. Feeling her flinch, the tribune glared at the tosspot, who was cheerily oblivious to him. But her chin rose in defiance, and she managed a small smile. He lifted his thumb; she knew enough of Roman ways to read his approval. He wanted to hug her on the spot but held back, judging it would only further ruffle her.

The chamber was small, but large enough. Marcus barred the door by the thin light of the promised lamp, which sat on a stool by the bed. He quickly set the brazier going; the room was shuttered against the chill outside, but an icy draft crept in regardless.

Alypia stood motionless in the center of the room while he did what was needed. When he took a step toward her, she started in such trepidation that he froze in his tracks. "Nothing will happen unless you want it to," he promised. With Roman practicality, he went on, "Warm your hands; it's cold as a frog in here." He moved aside to let her at the brazier. She stooped over it, taking him at his word.

Without turning, after a while she said, "Blow out the lamp." Scaurus did. The flame sprang up for an instant, then was no more. The dim-glowing charcoal in the brazier turned the whitewashed walls the color of blood.

He waited. She came to him slowly, almost defiantly, as if her body were a restive horse she controlled by main force. When he put his hands on her shoulders, she did not pull away, but lifted her face to him. It was a strange kiss; while her lips and tongue were alive against his, she stood so rigid he did not dare sweep her into a full embrace.

She drew back, studying him in the near-darkness. "How does a soldier make so gentle a man?" she said.

He did not think of himself so, but had learned she meant such questions seriously. With a shrug, he answered, "You know soldiering is not the trade I started with. And," he added softly, "I am not at war with you."

"No, never," she murmured. Then he did draw her close, and she came more readily into his arms. He stroked the back of her neck, brushed her hair aside to touch her ear. She shivered, but more from fear, he thought, than sensuality. She retreated a couple of steps, eyeing the bedding by the wall. "Please, you go first," she said to Scaurus, turning her back again. "I'll come to you in a minute."

As Safav had promised, the straw beneath the muslin ticking was fresh and sweet-smelling, the wooly fleeces thick and warm. Marcus lay facing the wall. Someone had scrawled a couple of words on it in charcoal, too smeared now to read in the faint red light.

From behind him, Alypia said, "And patient, too," with something close to her usual detached irony. There was a bit of silence, followed by a small, annoyed snort as a bone fastener on her dress refused to obey her fingers. The tribune heard the soft rustle of cloth sliding over skin. The mattress shifted as she let herself down onto it.

As his mouth found hers, she whispered, "I hope you will not be too disappointed in me."

Some time later he stared into her eyes; in the near-dark they were as unreadable as the scribble on the wall. "'Disappointed'?" he said, still dazed with delight. "You must be daft."

To his surprise, she twisted angrily in his arms. "You are kind, dear Marcus, but you need not pretend with me. I know my clumsiness for what it is."

"By the gods!" he said, startled into Latin for a moment. In Videssian he protested, "If that was clumsiness, I doubt I'd live through talent." He laid her hand over his heart, still racing in his chest.

She looked past his shoulder. Her voice was absolutely toneless. "*He* said there was no hope for me in such matters, but he would undertake to train me even so." She did not, perhaps could not, force the name out, but Scaurus knew whom she meant. Of themselves, his hands folded into fists.

She did not seem to notice; he might as well not have been there. "I fought him, oh, how I fought him, until one day he let me see he took pleasure from my struggles. After that," she said bleakly, "he trained me—aye, like a dog or a horse. Small mercies when I learned something enough to suit him. When I failed . . ." She shivered into silence.

"It's over," he said, and tasted the emptiness of words. Then he cursed foully in every tongue he knew. That did no good either.

After a while, Alypia went on, "Whenever he finished with me, he would curl his lip in disgust, as if someone had offered him a plate of bad fish. To the end, he despised me as couch-partner. Once I dared to ask him why he came back over and over and over, if I did not satisfy him." Marcus waited helplessly as she paused, remembering. "That was the only time I saw him smile, in all the months he kept me. He smiled and said, 'Because I can.'"

The tribune wished he had not wasted his curses before. He gathered her to him, hugged her close. "Listen to me," he said. "Vardanes, Skotos take him, savored your suffering."

"The very word," she said from against the side of his neck. "He was a connoisseur in all things, torment among them."

"Then why believe what he told you of yourself as a woman?" he demanded. "One more lie, to bring you affliction." He ran his fingers down the curved column of her spine, a long slow caress; kissed her with soft brush of lips. "For it was a lie, you know."

"I pleased you?" she whispered, doubting still. "Really?"

"If snow is 'cool,' or the ocean 'moist,' then yes, you 'pleased' me."

She gave a strangled hiccup of laughter, then burst into tears, clinging to him tightly. She wept against his shoulder for a long time. He simply held her, letting her cry herself out as he had with Senpat and Nevrat.

Finally she was spent and lay quiet in his arms. He tilted her face up to his. He had intended a gentle kiss, of understanding and sympathy rather than passion. But she responded with an intensity not far from desperation. A proverb he had heard somewhere, from the Namdaleni perhaps, briefly ran through his mind: "Tear-filled eyes make sweet lips." Then thought was lost, for Alypia clung to him once more, with a new kind of urgency.

They both gasped when it began again, gentleness forgotten. His lips bruised hers and were bruised in turn; her nails scored his back. She tore her mouth free, said half-sobbing into his ear, "What wonder, to want!" When she cried out in amazed joy, he followed an instant later.

After that, it was some time before either of them cared to move. At last Alypia said, "You're squashing me, I'm afraid."

"Sorry." Marcus shifted his weight; sweat-slick skin slid. They both laughed. "Who would have thought anyone could sweat in this hailstone of a room?"

"Who would have thought . . ." She let her voice trail away. She set her hand on his side, but did not speak.

"What, love?"

Alypia smiled, but answered, "Nothing." That was so patently untrue it hung in the air between them. She amended it at once. "Or nothing I know how to say, at any rate." He mimed scratching his head; she made a face at him. "Witling!"

She was serious, though, as he soon saw. "All I knew of man and woman was cruel sport. But Marcus, you have met with better than that. When you and—" She stopped, gestured in self-mockery. "The romances say one should never seek comparisons."

The romances, Marcus thought, knew what they were talking about. He realized he had scarcely thought of Helvis since fleeing the Amphitheater. Now he could no longer avoid it. Alypia stirred beside him; he saw his silence was frightening her. He said slowly, "The only comparison that matters is that you are here and want to be, while she—is in Namdalen by now, I suppose."

She sighed and snuggled against him. Her whisper sounded like, "Thank you."

But once reminded, he kept slipping back to the stepson he had come to care for, to his own son, to the child Helvis was carrying—or would it be born now? probably—and to the way that had been taken from him. "One thing more, after all," he said harshly. "You would never use your body as a weapon against me."

Her hand clenched on his upper arm, hard enough to hurt. She willed it open. "No," she said. "Never that."

She sat up. The brazier's faint red light softened her features, blurring her resemblance to her father, but she had her own measure of Mavrikios Gavras' directness. "Where do we go from here?" she asked Marcus. "If it pleases you that this should be the affair of an evening, to be forgotten come light, I will understand. That surely is safest."

The tribune shook his head violently, almost as frightened as she had been before. He had seen his life uprooted, all he relied on snatched away, and the prospect of abandoning this gladness filled him with worse dread than the familiar terrors of the battlefield. He and Alypia had cared for each other since not long after the Romans came to Videssos; this was no sudden seduction, to be enjoyed and then thrown aside.

She waved his stumbling explanation aside as soon as she had its drift, bent to kiss him. "I would not force myself on you, either, but I would have grieved to see what might have been, cut short." She abruptly turned practical again. "It won't be easy. You know I am hemmed in by ceremony and servants; chances to slip away will come too seldom. And you must run no risks for my sake. My uncle, did he know, would come after you not with a horsewhip, but the headsman's axe."

"By his lights, it would be hard to blame him," Scaurus said soberly. A mercenary captain—especially one with as alarming a record as the Roman's—the paramour of a childless Emperor's niece? Thorisin could not afford to ignore such a thing, not in Videssos where only intrigue rivaled theology as the national passion.

The tribune thought of the executioner's hot irons, back at Garsavra. He might come to beg for the axe, after a while.

That was the thought of a moment, though. He laughed and stroked Alypia's smooth shoulder.

"What is it, my astonishing, desirable beloved?" she asked, half-embarrassed by the endearments but proud of them as well.

"I was just remembering that a year ago this time, near enough, I was reaming Viridovix up one side and down the other for carrying on with Komitta Rhangavve and here I am playing the same mad game."

"Viridovix?" She frowned in brief puzzlement. "Oh yes, the big copper-haired wild man in your service—a 'Kelt' he called himself, did he not?" Not for the first time, Marcus was impressed by her memory for detail, sharpened, no doubt, by her historical research. He wondered what the Gaul would say about being in Roman service. Something memorable, he was sure.

Alypia suddenly giggled as she made a connection. "So *that's* why he disappeared off onto the plains with Goudeles and the Arshaum—Arigh." She found the name.

"Aye. He and Komitta quarreled, and she went crying rape to Thorisin. He didn't care to wait to find out whether she'd be believed."

Alypia's nostrils flared in an unmistakable sniff. "Komitta would quarrel with Phos as he came to bear her soul to heaven. And as for the other, your friend was hardly the first to know her favors—or the last. I think in the end my uncle was glad she grew flagrant enough to give him the excuse to be rid of her." She giggled again. "Truly, without it I don't think he'd have had the nerve."

Having seen some of Komitta Rhangavve's rages, Scaurus could well believe that. "What happened to her after she was caught with the Haloga?" he asked, recalling the first skit he'd watched in the Amphitheater.

"Thorisin packed her off to a convent outside the city—and a tidy sum he had to pay the reverend mother to take her, too; her reputation was there ahead of her. The northman—Valthjos his name was, called Buttered-Bread after their fashion of giving nicknames—had to sail for home. He was supposed to be in disgrace, but he carried a gold-inlaid axe and a jewel-set scabbard I know he didn't have when he got to Videssos."

The rough justice in that sounded like Thorisin, and the story explained more of the pen-pushers' jokes, but Marcus was grimly certain he would not escape so lightly if discovered with Alypia. She was no mistress of whom the Emperor had tired; until Thorisin bred himself an heir, she was the channel through which the Gavras line would descend.

Thinking along with him, Alypia said, "We must make sure you're not found out." She rose from the bed and walked over to the dress which lay carelessly crumpled on the floor. Her nipples stood up with cold; that icy draft was defeating the brazier. Scaurus admired her economical movements as she dressed, then he threw the sheepskins to one side and started to retrieve his own clothes.

"Wait," she said. "Best I go back alone." When he frowned, she said, "Think it out. I'll simply say I fell asleep over my scrolls. Everyone will believe that and pity me for it. Whereas if I returned with you at whatever hour this is, eyebrows would fly up no matter how innocent we were."

He put out his hands palm up, defeated. "You're right. You generally are."

"Hmm. I'm not quite sure I like that." She quickly ran a comb through her hair. "Anyway, no great hardship for you here. The bed is comfortable."

"Not half so much, without you in it."

"A courtier born," she said, but her eyes were warm. She dimpled. "What would your Viridovix say if he found out you'd been bundling with an Emperor's daughter?"

"Him? He'd congratulate me."

"Good for him, then." Alypia hugged the tribune, kissed him hard and quick. "Sleep warm and think of me." They walked to the door together. He unbarred it. Her hand on the latch, she looked up and said softly, "This is but a beginning, I promise you."

"I know that." He opened his mouth, shut it, and shook his head. "There doesn't seem to be anything else to say." She nodded and slipped out the door. He closed it after her.

ABOUT THE AUTHOR

Harry Turtledove is that rarity, a lifelong southern Californian. He is married and has two young daughters. After flunking out of Caltech, he earned a degree in Byzantine history and has taught at UCLA and Cal State Fullerton. Academic jobs being few and precarious, however, his primary work since leaving school has been as a technical writer. He has had fantasy and science fiction published in *Isaac Asimov's*, *Amazing*, *Analag*, *Fantasy Book*. His hobbies include baseball, chess, and *Playboy*, and beer.